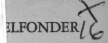
RAVE R... ELFONDER

...ING FOR A KNIGHT

"Will win your heart!"
— *Romantic Times BOOKclub Magazine*

"With history and beautiful details of Scotland, this book provides romance, spunk, mystery, and courtship . . . A must-read!"
— *Rendezvous*

"A very romantic story . . . extremely sexy. I recommend this book to anyone who loves the era and Scotland."
— **TheBestReviews.com**

MASTER OF THE HIGHLANDS

"Welfonder does it again, bringing readers another powerful, emotional, highly romantic medieval that steals your heart and keeps you turning the pages."
— *Romantic Times BOOKclub Magazine*

"A vastly entertaining and deeply sensual medieval romance . . . For those of us who like our heroes moody, ultra HOT, and SEXY . . . this is the one for you!"
— *Historical Romance Writers*

more . . .

"Yet another bonny Scottish romance to snuggle up with and inspire pleasantly sinful dreams . . . A sweetly compelling love story . . . [with a] super abundance of sexual tension."

—*Heartstrings*

"Welfonder brings the Highlands to life . . . Romance, mystery, action, and passion, combined with historical details, make *Master of the Highlands* a joy to read."

—Bookloons.com

"Another masterpiece . . . I can hardly wait to read Ms. Welfonder's next book . . . She never lets her readers down."

—ReaderToReader.com

BRIDE OF THE BEAST

"Larger-than-life characters and a scenic setting . . . Welfonder pens some steamy scenes."

—*Publishers Weekly*

"A wonderful story . . . well told . . . a delightful mix of characters."

—Romanticreviews.com

"*Bride of the Beast* is a thrilling story . . . It is so sensual at times, it gives you goose bumps . . . Ms. Welfonder spins pure magic with her vibrant characters."
—*Reader to Reader Reviews*

"Four and a half stars! . . . A top pick . . . Powerful emotions, strong and believable characters, snappy dialogue, and some humorous moments add depth to the plotline and make this a nonstop read. Ms. Welfonder is on her way to stardom."
—*Romantic Times BOOKclub Magazine*

KNIGHT IN MY BED

"Exciting, action-packed . . . a strong tale that thoroughly entertains."
—*Midwest Book Review*

"The perfect blend of intrigue, forbidden love, and danger."
—TheRomanticReadersConnection.com

"Ripe with sexual tension . . . Breathtaking!"
—RoadtoRomance.dhs.org

"Steamy . . . sensual . . . Readers will enjoy this book."
—*Booklist*

more . . .

DEVIL IN A KILT

"A lovely gem of a book. Wonderful characters and a true sense of place make this a keeper. If you love Scottish tales, you'll treasure this one."
—Patricia Potter, bestselling author of
The Heart Queen

"As captivating as a spider's web, and the reader can't get free until the last word. It is easy to get involved in this tense, fast-moving adventure."
—*Rendezvous*

"Four and a half stars! This dynamic debut has plenty of steaming sensuality . . . [and] a dusting of mystery. You'll be glued to the pages by the fresh, vibrant voice, and strong emotional intensity . . . Will catapult Welfonder onto 'must-read' lists."
—*Romantic Times BOOKclub Magazine*

"An engaging mystery . . . very fast paced with fascinating characters and several interesting plot twists . . . *Devil in a Kilt* is a keeper."
—Writers Club Romance Group on AOL

Only
for a
Knight

Only
for a
Knight

SUE-ELLEN
WELFONDER

NEW YORK   BOSTON

Cover design by Diane Luger
Book design by Giorgetta Bell McRee

Warner Books

Time Warner Book Group
1271 Avenue of the Americas
New York, NY 10020
Visit our Web site at www.twbookmark.com

Printed in the United States of America

First Paperback Printing: July 2005

10 9 8 7 6 5 4 3 2 1

ATTENTION CORPORATIONS AND ORGANIZATIONS: Most WARNER books are available at quantity discounts with bulk purchase for educational, business, or sales promotional use. For information, please call or write: Special Markets Department, Warner Books, Inc. 135 W. 50th Street, New York, NY 10020-1393. Telephone: 1-800-222-6747 Fax: 1-800-477-5925.

For the Legends of Lochindorb.
May they always walk in the joy of bright blue days and,
of a night, gaze only on the brightest shining stars. May
they ever be wrapped in sweet golden warmth and
contentment. And as it has thrived undiminished all down
the centuries, may their incomparable love bloom through all
their tomorrows and beyond, unending. These blessings I
wish them—with the whole of my heart and soul.

Acknowledgments

❦

Scotland ever holds my heart and is the wellspring of my inspiration, the passion behind every word I write. To walk there can feel like moving in a magical land where time stands still and centuries-old traditions of Gaelic heroic myth and legend still throb with life.

Even the most remote corners of Scotland are steeped with tales of larger-than-life men and women, true heroes and heroines so great of heart and spirit they could easily stride across the pages of any romance novel.

The opening scene for this book was inspired by one such heroic soul, Lieutenant Colonel T. W. Cuthbert of the Seaforth Highlanders. A well-respected man and devoted animal lover, he died while trying to rescue a drowning ewe in a lochan. I learned of him while staying at the Eddrachilles Hotel on Scotland's wild northwest coast. Colonel Cuthbert rests in the hotel's lovely rhododendron-filled garden, and it was there, as I paid my respects to him, that I decided how Robbie and Juliana should meet.

Special thanks as always to my editor, Karen Kosztolnyik, whose glowing warmth, expertise, and intuitive wisdom shine ever so brightly. Deepest gratitude, too, to my true-hearted friend, Roberta Brown, for being such a brilliant light in the dark.

And as ever, all my appreciation to my handsome husband, Manfred, my real-life knight, for his understanding, patience, and strength. And, of course, for wee Em, my own four-legged champion, who knows very well that I would not trade him for all the world's romance novel heroes combined.

*Only
for a
Knight*

The Legacy
of the Black Stag

❧

$\mathcal{I}$N THE MIST-SHROUDED FASTNESSES of Kintail, a rugged
country of sea lochs, wild heather hills, and moorlands on
the western coast of Scotland, one man has e'er held
sway. Since time beyond mind some might say, Duncan
MacKenzie, the famed Black Stag of Kintail, has called
this hauntingly beautiful place his own.

His, and the great house of MacKenzie, the most powerful clan in the region.

Truth be told, those who visit Kintail cannot help but
be awed by the grandeur and magic of the land, or the tall
tales circulated about its legendary chieftain. A deceptive
air of tranquility and timelessness clings to the dark peaks
and shadowed glens, a peace made possible only by the
puissant Black Stag's competent rule—and his formidable reputation.

Few are those who would cross him.

And most who have tried are no more.

Yet, of late, during long Highland nights beside the
fire, the more bold amongst the tongue-waggers declare

that the Black Stag has grown complacent and would surrender his lairdship to his only son and heir, Robbie
MacKenzie. A braw young man whose task would seem
tame, inheriting a land so favored, its people already
loyal and true.

But all is not as it seems in the soft Highland air and
broad, cloud-hung hills of Kintail, its purple moors and
empty glens.

For deep within the most remote corner of this expanse of hill and sea, change and disruption stir like an
ancient benediction chanted just beneath the surface to
echo across the heather until even one so mighty as the
Black Stag cannot deny its truth.

Or run from the burdens and memories of the past.

Robbie, too, must trod the path of fate.

A path indelibly inscribed on his destiny and unleashed by the whispered last wishes of a frail and dying
woman.

Chapter One

❦

Glenelg in the Spring, 1344

"*Repay Duncan MacKenzie?*"

Juliana Mackay stared down at her mother and reached to smooth the threadbare plaid tucked so lovingly about the older woman's thin body. She hoped she'd misheard the ill woman's unthinkable request.

After all, her mother had lost much strength in recent days. The words had been rasped in little more than a dry whisper.

Straightening, Juliana wiped her palms on the many-times-patched skirts of her kirtle and struggled against the urge to flee from the pathetic sight before her. She wanted to wrest open the rough-planked door and run from the mean little cot-house of sod, heather-thatch, and stone, until she'd put all her cares and woes behind her.

Instead, she drew a deep breath and fixed her gaze on the peat fire smoking beneath a heavy iron cooking pot. *Repay Duncan MacKenzie.* The very notion ignited her spleen and twisted her innards.

Aye, she'd surely misheard.

But in case she hadn't, she squared her shoulders and folded her arms. A stance meant as much to stave off any further appeal as to keep herself from yielding to her own panic and fears and raining a thousand well-peppered curses on the man whose family had brought such grief to bear upon her own.

Juliana clenched her hands. Duncan MacKenzie deserved a *hundred thousand* curses piled onto his head.

But she knew without asking that any such outburst would only plunge her mother into another coughing fit.

"The Black Stag is one of the most heavily-pursed lairds in all the land," she said at last, trying not to see the feverish glint in her mother's eyes—the desperate plea hovering there.

But even by the feeble glow of a lone tallow candle, the ravages of impeding death stood all o'er Marjory Mackay's once-beautiful face.

And the truth of it jellied Juliana's knees and brought out the worst in her.

Her fierce pride and her seething resentment that despite the monies and aid the MacKenzie laird had sent their way over the years, her mother—long-time hearthmate to the laird's unlamented late half-brother, Kenneth MacKenzie—had been forced to suffer raising her children in a one-room hovel, dirt-floored and divided only by an ox-hide curtain.

"Duncan MacKenzie has trod heavy-footed over you for all your days," Juliana bit out, using her own booted foot to nudge a loose pebble from the hard-packed earthen floor. "He ne'er acknowledged your bond to his brother nor cared that my father sired two bairns on you—the Black Stag's own niece and nephew!"

Frowning, she paused to grind the pebble back into the dirt. "He holds gluttonous feasts in his stout-walled Eilean Creag Castle yet e'er left you, his own brother's leman, to scrape the barest living from these hard hills, soothing his conscience by having a milk cow or a jangling pouch of siller delivered to us whene'er he recalled our existence."

"He had his reasons, child," Marjory Mackay wheezed from her pallet.

Juliana sniffed. "I mislike that you would even consider owing him restitution." Stepping closer to the pallet, she dabbed at her mother's brow with a damp cloth. "I have ne'er heard aught more . . . unnecessary."

Marjory closed her eyes, pulled in a ragged breath. "Times were worse than you ken, food scarce. Without the MacKenzie's largesse, you and your brother Kenneth would have had to endure an even harsher, more comfortless life. Think you I can . . . exit this world without repaying the man whose aid spared my bairns from hungering?"

"You are not going to die." Juliana wrung out the cloth, squeezing it tighter on each word before re-dipping it into a wooden bowl of cool spring water. "I will not allow it."

A delicately-veined hand, astonishingly strong, reached to circle Juliana's wrist. "The good Lord alone decides when a body is to join Him, lass, but I . . ." A bout of breathlessness stole Marjory's words, the flecks of pink-stained spittle she coughed up twisting Juliana's heart.

"If the good Lord or His great host of saints have any

mercy in their wing-backed souls they shall work their
wonders to see you well again," Juliana snapped, the
words coming sharper than she would have wished.

"You must do as I ask and deliver the monies to the
Black Stag for me. I have a missive for him as well, writ-
ten when I first sensed my end was near." Marjory half
raised herself from the pallet, her glassy-eyed gaze sliding to the rolled parchment on the cottage's sole table.

"I do not have much longer," she added, squeezing Juliana's wrist before letting her hand fall back onto the
plaid coverlet, the last of her strength clearly leaving her.
"I would know this done."

Following her mother's gaze, Juliana pressed her lips
together and said nothing. She'd seen her mother labori-
ously scribbling away on the precious piece of parchment—the saints knew where she'd obtained it. Or the
ink-horn and quill now resting so innocently beside the
curled missive. Such luxuries were scarce and few in this
narrow glen where they lived, all but cut off from the outside world.

"Duncan MacKenzie has siller enough of his own—
and to spare!" Juliana glanced at the rusted, iron-latched
strongbox where she knew her mother kept what coin her
brother Kenneth sent to them.

Hard-earned monies intended for their mother's use
and not to be hoarded, unspent.

And of a certainty, not to be delivered into the hands
of the notorious Black Stag for the singular purpose of
adding to that one's already overflowing coffers.

Her gall nigh choking her, Juliana glared at her
mother's pathetically battered money coffer, resentment
flowing through her like a deep and sullen river. Truth

was, if her mother had put the monies to good use, mayhap refurbishing the thatch of their cottage's leak-plagued roof or repairing the countless chinks in the stone and sod walls, perhaps then Marjory Mackay's ailing would not have taken such a ferocious turn for the worse.

As it was, Juliana could only pray to God for her mother's recovery—or a peaceful release from her travails.

That, and wish the Black Stag of Kintail to the lowest, most wretched of hells.

Bristling, she hoped her vexation did not stand writ upon her face. "The MacKenzie has not sent you aid since Kenneth and I are grown. Had the man e'er desired repayment, he would have surely demanded suchlike by now," she said, amazed by the steady calm of her voice.

She jerked her head toward the strongbox. "Yon coin comes from Kenneth—your son, I'd beg you to recall. And I vow, were he here, he would be of a like mind. Duncan MacKenzie is a hard and savage man. He has no need of restitution."

Biting her lip to tamp down the floodtide of heated epithets dancing hot-foot on her tongue, Juliana paused to press the cool cloth to her mother's feverish forehead. "On my soul, would you desire the truth of it, there are those who say Duncan MacKenzie has a devil in him and you ken he has e'er lived in fine style. I doubt he would even appreciate the gesture. So why deign him with such a boon?"

A long, shuddering sigh escaped Marjory's parched lips. "Are you so blind, lass? Can you not see the matter has scarce little to do with the coin—or even whether or

no the Black Stag appreciates the message I would have
you bring to him?"

"I see naught but sheerest folly and would wish you to
desist with such a foolhardy notion," Juliana countered,
her scuff-toed boot already worrying another pebble
imbedded in the well-swept earthen floor.

"Then I have not raised you to be as far-seeing as I
would have wished." Marjory's thin fingers clutched at
the plaid covering her. "Of more import than the good
man's acceptance or refusal of my offering is that the giving of it shall solace my mind. Whilst the breath of life is
still in me, lass, I plead you to heed my wishes."

"Good man." Juliana couldn't help but scoff, her
blood chilling with the implicated surrender in the words
she was about to say. "Kenneth will be sore wrath when
he learns."

"That is as may be, but your brother is not here and we
can ne'er ken when he shall choose to visit us. I would
know this done now so that—" Marjory broke off to raise
herself on an elbow. She fixed a determined stare on Juliana. "So that I may take my leave of this world in
peace."

"And I cannot take myself off into the heather and
leave you here alone . . . to . . . to die unattended." Juliana dropped to her knees beside the pallet, stroked a
sweat-dampened strand of hair from her mother's brow.
Fine, sunfire-colored hair, bright as Juliana's own. "I simply cannot do it."

"You can and you shall, for you are strong," Marjory
argued, reaching to take one of Juliana's fiery-red braids
in her hand. "Let us say Godspeed now, my dear heart,
and give me the closure of your word."

Juliana bit her lip, shook her head in staunch denial, hot tears spilling free now, each damnable one nigh blinding her.

"I ask this of you only so I may know peace," her mother persisted, letting go of the braid to touch tremblycold fingers to Juliana's cheek. "Promise me, lass. I beg you. Swear to me that you will do this—and be on your way by cockcrow on the morrow. So that I—"

"Pray God in all His glory, do not say it again," Juliana surrendered at last, pushing to her feet, amazed her watery knees could hold her upright. "If this means so much to you, aye, I shall go . . . I will see to this for you, I promise," she agreed, the words bitter ash on her tongue.

Swallowing hard, she squared her shoulders and pulled in a long, steadying breath. "Aye, I give you my word the deed is as good as done."

❧

Later, just as darkness settled on the coast of Kintail and the quiet hush of evening began curling round the stout walls of Eilean Creag Castle, loch-girted stronghold of Clan MacKenzie, Lady Linnet moved about the keep's well-appointed solar. She was a comely woman of middle years and the same flame-bright tresses as Juliana.

Ill ease niggled at her, dogged her every step. An unpleasant and cloying chill it was, and persistent as the inky shadows laying gleeful claim to those corners of the solar not fully illuminated by the crackling log fire blazing in the chamber's fine stone hearth.

Trying hard to ignore the frightfully familiar sensation, Linnet paused at one of the solar's tall, arch-topped windows and looked out at the pewter-gray surface of Loch Duich far below.

Most times, the view from this chamber soothed her. Indeed, she came here often, the lonely beauty of the empty shores and the great heather hills that stretched beyond in endless succession never failing to gentle any and all unwelcome thoughts.

Until now.

This night, far deeper cares than usual bore down upon her shoulders and occupied her increasingly troubled mind.

Truth be told, she scarce noticed the heart-wrenchingly lovely world whiling so still and tranquil beyond her windows. Nor did her ears catch much of the keening wind racing in from the not-too-distant sea to ruffle the loch's dark waters and whistle past Eilean Creag's night-bound ramparts and turrets.

For rather than the wind, the lady Linnet heard the sound of bees.

A multitude of buzzing bees.

The most dread sound to e'er plague her—the sound that always heralded one of her spells.

Her visions.

Seventh daughter of a seventh daughter, 'twas a curse she'd been spared in recent years, but one that seemed determined to return with a vengeance. This night should have been filled with naught but celebratory joy, for word had come at last that her stepson, Robbie MacKenzie, was finally returning home to Eilean Creag.

"Ten long years." She turned to her liege husband, Duncan MacKenzie, hoped her voice sounded level and firm. She could not tell for the din of the bees was nigh deafening now.

A nightmarish cacophony robbing her of her wits and making her weak.

Vulnerable.

Moistening her lips, she clasped her hands together, lacing her fingers to stave off the trembling. "Do you think he is truly coming? At last?"

Her husband set down the wine cup he'd been drinking from, wiped the back of his hand across his mouth. "Think you he would dare not come? Knowing his betrothed is on her way here? Even now as we speak?"

A chill streaked down Linnet's spine at the word *betrothed*—a deep-reaching, breath-stealing cold that spread clear to her toes, enfolding her.

Still fighting it, ignoring the tell-tale signs, she shivered, drew her woolen *arisaid* closer about her shoulders. "Think you it is wise to wed him to the lady Euphemia?" she challenged her husband. "The daughter of a man you yourself have called a scourge upon the heather?"

Duncan waved a dismissive hand, shook his dark head. "She was chosen *because* she is that lout's daughter, as you well ken," he minded her, coming forward to rest his hands upon her shoulders, kneading them. "'Tis a necessary alliance if e'er we are to enjoy true peace in these hills."

"And if the lad finds her not to his liking?" That, from a tall, scar-faced man lounging in the shadows of a window embrasure. "Would it not be more prudent to let Robbie first return home and resettle himself before fetching the lass to his side?"

"Och, but there speaks the eternal voice of caution."

Duncan aimed a dark look at his friend and good-brother, Sir Marmaduke Strongbow. "Euphemia MacLeod is already on her way here—as you well know. To send her back now would be an intolerable affront."

"Such insult might prove the lesser evil if Robbie finds the maid not to his liking," Sir Marmaduke gave back, ever undaunted by the Black Stag's scowling countenance. Indeed, he leveled a penetrating glance of his own at his long-time friend and liege laird. "Perhaps you have acted in haste."

"In haste?" Duncan's dark brows snapped together. With a huff, most decidedly issued for Marmaduke's benefit, the redoubtable Black Stag strode back to the table, poured out a fresh measure of the blood-red wine, and downed it in one gulp.

"The lad has traipsed about the land these last years, doing as he pleases and garnering a reputation of valor nigh as untarnished as your own," he said, his hot gaze pinning Sir Marmaduke, daring him to declare otherwise. "Robbie gave his promise, his solemn vow, to wed the MacLeod lass *before he left*. Think you he would despoil his honor now . . . by refusing to accept her as his bride?"

E'er a paragon of level-headedness, Sir Marmaduke kept his unblinking stare locked on Duncan. "I warrant he will uphold his promise," he said, folding his arms—and doing so with enough practiced leisure to bedevil Duncan beyond endurance. "Aye, he will no doubt keep his word, and his honor. I only wish he would have had some time to . . . adjust."

"Sacrament!" Duncan's dark blue eyes blazed. "He has had ten full years to adjust—or sample enough sweetness elsewhere, if you have forgotten. *Ten years*,"

Duncan said, his tone—and the rapidly beating twitch in his jaw—giving his friend no quarter. "The MacLeod lass will suit him well enough, I say you. She is pleasing to the eye and of sound wits—unlike her oaf of a father."

Some might argue that Robbie suffers such a sire as well, Linnet thought she heard Sir Marmaduke comment. And whether he'd spoken the words or no, Linnet's husband gave him a dark oath in response.

Or so she imagined.

Not that she could hear much of what either man had to say, for the droning buzz in her ears had reached a fever pitch.

Ignoring the men, for she was well accustomed to their ceaseless ribbing, she turned her back on them lest they note her discomfiture, the perspiration beading her brow. Determined to remain calm, she stared into the hearth fire, peering intently at the fiery-red flames licking at the well-burning logs.

Fiery-red flames that soon became a tall and lithesome maid's unbound cascade of shimmering red-gold tresses. Beautifully-waved tresses that spilled clear to the young woman's shapely hips, each shimmering strand shining bright as sunfire.

The lass stood tall and proud, untold happiness seeming to radiate from every glorious inch of her. And from someplace deep inside Linnet, a hidden corner far removed and safe from her hard-pounding heart and the sweat trickling cold between her breasts, Linnet knew she was staring at her stepson's bride.

A truth she would have recognized even if the lass weren't standing in front of the MacKenzies' famed Marriage Stone, a large blue-tinted stone incised with ancient

Celtic runes, a near-perfect hole in its center—the main piece and pride of every MacKenzie wedding ceremony.

A clan tradition all down the centuries.

The MacKenzies' most sacred talisman.

Aye, the lovely maid with the flame-bright hair could be no other.

Trembling now, her knees nigh giving out on her, Linnet struggled to keep standing, reached deep inside herself to maintain her composure even as she willed the lass to turn, to glance her way, so she could see the maid's face.

But such visions cannot be summoned nor steered, Linnet well knew, and even as she stared, the image began to waver and fade until the bright-shimmering tresses were once again nothing more than dancing flames, the beautiful young woman, and the celebrated Marriage Stone, gone as if they'd never been.

"Sir . . ." Linnet began when she could find her voice, forgetting herself in her flustered state and calling her husband by the title he loathed her to use. "Duncan," she corrected, careful to keep her back to him, feigning calm. "You say the MacLeod lass is fetching. I would know, is she . . . flame-haired? Perchance like me?"

"Nay, she is nothing like you." Duncan's answer came swift and, oddly, exactly as Linnet had feared. "Euphemia MacLeod is dark. A wee snippet of a lass with dark brown hair and eyes. She will make a meet bride."

"A meet bride," Linnet acknowledged, her heart sinking. *But not for our Robbie.*

That last she left unsaid.

Kintail.

Robbie MacKenzie reined in his sure-footed Highland garron on the crest of a windswept ridge and surveyed the wide heather wilderness spread out before him. He drew a deep breath, filling his eyes and half certain his heart would burst now that he'd finally crossed into his father's territory.

Wild, bright, and sunlit, the mountains, moors, and glens of home stretched in all directions, rolling endlessly to a broad, cloud-churning horizon. Sweet, fair lands he'd ached to see every night of the ten long years he'd been away.

Necessary years, needed to earn his reputation and valor, but a trial all the same. And now he was a man of full age and abilities, well able if not entirely eager to step into his puissant father's footsteps.

And, too, to accept the daughter of a rival clan chieftain as his bride, thus assuring peace in this rugged and mountainous land.

"God's mercy," he breathed, staring out across Kintail at its springtime finest, taken unawares by the deep emotion coursing through him.

Saints, even the thought of Euphemia MacLeod, the lass he'd agreed to wed but had yet to meet, could not dampen his spirits. Indeed, with good fortune blessing him, the lady Euphemia might prove none so ill a match. He might even surprise himself and find her to his liking: warm, voluptuous, large-bosomed, and . . . all woman.

And if not . . . then so be it.

He'd make do with his lot.

His honor demanded it of him.

But for this one blessed moment, the most perfect

noontide he could have wished, naught would mar his pleasure or steal the sweetness of his homecoming. The heather ridge he'd chosen for his outlook bore clutches of silver birches and tall Caledonian pines, whilst the hills more distant wore deep blue shadows and sparkling white cornices of snow.

And, joy upon joy, beyond them waited Loch Duich and Eilean Creag Castle, as yet hidden from view, but there all the same.

Calling to him until he was nigh ready to fling himself from the saddle, drink in great, greedy gulps of the tangy gorse-and-juniper-scented air. And, aye, even throw off his clothes, every last stitch, and roll full naked in the heather!

By the Rood, but it was good to be home.

Or so he thought until a short while later, furious shouts, the near-crazed *baa'ing* of a sheep, and the sounds of wild, *wet* thrashing broke through the birch scrub and juniper tangle to his left, the panic in the shrill *female* cries shattering his jollity at once and dashing cold, stark dread onto the peace he'd let slide all over him.

A dread that clamped icy fingers around his heart when, as quickly as the fracas had arisen, the earsplitting cries and loud splashings ceased.

From one lightning-quick blink of an eye to the next, naught marred the silence save the frantic *baa'ing* of the sheep, now joined by the equally distressed-sounding neighings of a horse, and the uncomfortable roaring in his ears of his own fast-thundering heart.

"Sweet holy Christ!" he yelled, spurring hard now as he sent his garron plunging through the prickly juniper bushes and gorse. *Saints have mercy,* he meant to cry when the beast burst free of the underbrush, but the words lodged in his throat, caught and held there by the horror of the scene before him.

Leaping out of the saddle, he looked about, but saw only the shaggy-maned garron whose neighing agitation had captured his ear. A sway-backed wretch of a beast, the aged creature watched his approach from near a jumble of boulders, wild-eyed, panting, and skittish-looking. A leather travel bag had been tossed aside, or mayhap slipped from its fastenings and now laid open atop a flattened clump of bell heather, a scatter of good Scots siller spilling from its depths to litter the peaty ground.

The *baa'ing* sheep, a drenching-wet ewe, stood beside a black-watered lochan, shaking water droplets from its oily fleece and looking more angry than frightened.

The *lass*, the one whose cries and thrashings had frozen Robbie's blood, stood a good ways into the lochan, submerged to her waist, the front of her gown ripped and gaping open to reveal a set of full, magnificent breasts, gleaming wet and with sparkling beads of water dripping from her tight-budded nipples.

But it was the crescent-shaped gash in her forehead that arrested Robbie's attention and had him tearing into the icy water, boots, plaid, sword, and all.

Bright red blood flowed copiously from the wound, discoloring to pinkish-red what surely had to be the fairest face he'd e'er laid eyes upon.

Swaying wildly in the peat-stained water, she stared at him from unseeing green eyes, her arms flailing, her mouth opened wide in a silent, ghastly scream.

"Hold, lass!" Robbie found his own voice as he

plunged forward, the silty bottom of the lochan and his clothes sorely hampering him. "I will have you anon!"

But just as he closed the distance between them and reached for her, her oddly blank eyes rolled back into her head and she slipped beneath the surface, disappearing completely save the billowing skirts of her ruined gown, the top crown of her head, and two red-gold braids.

Nay, Robbie corrected himself as he gathered her in his arms and carried her, blessedly still breathing, out of the lochan.

Not mere red-gold, but a rare and shimmering flame-bright color.

Aye, that was it.

The lass had hair of flame.

And as he eased himself to his knees and gently lowered her to a grassy patch of delicate little flowers, yellow tormentil and buttercups, Robbie knew only one thing—he wanted her.

Chapter Two

❧

THE FLAMES OF HELL ROAST HIM if he'd e'er desired aught more fervently. Frowning, Robbie glanced upward and repeated the oath to the great dome of the sky, his pulse racing even if the fiery-haired beauty met his astounding revelation with supreme indifference.

Indeed, she made no response at all.

He could not be more reactive.

Awareness, sharp and immediate, tingled along his spine and clawed at his guts as he stared down at the lass, watching her as if they were both caught up in some eerie silent dream. A world gone deathly still. The wonder, awe, and magic of earlier now tinged with something . . . unnameable.

Unnameable yet real enough to split him open and lay him bare.

Robbie's heart thumped. He moistened his lips. "God in Heaven, lass—can you hear me?" he pleaded, struggling against the urge to shake the silence from her.

He blinked, his throat tightening as disbelief thickened the air. He hadn't come all these heather miles for . . .

this. To see a lass's light extinguish beneath his hands when 'twas plain she was a maid whose beauty and joy of life should have burned bright as a star. Yet her fine-drawn features remained without expression, her wide, generous mouth slightly parted but unspeaking. And the striking moss-green eyes, glimpsed so briefly and fringed with such thick black lashes, stayed decidedly closed.

Frightfully still.

Robbie set his jaw against defeat, moistened his lips again. Saints, he would have sworn his mouth had filled with stone dust! He winced. *Her* mouth looked anything but dry. And her lips, deeply sensual in their fullness, held a definite hint of seduction. Even now, in her unconscious state.

"Jesu—" He shivered—and not from his cold, wet clothes. With effort, he forced his thoughts elsewhere, silently vowed not to glance lower than her nose again.

A most delectable nose he couldn't help but note.

Steeling himself against the notion that the self-discipline he so prided himself on was ebbing inexorably from his control, he reached to ease a few locks of clinging, blood-soaked hair from her forehead. A great sweep of relief surged through him when she made a soft moan.

Sweet assurance that she lived, a hopeful sign called forth by the clumsiness of his touch.

A bumbling unsteadiness that had ne'er plagued him when gazing upon or tending much angrier wounds than the crescent-shaped gash one of the ewe's flailing hooves had engraved so close to the lass's hairline.

A blessedly shallow gash, but troublesome nonetheless.

As was his oafish ineptitude.

His inability to rouse her.

Robbie grimaced, his mood darkening. From some uncomfortable place inside him, emotions writ deep on his soul wakened and stirred as if rising from a long winter's sleep. Knowing he'd be wiser to ignore them, he pulled in several long, grounding breaths. But when the sought-for calm evaded him, he muttered a wicked oath and opted for sheer iron will to make his hands stop trembling.

It would help, too, if her ripped bodice didn't offer tantalizing glimpses of her full creamy breasts and tight rosy-brown nipples. If her sopping, bunched skirts hadn't fallen away to reveal the sweet curve of her hips and the shapely nakedness of her thighs.

And, saints preserve him, he'd know even greater comfort if he did not have the sinking conviction that somehow the very earth was about to crack open and swallow him whole.

Him, the dripping flame-haired vixen, and every shred of honor and chivalry he'd managed to amass over the last ten years!

But like a self-fulfilling prophecy, the harder he sought to school his wits, the farther any shimmer of control spun from his grasp until he knew with humbling certainty that even his fullest reach would prove futile.

Just as he knew with equal surety that his fingers trembled as much from the shock of *her* as from his head-long plunge into the chilly-watered lochan to rescue her.

Soon, a niggling foreboding warned him, *he* would be the one in need of rescue!

Narrowing his gaze on her, Robbie took one of her chill-reddened hands between his own and began briskly rubbing her fingers. Icy elegant-shaped fingers with neat, short-clipped nails. Lovely hands marred only by the work-roughened skin of their undersides.

Calluses.

The mark of a peasant.

As were the patches on her well-worn skirts and the pitifully scuffed, thin-soled boots gracing her feet. Robbie shot a glance at her ancient-looking money purse and the scatter of good Scots siller spilled across the tussocks of coarse deer grass. The coins glinted in the sunlight and to his amazement—or mayhap not—he puzzled more as to how the afternoon could still be so bright than where a lass of obviously meager means had happened upon such wealth.

Aye, knot-twisted as his innards were, as besieged his wits and hard-pounding his heart, he deemed it a wonder thronging clouds hadn't spread o'er the land and that raindrops weren't stippling the lochan's smooth, indifferent surface.

But naught had changed beneath the slanting Highland sun or in the day around him—only within.

His mouth still tinder-dry, he tightened his fingers on hers and massaged her cold, chapped palm with increasing vigor. Blood yet flowed from her forehead, so he reached one hand to the side, dug a thick clump of moist sphagnum moss from the yielding ground, and pressed the spongy, crimson-colored moss against the wound. Then he prayed God the sphagnum would work its usual good and stanch the bleeding.

He leaned close, peered fiercely at her as if by the penetration of his stare alone he could reach her. "Lass . . .

merciful saints, bestir yourself!" He tried again to revive her, and failed.

Save for a faint fluttering of her thick-lashed eyelids and another barely audible moan. A tiny breathy sigh. But reaction enough to give him his first true lift of the heart since he'd glimpsed her.

And what an eyeful she was!

Forgetting his impossible vow not to look lower than her nose, he let his gaze devour her, the neck opening of his drenched tunic seeming to grow tighter with each slow beat of his heart. Frowning, he reminded himself to breathe. But, holy saints, even wet and bedraggled, there could be no denying the splendor of her. A high-colored beauty, ripe promise limned her lush curves in ways he ought not be noticing.

Especially under the circumstances of his return to Kintail and the unavoidable duties awaiting him at his father's Eilean Creag Castle.

In particular his responsibilities to one Lady Euphemia MacLeod.

His betrothed.

A lass he suddenly knew would prove as cold and unforgiving as a long dark winter—if she even perceived herself wronged.

"Aye, well . . ." Robbie muttered to himself, the softly spoken *acceptance* slipping off his tongue before he even realized its portent.

But before certain relevant conclusions could assail him, he relegated Lady Euphemia to the farthest reaches of his mind—for the nonce, at least—and returned his fullest attention to more immediate concerns.

Ill-placed attraction or nay, the wild possibilities of

every glorious inch of this golden, voluptuous maid whirled inside him, quickening his pulse and sharpening his senses. Keening, too, a needful urgency he hadn't known himself capable of rendering—until the sheer impropriety of his longing caught hard at the back of his throat.

Tearing his gaze from her, he stared across the lochan at the cloud shadows teasing their way across the braes— stared until he'd better steeled himself.

Thus fortified, he touched her face again, used the edge of his dampened sleeve to wipe her blood-stained cheek. "Have no fear, all will be well," he murmured, willing it to be so, hoping his assurances weren't just empty blundering. "You wear your good health as robustly as your high looks—a single wee cut from a ewe's hoof will not be enough to have done with such a braw fine lassie."

His heart thudding, he lifted the clump of sphagnum and peered at her forehead. Praise the saints, the bleeding appeared to have lessened. But as if his ill ease had not yet been fully unfurled, the moment he pressed the moss to her wound again, a great shudder tore through her and she began to shiver.

Uncontrollably.

Truth be told, she shook so fiercely that just by holding her he could feel her every tremble echo down the length of his own over-chilled body.

Her teeth chattered, too.

At once, stinging heat shot up Robbie's neck. He ought be scorned with a thousand Gaelic curses! The lass was dripping wet, freezing, and like as not catching a surer death than a single ewe's kick could e'er hope to give her, and he'd done naught but slap a clump of quickly-dug healing moss onto her forehead.

His own head beginning to throb, Robbie pushed to his feet, already unbuckling his sword belt. Casting it aside, he drew in a deep, shoulder-bracing breath, prepared himself for what he was about to do.

The lass needed to be stripped naked, rubbed dry, then held warm until she stirred.

Just as he, too, ought—and soon would be—shedding more than just his sword belt.

To prove it, he shrugged out of his drenched plaid, yanked off his boots, and made admirably short work of any other piece of cold and cloying garb yet clinging to him until naught clothed him but the afternoon's gilding sunlight and the fine Highland breeze.

Full naked, and with the living air around him crackling with expectation, he strode to his horse, his purpose soundly fixed. And damn his unchivalrous hide, but he thrummed with excited anticipation as well.

A fool could see the lass wore no undergown and that once freed of her soggy kirtle, naught but her fiery braids would cover her luscious breasts. A splendid bounty he'd already feasted his gaze upon. And he wouldn't be a man if he hadn't noted that she lacked hose as well—naught but the smooth, sleek skin of her bared calves showed above her sadly scuffed boots.

"Blessed Saint Columba!" Robbie muttered as he rummaged in his traveling gear, pulled out a voluminous plaid and two clean linen tunics.

Wheeling about, he returned to her, dropped the items on a patch of high-growing deer grass, and, once again, promptly forgot the wholly absurd vow he may as well have scribbled on water. Driven by a force he did not even consider schooling, he let his gaze drift lower than her nose.

A good deal lower.

Ignoring any shades of reproof his honor might hurl at him, he listened only to the rapid *clacking* of her chattering teeth and, sinking to his knees, reached for the edges of her torn bodice. Already, the ragged cloth gaped wide, exposing her in all her lush plentitude. Robbie swallowed, his heart pounding as he began easing the drenched gown down her shivering body.

Glistening droplets of water sparkled on her full, perfectly formed breasts and tiny rivulets formed, rolling down the wet-gleaming skin of her stomach to form eye-catching little pools where the bundled mass of her soaked skirts yet bunched about her naked hips.

Robbie gave himself an inward shake, and summoned all his strength. Then, with a quick downward tug, he freed her of the sopping garments.

Again, the sheer impact of her hit him like an iron-balled fist to the gut, her ripe lushness stealing his breath and firing him in ways that had his every muscle tensing. Setting his jaw, he tried not to glance at the wet, garnet-red curls springing betwixt her thighs—and failed.

There, too, water droplets glistened in a nigh irresistible beckoning. More tempting still, the faint spice of her *female* scent wafted up to him, and catching it, he looked away at once. The musky scent's tang beguiled him, especially laced as it was with the freshness of heather and the dark sweetness of peat. His heart thumping, Robbie pulled in a slow, steady breath—the best he could manage with his throat and chest constricting so acutely.

And if any other part of him tightened more than he would wish, he strove to ignore it.

More difficult was ignoring his fierce urge to look at her *secret charms* again. And look right well. So he gathered her in his arms and pulled her tight against him, shielding her delights from immediate view, but promptly delivering himself a whole new batch of woes unleashed by the startling intimacy of the over-close embrace.

Frowning at the necessity of such a measure, he snatched up the dry plaid he'd retrieved and swooped its generous folds around their shoulders, letting its wooly length warm them both.

Not that he needed much warming.

His trembling had little to do with chilblains.

Saints, but the maid was fashioned to grace a man's most heated dreams.

And *he* ought be made of a finer metal!

A better tempered steel, hard and resistant.

Run steely-hard indeed, Robbie gritted his teeth and began massaging the lass's naked back beneath the cover of the plaid, rocking her gently to and fro as he did so. He also wished himself a better master at the fine and much neglected art of *ignoring* and wished even more that on his long journey home he'd availed himself more often of the buxom tavern wenches and warmhearted young widows who'd offered him all manner of salacious comfort along the way.

But only one of the fulsome lassies had truly captured his interest—an ale-keeper's plump and gap-toothed daughter. And because of her and what she'd offered him, the progress of his journey had dwindled to a snail's pace.

Aye, he ought to have been home days ago—and

would have been—had not the persistent serving maid pressed *other wares* on him when he'd repeatedly rebuffed her amorous looks and bawdily proffered favors. Clearly bent on winning some coin from him, however achieved, she'd listened to his excuses about hurrying home to wed his betrothed, then seized his hand and led him to a smoky corner of the low-ceilinged alehouse.

With a triumphant flourish, she'd pointed behind a trestle bench piled high with kegs and flagons to where a clutch of tiny fat-bellied puppies frolicked and tumbled amid the strewn bones, onion peels, and other refuse littering the soured floor rushes.

A wee puppy, she'd declared, all fluff and floppy ears, would delight his new bride and surely soften her heart . . . if indeed the lass needed a bit of taming.

And Robbie had agreed.

But not because he felt he required any assistance in wooing Euphemia MacLeod. Like most MacKenzie men, Robbie suffered more trouble fending off willing wenches than attracting them.

Nay, he'd simply been charmed by the wee pups— losing his heart to a chubby little round of brown and white fur he'd dubbed Mungo because the alehouse stood not far from the mighty cathedral church of St. Mungo in Glasgow.

Remembering, he slid a glance at the small wicker hamper affixed to the back of his saddle. Even now, the wriggling little fellow peered at him over the side of the tiny basket, the pup's bright brown eyes quizzical.

Praise be the saints, the mite's gaze appeared only curious and not . . . *urgent*.

Wee Mungo had piddled and soiled his way all

through the Great Glen into Kintail, the necessary pauses not only delaying the journey, but without doubt causing Robbie to have passed by this lochan at such a propitious moment.

At the thought, Robbie paused in his circular rubbing of the maid's back, a quick stab of guilt piercing straight to his conscience. Many were they who'd claim his encounter with the fiery beauty anything but propitious.

Vowing to hush any such tongue-clacking should the like arise, he compressed his lips until the moment passed, then resumed kneading the cold, smooth shoulders pressed so close against his heart.

"Fear not, lass, I will let naught befall you," he murmured against her hair. "No matter who you are or what troubles follow you. Just waken, you fine braw lassie, and I promise all will be well. . . ."

All will be well.

Ne'er forget you are a fine braw lassie . . . naught will befall you while I am away.

I promise. . . .

The familiar words slid past Juliana's ear, softly spoken but strong enough to penetrate the cold darkness pressing all around her, powerful enough in their dimly remembered assurances to echo in her mind with the same throbbing insistence of the pain pulsing in her forehead.

But then the voice faded, leaving only a dull ache and blackness. That, and a sweet, all-enveloping warmth that cushioned her from the little nigglings of dread licking at her from the whirling shadows.

Dread, and a maddeningly elusive sense of . . . *purpose.*

Something she must do.

If only she could remember.

Or stop the red-hammering agony in her head.

"Come you, lass. Open your eyes," the man spoke again, his voice still close by her ear yet louder this time, more clear. And laced with a definite tinge of concern.

Deep inside Juliana, a part of her still hazed and sleeping reached toward him, yearned to soothe his worry. All the saints knew, he bore a heavy enough weight upon his shoulders without her adding to his burden.

And he'd spoken naught but the truth. She'd always fared well during his absences for she was indeed strong—steely-backed, he'd often declared in jest, his dark blue eyes twinkling when he teased her.

But much as she wished to reassure him, her lips wouldn't form the words.

Truth be told, she couldn't move at all.

Not until he touched probing fingers to her forehead and a lancing pain such as she'd never known streaked clear to her toes.

"Eeeeeeeee . . . ow!" she cried, jerking violently in his arms.

Arms that had only ever held her in loving, joyous reunion or sad, parting embraces—till now.

She blinked, peered through stinging eyes at the beloved face. But billowing red-tinged fog still swirled all around her, blurring the edges of everything and even making the familiar features appear somehow different.

She just couldn't say *what* was different.

"Whate'er have you done to me?" She pulled back from his tight embrace, fixed all her confusion on the concern-filled eyes watching her so strangely.

"My head—" She raised trembling fingers to her forehead, felt the tenderness and pain, the warm stickiness of congealing blood. "I am bleeding," she stammered, more startled than anything. "What hap—"

"Hush, sweeting, dinna you fret," he soothed, brushing his cheek so closely against hers she would have sworn he kissed the tip of her nose.

Something he always did when he meant to tease or comfort her.

At the remembrance, the sweet golden warmth of familiarity swept through her again and she leaned into him, wrapped her arms around his broad, naked shoulders.

Naked shoulders?

A tremor of . . . *something* . . . skittered down Juliana's equally unclothed spine but the throbbing in her head wouldn't let her make sense of what bothered her.

What was so different and . . . wrong.

So she gave herself defeated and sank back into the cushioning warmth, nestling her head against the welcome strength of his shoulder. Whate'er plagued her, he'd fix it. He always did, e'er knowing her very thoughts before they even left her lips.

They were so alike.

Almost adrift on the blessed peace his mere presence lent her, she dared to stretch gingerly testing fingers along the top of her forehead again, measuring in silent assessment the damage to her brow.

She sighed. A lifetime spent living close to the land had stripped her of embracing anything but the cold, hard truth. But hurtful or nay, there was e'er room for hope.

And Juliana collected hope, seizing every wee shimmer of goodness that she could, stashing each precious blessing in her heart like bright water-washed pebbles.

Aye, she'd learned early on to always look on the more felicitous side of whate'er life laid at her feet.

So she reached inside for her deepest strength, then eased herself back to look into the face she so cherished. Touching her head wound again, she tried to give him a not-too-wobbly smile.

But when even that small effort proved too difficult, she contented herself by lighting her cold lips to his cheek in the dearest kiss she could muster.

"See you, Kenneth, now we shall be truly alike," she whispered, her voice shaky. "Now we will have nigh matching scars."

"Kenneth?" The man's deep blue gaze, so familiar and yet not, sharpened. He stared at her, his brows drawing together in a frown.

Nay, more a look of total perplexity—an expression that nowise detracted from his dark good looks or hid what she only now noticed.

The irrefutable truth that his handsome face bore nary a scar.

Certainly not the three vertical slashes she'd expected to see marring his left cheek.

There was simply nothing.

Naught save his undeniable handsomeness and the intensity of his questioning gaze.

Juliana bit her lip. For the first time since she'd wakened, an icy chill sluiced through her. "You are not—"

"Kenneth?" he repeated, pushing to his feet. "Nay, to be sure, I am not, though I once had an uncle of the name." He sketched her a quick bow.

A fully unabashed naked bow!

Juliana stared. Faith, she could even feel her jaw dropping. Foggy-headed or no, she was quite certain she'd ne'er seen a more . . . *naked* man. She blinked. Her heart began to pound in her throat and she started shivering again—even as her cheeks flamed hotter than two clumps of red-glowing sea coal.

"Sir Robert MacKenzie at your service," the strapping knight said, wearing his nakedness as boldly as she sought to cover hers. "But 'Robbie' will suffice."

Staring at him, Juliana drew the great plaid closer about her chilled body. *"MacKenzie?"*

She blinked again. Faith, but the name gave her an inexplicable jolt.

He merely nodded. "The MacKenzies of Kintail. My father is Duncan MacKenzie, the Black Stag. Mayhap you ken the name?" He paused a moment, then continued when she only gaped at him. "I am his son and bound home to wed my betrothed."

This time it was her turn to nod. But she couldn't speak for her mouth had gone ash-dry. And something— a swift-descending emotion best described as a sharp stab of resentment—made her insides tighten and quiver like a well-wrung cloth.

Most disturbing of all . . . she didn't know why the name MacKenzie distressed her. As did the name of his family's stronghold, even though he hadn't spoken it aloud.

She knew the name regardless.

Eilean Creag Castle.

Juliana shuddered, just the whisper of the dread place sent hot bile rushing to her throat. She curled her fingers deeper into the soft woolen folds of the plaid and looked at the knight, the knifing pain in her head clearly addling her wits.

As with his name, she had no idea why the mere thought of his home so repulsed her.

". . . and you?" he was asking her in a friendly enough tone but with a definite hint of easy command lacing the gentle question.

Hearing it, some inborn thread of rebellion made Juliana straighten her back and square her shoulders—despite the agony the brisk movements cost her.

Biting her lip rather than cry out again, she tugged the great plaid a wee bit higher up her breasts. Whate'er had brought her to this miserable pass, she would not sit on the grass and cower before him like a frightened rabbit.

"I asked your name," he repeated, still quite naked and coming forward with a length of cloth he'd ripped from the hem of a clean, dry shirt.

Juliana swallowed, tried to keep her gaze on the improvised bandage in his hand.

With deft movements, he began securing the linen strip around the top of her head. "Who are you and whither were you bound? Before you decided to take a swim with yon grazing ewe?" He jerked his head toward the still-dripping animal. "Saving her life nigh cost you your own."

"Then I offer you my profoundest gratitude, Sir Knight." Her voice held just a bit of a quiver, as if she couldn't quite wrap her tongue around the words.

Or didn't want to—but that was ludicrous.

She had no cause to dislike him.

His nakedness forgotten, Robbie raked a hand through

his damp hair, watched as a variety of emotions played across her lovely face. And the longer he studied her, the more he couldn't quite shake the impression that she half expected him to sprout horns and a tail.

"Robbie will serve," he minded her again, deliberately keeping his tone light. "Pray do not call me *Sir Knight*. For you, my lady, I am simply Ro—"

"I heard the name, good sir," she blurted, inching the fool plaid nigh to her chin. A most fetching chin with just a flavor of defiance in its pert lift. "As to my name and where I was going . . . I . . ." She faltered, let the words tail away as her wee spark of oh-so-appealing boldness faded to dismay.

She glanced at the mounded heap of her ruined kirtle. A carefully stitched-on patch showed conspicuously amongst the soggy folds.

"My name—" she began again, then promptly bit her lower lip, stared at him. "Ach, I can tell you that I am not a lady. That much I know." She poked her foot at the wet gown. "I vow you will agree that no gently born lass would suffer to wear mended skirts?"

Robbie's jaw tightened. True lady or nay, he'd but meant to accord her the courtesy. And would. "Even so, fair maid, I would still learn your name."

"Think you I would not tell you if—" she started again, only to break off once more, this time pressing her lips together in clear consternation.

Her lovely moss-green eyes clouded and she looked past him toward her ancient nag of a garron. But when her gaze left the shaggy beast to light briefly on the spilled coins and her raggedy money purse, Robbie could see her confusion mounting—just as he also would've sworn she was inwardly steeling herself before she looked back at him.

"You needn't fear me," he said, deciding she must indeed be afraid of him, for whatever misplaced reason. "I have ne'er harmed a woman in my life and would sooner cut off my sword arm than cause any female even the most fleeting moment of distress. Gentle-born, cot-reared, or otherwise. You have my word on it."

"I am not affrighted of you, sir," she declared, her voice a shade stronger. "'Tis only that I have dire need to be on my way."

"Unclothed, my lady?" Robbie couldn't resist teasing for she'd lurched to her feet so quickly she'd forgotten to hold fast to the plaid.

"Oh!" Frozen in shock, she flattened one hand across the lush triangle of red-gold curls at the top of her thighs and jammed the other, spread-fingered, against her well-rounded breasts.

Snatching up the two linen shirts he'd also thought to gather, Robbie thrust them at her, indicating the one he'd ripped to make a bandage for her head.

"You can use the torn shirt to dry yourself and the other . . . that one, you can wear to cover yourself unless your travel bags hold better?"

But a glance at the two leathern satchels assured him they did not.

As did the lightning-quick flash of perturbation flaring in her magnificent eyes as she clutched both tunics to her wet-gleaming nakedness.

"And you, sir?" she challenged, the slant of her gaze reminding him at last of his own . . . exposure.

But, a true son of his father, Robbie could not keep his

eyes from crinkling with reluctant amusement as he donned his own fresh garments. Then, having refastened his still-damp sword belt low on his waist, he folded his arms and waited in appreciative silence as she struggled into the undamaged tunic.

Knightly honor or nay, fetching lass or otherwise, an insistent cribbling along the back of his neck warned he ought not let her out of his sight—not even for her modesty's sake.

She also warranted a close eye because her deliciously creamy skin held an unnatural waxy pallor. Equally alarming, she swayed on her feet. And despite all his precautions and care, she still shivered.

More vexing still, at least for him, she also seemed to have tangled her arms in his much-too-large-for-her tunic.

Robbie heaved a great sigh, knew himself lost. Looking on as she twisted and turned in her efforts to don the garment proved both an immeasurable delight and a torture beyond all imagining.

Unable to endure watching her innocently sensual windings a moment longer—or mayhap worse, not wishing to imagine how easily he could bring a cessation to her trembling if only he'd forget his honor long enough to pull her lushness flush against his body and *un*chill her with a searing, soul-stealing kiss—Robbie drew a stiff, bracing breath and strode forward.

He closed the short space between them in two long strides and, with one practiced flick of the tunic's hem, urged its cloaking length down over her charms until the soft linen folds molded seductively to her bounty but also shielded each golden inch of her from prying eyes, including his own.

Especially his own!

Even so, he purposely lifted one corner of his mouth in a way he knew brought out his best dimpled smile.

Better to capture her attention with a look he hoped she'd find charming rather than risk her noting how intensely the temptation of her unclothed twistings and turnings had affected him.

There were some things a man simply could not hide.

Things even the best-draped plaid failed to disguise.

Careful to keep his gaze on her, and well above her fetching nose, Robbie willed her to look at him, to notice his smile. But she paid him scant heed. Not to his focused gaze, his dimpled smile, nor the unruly evidence of his *admiration*.

Indeed, she'd scarce smoothed the folds of his shirt in place o'er her sweetness before she began looking from side to side, her beautiful eyes troubled as if she sought something she'd lost but didn't know what.

When she dropped to her knees and began searching through the wet heap of her ruined kirtle, Robbie could bear no more. "Come, lass," he urged, his dimpled smile receding as he drew her to her feet. "Your kirtle has served its purpose—"

"You do not understand," she protested, jerking free. "I'd hidden it for safekeeping . . . here, in the folds, see you? But it is gone."

"*It?*" Robbie eyed the sodden gown, cocked a dubious brow. Save a wealth of patches and too many years of use, the kirtle had scarce little to offer. "What, lass? What are you searching for?"

"I— . . . cannot tell you . . ."

Robbie arched a brow, strove to ignore the increased surge of icy tingles spreading up and down the back of his neck. His gaze slanted to the spilled coins still fanned haphazardly across the grass.

Coins that, despite his noblest efforts, loosed his tongue.

Any maid with such reddened, work-worn hands would need a lifetime to gather even half as much siller. Truth be told, many a landed man he'd encountered o'er the years would rub their palms in glee to possess a lesser sum!

"Whether you can tell me or no, I think you should," he suggested, eyeing her. Holding her gaze, he folded his arms in a way that mirrored one of his father's favorite postures—the Black Stag's I-am-the-laird,-tell-me-or-die pose. "Aye, I find myself desirous of knowing."

"The coin is not ill-gotten," she huffed, meeting his challenge with a defiance most surprising in one of humble birth.

But low-born or nay, Robbie's heart clenched when she drew a deep, shuddery breath and clutched her middle against the chills still racking her.

"I only wish to help you," he said, uncrossing his arms at once. "But I canna if you refuse—"

"I am not a thief." She hurled the words at him, a bit of pleasing color coming back into her cheeks with the brisk denial. "Aye, that I know beyond a doubt. I would not steal a bannock were I starving. 'Tis only that I— . . . I promised and I have e'er taken care—"

"Och, lassie, do you not see 'tis *you* who are in need of care?" Robbie's smile returned, his own niggling doubts forgotten. Every last one of them banished by the snapping indignation in her beautiful eyes and the returning vibrancy not only staining her cheeks but beginning to thrum all through her.

Already a rare beauty, her vexation set her aflame and Robbie found himself sore smitten.

Besotted enough to take a chance.

Sliding an arm around her waist, he pulled her as close as propriety allowed—now that they were both more or less clothed and she fully wakened and by her senses.

But she only stiffened and flashed him an indignant stare. "I did not steal a single coin of yon sillers," she repeated, clearly mistaking why he'd seized her.

Robbie heaved a sigh. "You err, lass. I care not whence you obtained the coin," he said, seeing no reason to lie. Truth was, she could be transporting a whole coffer brimming with shiny fripperies of mysterious origin and he'd feel the same. "'Tis seeing you well cared for that concerns me—naught else," he sought to reassure her. "Ne'er you worry."

"And neither should you, good sir. I can assure you that it is not every day that I seek to save a drowning ewe . . . nor do I wish to burden you." She tried to wriggle free of his grasp, then narrowed her eyes at him when she couldn't. "Leave me to while here a bit and I shall soon be well enough to be on my way—alone," she insisted, the shakiness of her voice belying her every spoken word.

Robbie cocked a brow. "I vow you ought not be left alone here or elsewhere." He glanced at her tired nag. "Nor do I believe your mount is fit to carry you where'er it is you wish to go."

To his considerable amazement, she gave a great heaving ruck and broke away from him. Determination pouring off every sweet inch of her, she walked purposely if somewhat wobbly to her horse.

"Whate'er ailings and laments may trouble me, I shall tend them on my own. As I have e'er done," she said, reaching for the pommel and trying without success to slip her foot into the stirrup.

A burst of annoyance rose in Robbie. He tried to quell a frown and couldn't.

Not after her bold stride across the grass.

Such a saucy piece ought be safely married and with at least two bairns a-tugging at her skirts. Or, better yet, tucked away behind cloistered walls where she proved no danger for unsuspecting knights haplessly riding through the day!

And dangerous she was, for just looking at her nigh robbed his ability to breathe.

Scarce a wonder since he'd ogled the wet-gleaming expanse of her naked breasts. Seen even more, truth be told. Aye, and hadn't he savored the enticing sweep of her unclothed curves pressed flush against his own naked flesh?

Saints help him, but with her abundant flame-bright hair and long-legged lushness, she was temptation incarnate. He narrowed his eyes at her, keenly aware of the tightening in his jaw.

And elsewhere.

Worse, his borrowed shirt only underscored her charms. Each fold of the linen clung provocatively to her ripeness, her every sweet curve offering more sensual promise than a man ought be made to suffer.

Robbie scowled. At her bounty. And at himself. Especially at himself. After so many years spent building his chivalry and honor, ne'er would he have believed he'd succumb to folly so easily.

And a great folly it was.

The absolute foolhardiness of riding into Eilean Creag Castle with such a ripe sweetmeat at his side. The lass good as unclothed, her moss-green eyes full of fire and indignation. Not to mention his own soon-to-be bride awaiting him, wholly unsuspecting and, without doubt, sure to be mightily displeased.

The repercussions did not bear thinking on.

Living them before this night came to a close would be penance enough.

And he did not even know the maid's name.

Chapter Three

HER NAME.

Robbie's need to know it burned through him like a fast-moving firestorm raging out of control.

Her refusal to tell him scalded with equal heat and proved an unacceptable omission he meant to correct—now.

"Lass." He pinned his gaze on her. "I would hear your name and learn why you are riding about—fully unescorted?"

She met his gaze with annoying calm. "Have you e'er seen a simple lass of the glens travel with a great entourage?"

Unable to refute her logic, Robbie gritted his teeth and rammed his fingers through his damp hair. "Then tell me your name and how, amongst the great heather hills, you just happened to be in the lochan when I rode past?"

"Because the ewe just happened to be drowning when I rode by," she said, giving him a small, noncommittal smile—and making no mention of her name.

Robbie shifted—stepped closer to her. "You may as

well tell me for you are accompanying me to Eilean Creag whether or no you grace my ears with who you are."

"Och, nay, and I will not be going with you." She lifted her chin, gave him an amazingly bold stare. "And I cannot tell you who I am, or my purpose for riding about, because I do not know," she said, a sparking flash of agitation lighting her eyes. "I canna remember."

Robbie's heart stopped. Then immediately began to thunder as the implications penetrated his surprise.

"You recall naught?" He stared at her, stroked his chin.

"Only hazy bits."

Robbie nodded, not trusting himself to speak.

Wild possibilities spun inside him, each one sending little bursts of excitement flickering across his skin— even as his chivalry damned him for seeing his own good fortune in her sorry plight.

But, of a saint's mercy, what man of honor could abandon such a sore-stricken lass to Glenelg's vast upland wilderness?

In especial, a *wounded* and clearly dazed lass?

Nay, to leave her would be . . . unconscionable.

Unless she sought to cozen him.

Unable to ignore the possibility, Robbie narrowed his eyes at her, studied her with a look that would've made a less daring chit's insides quiver.

"Only . . . *bits*?" He took another step closer, cocked a brow. "Yet you claim you can care for yourself and that you must hasten on your way? That much you profess to know?"

"Aye, to be sure and I do." She met his stare, unblinking. "I feel it in here," she added, and pressed a hand over her heart to underscore her words.

His own heart thundering, Robbie watched her begin collecting the spilled coins. With surprising calm, she gathered and stuffed them one by one into her pathetically worn money purse.

"I have naught to fear in this glen," she told him with a quick, sidelong glance. "I am safe here—you needn't fret for me."

Coming closer, she waved one of the coins at him. "But mayhap you will accept recompense—"

"God's eyes—but you can set a man by his ears!" Robbie accused, though with enough good humor to take the sting from his words. "I do not want nor have need of your siller. As for you traipsing about these hills alone, I warrant you could not venture far in your present state, if your sweet life depended on it."

He tilted his head to the side, gave her his best smile again.

She remained unmoved.

"My life, sir, is my own concern," she said. "And my good conscience depends on reaching my destination—a task I cannot accomplish if you persist in keeping me from the solitude I need to recover my wits."

Robbie glanced up at the gathering clouds and tried to keep the corners of his mouth from twitching. Any village idiot could see the lass had wits enough to spare. She suffered no need to recover them. They were merely . . . misguided.

"What you need, my *lady*, is warmth and comfort," he said in a tone of absolute reason. "You shall receive suchlike a-plenty at Eilean Creag, that I promise you."

"And who shall you charge with spending me this . . . care?" She fixed another penetrating stare on him. "Mayhap your soon-to-be lady wife?"

"If I tell her to see to your comfort, aye," Robbie declared, knowing he'd ne'er spoken more untrue words. "But it is my stepmother, the lady Linnet, who will lend you the greatest service. She has a healing touch and a kind heart."

"And you think to simply take me there? To your home? To these women—these *ladies* who neither expect nor know aught of me? In especial with me all but mother-naked and wrapped in naught but your shirt and borrowed plaid?"

Robbie nodded. The plan seemed more than logical to him.

Unless there was someplace else he ought better take her.

A notion he did *not* like.

"You lack adequate provender and plaiding to journey far on your own and your coin will serve you scarce little in these rough bounds. Or"—he waited just the sliver of a heartbeat—"were you heading someplace none too distant? To Kenneth perchance?"

She glanced away, her gaze settling on the dark-watered lochan, each tension-fraught moment of silence making Robbie feel all the more a doltish lout for mentioning the man's name.

A name that clearly disturbed her.

But he had to ask.

He could not keep her with him if she was bound to another.

That much honor he did possess.

"Is Kenneth your husband?" he asked into the stillness. "Were you taking him the siller?"

Or perchance running from him?

Leaving that last unspoken, Robbie folded his arms and waited.

She impaled him with a gaze that bespoke more answers than any words.

Urgency shimmered in her beautiful eyes and the luminosity of her unyielding, leaf-green stare made his heart beat fast. But above all, her eyes held a truth that sealed her fate and charged the living air with enough promise to encourage him to press her yet again.

"Kenneth," he repeated, his dread of her answer lying like bitter ash on his tongue. "Who is he?"

Juliana blinked, something inside her beginning to waken and focus . . . but not quite enough.

"I do not know who Kenneth is," she spoke true, her heart clenching on the name. "I do not remember . . . save that he is dear to me and that he is not my husband. Of that, I am in no doubt. He feels . . . otherwise."

The knight nodded, his expression unreadable. "And the coin?" he probed, the pulse hammering at his throat revealing everything his face did not—in especial, how unpleasant he found the question.

Or the possibility she might be a thief.

"You understand I must ask?" His voice was deep but surprisingly gentle. Soothing. "I assure you it shall make no matter to me what you say."

"I can tell you naught about the coin." Juliana's fingers tensed against the soft leather of the money purse. "To be sure, though, no ill deeds brought such wealth into my care."

Raising her chin again, she narrowed her eyes at him in her best challenge. But he only smiled—a dimpled smile that slid through her like sun-warmed honey, its distraction almost swaying her from her purpose.

"Smile as you will, I have done no wrong," she said, her tongue sharper than she'd wished.

"Och, I believe you well enough." Robbie's smile deepened and somewhere inside him a steady point of warmth began to pulse and grow. "I but needed to hear the words."

And now that he had, layers of tension started slipping from his shoulders. Truth be told, she filled him with a poignant longing such as he'd never known. Even the steel in her voice enchanted him and the defiant bravery in her snapping green stare only made her all the more appealing.

Since he could remember, he'd liked women with spirit.

Relished and savored them.

And this one's flame was only beginning to burn.

As if sensing how much her spark captivated him, she straightened her shoulders and favored him even more when a light flush colored her cheeks. Her gaze not leaving his, she drew a deep breath.

But not deep enough to pull more than a hazy image of Kenneth's face from the draughty emptiness of her memory.

'Twas a beloved face.

And well trusted.

A face triple-scarred yet still so handsome. And so eerily like Robbie MacKenzie's that she half expected the two men to merge into one.

But the strapping young knight's deep blue eyes speared her in a way Kenneth had ne'er looked at her. That much she knew. But who *was* Kenneth? And what was he to her?

Whoe'er he might be in her life, the penetrating stare he sent piercing through the mists clouding her mind assured her that he would not approve of her accompanying Robbie MacKenzie to Eilean Creag Castle.

Be he a good and noble-seeming knight of the landed classes or nay.

Eilean Creag Castle.

Juliana shivered. The stronghold's name disquieted her, spilling chills down her back and letting her feel . . . queasy. Nay, she could not go there. To do so would be to cause a great stir and much . . . unpleasantness.

Disaster deep as oceans.

"Good sir," she began, determined to dissuade, "with all gratitude and respect, I must decline your offer to take me to your home. I have assured you that I can care—"

"For yourself?" His dark brows shot upward. "Lass, be well certain, for the nonce, at least, you are not capable of caring for a flea. But mayhap you will manage to cosset wee Mungo? He is not much larger than a flea, I vow."

She peered at him, looking curious despite herself. "Mungo?"

Robbie tamped down a smile.

He had her now.

"Ach, you shall meet him soon enough," he promised, letting his eyes twinkle with amusement. "He will appreciate your attentions on the remainder of our journey."

"Our journey?" The color in her cheeks deepened at once. "You mistake yet again, sir. I am not going with you."

"Ah, lass, but I am thinking 'tis you who err." He stepped forward and the very air began to vibrate with what he was about to do. Trying his best not to grin, he seized her by the waist. "Think you my knightly heart will allow you to continue down the glen . . . injured as you are? And alone?"

Now he did smile. "Nay, my lady, 'tis for your own good that you must accompany me," he said, capturing her hand and turning it over to boldly kiss her palm.

"Oh!" She snatched her hand from his, glared at him.

"O-h-h-h, indeed," Robbie agreed, lifting her onto his garron's back before she could even think to sputter a protest. "Best ride pillion with me—until your own beast has been properly curried and fed."

More pleased with himself than he cared to admit, he snatched her nag's reins, drew the raggedy creature near. "Aye, this poor beast will benefit from a stay at Eilean Creag."

"You are a knight," she argued, clutching the pommel so tightly her knuckles gleamed white. "Your chivalric oaths bind you to save women, not abscond into the heather with them, unwilling."

"I did and I am saving you. From your own stubborn self—at least until you are well enough to be on your way again," Robbie countered, vaulting up behind her.

And praying the saints wouldn't strike him dead at the lie, for were the truth known, he ne'er meant to let her go.

Feeling a near irrepressible urge to enforce that desire, he slid his arm round her waist, pulling her firmly against his chest. "Once we've reached Eilean Creag and you've received proper rest and care, you will see the rightness of my taking you there."

"Nay, no rightness," she shot back, her voice tight with conviction. "It has naught to do with you—I simply have no wish to go there."

Robbie lifted a brow . . . not that she could see his face as he swung the garron away from the little lochan. Clicking his tongue, he nudged the beast's sides and urged him forward.

With good fortune and no further mishaps, they'd reach Eilean Creag sometime well after compline.

Eilean Creag, his waiting betrothed, and a homecoming he now both relished and dreaded.

❧

Much later and still a goodly distance from Glenelg's narrow, green-wooded fastnesses, darkness began enveloping the walls of Eilean Creag Castle. Each passing hour sent more veils of shadowy-blue mist to curl round the stout stone towers and slide gently across the quiet, night-bound ramparts.

Indeed, all seemed at peace and only the most observant passerby would have caught movement atop the battlements, noting perhaps the pacing figure of a lone, broad-shouldered man. An imposing-looking figure of great height and impressive build who repeatedly lifted a hand to his brow to better scan the distant horizon.

But not even the most sharp-eyed onlooker would know that high above the dark and rippling surface of Loch Duich another, much slighter figure paced as well.

A decidedly female figure.

Soundly ensconced within a stuffy little tower room, this figure paid no heed to the horizon. Truth be told, the unusually tiny woman had taken measures to hide the loathsome loch and its foul night vapors from her view.

Resenting those oh-so-necessary efforts, she slid a sidelong glance at the chamber's one rude table and eyed with increasing weakness the beckoning ewer of fine, strong ale. But such fortification could wait.

She needed her wits.

And, for the nonce, naught threatened her.

Loch Duich in all its silent bleakness lay harmlessly beyond the deliberately secured window shutters.

But even that precaution could not keep the chill night wind from blowing through the cracks in the shutter slats. Again and again, cold draughts whistled round her ears—finding and taunting her no matter where in the mean little room she tried to flee.

Still pacing, the quick-striding figure pressed her lips together in a tight line of perturbed irritation. Each wretched blast of the icy air proved a damning reminder that Sir Robert MacKenzie was taking his merry good time to make his way home to do his duty.

His duty to his father and his clan . . . and to her, Lady Euphemia MacLeod.

Not that his delay surprised her.

He'd already kept her whiling ten long years.

Ire consuming her, she paused to glare down at her betrothal ring. Its winking ruby, so large and heavy on her tiny finger, made cruel mockery of her diminutive stature.

Its size and worth, an obscene and contemptuous reflection of the rude little chamber, of how low in esteem the MacKenzies held her.

Her agitation mounting, Lady Euphemia touched a hand to her dark hair, patted the braids so tightly wound on either side of her face. Perfectly fine dark hair, even graced with a few strands of burnished red.

But only a few such strands and in tresses unfashionably thin and . . . *lank.*

Hair as lackluster as her quite ordinary brown eyes.

As unimpressive as her embarrassingly flat bosom.

Anger, venomous and hot as bile twisting through her, Euphemia snatched up the ewer of ale and treated herself to a generous swig of strength—straight and fast-flowing from the ewer's rounded lip.

Slamming down the jug with a loud *crack,* she could not control a quaver as her gaze darted about the pathetic chamber. A blasphemous excuse for a room, and—supposedly—given to her because it'd been Sir Robert's boyhood quarters.

And because of her . . . ailments.

Or so her betrothed's saintly-seeming stepmother had suggested the first time she and her two clack-tongued daughters had escorted Euphemia to the room, leading her up more stone steps and through more dark and chill passages than a single stronghold aught contain!

Only here, in Eilean Creag's most remote and desolate corner, the lady Linnet had explained, would the delicate Lady Euphemia be secure from the various 'air disturbances' supposedly permeating every other inch of Clan MacKenzie's formidable ancestral seat.

The Flemish tapestries and heavy brocade bed curtains adorning all other chambers.

The continual annoyance of the wafting smoke penetrating every nook and cranny of the stronghold—thick, choking ropes of eye-stinging unpleasantness e'er pouring out from the permanently overcrowded great hall with its ever-burning log fires and unfortunate proximity to the kitchens.

And then there were the dogs.

Duncan MacKenzie's many dogs.

Euphemia scowled and pressed a hand to her breast, half expecting just the *thought* of the mangy beasts to unleash a bout of painful, hacking coughs.

Aye, she'd while better here, the lady Linnet had insisted, not batting an eye as she'd whisked Euphemia into the disgraceful little room and immediately set about stripping away the chamber's every embellishment until only the barest furnishings remained.

Her chest tightening in vexation, Euphemia glared at the piteously naked floor, rubbed her small, fine-slippered foot back and forth across the well-swept and scrubbed wood planks. Nary a single bit of straw or dried herbs remained to lay siege to her sensitive nose.

Just as every other dust-collecting adornment and frippery had been gathered up and spirited away.

Misery washing over her, she flung herself down on the bare-stripped window bench, its cold, cushionless stone seat underscoring the bitterness roiling in her heart. A seething anger that had grown and festered ever since Sir Robert MacKenzie had sallied off to make his mark in the world so many long years ago—leaving *her* to brave the shambles of her fate.

A cruel destiny that had now landed her amongst

her enemies and in this mean and shabby excuse for a chamber.

Fisting her hands in her lap, she bit back the urge to hurl a string of blackest oaths at the room's damning bleakness.

Truth tell, she doubted hermits and anchorites lived as frugally.

But whether she secretly yearned for the beauty and rich trappings so evident throughout the rest of the MacKenzie stronghold or nay, fate had visited her with a condition that made this dismal little chamber her best refuge.

Even if she suspected the lady Linnet harbored other, more surreptitious reasons for sequestering her here, so distant from the teeming life and bustling activity pulsing through less remote corners of the loch-girt castle.

Euphemia sniffed, smoothed her tiny hands down the flat of her stomach. She, too, could be . . . devious. Knew ways to strike revenge into the most unsuspecting hearts.

Cold and cruel hearts.

Hearts that had cost her the very life-beat of her own.

At the thought, disembodied voices rose up to swirl in her head—accusatory snatches of converse, vile things whispered by the castle servants when they'd thought she couldn't hear.

Cold-eyed malcontent.

A mealy-mouthed slip of beggarly bitterness too wee and thin-hipped to even think about meeting her soon-to-be husband's conjugal demands—much less attract him into desiring their consummation.

Haughty and long-lipped.

"A shrew, they called me," she swore, her voice a curdled whisper. "And mayhap I am . . . but with good reason," she added with a tight little smile.

A contemptuous smile that remained in place as she stared into the gloom, her hands clenching and unclenching on her lap until, at last, the chill dampness from the window seat began creeping through her skirts, making her cough and shiver.

"Shrews can be clever," she wheezed as she pushed to her feet, her breath labored with the effort.

Crossing the room, she sank onto her bed without even attempting to remove her clothes or even her finely-tooled kid leather shoes. She laced her fingers across her stomach and glared holes into the dark wood of the unadorned bed ceiling, hating her weakness and damning the need that sent her into sleep garbed so uncomfortably.

But undressing would expend too much energy, and along with her wits she needed her strength.

Only so could she wreak the worst revenge on Sir Robert MacKenzie.

"Bleed him white, I will," she vowed through her teeth.

And to the last inch of his odious self-pleasing soul.

"I knew the maid would not prove pleasing."

Sir Marmaduke Strongbow folded his hands on the high table and slid a pointed glance at the lady Linnet, one of the few other souls yet awake at this late hour. Most of the castle folk already slumbered where they could, their plaids and pallets providing their bed-places, their snores and various shuffling noises rising up to herald yet another tedious night's passing in the smoke-hazed cavern of Eilean Creag's once so joyous great hall.

Joyous until the arrival some days past of Euphemia MacLeod and all her aggrieved sighs and posturings.

Wishing fervently that she felt otherwise about a lass who aught stir one's pity at the very least, Linnet refrained from commenting on her long-time friend's remark and continued to sip her wine in carefully controlled silence.

"I know you knew it, too, my lady."

Linnet's brow knitted. She took a deeper sip of the blood-red Gascon wine.

"You do not fool me, lady, and never could." Sir Marmaduke gently took the wine cup from Linnet's hand and returned it to the table. "Will you not tell an old friend why you seem so . . . untroubled by her?"

Linnet sighed, began tracing circular designs on the high table's pristine white linen covering. She also did her best to resist being captured by her friend's penetrating, all-seeing gaze.

"She would banish the very birdsong simply by walking through a wood, wouldn't she?" she finally said, making the words a statement.

"I am loath to speak ill of any woman, as you well know," he said, clearly picking his words with care. "But the devil burn my bones if I do not at least voice my . . . concern."

He looked at her, the expression on his face almost loosing her tongue. "I love Robbie as my own son, see you. I would know him pleased with his given bride."

"Then do not suffer yourself to worry, for I promise you he shall be more than content with his chosen mate,"

Linnet said, fixing her own gaze on the fat, red-glowing fire log still burning in the hearth. "The fullness of time will resolve any missteps the fates may visit upon the lad."

"Think you?" Sir Marmaduke sounded skeptical. "Some would say the fullness of time seems to have run its course," he groused, his brow lowering in a rare expression of ill humor. "I would not mention it did I not desire the lad's best—and I warrant he has exhausted whatever largesse of time the good saints would allow him. He ought to have been here days ago and his betrothed frets and paces in her quarters nightly, eager and impatient for his return."

"She is impatient, aye," Linnet conceded, not adding that she suspected the maid's irritability had little to do with a fierce yearning to welcome Robbie into her conjugal embrace.

"And none of this . . . disturbs you?"

"I have told you it does not." Linnet placed a reassuring hand on her friend's well-muscled arm. "Let that be enough for you."

"Let it be?" Sir Marmaduke snorted. "As *he* is letting it be?" He aimed a deliberate gaze at the smoke-blackened ceiling. "I vow your lord husband is wearing the soles from his boots pacing the parapet-walk day after day, night for night, scanning the horizon. To be sure, that one has not wasted a second glance at the MacLeod lass since her arrival, is scarce aware of her *influence*."

"My lord Duncan has other matters on his heart," Linnet agreed, pouring a measure of wine for Sir Marmaduke and setting the pewter cup in front of him. "The return of his son and, too, the undoubted success of sealing his alliance with Hugh Out-with-the-Sword MacLeod."

She tapped Sir Marmaduke's shoulder, slid the wine cup closer to his hands when he continued to ignore its offering.

"Observant as you are, even you cannot deny that nary a galley has been turned back from the narrows of the Kyle of Lochalsh since the lady Euphemia's arrival. Nor has a single fury-spitting complainant darkened our door, seeking redress against the MacLeods," she said, pleased when her friend lifted and drank the wine.

"As clan chief, such welcome peace will be clouding my husband's eyes and ears to any misgivings others may hold against Out-with-the-Sword's daughter."

Sir Marmaduke slammed down the wine cup, swiped his sleeve over his mouth. "In days of old, your liege husband would have dealt with Hugh MacLeod using naught but cold steel and a torch flame."

Reaching for the wine jug, he replenished his cup and tossed down its contents in one agitated gulp. "Often enough were the times Duncan kept that lout of a MacLeod from stretching his fool chain across the narrows, imperiling every hapless galley attempting to sail through these waters lest they surrendered an outrageous toll into Out-with-the-Sword's greedy hand," he said, his deep-seeing stare daring her to deny it.

And she couldn't.

The mighty Black Stag of Kintail *had* kept a watchful eye on the MacLeods in recent years, his far-reaching shadow and reputation enough to prevent the rival clan from making all too frequent use of their nefarious underwater chain.

The MacLeods' Girt of Strength, Hugh was fond of calling the chain whenever his affinity for drink put him in a boasting mood. Or, more often still, the prattle-mongers insisted, when his voracious appetite for light-skirted lasses left him desiring to impress.

To be sure, with its far end secured and hidden by a great cairn of stones, the heavy-linked chain could be raised and lowered at will from Hugh's castle's gate-house. Only a fool thought to slip past Castle Uisdean without rendering a tribute for the privilege.

A fool, or a shipmaster who stood in high favor with the Black Stag of Kintail—for all galleys bearing the MacKenzie banner were left to pass in peace.

Most times.

Linnet shifted on the hard seat of her chair, struggled to ignore the unpleasant tingles erupting along the nape of her neck.

Sir Marmaduke leaned close. "If the gossip in the glens can be believed these days, Hugh has grown too weak and addled to keep his many mistresses well-tended, much less raise and lower his dread water-chain," he said, slapping the flat of his palm on the table. "'Fore God, a bit of good swordery would be all the lout needed to be put back in his place should suchlike be required—not the marriage of his shrewish get to our own Robbie. The lad needs a bold-eyed, high-colored lass with curves a-plenty to warm him, I say!"

Linnet looked at him sidelong. "There have been other difficulties with the MacLeods," she said, hoping the smoothness of her tone would ease his irritation. "Little things, to be sure, but . . . annoying."

"Precisely," Sir Marmaduke agreed. "Countless trivialities that could all be addressed without saddling Robbie with a pinched-face maid lacking the charms to challenge even the least discriminating man's masculine susceptibilities."

"You surprise me, Sir Marmaduke." Linnet raised her brows. "Ne'er have I heard you speak so harshly of a woman."

He had the good grace to appear chagrined ... but only for a moment. "Then perchance you have spent too little time around me when I see those I love sinking into a bog of their own digging."

Linnet made no response.

She could not tell him of the fine flame-haired lass she'd glimpsed in the hearth fire. For meant to be or nay, in the end, a soul must choose its own freely followed path. She could only pray Robbie would choose his heart's path and not the road paved by duty.

Linnet's scar-faced champion of old gave something like a sigh.

"I crave your pardon, lady," he said, sounding anything but contrite. "'Tis only that in earlier times, Duncan would have never tolerated such deep-reaching changes to his household."

He made a great sweeping gesture with his arm, drew her attention to the cold stone floor, now swept free of the thick layer of rushes so crucial to lending warmth and comfort. A necessity, too, in absorbing the worst of the hall's ceaseless din.

"Nay, nay, nay, I say you, in days past, he would have stormed through here bellowing rage like a goaded bull." He looked at her. "And the worse for any who may have tried to stop him. Yet now, on my soul—"

"My lord only wishes the best for his son. And Kintail. His people," Linnet broke in, her fingers tightening on her wine cup. "And mayhap, too, he has simply grown weary of strife."

She looked toward the hearth again, stared at the small flames yet curling along the bottom of the fire log.

"He is not overly concerned because I have assured him all will be well with Robbie's marriage—despite Lady Euphemia's tight-lipped scowls." She slanted a glance at her friend. "Can you not trust me as well?"

Sir Marmaduke drew a deep breath, pulled down a hand over his mouth. "I should have faith when, by God's good graces, you and all within these walls seem bent on allowing this keep to be turned into a castle of gloom?"

He leaned close again, so near this time that his breath hushed against her cheek. "Dear lady, even your husband's precious hounds have been banished from the dais. Think you Robbie will not notice that change alone? You know how he favors dogs."

"Och, to be sure and I do," Linnet agreed, remembering Robbie's childhood devotion to old Mauger, the grandsire of nigh every dog within Eilean Creag's stout castle walls. And mayhap a goodly number beyond!

But in truth, she'd scarce heard her friend's words for her attention had drifted . . . elsewhere. Cold sweat beginning to trickle between her breasts, she pressed her feet against the unyielding stone of the now-bare dais floor and focused on connecting herself to her surroundings. Anything to distract her from the increasingly persistent chills and tingles.

The unsettling drone of approaching bees.

"Is aught amiss, lady?" Sir Marmaduke laid a hand on

her arm, the friendly contact pulling her back from the loud-buzzing abyss.

"I am . . . well," she lied, not wishing to alarm him— nor hearing a word of his concerned response.

The buzzing noise would just not go away.

Refusing to tremble, she managed a glance to the far end of the hall where her two daughters lay sprawled across the twin-facing benches of a deep window embrasure. They, too, sometimes possessed the power to call her back, her love for them strong enough to stave off the dread visitations before they could manifest.

If she could focus well enough.

Something she hadn't been able to do in recent days.

Hoping desperately that she could now, she peered deep into the window alcove. The flickering glow of a nearby pitch-pine torch cast sparse illumination into the arched recess. Not much light, to be sure, but enough to gild the sleeping forms of her daughters.

But her two precious girls were not alone.

A closer look revealed that nigh every four-legged beast to populate Eilean Creag had deigned to join them!

Linnet's heart lifted at the sight and, at once, the droning buzz of bees withdrew from her ears, and even the chills sliding up and down her back began to recede. And beneath the table, the tensed muscles of her feet and legs slowly relaxed.

She drew a shaky breath. This night, at least, the flame-haired beauty she knew could only be Robbie's meant-to-be bride would not be making an appearance.

Nor would any other harbingers her gift might have attempted to visit upon her.

Sighing with inward relief, warmth flooded her as she stared at her slumbering girls.

They, too, had kept a long vigil, waiting in vain for their brother's return. The older lass, raven-haired Arabella staring morosely at the hall's massive, iron-shod door the whole night through. And the younger Gelis, a lively girl with the same bright coloring as her mother, had forgone her supper in favor of brisk, ceaseless pacing.

Untiring and determined, she'd turned deaf ears on all pleas to return to the dais and had stubbornly made one circuitous sweep of the hall after the other, until the lateness of the hour finally wore down even her quick-thrumming exuberance.

"They have their hearts in the right place," Sir Marmaduke said, following her gaze. "You will not punish them?"

"Punish them?" She laid a deliberate lightness to her tone. "Chide them for staying below? For seeking and giving warmth and comfort when, of late, such . . . *disquiet* has surged into their world?"

Picking up a horn-handled table knife, she shook her head as she cut herself a thick slab of brown bread, smeared it with sweet, heather-flavored honey.

"Nay, I shall not chastise them, nor shoo them to their bed. I would sooner toss plaiding o'er the lot of them and scatter handfuls of comfits for them to find upon waking."

"Reward for their fortitude?"

"Aye, that would be the way of it," she admitted, touching the rim of her wine cup to her friend's.

Truth be told, she'd ordered the girls abovestairs hours

before—but to no avail. Should she waken them now, they'd simply claim they'd *had* to stay where they'd fallen asleep.

To move would have meant disturbing the equally slumbering canines and hadn't the poor beasties been trod upon enough of late?

And Linnet would not have been able to argue otherwise.

Besides, she, too, would relish snuggling in the cozy confines of one of the hall's deep window embrasures, a brace of soft, embroidered pillows and warm, adoring-eyed dogs to shelter and soothe her into a good night's sleep.

Something she'd missed in recent days with her lord husband spending his nights stalking the ramparts, no doubt repeatedly scanning Loch Duich's eastern shore and the enclosing, hills rising so close behind the loch's long-curving, shingled strand.

"Your stepson will show no less fortitude than your bonnie daughters," Sir Marmaduke said into the stillness, his deep voice so soft Linnet wasn't certain she'd caught the words aright.

"Beg pardon?" She blinked, hoping she'd misheard the ill ease in his tone.

"Robbie did not spend all these years away to return a spineless cockerel. He will do his duty by the MacLeod maid, seeing himself honorbound to marry her," he said, looking at her. "And that, dear lady, is what plagues me this night."

And those very concerns trouble me, too, Linnet's heart cried in response.

She simply nodded and gave him her most sincere smile of commiseration.

'Twas the best she could do.

That, and pin all her hopes on the maid of flame.

Chapter Four

HOME.

Robbie's first real glimpse of Eilean Creag Castle lanced his soul. His heart slammed hard against his ribs and for one startled, disbelieving moment he wondered what dastard had dared deliver such a ferocious, knock-the-wind-from-him blow to his chest.

But then he knew.

'Twas only all the wonder he'd been feeling earlier, spiraling back to enchant him anew.

His most intimate and beloved corner of Kintail welcoming him, with arms flung wide. Breathing deep of the damp, gorse-scented air, he tightened his hands on the reins, hot emotion pulsing through every inch of him.

Soon he would sit at his own fireside and the sweetness of that prospect possessed him, as did the incredible panorama of deeply-indented coastline and wide horizons spread before him.

E'er a wild country of sea lochs, broad heather slopes, and high mist-filled corries, Kintail with its rugged peaks so oft hidden by swirling clouds had always held his heart. Mayhap even since beyond the reaches of time, so great was his passion for this land. But tonight, his *true* home, this lonesome stretch of Loch Duich, squeezed the very breath from him.

Drawing up on a high, boulder-strewn knoll, he stared out across the black-frowning water, his gaze stretching past a scatter of kelp-strewn islets to the great loch-girted stronghold that had consumed his every waking and sleeping hour for more years than he wished to count.

Moonlight gilded the long stone causeway leading out to the island fortress. Looking at it, Robbie swallowed hard, a whirl of soul-deep longing welling inside him.

Saints, just the silhouette of Eilean Creag etched dark against the hills thickened his throat so fiercely he doubted he could speak if his life depended on it.

And to his manly shame, or mayhap not, red-hot fire needles jabbed into the backs of his eyes, making them sting and blur until he accepted the tears for what they were and used a fold of his plaid to swipe the telltale dampness from his cheek.

Aye, 'twas a night of magic.

A night filled with beauty and sparkling crystal stars—the brightest, loveliest of them all melted so softly against him in her sleep. He leaned down and pressed a light kiss to the top of her head, let his lips graze her sun-fire hair.

A liberty that would surely have cost him a *true* fist to his gut were she awake.

Mayhap even worse if she realized how very much he relished the simple liberty of just breathing in her fresh, heathery scent.

Unthinkable if she suspected how often, since leaving

the lochan, he'd remembered the musky tang of her womanhood. How that one wee whiff of her most intimate femininity had fired his blood. Sweeter than any rose, her scent intoxicated him beyond all good bounds of knightly restraint—and made him burn for more.

Much more.

He looked down at her, his gaze focusing on her thick, shining braids and fought against a raw need that wound tighter with each pounding beat of his heart. Knowing himself lost, he pulled in another great, lung-filling breath of the damp night air and let it out slowly.

Saints, but she'd bewitched him. Her hair alone held him in thrall, the gleaming red-gold plaits shining gloriously bright even in the pale moonlight of the windswept knoll.

Increasingly aware of bestirrings of a most ungallant and demanding sort, he cast a deep sigh and adjusted his hold on her. Just a slight shifting of her warm weight in his arms—enough so that, should she waken, she wouldn't be shocked by his . . . *condition.*

Though, in truth, he doubted anything would astound the lass. He knew without question that she was made of a finer, stronger metal than most.

Still, he did not want to unduly trouble her.

At least not until he'd figured out a way to keep her, *have* her, and do so without shaming her.

A heart's desire his honor alone declared an impossibility.

Emotion surging through him, he looked back out across the loch. The night-bound waters gleamed black as rare, polished glass and the moon spilled a rippling path of molten silver to the farthest shore, to Eilean Creag and . . . home.

He stared hard at the island stronghold, let his gaze caress the massive walls seeming to rise from the loch's glinting surface. He swallowed again, indecision beating through him with the same erratic pumping of his heart. Little nigglings of ill ease to temper the elation of his homecoming and send chills of foreboding sliding down his spine.

If only he'd taken a different route, hadn't happened upon this beauty.

If only he could peel back the hours and ride home with his heart as unsullied as his valor, rid himself of the enchantment she'd wrapped around him.

He cursed softly. As if he would change a single moment of the day even if he could. Nay, he'd keep her— even if he paid the highest price!

With an inward grimace at the trials awaiting him, he glanced up at the broad night sky. The clouds had thinned to wisps and a swath of twinkling stars glittered across the heavens, nary a one winking him mercy. Far from showing sympathy, their cold brilliance, so distant and aloof, only underscored his plight.

A dilemma he could easily solve by wheeling round his garron and riding away with his beauty. Absconding with her across hill and moor until they'd reached the edge of the world—a place where no living soul would care if she bore a name or no, and where he could do as he was wont without calling down certain ruination upon his clan.

A folly of a notion he considered no longer than the space of a breath and an exhale.

"Would that it could have been otherwise," he swore again, the softly muttered words snatched away by the wind before they could fall upon impressionable ears.

Then, without further thought, he tightened his arm around his treasure, dug in his spurs, and set his mount thundering down the rugged slope, into the night—and in the only direction his honor allowed him.

Honor.

The word slipped through the darkness, teasing the edges of Juliana's sleep but not quite waking her.

She tossed uncomfortably, snuggled deeper into her unusually soft plaid, and wondered when the Highland wind had started gusting so ferociously that it shook not only the rough-planked door of her mother's cot-house but also the hard-packed earthen floor beneath her bed-pallet.

Faith, even the heavy iron cooking pot swung on its chain—she could hear the commotion, an incessant jangle. And, surprisingly, the unmistakable creaking of leather.

But before she could puzzle over *that* oddity, or the unaccustomed solidity and warmth of her most-times cold and lumpy pallet, the voice she'd heard earlier spoke again, penetrating her dream.

Her brother Kenneth's voice, it was, and he was at home once again—however briefly. A journey he made whene'er he could, generously delivering the siller he'd earned at sea and supplying them with provender and goods he'd gathered in the months he'd been away.

His usual type of visit in which he'd stay only long enough to address whate'er tasks required a man's strong arm. But also taking precious time to reassure them of his love, see to their well-being, and, he would always insist, to steel Juliana's backbone.

To fire her mettle and make her strong . . . lest any smooth-tongued fool dare attempt to hurt her.

Use her as their mother had been used, however willingly.

"See you, lass, honor belongs to all whose heart is pure. Never you forget it, for I tell you true. Such glory is not the sole privilege of knights and lairds," his well-loved voice minded her, the comfort of his words making her forget the annoying rolling motion of the floor.

He'd caught her muttering dark oaths as she'd stitched yet another patch onto her best kirtle's thread-worn skirts. And, as he was e'er wont to do, he'd fixed her with a calm and steady gaze, then assured her she possessed sound wits and a stout, goodly heart—a generous heart.

Qualities that cloaked her in honor as shining and true as any nobly-born maid gowned in finest raiments.

And as always on hearing such words from him, her cheeks would flame and she'd glare at her patched skirts or her work-reddened hands before lifting a doubting brow.

But then she'd smile and promise to make him proud—to be as honorable as she could.

Yet now, she'd been given a task of monumental import and could not rouse herself from her pallet and its inexplicable jostlings—something harder than a band of steel held her in place. And even more unsettling, she couldn't escape the sure knowledge that following the path of honor would lead her straight into the devil's own lair.

A conviction that seized her with shocking clarity when, at last, she broke free of her dreams and awoke.

"You!" she spluttered, realizing at once the source of her dream pallet's odd rolling motions, the reason her humble bed of heather and bracken had seemed so . . . solid.

So hard and unyielding.

"Ha—the valiant knight-rescuer! I see you abducted me in my sleep," she accused, using snapping fury to disguise her surging confusion.

"Havers, lass, if that is what you think," came her only answer. That, and a decidedly masculine snort.

Irritation brewing, she struggled against him, curled her fingers around the arm he'd clamped around her waist as she tried in vain to loosen his iron-firm hold on her. "A base-hearted paladin who'd carry off a poor lass unable to defend herself!"

"Not so. You err. That was not the way of it," he disagreed, splaying his hand across her midsection in an obvious—and brazen—attempt to keep her from squirming. "I—"

"Your fingers are jabbing into my breasts," she seethed, keenly aware that they weren't poking her at all. Rather, they rested perfectly still, there, in the softness beneath the rounded lower swells of her bosom. "You are hurting me."

"Say you?" His deep voice held a trace of amusement. "Some would say I am only trying to keep you from falling headlong from this horse. I vow suchlike would cause you far greater pain than the tips of my fingers brushing against your . . . tender parts, my lady."

Juliana stiffened at his logic.

She could not gainsay him.

Not without appearing mushy-brained or ungrateful.

She *had* slid sideways in her silly efforts to claw free of his viselike grip. And he'd righted her with lightning-quick speed, only then sending his fingers spreading into . . . intimate places.

Not wanting to admit she recognized he'd saved her from what could have been a disastrous fall, she bit down on her lower lip and let silence convey her annoyance.

Truth be told, he wasn't moving his hand at all. Not now that she'd ceased tearing at his arm. But, more distressing still, the warm press of his oh-so-motionless fingertips seemed to be sending countless little threads of tingles twisting through her abdomen, and lower.

Especially lower.

Pleasant tingles, they were, and the likes of which she'd never experienced. A sensation both wildly exhilarating and vastly . . . disturbing.

She drew a deep breath, squared her shoulders. Anything to keep him from noticing the effect his flattened hand was having on the deepest region of her belly.

The *tingles* she feared might be glowing all over her abdomen as well as firing her within.

"I would ask you to remove your hand." She made the clipped words a statement. "It bothers me."

"I imagine it does, for it bothers me in the same way," he said, his voice a shade huskier than usual. *Softer.* "Nevertheless, I shall continue to hold you. Simply so you do not—harm yourself."

Juliana frowned. Faith and mercy, his richly-smooth voice slid through her in ways almost as unnerving as the heated tingles he ignited in her soft parts!

Hot indignation streaking up the back of her neck, she twisted round to glower at him. "You took advantage of a sleeping woman! You are still taking—"

"Mind it well, lass—I have ne'er had need to take advantage of any woman," he shot right back, matching her glare with a dark look of his own. "You were full awake and spitting worse fire than you are now when I plunked you onto this saddle. You only fell asleep after we'd ridden many leagues. And it was a much needed slumber, I am thinking. A rest only made possible because I held you so securely before me."

The truth of his words fueling her ire, she lifted her chin, tried her best not to blink. "And how do I know you were not doing more than holding me?"

"I vow you cannot know—so you'd best believe me. My knightly word ought be enough to quell your doubts. If you are wise, you will recall that I have already seen you mother-naked—bare-skinned in all your fine-glowing magnificence. Were I a less noble man, I would have partaken then, had I wished to do so. Do not think I wasn't tempted."

Juliana blinked after all.

But she said nothing.

Her mouth had gone too dry to speak and it cost her too much effort to convince herself that the shivers sliding through her just now were summoned by the freshening wind and not his bold words.

Or that some shockingly brazen part of her found it exciting that he'd called her naked body her *fine-glowing magnificence*.

He tilted his dark head to the side. "Shall we say it a truce?"

Recognizing defeat, Juliana nodded.

She also swung back around and trained her gaze straight ahead, preferring to stare into the ever-thickening night mist rather than suffer another moment of his cheeky dimpled smile and the mischievous twinkle that could light his dark blue eyes so . . . annoyingly.

"'Tis well, then, that we are at peace. For your good and mine." The words came low-voiced and just above her ear. "See you, we are almost there."

"There?" Juliana couldn't help the response from tumbling off her tongue, unnecessary as the question was, for she saw indeed the island stronghold.

The most formidable holding she'd e'er imagined.

"Eilean Creag," her rescuer-captor confirmed, the thick emotion warming his voice at odd contrast to the cold, unwelcoming look of his home.

A devil's lair, to be sure, the whole of it seemed to glower at her from the depths of her most gloom-ridden nightmares. High curtain walls and heavy, battlemented towers rose up from the mist, every dark stone of its massive strength resonant with threat and droning menace.

Juliana's breath caught in her throat. Eilean Creag looked to be a dismal place fit to be inhabited only by ghosts.

Or worse.

Finding Robbie MacKenzie less intimidating than his home, she leaned backward into his sheltering embrace, for once blessing his close grip on her, even welcoming the light kiss he dropped on the top of her head in response to a gesture he'd surely misunderstood.

As they rode on, she started to grow cold with a numbing chill that came from someplace deep inside her. A disconcerting notion that Eilean Creag awaited her arrival, even crouched ready to smote her. Trying to ignore the sensation, she glanced heavenward, pleaded the saints that the castle would prove as empty, barred, and deserted as it appeared.

Nary a flicker of light glimmered from its narrow, arrow-slit windows and not a single horn blast ululated their arrival on the lochside.

But someone—or something—watched them.

She could feel devil eyes boring into her, assessing her critically and willing her gone.

Quite certain of the malevolent stare, Juliana drew the borrowed plaid closer about her shoulders. Faith, even her stomach churned now and her palms were running slick with clamminess.

Her knight appeared oblivious.

Seeming to have forgotten her completely, he dug in his knees and sent his mount spurring ever faster down the shingled strand toward the stronghold's massive portcullis-hung gatehouse.

A manned gatehouse, after all, for at their thundering approach, the iron-spiked barrier began to rattle upward with a night-splitting screech of pulleys and chains. Light shone at last, too. A double row of low-burning pitch-pine torches lined the entry's narrow, tunnellike pend, the smoking flames casting weaving pools of light and shadow onto the dark cobbles.

More torches burned at intervals along the stone causeway looming beyond. And a second, equally for-bidding gatehouse at the causeway's end stood open, its portcullis already raised. Soft, yellow-flickering candlelight showed at each arrow-slit window in the twin-flanking towers.

But Juliana paid these details scant heed beyond fleetingly registering the general air of gloom and oppression. Nor did she note or care that her fingernails were digging so fiercely into Robbie MacKenzie's arm that she'd drawn his blood.

Something else held her rapt attention.

A vision so disturbing she would have sworn the world was about to come to an end—could she find her tongue! At the very least, a great shudder ripped through her and her heart plummeted to her toes.

For the devil paced the parapet-walk of the keep's highest tower.

A great, glowing-eyed demon of the night, he stopped his stalking the instant they clattered out of the arched pend beneath the first gatehouse. A nightmarish threat in the swirling mist, he leaned out over one of the merlons in the parapet's crenellated walling and stared down at them, his dark wings flapping about him like oversized raven sails.

Colder-looking than the longest winter night, and taller than any true man she'd e'er seen, his feral stare unleashed all Juliana's deepest fears, hurtling them at her one by one to skitter across her every nerve and lodge in the pit of her belly.

"Jesu God," she cried, certain she'd caught a whiff of sulfur on the chill night wind. "'Tis the devil himself . . . there on the battlements!"

Behind her, Robbie MacKenzie hooted a lusty laugh, gave her a quick, exuberant squeeze. "Aye, by the saints, more than a few have called him just that—and worse, at times!"

But his mirth went unappreciated, and his words chilled Juliana to the bone. Each one, an icy blast loosed just above her ear to banish all silly notions of black-winged devil-demons and restore her mettle.

But before she could gather her wits and sharpen her tongue, her knight gave a great whooping cry that sounded like *Cuidich' N' Righ!* . . . *Save the King!* . . . Clan MacKenzie's battle cry some dim memory assured her.

Roaring the slogan again, and with such fervor her eardrum nigh burst, he slapped his horse with the flat of his hand and sent them pounding across the cobbled causeway. They thundered straight through the second gatehouse's great portcullis arch, not halting until they reached the shallow steps leading up to the keep's massive iron-studded door.

"Och, fair maid, do you not see? Your ill ease is sorely misplaced," he assured her, lifting his voice above the sudden ululant winding of a horn. "Unless another has taken this holding, yon *devil* you glimpsed is none other than my own good sire, Duncan MacKenzie. The Black Stag of Kintail."

But Juliana had already guessed.

And with the guessing came the faintest tinge of certainty that her knight's imposing father had much to do with her own secret tragedy.

❧

Linnet came awake at once.

She sat bolt upright at the high table, blinked the heavy

sleep from her tired eyes. Where moments before the hiss
and sputter of a guttering torch had been the only sound
to penetrate her fitful dreams, now the stir all around
proved deafening.

Throughout the great hall, clansmen pushed to their
feet, some stumbling over trestle benches in their haste.
Eilean Creag's ageless female seneschal, Elspeth, Linnet's childhood nurse, sent wide-eyed spit boys scamper-
ing about with heavily-laden platters fresh from the
kitchens.

The old woman's iron-gray curls bobbed and her
apple-red cheeks glowed bright as she stood mid-hall,
clapping her hands and keeping a good-natured but stern
eye on the wee lads as they hurriedly placed viands, ale,
and wine on the long tables.

Closer by, Elspeth's grizzle-headed husband, Fergus,
slept at the end of the high table, his undisturbed snores
filling Linnet's ears — as did the excited barking of dogs
and the ceaseless shrilling of horns. And from somewhere
in the tower high above, fast-pounding footsteps and
shouting could be heard.

A cacophony that could only mean one thing.

Robbie had been sighted.

Her stepson had returned at last.

His arrival imminent.

Beside her, already standing, her one-time champion,
Sir Marmaduke, drew her to her feet. "I will not let you
fall," he promised, taking her elbow.

"I know . . . th-thank you."

Linnet pressed his hand, welcoming the firm, steadying grip — blessing the long years of friendship that let
him know her knees had grown weak over time. She re-

mained grateful as well for his undiminished ability to sense when her gift plagued her.

As if he, too, could hear the drone of bees buzzing furiously at the outer edges of her perception—or perhaps caught a fleeting glimpse of the tall, lushly-curved figure she'd seen briefly outlined against the flame-shadows of the hall's cavernous hearth.

"Lady." Sir Marmaduke gently squeezed her arm, gestured at her untouched cup of wine. "If there is aught troubling you, mayhap you should have a sip before yon door bursts open?"

Linnet raised arching brows at him, but she knew in her heart that her bravura did not fool her old champion. Not for the sliver of a heartbeat. He knew her that well— and cared that deeply.

"It is my hope that there will be no difficulties, dear friend," she said simply, reaching for the wine.

But the moment she lifted the cup to her lips, a jolting current of icy-cold pinpricks spilled down her spine. The air around her became so thick with the scent of damp earth, heather, and gorse, she would have sworn she stood in the middle of the purest Highland glen and not on the dais of her own smoke-hazed great hall with its usual less-than-pleasing smells.

More strange, the comely lass, so generously made, no longer stood so proud yet insubstantial, in the crackling flames of the hearth fire.

Nay, she now stood beside Robbie in the open keep doorway—a vision come to life on the arm of an incredibly handsome young man whose likeness to his father had only increased in the years he'd been away.

Her breath catching in wonderment, Linnet stared

across the hall at her stepson, now a man of full years and every well-muscled inch of him as impressive as his sire.

With his plaid slung oh-so-casually across his shoulder and his sword belt fastened fashionably low on his hips, he'd acquired an irresistible air of twinkling-eyed confidence and pride that warmed Linnet to the roots of her soul.

For unlike her lord husband's still-daunting air of ferocity, Robbie MacKenzie's well-defined dimples and crinkly-eyed smile spoke for a man who wore his name and power with ease, but who tempered his strength with a pleasing measure of good humor.

The long years had been good to Robbie.

Not so, the proud beauty at his side.

Even if one ignored the borrowed shirt and plaid clinging so fetchingly to her generous curves, the maid's scuffed boots told a tale of their own—as did the determined lift of her chin and the heated flush on her cheeks.

The way her bold green gaze took probe and measure of every MacKenzie eyeing her so curiously.

Linnet stared, too, may the good saints forgive her. And her heart thudded heavier the closer Sir Marmaduke escorted her to this living vision she'd glimpsed only in hazy dreams and quick-passing instants of brilliant but fleeting clarity.

Whate'er had befallen the lass, she wore a strip of linen bandaging around her head and dear Elspeth, without doubt having noted the maid's disheveled state, already fussed over her, clicking and tut-tutting her tongue, and shaking her gray head like a mother hen.

Yet through all the stares and old Elspeth's attentions, the lass stood tall and kept her head held high, her shoulders and back straight and unbending. She clutched a tiny brown and white puppy in her arms, her fierce hold on the wee ball of fluff the only indication of the great strength of will it cost her to remain so calm.

Indeed, her remarkable self-possession and lissome grace claimed the hall and all within, hushing even the most boisterous clansmen to momentary silence and changing the penetrating stares to looks of interest if not outright welcome.

Even Linnet's erstwhile champion appeared smitten.

"There is the bold-eyed, high-spirited lass Robbie should wed," he decided, speaking the words just above her ear. "And with enough curves to warm him of a long winter's night . . . just as I said he needed."

But Linnet scarce heard him for in that moment the light of a flaring torch caught and shone on the maid's coppery braids. As if lit by an unseen hand, the gleaming plaits took on all the bright-shimmering colors of a thousand sunbursts, giving Linnet the surety of what, to that very moment, she'd only suspected.

And hoped.

The lass's sunfire hair was unmistakable.

"She *is* the lady of flame!" Linnet gasped as the forgotten wine cup slipped from her fingers, its spilled contents leaving a blood-red trail across the bare-swept floor. *"Robbie's bride—"*

"—is abed and will be sleeping!" Sir Marmaduke's deep voice rose above her blurted words. "In her frail health 'tis surely best if we do not disturb her slumber," he added, propelling her past the wide-eyed scrutiny of those near enough to have heard her strange outburst.

He glared round as he elbowed a path through the

jostling throng, letting the confidence of years and the look on his face warn any clansmen whose noses might be a mite too long to hold their fool tongues.

Her blood still roaring in her ears, Linnet pressed his arm. "You are ever my champion," she said. "My thanks to you, truly." She slid another glance at the fiery-haired lass, then jabbed a warning finger into Sir Marmaduke's ribs. "Yet, I say you, she is—"

She broke off when a sudden *whooshing* rush of air swept past them. A gusting blast of black-winged wind so strong its passage whipped the wall hangings and set the torches to hissing and sputtering in their iron brackets.

"Saints, Maria, and Joseph! Where have you been, laddie?" Duncan MacKenzie cried, his great plaid still flapping round his shoulders.

Breathing heavily, he grabbed his son's arms and stared, his dark eyes spilling over with a brightness that belied the bluster of his greeting—and explained the unusual roughness in his voice.

A telltale gruffness that instantly wiped out more childhood hurts than Robbie had managed to eradicate in all his years away.

Blinking the hot moistness from his own eyes, he reached down to tousle the head of one of the many hounds running circles round his legs, their tails wagging furiously. Only then did he dare cast another look at his father, pretending not to see the strands of gray at the older man's temples, the deep-creased lines of worry that hadn't been there before.

Blinking again, he tried his best to speak past the thickness in his throat. "I . . . my journey—"

"Your journey took far too long, but never you mind,"

the Black Stag declared, dragging Robbie into a bone-crushing embrace, his still-authoritative voice buzzing in Robbie's ears. "You are here now, and your bride—"

"Shall we fetch her, Papa?" Two innocent voices chimed at Robbie's elbow.

Breaking free of his father's bear hug, Robbie wheeled around to stare at the girls.

His sisters, and near full grown!

"Arabella? Gelis?" His voice caught on the impossibility that these two burgeoning lovelies could be his scrawny, flat-chested sisters. "Can it be?"

Two deep dimples appeared in Gelis's rosy cheeks. "Do you not recognize us, Robbie?" She twirled in a circle, white teeth flashing delight. "Though I admit we have surely changed . . . a wee bit. You, though"—she rose on her toes to plant smacking kisses on either cheek—"you appear to have turned *rogue*."

She slid a sidelong glance at her raven-haired sister. "Do you not agree, Arabella?"

That one said nothing, but nodded.

Not that she needed words after the look she'd exchanged with her younger sister.

A *mischievous-eyed* glance Robbie recognized.

He almost gave a short, mirthless laugh, but opted to brace himself instead. Throwing back his shoulders, he curled his hands around his sword belt as casually and demonstratively as he could. A wise move, too, for the light of a thick wax table candle revealed the girls' expressions and told him they were about to pour fat onto the fire in earnest.

"Who is *this*?" Gelis demanded, turning to Robbie's beauty to begin the assault. Her glee barely disguised, his youngest sister attempted to school her pretty face into an expression of mock concern. "She appears to be wearing one of your shirts? Shall I not fetch down the lady Euphemia so she can perhaps lend your . . . eh . . . *friend* something more suitable?"

"This lass would ne'er fit into Lady Euphemia's gowns," the more quiet Arabella declared. "And I doubt she'd thank us for disturbing her . . . she was feeling out of sorts earlier—"

"No doubt she will be feeling even more poorly when she wakens. All the better reason to leave her be," Elspeth declared, taking each girl by the elbow and maneuvering them from the hall.

Before the arched entry to one of the stair towers, she paused just long enough to glance back over her shoulder at Robbie. "After I've seen these two long-noses to their beds, I shall return to escort your lady to a decent chamber where your stepmother and I can see to her properly."

With that she was gone, vanished into the shadows of the stairwell and leaving only her seal of approval behind.

She'd called Robbie's beauty *his lady*.

And unless things at Eilean Creag had changed drastically during his absence, there was nary a soul within its walls brave enough to gainsay old Elspeth.

Save perhaps the Black Stag himself.

And *he* looked anything but eager to voice an objection.

Far from it, Duncan MacKenzie stared wide-eyed at Robbie's beauty, his still-handsome face blanched white as new-fallen snow.

"I—I know you," he said, the hesitation in his most-times booming voice making plain that he did not.

Truth be told, nothing about the mighty Black Stag of Kintail's behavior appeared plain at all.

Nothing except the surety that he looked as if he'd just seen a ghost.

❧

Lady Euphemia stood in the darkness of Eilean Creag's least-used stair tower and eyed her betrothed through narrowed lids. Sir Robert MacKenzie—for she refused to call him *Robbie*—held court near the hall's arched doorway, beaming delight, as all around him a great buzz of talk and conviviality broke out and fleet-footed servitors scrambled over themselves and each other to set every torch and sconce ablaze.

Aye, Sir Robert appeared well pleased.

His soon-to-be bride seethed.

"A pox on the varlet and all his charm," she hissed, contempt winding through her. "A worse plague on his . . . *companion*."

Her lips tightly compressed, she fisted her tiny hands against skirts still mussed from hours of uncomfortable, fitful sleep. Skirts that, no matter how well-cut and fine, would ne'er drape her slight form so alluringly as the indecently revealing man's linen shirt clung to the brazen curves of the bold-eyed whore standing beside Sir Robert.

Grinding her teeth, Euphemia slipped into the deeper gloom of the stair foot. There were other, more subtle ways to avenge herself than to be caught glaring fury at a blowsy, fiery-haired light-skirt who could be naught but a peasant from the looks of her.

A tavern wench.

Or Sir Robert MacKenzie's leman.

"A thousand deep plagues on her," Euphemia sniffed, then pursed her thin lips all the harder.

Even the MacKenzie plaid swirled oh-so-loosely round the bawd's shoulders couldn't hide the magnificence of her breasts. Full, firm-looking, and most obviously hard-tipped, the oversized orbs threatened to spill from the linen shirt's low-dipping neckline—a spectacle Euphemia suspected every gog-eyed MacKenzie male gawking about the hall prayed would happen any moment.

Equally vexing, the woman held a bundle of squirming brown and white fur in her arms—and despite the proximity of the wriggling, four-legged beastie, her nostrils did not appear to twitch at all.

The flame-haired bawd not only possessed more curves than a Highlander-in-rut's dreams could hold, she did not suffer Euphemia's need to sneeze and wheeze if a dog even glanced her way.

Indeed, the hall's arched vestibule already reeked with the rank-biting smell of the mangy beasts romping round her betrothed and his whore. The dogs jumped on them both, wagging their scruffy tails and barking.

The sight made Euphemia's skin crawl. She shuddered, her brows snapping together as her temper rose like a hot tide. Worse, her nose began to itch! And her eyes watered and . . . stung.

Dabbing at them with the edge of her sleeve, she leveled all her anger at a hapless MacKenzie pushing his way through the throng. His ale-bleared gaze fixed on the bawd's welling bosom, the man's tongue nigh lolled from his head.

To Euphemia's annoyance, he paused just outside the stair tower, raised a booming voice. "Heigh-ho!" he roared, slapping a kinsman on the shoulder. "That one will go to his bed naked, eager, and purring her pleasure—unlike the dried-up stick of a shrew he is to wed."

Purring her pleasure.

The words curled through Euphemia's gut like soured milk. She stared after the man as he moved away, fury pulsing through her, seeping into blood and bone.

A dried-up stick of a shrew.

How little the man knew.

How little any of them knew.

But *she* knew, and her confidence in her special skills lessened some of the burning tightness in her chest and even helped ease the streaming of her eyes.

Only her hatred continued to burn, banking now to a white-hot smolder. Needing support, she leaned against the cold stone wall beneath a narrow window splay, risked a deep breath of the damp night air.

Even the loch's dangerous vapors were preferable to the choking stench of the hall's thick-drifting wood smoke . . . the sharp odor of the many dogs.

Purring her pleasure, indeed.

Euphemia scowled. The lout's sarcastic witticisms cut deep, the slurs refusing to leave her ears. Closing her eyes, she forced her mind to dwell on other things.

Such as how she would have brought Sir Robert to his knees, had *him* purring in his ease and begging release—if only she'd had a chance to lure him to the bit!

An opportunity she doubted she'd have the chance to exploit with other, more lavish feasting hanging on his arm. Hot anger thrumming inside her, she pressed a hand to her roiling stomach and wished the fiery creature to the lowest pit of hell.

"So-o-o-o! I find you here, sweet lady," a husky-deep voice penetrated her anger, its mellifluous familiarity both irritating and exciting her.

Big Red MacAlister.

Euphemia's eyes snapped open . . . her woman's parts flamed and began to moisten.

She wet her lips, tried to smooth her rumpled skirts. Then, willing herself not to wheeze, she tilted back her head to gaze up at her father's most trusted guardsmen, a man prized for his skill and brawn.

A ruggedly handsome giant with a mane of thick, bronze-colored hair and twinkling blue eyes, Big Red MacAlister made a resplendent figure. And since the day he'd appeared at her father's door some years before, he'd proven himself not just Hugh Out-with-the-Sword's most stalwart man, but also her own most faithful and obedient . . . servant.

Every tall, golden inch of him.

Ignoring the chattering throng inside the hall, he looked down at her, his blue gaze almost a physical touch. "I rejoice to see you, lass," he said, stepping closer.

Euphemia blinked.

Her heart thumped wildly against her ribs and heat suffused her cheeks.

"W-what are you doing here . . . now?" she got out, the hot pulsing between her thighs damping her more the nearer he came. "Shouldn't you be with our other guards-men? Out in the hall with all the rest—or in the stables with our horses?"

Big Red cocked an auburn brow, his light blue eyes filling with amusement and . . . need.

"Och, see you, lassie, I thought I'd be a-doing what I do nigh every e'en." His voice dropped to an even silkier depth. "Aye, I was a-looking for you. Thought you'd wish to be attended. But you were not abed," he added, adjusting his plaid to better display his rising *enthusiasm*.

"I was abed, but I did not sleep well. As you can see he is returned and . . . and not alone." Her chest tighten-ing again, Euphemia shot a quick glance at her betrothed and his whore.

They still stood near the keep doorway, with none of the MacKenzies paying heed to her or any other shadows-in-the-night who might be lurking in the blackness of the stair tower.

"A notable surprise, eh?" Big Red agreed, following her gaze. "But not a tangle that ought turn his head over-long once you've shown him your talents." He lifted a finger to her lips, rubbed gently. "'Twas an ache for your *specialties* that sent me to your chamber."

Taking her hand, he pressed her palm against the hard ridge of his manhood, curled her fingers around its thick-ness. "I missed you the last few nights. Stroke me, lassie. Long, slow strokes, through my plaid."

Euphemia stared through the darkness at him. "This is crazy-mad. I cannot . . . *service* you here," she whis-pered, her hand beginning to move up and down on him all the same. "We are in fullest view of the hall. If any-one—"

"If anyone looks this way, my sweet, they will see naught but darkness. Or the broad back of Big Red MacAlister as I peer out the window splay. Mayhap they will think I am relieving myself? That ought keep them away long enough for you to relieve me in truth."

Fearing discovery, and chiding herself for it, Euphemia hesitated. She slid another glance at the noisy crowd in the vestibule, weighing the risk of getting caught against the urgent tingling between her thighs.

She glanced up the narrow turnpike stairs winding upward into the gloom behind Big Red's wide-set shoulders. She alone occupied a chamber in the forgotten tower above them.

Nary a soul would saunter down the steps and stumble across her . . . pleasure.

E'er bolder than people credited her, she pulled another deep breath of the damp night air into her lungs, filling them as best she could, her ailments considered. She took great pride in her daring. Her ability to wrap the brawniest, most fearsome clansmen around her fingers.

Bend them to her will.

Or snatch their affections from lasses graced with more obvious charms.

Another furious look at the flame-haired *plentitude* hanging on her betrothed's arm decided her. Turning back to Big Red, she resumed massaging his swollen tarse.

"Och, aye, that is what I was a-wanting." He looked down at her, his smile broadening into a grin. "But with your mouth, sweetness," he added, circling his fingers around her wrist, easing her hand away just long enough to toss aside his plaid and free himself. "Lick and suckle me as you e'er do—you promised you would when'er I have need."

Euphemia almost refused, but the strong musk of his potent male scent rose up between them, its earthy headiness intoxicating her and weighting her most tender parts with a hot-throbbing need all her own. She stifled a groan, tiredness and resentment warring within her—but also giddy, carnal excitement.

"Come, lass, touch your tongue to me . . . give me ease."

This time she did moan. No longer holding back, she met his gaze, wished the intensity of his deep-seeing blue eyes didn't have such power to melt her. If he had needs . . . hers were surely greater.

And she *had* promised.

But her sundry ailings were plaguing her this night, making her chest so tight and achy each breath pained her. Especially the deep ones she'd needed to becalm herself.

"Lick me."

Capitulating, she began to tremble, the two hungrily-spoken words and her own tingling lust pushing her over the precipice.

With a sobbing cry of want, she knelt before him, nuzzling her face against his groin, then pressing her nose deep into the springy cinnamon-colored curls that held his musky scent, but her joints cracked loudly as she positioned herself. The pitiable sound came overloud in the closeness of the stair tower, even echoing off the dank walls, damning her and calling attention to her lacking.

"I—I cannot . . . not this night," she stammered, pushing awkwardly to her feet. "On the morrow, mayhap."

"Then I shall lick you," Big Red vowed, already dropping to his knees, shifting their positions before she could naysay him. "You should have told me you were feeling more poorly than usual," he added, his deep voice going a shade lower, more intimate.

Too infinitely sweet for her to resist.

"As you wish," she acquiesced with a sigh, her assent rippling through her as he raised her skirts and began stroking his fingers over the puffy flesh of her nigh hairless woman's parts—a fault of her femininity she'd e'er detested but that he claimed to relish, insisting her scant covering of nether hair made her appear . . . virginal.

Feeling anything but, Euphemia opened her legs wider, giving him better access as he brought his auburn head closer to the exposed vee of her thighs. He blew gently on the sparse tufts of soft dark hair, tugged lightly on a few damp curls.

He looked up as he rubbed her, catching and holding her gaze. "I will lick you now, Phemie. 'Tis my wish to lap at you until you are better," he promised, touching his tongue to the fleshiest part of her womanhood, swirling it again and again over her quivering heat, finding the hard little nub of her pleasure and—suckling.

Nibbling and drawing on her until her entire body went taut and her innermost heat clenched tight, then shattered. "*This* is what you need," he murmured, rubbing his face back and fore against her hot pulsing flesh as her release washed over her and a low sob tore from her throat.

"You need me—not yon high-born spawn of the devil," he vowed, his hot breath searing the words onto the naked skin of her exposed belly. "You are mine, Phemie. Do not say me otherwise."

And she did not.

Not when he'd spent her so thoroughly she could scarce draw breath much less gainsay his illusions.

And illusions they were.

As he would know if he possessed wits to match his brawn, his incomparable skill at . . . pleasuring a woman.

Big Red MacAlister was sorely mistaken.

Lady Euphemia MacLeod belonged to no man.

Not her golden giant of a most-favored lover, nor her fool-preening rogue of a betrothed.

Neither man possessed her, but she needed them both.

Needed them badly.

And for her own good purposes.

Chapter Five

❦

"*WHAT FOOL PURPOSE WOULD I HAVE for lying to you?*"

Duncan MacKenzie, the redoubtable Black Stag of Kintail, proud laird of the great Clan MacKenzie, and irrefutably one of the most feared and respected men in all the West Highlands, paced his well-appointed solar and, most uncharacteristically, appeared too edgy to meet his own son's brooding eye.

And from where he stood in the deep alcove of a window embrasure, Robbie obliged his father's apparent ill ease and continued to gaze out through the open shutters at the thin drizzle of rain and the silent waters of Loch Duich far below.

His hands clasped behind his back, he repeated the words he'd been saying ever since he'd entered his sire's privy quarters.

"You did say you knew her—I heard you."

"Saints preserve us—use your head, laddie!" The Black Stag was on him in a heartbeat, grabbing his arm to spin him around. "Look at me when we speak, not out the fool window! Think you I would ruin your homecoming by fouling it with untruths?" he demanded, eyes blazing. "I swear to you I have ne'er seen the lass before this night."

Robbie shook himself free, readjusted the fall of his plaid. "Mayhap not, but you *thought* you knew her," he pressed, not at all surprised when his father started pacing again. "I would know why."

"A God's name—why not?" Duncan huffed with suspicious vehemence. "The lass is a fetching piece, many were the maids I . . . *sampled* in the days before I married your stepmother. Like as not your sweet bloom brought one of them to mind."

"The day I believe that is the day pigs will fly." Robbie folded his arms. "I saw your face run white when you looked on her. I will not leave be until you tell me why."

"Guidsakes—whene'er did you become so stubborn?" Duncan shook his head, ran a hand through his hair. "Forbye, I do not ken what devil-damned bog you visited to lay on such an annoying trait!"

"To be sure the devil had his wily finger in it," a deep voice put in from the shadows. "Though I doubt the devil in question was a bog-dweller."

"When did *you* find your way in here?" Duncan whirled on the tall, scar-faced figure lounging in a chair beside the well-doing log fire.

"See you, laddie," the Black Stag groused, tossing a quick glance at his son, "some things ne'er change. *That one* still has eyes and ears everywhere. Mind it well if you are wise, and be wary of him."

"You wound me, old friend," Sir Marmaduke said, clearly unruffled despite his words. Looking most comfortable indeed, he gestured to a platter of honeyed oatcakes on a nearby table. A fresh jug of ale and clean drinking cups rounded up the simple but tasty fare.

Sir Marmaduke helped himself to one of the oatcakes. "I do not seek to sow unrest. I was but ordered to deliver refreshments since the sun will soon rise and Elspeth and your good lady wife are yet occupied tending Robbie's . . . *companion*."

"She is not my anything," Robbie amended, lifting his voice above a sudden gust of wind rattling at the shutters. A cold, rain-damp draught rushed into the room, chilling him as surely as having to admit the maid was, and could not honorably be of lasting importance to him.

The notion galled and proved . . . unacceptable.

He wanted her with an urgency that stretched beyond all reason. Saints, he even felt an inexplicable oneness of spirit with her, as if she alone could make him whole.

Just thinking of her enflamed and heated him like a sheet of fire blazing all around him.

Even in the face of his father's strange behavior.

Cold no more, despite the gray chill of the wet new day just beginning to lighten outside the solar's tall, arch-topped windows, Robbie tossed off his plaid, dropping it irritably onto one of the twin-facing stone benches set into the sides of the window embrasure.

With more patience than he knew he possessed, he pushed up the sleeves of his tunic, not caring if his scowling-faced father or his e'er complacent Sassunach good-uncle noted anything unusual.

He eyed the matching rows of red half-moon nail marks on his forearms with pulse-quickening satisfaction.

His flame-haired vixen had scored him with the marks

as they'd thundered across the causeway to the castle's second gatehouse. And just looking at them, at the tangible proof of her fiery nature, was enough to tighten his loins and fill him with hot-crackling desire.

He knew instinctively that any man to lie with her would bear similar marks all down his back. And that fortunate lump would no doubt leave her bed more sated and drained than if he'd enjoyed the simultaneous attentions of a full score of the best-skilled courtesans in the realm.

He knew, too, that he had to have her.

In his bed and, even more so, in his life.

Aye, especially in his life.

But he thrust all such thought from his mind—for the moment—and fixed his father with a look he hoped would not appear disrespectful.

"You e'er favored oatcakes," he said, gesturing to them. "Mayhap a bit of sustenance and ale will make our discourse less unpalatable for you."

"I have no stomach for food," Duncan snapped, his furious glance at the hapless mound of oatcakes more telling than he knew.

"You also lack appetite for answering the simplest questions, it would seem." Sir Marmaduke stretched his long legs to the fire, dusted a scatter of oat crumbs from his knees. "If you would speak true and have done with your bellyaching, we could all snatch at least a semblance of sleep before the day begins in earnest."

His face darkening, Duncan slid a pointed look at the door. "Naught is keeping you from your bed, you great lout of an Englishman," he grated. "And I have told Robbie all I can. I have ne'er before seen his fiery-haired lass and her name is not known to me. Would that it were."

Robbie gave his father an assessing look. He did not like the tone of those last four words. "How so?"

"How so?" Duncan repeated, his exasperation palpable. "For many a good reason, never you doubt it."

"Save the obvious—the maid's own well-deserved sanctity of mind, I would hear the reasons," Robbie declared, not missing the barely there twitch of a muscle just beneath his father's left eye. Or the tight-thrumming tension deepening the lines bracketing the older man's mouth.

"What are those reasons, h'mmm?" Robbie persisted, well aware he treaded dangerous ground but unable to stay his tongue.

Something in his father's expression curdled Robbie's blood and made him almost certain that his beauty's identity, or momentary lack thereof, troubled his sire near as much as it vexed him.

Narrowing his eyes at his father, he dragged in a tight breath and wished the insistent pounding at his temples would stop—or at least lessen.

"Can we not cease this senseless beating of the air and be open with one another? Now, after all these years?" Robbie kept his tone level, maintained a calm that was entirely feigned.

But at his father's silence, he ventured farther onto the thin ice he'd been purposely avoiding.

"Ne'er have I seen you so sullen," he said, the throbbing in his forehead making it ever more difficult to resist returning his father's glare. "Does your perturbation have aught to do with the name *Kenneth* being the only one the lass can recall?"

The Black Stag jerked at the reminder of his long-dead

bastard half brother, bane of his existence and, in the knave's nefarious lifetime, scourge of all Kintail.

"My half brother—may he be roasting on the hottest hob of hell—was not the only Highlandman to bear the name Kenneth," he said of the one-time friend who'd repaid youthful love and camaraderie by seducing Duncan's first wife, Robbie's own equally dead mother.

Even worse, when confronted with his treachery, the blackguard had used his excellent sword skills to carve out Sir Marmaduke's left eye and maim the Sassunach for life. And by the time he'd finally breathed his last, just a few blessedly short years later, the stain of his sins had steeped all of Kintail in shame and sorrow.

His face going dark as the cloudbanks e'er brimming o'er the moors, Duncan went to stand at one of the windows where he flexed and unflexed his fingers a few times before he spoke.

"Aye, son, 'tis true enough that the name *Kenneth* has not passed the lips of anyone beneath my roof in some years," he admitted, tight-voiced, his rigid back to the room. "Most good men know better—and womenfolk would not dare."

That said, he turned on his heel and, set-faced, strode to the table to pour himself a generous measure of heather ale. He downed the fine, frothy brew in one long swallow.

Looking back at Robbie, he wiped his mouth with the back of his hand. "For truth, son, in all your years away, have you not yet learned that it serves nothing but ill to stir peacefully slumbering waters?"

"And if those waters have already been disturbed?"

"So-o-o!" Duncan all but snorted. "That is the way of it. I thought as much," he said, the words charged with meaning. "As for those waters, my son, the dimmest of fools ken that even the most turbulent sea will settle again—given time. E'er poking into matters best left alone brings naught but grief."

Robbie opened his mouth to counter that, but thought better of it. Instead, he pressed his lips together, his gaze fastening on a large blue-tinted stone half-hidden in the shadows of a deep-set alcove in the corner.

Clan MacKenzie's Marriage Stone.

The sacred main piece of every MacKenzie wedding ceremony since time beyond mind.

Tall and phallic in shape, its entirety carved with ancient Celtic runes, the clan talisman, or swearing stone, bore a hole in its center—a hole through which a couple could clasp hands thus ensuring the blessing of their marriage.

A union the MacKenzie graybeards swore would then be joyous beyond all bounds and filled with love, harmony, and many healthy bairns.

Robbie frowned.

He could not imagine the famed Marriage Stone vibrating with paeans of praise and joy on his wedding day. Nor could he see the fabled stone casting even the faintest smile on his union with Lady Euphemia MacLeod.

With all surety, *he* could not smile on the marriage.

Not now.

A stance he would uphold even if he had not happened upon his beauty.

For tumultuous as his arrival and the exuberant greeting of his kinfolk had been, so loud with good cheer and the drinking of healths, he had not failed to note that his bride-to-be had not shown her face—had kept demonstratively to her room.

Robbie's jaw locked in a frown.

Such behavior alone disqualified her as a suitable bride for any MacKenzie much less the future laird—the very grit of MacKenzie males and the e'er-present gloom permeating Eilean Creag required hearth-mates with steel in their veins.

Not women so spiteful or meek they take to their beds at the first quiver of adversity.

Robbie glanced at the Marriage Stone again, almost felt its grainy displeasure. Sakes, would he credit the prattle-mongers, all of Kintail already disapproved the match. Rampant were the whispered frettings and resentments of the castlefolk, kinsmen, and servitors alike.

And he'd seen the changes the supposed tight-lipped shrew had wrought to his father's hall.

Unwelcome alterations *he* would not tolerate regardless of whether others at Eilean Creag had accepted them in goodwill or nay.

His mind set, he took a few steps toward his father, held up a hand. "Sir, I crave your pardon," he began, determined to seize his happiness. "See you, I am no longer a whelp or stripling to cringe in my boots. However much I would avoid causing undue strife. Still, I cannot ignore certain sentiments when they are burning a hole inside me."

His father glowered at him from beneath down-drawn brows. "By the grace of God," he railed, clearly provoked to frothing anger, "when I saw how close you held the flame-haired lass as you rode into the bailey, I knew

the way the wind blew . . . that disaster would soon befall us."

Robbie half turned away, bit back a hot retort. "Think
you I would willingly bring down disgrace on our house?
Blacken the honor I worked so hard to accrue?" His every
muscle strained and taut, he glanced up at the stone-
vaulted ceiling, blew out a quick breath.

Looking back at his father at last, he threw down the
gauntlet.

"Even so, I do not wish to keep my vow . . . I would
see my betrothal broken," he said, an incredible *rightness*
flowing over him upon putting voice to the words.
"Would that I could feel otherwise—but you should ken
where my heart lies. I give you my word that I shall do
naught, say nary a word, until I can think of a way to
spare the lady Euphemia undue hurt and so that nothing
goes ill with the MacLeods. I—"

"Faugh, you say!" The Black Stag fumed, wrath
rolling off him in almost visible waves. "In the name of
all that is holy, I have ne'er heard such folly! All in the
land will esteem such a breech of vows as the basest affront. Do you have any idea how many seafaring friends
I have promised they'd ne'er again be harassed by
MacLeod's foul chain? His hordes of murdering wreck-
ers? Ne'er will we—"

"I will deal with MacLeod, though I pray it needn't be
with weaving steel." Robbie took a deep breath, ignored
his father's fierce scowl. "But I am . . . sorry."

Ignoring him, Duncan rounded on Sir Marmaduke.

"Did you know aught of this? Saints, save us! The lad
prays he mustn't draw his blade! Yet his own doings
would shake a fist at the first true glimmer of peace

we've seen in years." He made an impatient gesture, glowered at his old friend. "This is an ill day, and such perfidy smacks of your kind of interference and machinations."

Still reposed in the chair by the hearth fire, Marmaduke shook his head and spread his hands palms outward.

"God keep me from e'er meddling in the business of others," he drawled, seemingly unfazed by his liege's outburst. "In especial the privy doings of such a puissant and goodly young man as our Robbie."

"Ho! There speaks the most meddlesome beast to e'er walk this earth," the Black Stag shot back. "I ought have you tossed in the pit beneath this keep's west tower for your prattle and denials." He jabbed a finger at his friend. "'Tis fell deep our dungeon is, if you've forgotten. Hewn into the living rock by my own great-great-grandsire, and so narrow a poor body thrown in there can do naught but stand till the flesh rots from his bones—or he loses his mind."

"Then I suggest we all seek our beds before your bellywinding gives us collective nightmares," Sir Marmaduke suggested as he pushed to his feet, stretched his well-muscled arms above his head.

Crossing the solar in long strides, he slung a friendly arm around Robbie's shoulders. "Yon devil's tail is well clipped these days, never you worry," he said, speaking as though Duncan weren't standing there glaring firedaggers at them. "His vexation will soon be by with, and meantime, if no one has told you, you can bed down in my old chamber—'twas your father's own quarters before he relinquished it to me, and the only rooms standing vacant at present . . . or so I am told."

He sent a questioning glance at Duncan, but that one's only response was a curt nod.

Until Sir Marmaduke started guiding Robbie to the door.

"Stay your feet, you two—a word yet before you go," the Black Stag called, the sheer authority in his voice halting them despite Sir Marmaduke's casual airs and Robbie's own determination to see his will done.

"There will be no breaking of vows, Robert MacKenzie," Duncan said, the close-checked anger in his voice more ominous than any thunder echoed from high. "Too many high altercations would ensue—and too many promises of peace have indeed been granted to my people and allies. You *will* wed the lady Euphemia and at the soonest."

"Damnation, Father, but I say you I cannot," Robbie swore, clenching his hands. "I—"

"You can and you shall," the Black Stag decreed. "Make the saucy wench you rescued your leman if you desire her so hotly—though, such a dalliance, too, is something I would frown upon. But anything else, and it shall be the worse for you."

His lairdly word spoken, Duncan MacKenzie gave his friend and his only son another of his famed black scowls and made for the door, striding out, and slamming it hard behind him.

The walls of the solar vibrated for a long moment, then seemed to contract, closing in on Robbie. His gut clenching, he lifted a hand, swiped dampness from his brow. More shaken than he was willing to admit, he snatched the ale jug off the table, tipped it to his lips, and drank deeply.

Then, and without a further word or even looking at Sir Marmaduke, he exited the solar.

But much more quietly than his father's leave-taking, and with a heavier heart than he would have believed.

Cares and regret weighting his shoulders, he made his way down the winding turnpike stair. His oh-so-dearly-longed-for homecoming had fallen out worse than he'd imagined and he should have taken his beauty when he'd had the chance . . . riding away with her to the edge of the world.

A possibility he might yet explore.

And fie and damnation on any who might think to try and stop him.

❧

About the same time, nestled deep in the quietude of another tower, Juliana tossed and turned in a restless sleep . . . a fitful slumber held in sumptuous quarters once belonging to the Black Stag himself and latterly to Sir Marmaduke Strongbow, the puissant chieftain's good-brother, most well-loved friend, and self-proclaimed non-meddler into the privy doings of others.

Quite unaware of whose one-time chamber now sheltered her, Juliana's exhausted body welcomed the smooth, fresh-scented linens of the great four-postered bed, every inch of her savoring the indescribable comfort of the bed's mound of cushiony-soft feather mattresses and silken pillows.

But untold luxuries or no, her brow furrowed and,

even asleep, some hidden part of her stirred with awareness. Something ominous lurked in the shadows of the
grand chamber's silent, inky corners.

A sinister and watching presence, crouching in its lair,
waiting.

And even the soothing ablutions spent her earlier by
the lady of the keep and her oh-so-capable female
seneschal could not prevent the dark little nibbles of foreboding nipping at the edges of Juliana's troubled dreams.

Dreams she'd surely slipped into so deeply thanks to
the ne'er-before-bliss of having two sets of caring hands
settle her into a tub of heated rainwater. Hands that then
scrubbed the travails of her journey from her tired limbs,
and with skilled fingers, massaged her head to toe with
sweet-smelling essence of lavender.

Faith, the two women had even washed and combed
her hair, rubbing each curling tendril with thoughtfully
warmed drying linens before brushing Juliana's some-
times-unruly mane to sleek, bright-gleaming brilliance.

At last satisfied with their ministrations and pamper-
ing, they'd slipped the softest wisp of a night-camise over
Juliana's head and tucked her into the cocooning embrace
of the magnificent canopied bed, leaving her, they'd
surely hoped, to a restorative slumber . . . and not the
whims of terrifying, clutching nightmares.

Never-ending horrors even the four-poster's carefully-
closed bed curtains could not hold at bay.

"Blessed Jesu . . ." Juliana breathed, rolling onto her
belly and tangling her limbs in the constricting welter of
mussed sheets and encroaching darkness.

Ill ease descended, a dank and cloying curtain of dread
as chilling as the cold, damp air permeating the bed-

chamber, and persistent as the sluicing rain pounding the stone window ledges.

Somewhere not too distant a loose shutter banged, its loud thumping an unwitting echo to the hammering of Juliana's heart, the futile pounding of feet that ran but could not speed her from the reach of the raven-winged devil-demon racing along behind her, so close on her fleeing heels.

A creature fashioned of wrath and brimstone, he spewed fire and chased her, damning her with white-faced fury and red-glowing eyes. Hurling slurs she could not escape.

Curse you, wraith of the past, for daring to come here. Be gone and away—now, this night!

You will know no peace if you stay . . . not so long as I have breath in my body . . .

But then the bitter, sulfurous wind swirling round the savage-staring ogre shifted and changed, and the biting sting of hell's own fumes faded away to leave naught but a sickly-sweet sourness . . . the telltale stench of nearing death.

The chamber's rich trappings and even the seductive haven of the massive oaken bed vanished as well, every tinge of wealth and refinement replaced by the ravaged weariness of a tiny cot-house of sod, heather, and stone.

A place dark and smoky with burning peat, where times were rough and food scarce, but where Highland honor flourished nevertheless and every harsh-spent hour came blessed with soul-deep smiles and boundless love.

A legacy now marred by the crushing heartbreak of life almost spent and urgent wishes not yet fulfilled.

Juliana sobbed in her sleep, her throat tightening nigh

enough to suffocate her. Searing heat pricked the backs of her tight-pressed eyelids, but even trapped inside her most wrenching sorrows, she wore a bold and determined countenance, refused to allow the teensiest tear to slip down cheeks gone icy cold.

Near as cold as the thin, blue-veined hands reaching out, imploring her.

"No-o-o," Juliana cried, flipping onto her back and wrestling with the tangled binds of her stubbornness. "I will not go there . . . cannot carry *recompense* to one whose callousness caused you naught but pain . . . a heartless dastard who considers us little more than a ragged brood of beggars—"

"You err, Juliana," her mother lamented from the darkness, her words scarce audible above the iron clang of the bells tolling her end.

"See you, it was my own beloved hearth-mate who proved pernicious, *his* wickedness that closed the hearts of others," she rasped, her tired voice breaking. "Do not blind yourself to your destiny for railing o'er ifs and might-have-beens. Do not fear—"

"Och, I see well enough," Juliana sniffed, a sharp-taloned fist squeezing her heart. "You have been deluded by a man without the least tincture of virtues. A blackguard whose hardness and tyranny has earned him an eternity of contempt."

Her saturation point well reached, she kicked at the bed linens holding her captive, clawed at her wispy-thin camise until nary a shred of its borrowed fineness yet clung to her riled and hot-flushed body.

"And let it be known I fear naught," she added, sitting bolt upright, impotent fury coursing through her as her mother's gaze began to glaze and grow unfocused. "I am not affrighted of the greatest hardship or misery, nor this black-hearted scoundrel you speak of as a friend—and if he and a full legion of his horned minions should come hallooing down the glen!"

Marjory Mackay's face loomed over her then, infinitely sad and impossibly near, the sunken eyes bright and pleading.

"Juliana . . ." she began, only to fall silent when everything shifted and the devil-demon himself stood leering at her again.

Nay, not . . . leering.

He no longer stared with narrowed, anger-filled eyes, all red-rimmed and spitting fire, but looked at her in terror . . . as if *he* feared her.

A vulnerability that wiped away his horns and hid his forked tail, the haunted look on his handsome face making him appear almost human.

Sympathetic and . . . *needy.*

A prospect that chilled Juliana to the marrow of her bones.

❧

Robbie walked into Sir Marmaduke's erstwhile quarters and froze. The entire bedchamber, dark but for the dim glow of a low-burning fire, reeked of essence of lavender—a scented oil his stepmother e'er favored for her baths.

Only, as all at Eilean Creag knew, the lady Linnet indulged her ablutions in the seclusion of her own chamber's tapestried walls.

Suspicion beginning to tickle the sensitive skin at the back of his neck, Robbie peered deeper into the gloom, his keen wits and sharp eyes probing the darkness for evidence of his good-uncle's . . . meddling.

He found what he was seeking almost at once.

The validity of his instincts roundly confirmed by the large, cloth-lined bathing-tub whiling innocently in the shadows next the hearth. Cooled, oil-slicked water and the little half-emptied jar of lavender-scented soap a-winking at him from a three-legged stool conveniently placed nearby told the rest of the tale.

His own linen shirt and the MacKenzie great plaid hanging on a wall peg gave him irrefutable surety.

For whate'er his reasons, Sir Marmaduke Strongbow, master of mischievous subtlety but oh-so-good of heart, had sent Robbie strolling straight into a lavender-scented trap.

His beauty held her sweet, lush self somewhere within these thick, expectant walls and a quick, assessing glance around the dimly-lit room told him she could be but one place . . . ensconced behind the tightly-drawn curtains of the four-poster bed.

Reposed there alone and freshly bathed, her voluptuously curved body oiled and scented.

Mayhap even naked.

The thought sent heat pouring into his loins. Need and want flared within him, an inexorable force blazing hotter than a thousand bonfires. His heart swelled, too, the whole of it welling with an ache of yearning such as he'd never known.

Scarce aware of his actions, he unbuckled his sword

belt, letting it drop to the rushes before he turned back to the closed door and slid its drawbar soundly in place.

The only other corner in all Eilean Creag not crowded with slack-mouthed, loud-snoring kinsmen at this hour were the deep vaults cut into the living rock far beneath the keep. The foul place his father had used to goad Sir Marmaduke.

Dungeon pits where naught but ghosts and water rats might find a decent sleep.

Robbie shuddered.

He would take his rest here.

Mayhap even steal a goodnight kiss.

Or more.

Desire thundering through him at the notion, he stripped off his tunic and crossed the room, his hands reaching for the closure of his leggings until awareness and a decidedly sharp prick of conscience halted him.

He might have just faced down his formidable father, and would surely do so again soon, and he most definitely possessed the cheek, and bone-deep weariness, to bed down in this chamber no matter who presently occupied it.

But he was not so bold-hearted and calloused to allow a possibly untouched maid catch him parading about with a lancelike protuberance rising in his braies!

Clenching his hands, he stood stock still, heated tension twisting through him, the whole of his tight-drawn body as granite-hard as the pulsing need at his groin.

Grateful for the shielding barrier of the closed bed curtains, lest his beauty waken and discover him in the all-too-obvious throes of such *un*knightly behavior, Robbie began slowly counting backward from one hundred and willed his raging *ache* to subside.

And so soon as it did, he'd gather up his discarded sword belt and tunic—along with his almost-abandoned honor—and exit the chamber as swiftly as he entered. He'd make his pallet in the hall with the rest of his father's men and kinsmen . . . as all goodly knights ought do.

And where naught but moonbeams and snores might keep him from his sleep.

Aye, that is what he would do—after having words with a certain one-eyed Sassunach champion who just happened to be his good-uncle.

Or so he thought until he heard his beauty's first moan.

Chapter Six

✤

"*No-o-o . . . I DINNA WANT . . .*"

The muffled cry came from behind the drawn bed curtains, the anguish marring the cadence of the softly-lilting voice wrenching enough to lance the most hardened of hearts.

Robbie's plummeted to his toes.

"God's wounds!" His blood freezing, he sprinted across the rushes to the great four-poster and yanked open the enclosing curtains.

The sight within squeezed his best restraint with a hard and heavy hand and sent all his just-banished licentious cravings crashing back over him in a surging, unstoppable *whoosh*.

His beauty knelt in the middle of the bed.

Full-naked and singularly sweet, her bright-gleaming tresses spilled free to her hips and every gold-gilt inch of her shimmered in the dim light of the hearth fire.

Robbie stared at her, hardly able to breathe.

She scarce noticed him.

Clearly caught in the grasp of troubled dreams, she

looked past him, her beautiful eyes opened but unseeing. She held one hand pressed tight against her breasts and flailed the air with the other, waving it before her as if to stave off a blow.

Or block out something she did not wish to see.

He saw . . . *everything*.

A welter of bold and minute details seared themselves into his consciousness, rooting him in place and making it impossible to look away.

"Holy saints . . ." He smoothed a hand down over his mouth, his entire body thrumming with a fervency that stunned him.

Certain he could now be styled the most execrable rogue to e'er stalk the heather, he continued to stare, well aware of the scalding flush creeping up his neck. More damning still, hot blood scourged his loins until a certain roguish part of him swelled and lengthened, running full-stretch to boldly lift the fine-woven linen of his braies.

And this time he doubted he could quell even one unrepentant inch his body's . . . masculine determination.

He *did* try not to let his gaze fasten on the red-gold curls beckoning so enticingly from betwixt her thighs. Nor did he risk more than a quick glance at the deliciously hardened nipples cresting the full rounds of her naked breasts.

Even more difficult was pretending the cloud of lavender-scented air drifting out from the confines of the bed recess did not hold a wee bewitching tinge of a darker, muskier scent.

A thread of wafting temptation to water his mouth and make his tongue itch to . . . savor and taste.

He wisely ignored what the scent did to his nether parts.

But then the very air seemed to quiver and her gaze cleared, fixing on him with slow-breaking comprehension.

"You . . ."

She peered at him, her luminous eyes, moss-green pools of distress, her dazed expression worlds different from the snapping indignation she'd bristled with on their journey.

A pink flush rose on her cheeks, its poignant innocence unraveling him as his breath caught at the transformation. He swallowed, his heart tumbling uncomfortably as he waited for ire to spark in her eyes.

For her to cross swords with him again as she'd done beside the lochan. Perhaps upbraid him for being a high-minded knight. Or chastise him for disturbing her night-rest by brazen-heartedly invading her bedchamber and accosting her when the full shapeliness of her, all her unclothed curves and hollows, fair beckoned for a man's touch.

His touch . . . his caresses and warmth.

A deep silence bloomed between them, deafening but for the heated anticipation pulsing so loudly in Robbie's ears. No other sound save the pelting rain and wind stirred in the great black-raftered chamber. He simply stood, still as stone, and rooted to the rushes.

Slack-jawed and smitten.

Almost forgetting to breathe.

"What are you doing here?" she spoke at last, her cheeks flaming with color, the agitated rise and fall of her rounded bosom driving him to madness. "Your eyes talk plain enough, but I would hear the words from you."

"I—" he broke off, held up a hand. "It is not what you think," he said, wishing he could reenter the room and begin again.

She made no response, simply peered up at him from within the canopied bed.

Robbie shifted his feet, then immediately wished he hadn't for the crackling noise of the dried floor rushes only underscored the nervous shuffling.

She appeared none too troubled . . . merely vexed by his unexpected presence.

But then she moistened her lips and her eyes began to focus on him most intently.

Robbie squirmed.

Aye, to be sure, any moment she'd pull back her magnificently bared shoulders and rant at him for standing before her roused to bursting like a stag in rut.

Even wee Mungo, nestled in a welter of pillows at the foot of the bed, stared at him from bright quizzical eyes, his tiny jaws opened in silent reproach.

Saints of mercy!

Realization, cold and stark, cuffed Robbie soundly round his ears . . . an icy clump of good, knightly conscience reawakened, landing with a dull and damning *thud* in his gut.

There could be no denying it.

He *was* standing before her like a rutting stag.

And the dim lighting in the room was nowise poor enough to conceal his . . . depravity.

His face burning, he latched his gaze on hers, willing her not to even dare glance downward as he snatched one of the many pillows strewn across the bed and positioned it strategically. That feat accomplished, he heaved a great sigh of relief when she remained seemingly oblivious to how very near he'd come to disgracing himself.

"See you, lass, I did not know you'd been brought to this chamber," he said, hoping to explain his presence before he blundered into an even more impenetrable mire. "I meant only to bed down here—alone—but now . . . I heard your cries and would but comfort you."

She raised a brow, looked anything but convinced.

"You sought to solace me by coming to within a handbreadth of my night-nakedness—storming in here to ogle my breasts?"

Robbie bit back a curse, shoved a hand through his hair.

"Nay, by wishing to *soothe* . . . if you will let me," he offered, not about to admit that he had indeed been eyeing her breasts.

Admiring them.

In particular, her fine, tight-thrusting nipples.

He swallowed a groan. Then, hoping she hadn't noticed, he lifted her torn night rail from the bed and draped it round her shoulders. To his annoyance, a certain unacknowledged part of him jerked to attention when his fingers inadvertently brushed across a pebbled nipple as he smoothed the ruined camise over the very bosom he was supposed to be ignoring.

She jerked, too.

But only in surprise at the unexpected contact . . . nary a hint of affront clouded her expression. Indeed, although she seemed appreciative for the gesture, she made no move to draw the night shift more fully over herself—nor did she appear overly concerned that the triangle of red-gold curls topping her thighs still loomed in fullest view.

Truth tell, there was even more to be seen a-winking at him from betwixt her shapely legs, spread oh-so-slightly as they were, and just that wee delicious hint of her sweetest nectars clamped a white-hot vise around his man-parts . . . a fiery grip so tight and relentless, he could scarce breathe.

Blissfully unaware of his discomfort, she lifted her chin. "See you, sir, I am no sheltered maid taught to feel shame in my unclothed flesh," she said, pride in her voice, her green eyes reflecting the fire glow.

"But neither am I wont to suffer such fearsome dreams that I shred my night garments." She looked down, fingered a strip of the torn camise. "So, aye, you have the right of it, to be sure. I am in need of comforting. This night, mayhap even from you."

Robbie looked at her, not trusting himself to speak, for although the carefully positioned pillow quite hid his *problem*, the matter at large still raged fully out of control.

A circumstance worsened by the way the firelight played over her, illuminating her skin with a soft glow of reds and golds, each wavering flicker of light enhancing her loveliness more than any silken raiments or jewels.

Whoe'er she was and where'er she hailed from, she required no such fripperies and embellishments to turn a man's head.

Or bring the most stalwart knight to his knees.

She held his gaze, pulling in one deep, bosom-lifting breath after the other, a cascade of visible shivers rippling through her, delicate and sweet. But then her face clouded again and a shadow crossed her brow.

"Oh, dear saints, so long as I live, I p-prefer him to be a devil," she blurted, the hitch in her voice sealing Robbie's fate. "He *is* a hellhound—the truth of his callousness resounds on every lip up and down the glens."

"Hush you . . ." Robbie took a step forward, touched her shoulder. "If you mean my father, you have no cause to fear him." He lifted a tendril of her hair and twined its silk around his fingers. "Ne'er you worry. See you, he loves naught more than his family and his home and comfort. Beyond everything."

"To be sure he must love it well," she said, indicating the bedchamber's opulence with a sweep of her hand. "Even without my full awareness, I know this keep to be the Black Stag's own lair . . . and I know, too, that Kintail is a land of ancient strongholds and still older traditions, a place e'er ruled by iron-fisted men with hearts of stone. Your father does not wish me here. He will put up stout resistance, will not take kindly to—"

"Hearts of stone?" Robbie stared at her, a thousand contradictions making his own heart seize in objection. "I say you err, lass. All other faults considered, my father and men like him have more heart than is healthy for them."

He glanced at the deep-set window embrasure across the room, not hearing the whistle of the damp, bitter wind nor seeing the rain that blotted out the great hills looming so close they seemed to hug Loch Duich's shoreline.

In his heart, *with* his heart, he saw a day of bright sun and birdsong high on the braes, breathed in the darkly-sweet solace of wafting peat smoke, and felt a fresh heather wind riffling his hair. A day still new, its beauty vibrating the air, its wonder splendorous enough to bring a tear to even the most fierce Highland chieftain.

He remembered the wee pebble tucked into his own money pouch, a small stone he'd snatched from the edge of Loch Duich the day he'd left so many years before—and e'er carried with him because just closing his fingers over its smoothness took him back to this wild country of moors, mists, and hills that so possessed his soul.

And in all its moods and seasons—whether in spring when the broom and gorse are golden and the whole of the land lies bathed in soft sunlight, or deeply silent in winter, with great drifts of glittering snow covering each fold of the higher hills and icy-black squalls driving up the loch.

Aye, he loved the land well, as did all Gaels.

'Twas a soul-deep passion with no beginning and no end . . . it was simply always there inside him, writ across his heart and engraved forever on each breath—a vivid, palpable sense of belonging so profound just *thinking* of Kintail made his heart warm with a brilliance wide and radiant as a sunset.

And he doubted a Highlander was e'er born who would not understand his passion.

Not even the green-eyed minx who seemed to enjoy frowning at the bedchamber's more luxurious trappings—as if his family's wealth and power had fossilized their hearts and, saints forbid, might even taint her own.

He looked back at her, lit his fingers down the edge of her cheek. "I will not argue with you about iron-fisted men who spend their days stalking about with swords at their belts," he said with a nonapologetic glance at his own brand, so casually discarded on the floor rushes near the door.

"Strength and, in especial, the showing of it have e'er been needed to keep a semblance of peace in a land where ancient clan loyalties often end in blood feuds," he went on, half expecting her to interrupt him with an indignant *harrumph*. "But I will say that you do not speak the language of these hills if you can honestly claim such braw men are without hearts."

She blinked at that, belligerence flashing in her quickly narrowed eyes, the saucy tilt of her chin.

"You insult me if you think I do not know Highland ways. I vow I was reared closer to the land than you." She flicked a richly-embroidered bed cushion with a slender but work-chapped finger. "I but meant your father. He appears . . . different than most."

"Aye, and that he is," Robbie agreed, trying not to notice how her curves beckoned . . . how very much of her he could see.

Saints, already the fool night shift he'd draped round her shoulders had dipped low enough to fully expose one deliciously taut nipple. And if he craned his neck just a wee bit, he could see a goodly portion of the other one's tight-puckered rim!

"Hear me, lass," he began, letting go of the curling tendril of her hair as if it'd bit him. Sakes, just fingering its smooth silkiness made his fingers ache to pluck and toy with her *other curls*.

"My father will not stir discord by shunning you," he rushed on, certain he'd found a topic guaranteed to cool his ardor. "Because of the very traditions you name, he would ne'er risk the stain such a breach of Highland courtesy would call down around his ears."

Nor will he look with charity on the breaking of betrothal vows.

But that particular facet of the Black Stag's obsession with lairding it rightly he kept to himself.

If he'd learned aught in his years of traversing the land, it was that each new day brimmed with endless possibilities.

Naught under the heavens that e'er was or might yet come to be could not be turned over again, made good. Some worthy new use found for it. Even the matted and smoke-congealed thatch of the humblest cot-house roof, when replaced, proved fine nourishment for barren fields, a much-prized fodder to replenish and strengthen Highland crops.

There had to be at least one possibility that would allow him to solve his dilemma without bringing turbulence to his clan or Lady Euphemia's.

Aye, sure as rain fell downward, he'd find a way to turn his fortune . . . and if he had to single-handedly sail a galley to the distant isle of Doon and seek the supposedly infallible aid of Clan MacLean's famed wisewoman, the inimitable old Devorgilla.

Regardless of howe'er he'd have to conciliate the crone's much-prized favor.

Feeling better already, he touched his beauty's face,

taking care not to disturb her fresh bandaging. A faint whiff of some pungent herb wafted up from the clean linen wrapping, testament his stepmother or Elspeth had applied a healing poultice to the gash.

Seemingly untroubled by the wound, his beauty glanced up at the dark-raftered ceiling, fire glow playing over the exposed skin of her neck. But when she looked back at him, her gaze was burdened.

Robbie frowned, struggled against the urge to sit down, draw her onto his lap, and cradle her in the soothing warmth of his arms.

Instead, he lit gentle fingers across her temple. "Does the wound still pain you?" he asked, doing his best to ignore the tantalizing proximity of her near-nakedness.

"There is only a dull ache now . . . I scarce feel it." She touched careful fingers to the bandage. "'Tis other . . . concerns that trouble me."

"Have I not convinced you, then? About my father?"

She sniffed. "All ken it is not meet for any Highlander to turn a guest from his door, welcome or otherwise," she said, sitting up straighter, the brisk movement sending the night shift dipping even lower.

Leveling a piercing look at him, she made no attempt to cover her now fully bared breasts. "Ach, see you, we both ken that so long as the wind blows and water runs, the old ways will flourish—as well they should," she said, a wistful smile playing about her lips. "Even so, I warrant your father's displeasure in me runs deeper than mere concern to uphold the etiquette of these hills."

Suspecting she had the rights of it, Robbie tamped down his own doubts about his father's overblown reaction and reached to skim the backs of his knuckles lightly down her cheek.

"You do not know him," he told her, inordinately pleased when she did not pull back from his caress. "He has his reasons for seeming to live in a foul wind. He has rebuilt his life—the unity of this clan—upon the ashes of much strife and ill doings."

She caught her lip at that, something indefinable flaring in her eyes. "I have faint . . . memories of strife connected with this house. Impressions of sorrow and anger. Grief. I am also quite certain I ought not be here, yet . . ." She let the words tail off, swept a coppery spill of flame-bright hair behind her ear.

"Can it be . . . see you, in my dream I saw him. . . ." She faltered, stumbling over the words. "Is it possible that your father lives in . . . *pain*?"

Robbie all but snorted. "Ach, 'tis long past and best forgotten."

Still, he slid a glance at the hearth fire, then the carefully bolted door. His nerves tightened at giving voice to something his father would surely view as a weakness.

The Black Stag's little-glimpsed vulnerability.

An elusive quality Robbie himself was none too sure of most days.

"Whate'er pain he has known is long by with," he said, wishing her full, firm breasts weren't so glaringly apparent. "I am told he is the happier to while by his hearthside these days, his greatest foe the threads of peat smoke e'er drifting through the hall and a-stinging his eyes—"

"But he still bears the scars," his beauty persisted. "To this day."

Robbie shrugged, waiting until a low rumble of distant thunder faded away before he spoke.

"Aye, that is the way of it, true enough. He fashes o'er the slightest menace from without—anything he perceives as a threat to the good of his people," he explained, stepping closer to stroke her face with his fingertips. "But you needn't seek the shadows in his presence. He only gives himself quarrelsome—that I vow! Inside, he is soft as wee Mungo's belly. You must trust me on this . . . will you?"

Not looking at all convinced, she flicked a glance at the tall windows across the room where one shutter in particular rattled in the gusty wind.

Black-glowering fragments from her interrupted sleep rose and blew about as well, but she steeled herself against them even as they pressed close, pushing and prodding her ever nearer the unseen edge of a treacherous drop.

Her heart beginning a slow hard beat, she struggled to forget the Black Stag's dark blue eyes boring into hers from the depths of her nightmare. Strove to *un*-see how he'd looked at her in a way that shredded her soul, his silent regard filled with both regret and dread, branding her.

'Twas a susceptibility she had ne'er expected or desired to find—a threat insidious enough to slip through her resistance and spear her most tender parts . . . her own welling empathy upon witnessing suffering of any kind.

"Well, my lady?" her knight prodded, his voice full of persuasion, its husky-rich depths softening her. "Will you believe me—or do you mean to heed the prattlings of loose-tongued rabble?"

"I do not fear your father. That much I can swear to you. But neither ought I stay here. Not now . . . after my dream," Juliana said, glancing down the bed to where wee Mungo tumbled about on his short legs before burrowing beneath the mussed bedcovers.

His brows drawing together, Robbie snatched him and lowered the wriggling pup to the floor, settling him on a pillow that'd fallen off the bed.

But having none of his displacement, the little bugger showed needle-sharp teeth. Full of bristling ingratitude, he even tried to sink them into Robbie's fingers before he could withdraw his hand.

"Have a care, mite." Robbie fixed him with a look of mock sternness. "Or next time I shall be tempted to drop you onto the prickly rushes and not a fine, plump pillow," he added, tousling the pup's floppy ears before he turned back to his beauty.

"As for *you*, I promise, my father only blusters," he said, tracing the smooth line of her jaw. "Some, like my good-uncle, swear he is made of naught but bellywind and scowls."

Robbie watched her as he stroked the side of her face. He'd hoped his jesting would win a smile, if only a wee one. But she only shook her head again, the subtle straightening of her back and shoulders screaming her refusal to be cajoled.

"He is not the sole reason I cannot stay here." She looked up at him from beneath a sooty fringe of thick, curling lashes. "You do not understand."

"Then make me." Robbie let his fingers glide down

the slope of her neck, bit back a smile when the soft gentling touches wrested a tremble from her. "I want to help you."

"Help me?" Her brows shot upward. "Is that what you call this?" She captured his hand, removing his fingers from her nape, her firm grip deftly halting any further exploratory caresses. "Some would say it . . . otherwise."

Robbie choked back the denial rising in his throat.

He would not lie to her.

For she had the rights of it—touching even a wee fingertip to her proved . . . *otherwise.*

He blew out a slow breath, his entire body tightening with increased awareness. Saints cherish him, even wet and bedraggled as she'd been when he'd found her, garbed in scruffy shoes and rough-spun clothes, her high coloring and shapely, vigorous femininity had transported him.

Now, full naked but for the scant covering of torn night rail, she disarmed him completely.

Sakes, his hand trembled in hers—his fingers tingling to return to the silken skein of her unbound hair. Or, better yet, cup and caress the soft, plump weight of her breasts. Even more vexing, his *problem* jerked against the fool pillow with such vehemence she'd have to be blind not to notice.

"So you would . . . help me." Her smoky-rich voice cut through his lust-driven haze and made his heart thump.

"Aye, to be sure," he got out, the words strangled-sounding to his own ears. "Help you, help myself . . . us both."

"How?"

"I think you know," he said, his gaze meeting hers, probing.

All man again save his annoying inability to keep a steady grip on a ridiculously plump square of goose down.

For one moment of scowling frustration, he almost tossed aside the wretched pillow and yanked her to him. Truth be told, the urge to slant his mouth over hers and *feast* on her nigh overwhelmed him.

His desire to see her all beaming smiles and joy, with nary a tinge of darkness in her heart, raged equally compelling.

He grimaced. Behaving like a Highland stirk with his spring-juices rising would get him nowhere.

Nevertheless, the warm vitality of her, her vehement womanliness, made him burn for more of her—all of her. His senses in a whirl, he slipped his hand from her grasp and began deliberately caressing the sensitive skin beneath her ear.

If the fates were kind, the careful caress would summon another shiver, pour the same sweet, molten warmth through her as engulfed him just being this close to her, breathing in the same air.

But she only stiffened and frowned.

"Do not touch me . . . please," she murmured, the soft quiver in her voice and the pink bloom on her cheeks standing in stark contrast to her protest.

And giving Robbie hope.

"Och, sweetness, I am thinking you need to be touched," he said, his voice a shade deeper than usual. "Your body is telling me so."

Indeed, she trembled beneath his circling fingers. Denials or nay, she wanted to be gentled and touched. Undisguised need darkened the green of her eyes, and seeing it, a little thrill of conquest flipped Robbie's heart.

She wanted him.

There was nothing surer.

Even so, he wavered, the weight of honor and propriety crashing down all around him, the shattering of his scruples loud and accusatory in his ears.

But then she gave a soft little sigh, and leaned toward him, her body yielding a heartbeat before stubborn acceptance shuddered the length of her.

Seeing her capitulation near sent him over the edge. Lavender-scented heat rose and shimmered between them, beguiling his senses, while her warm curves and creamy expanse of smooth, bared skin stole his ability to think.

He dragged in a ragged breath, his need verging on desperation when she touched questing fingers to his own naked chest, her soft, heated nearness, so sweet-smelling and acquiescent, banishing even the staunchest of his knightly virtues.

The boundary overstepped, he tossed aside the pillow and slid his arms around her, drawing her warmly pliant curves flush against him.

"Lass," he whispered as another shivery tremble rippled through her. "Sweet precious lass."

His own body tensed, grew hotter, as he lowered his head and brushed his lips back and forth over hers in the sweetest, most tender of kisses.

Once more, she stiffened, withdrawing, but then she

gasped, the sound more like a *purr* this time, as she parted her mouth beneath his, instinctively seeking a deeper, more intimate joining.

Letting the ruined nightshirt slip to the floor, she slid her hands up between them, exploring his well-muscled chest and rubbing her flattened palms back and forth against the dark, glistening hairs sprinkled there. Robbie's loins tightened, the seductive friction of her hands moving across his chest hair unleashing a welter of lust and want of indescribable proportion.

He took her face between his hands, used his thumbs to caress her soft, creamy skin, the fine sweep of her cheekbones. "If you could but tell me your name, sweet minx, I swear to you I would carve it across the heavens . . . write each letter in stars," he vowed, whispering the words against her mouth, drinking in the warm sweetness of her breath, headier than wine. "I would—"

"My name is Juliana," she murmured suddenly, breaking the kiss, her voice less than steady, as if she needed to test the name's cadence on her tongue. "I remember . . . from my dream. Naught else, though, only the name."

Juliana.

Robbie's breathing stopped. Exhilaration pumped through him, the beauty of her name wrapping round his heart and sending flickering excitement skimming along his nerve endings.

"For truth"—a slow smile spread across his face, deepening his dimples—"I have ne'er heard a lovelier name. We shall soon discover the rest, I promise you."

"Aye," she agreed, some fleeting emotion in her expression reminding him that perhaps merely Juliana, a name without a past, might be best.

A deeper knowing might bring an insurmountable burden to lie upon them—and, at the moment, with his heart full to overflowing, he could think of naught but lying upon her . . . with her.

"To be sure, and we will," he agreed, meaning anything but delving into the mysteries of her past.

He wanted the unwritten days stretching before them.

Days he meant to shape and claim.

Somewhere thunder rumbled, nearer now and loud enough to rattle the shutters and jangle the chain of a hanging cresset lamp, long guttered. A burst of sudden lashing rain buffeted the walls, the fierce pounding almost deafening, but he took scant heed.

The wild fury of his own passion consumed him, pushing him past reason and dulling his senses—all save his sharp awareness of her.

Nigh drink-taken by feverish desire, he tunneled his fingers into the heavy silk of her hair, holding her close as he slanted his lips over hers in a slaking, soul-claiming kiss. A heated melding of soft breath and teasing, hot-gliding tongues.

Like one drowning, Juliana melted against him, angling her head to deepen the kiss, some half-coherent part of her wondering when and how he'd pulled her to her feet, for they now stood.

Toe to toe, skin to nigh-naked skin, intimately entwined.

And, saints preserve her, but she relished the contact, ached for every hot-pressing inch of their closeness, even opened her lips wider to allow his addictively stroking tongue greater access!

Molten heat streamed through her and her heart thundered, the whole of her quivering, savoring the hot, wet glide of his lips down her throat, across her collarbone and lower. Sweet kisses to the top swells of her breasts, each warm, moist touch of his lips and tongue scorching her and intensifying the slow, heavy pulsing low by her thighs until all resistance spun away on a rushing tide of need so demanding she could sooner have kept the sun or the moon from shining.

Sighing, she leaned into him, pressing closer still.

She did not want him to stop, could not bear it if the bliss-spending warmth spooling through her should come to an end. Willing its tantalizing heat to ne'er extinguish, she lowered her head to his chest, nuzzled the smoothness of her cheek against the warm, hair-roughened skin of his broad, hard-planed chest.

She craved the soothing of him, every sweet golden shimmer.

But dark wisps from her dream yet swirled around her, deep blue ripples of uneasiness caught on the eddies of the rain-damp air blowing in through the shuttering . . . a ceaseless distraction, its menace condemning and tormenting, making her . . . needy.

Decidedly vulnerable to the caresses of her knight's stroking fingers, the whisper of his kisses across appreciative skin.

And, for this blessed moment, ever so grateful for the sweet, mind-numbing solace trailing in the wake of his every touch. Each smooth glide of his hands along her naked flesh—the pleasure he spent her—proved too seductive to resist.

Clinging to his wide-set shoulders, with him raining soft kisses on her, such bliss seemed a wonder she could almost believe in. Even his simplest caress gilded her as if the angriest heavens had parted to let beautiful, golden light spill down all around her. Blessed warmth that flowed into her, enchanting her from within.

Illuminating her and chasing away all darkness.

"You tremble, sweet Juliana," he murmured, his hands still moving over her, stroking down the slope of her back to her hips and lower where he cupped and kneaded the curving fullness of her buttocks.

Splaying his fingers across her cool, smooth skin, he drew her closer, molding her against him until she no longer just imagined she'd felt the hard thickness of his desire. Nay, without doubt, every blatant inch of him pressed hotly against her belly!

But then he released her, stepping back as if she'd transformed herself into the most grizzled of crones.

"I am sorry, lass," he said, his eyes almost black with stormy emotion. "I only wished to hold and caress you, *soothe* you. It was ne'er my intent to seek my ease with you. On my heart, I would not see you dishonored."

. . . *would ne'er see you dishonored . . . ill-used . . .*

The words came from nowhere, yet everywhere, startling her and ripping through the desire and confusion to prick at her conscience with insidious persistence.

Nay, *well-meant* persistence.

Caring words e'er drilled into her by another husky-deep Highland voice, gently melodious and eerily simi-

lar to Robbie MacKenzie's but way too faint and far
away to have passed that one's bonnie, unsmiling lips.

Her brow furrowing, Juliana.stared at her knight. He
looked even more uncomfortable than she felt, but oh-
so-darkly handsome standing half naked in the flickering shadows, his braw presence dominating the whole
chamber, making it—and her—his own.

"How do you mean . . . dishonored?" She laced the
words with challenge for what he'd meant was painfully
obvious—it still loomed hard and throbbing against the
finely-knit linen of his loose-fitting braies.

"I will not dishonor either of us by expressing what I
meant in words," he said, retrieving his discarded tunic
and donning it with a careful grace.

Juliana bit her lip, not wanting to admit how much
she admired his self-possession—considering she stood
full naked before the bed, watching him.

He adjusted the fall of his shirt with equal care, his
gaze fastened on hers as he made certain the shirt's folds
covered the evidence of his arousal.

Satisfied at last, his expression turned assessing. "I
would think you know full well the kind of shame I
wished to spare you?"

"And if I do?"

Juliana fixed him with her best bold-eyed stare.

Some demon inside her refused to let her snatch up
the bed coverlet or even the remnants of her borrowed
nightshirt, to cover herself as he'd so pointedly done.

For good measure, she flickered a quick glance at the
still-apparent rise beneath his shirt. Anything but cry out
in frustration because, dear sweet saints, for the nonce,
at least, she'd *wanted* to be dishonored as he called it.

Aye, he'd ripped open a fissure inside her she'd ne'er known existed, and to her dismay, she found herself reveling in this hot-spinning tide he'd so surprisingly unleashed inside her.

Some wild wanton part of her burned for fulfillment . . . a blessed release of the dizzying whirl of tingles that had built to such a wild crescendo so low in her belly.

Deliciously sweet tingles that weighted the soft place between her thighs . . . the place where she now blazed the hottest.

"Well?" she pushed when he continued to gawp. "If I do ken what you meant?"

"Then, my lady," he said, stepping closer, "it falls my duty to say you that, in future, you'd best be more careful where you bed down alone and naked . . . lest you wish to give over your body, heart, and soul and be glad in the surrendering."

From some dark place hidden deep inside her, there was an inner knowing of the wrong she was about to do but also a strange acceptance of how alluring such irresistible impulses can be. Acknowledging them, she closed the few inches between them and snaked her arms around his neck, arching herself unashamedly against him.

"And if I say you that I did not wish you to stop?" she pushed, the smoldering attraction between them almost palpable. "What then, Sir Knight?"

"That would be unwise, lady—now, this night."

"Then why did you bring me here?"

"Because I could not leave you there in the glen— alone, injured, and helpless."

"And because you wanted me," Juliana spoke the truth she saw writ all over his face, even if he would not put it to voice. "You desired me as your leman."

"Nay!" That burst forth without the slightest hesitation. "Ne'er that," he objected. "Think you I would . . . pull back now, deny myself our passion and need, if I wished—"

"Yet you are as good as wed—your soon-to-be wife within these walls. What else—"

"I am not a jackal to stoop to such misdeeds," he jerked, setting her from him. "Even if—God helping me—I'll admit to burning for you!"

When a man burns for a woman, in especial one he can ne'er take to wife, 'tis always the lass whose life ends in sorrow and ash . . .

The other man's voice came again, so clear in her memory he may well have stood before her, even shouted the warning into her face.

Words spoken to her in another time and place, and by Kenneth—her brother.

That realization recognized now in full wakefulness, poured sweetest relief through her, welling her heart. A reassuring bliss marred only by the other fragmented terrors still leering at her from the shadows.

Unpleasing harbingers to remind her of things she'd rather forget—or best not even know. Dark, shameful things rising up unbidden to slay her.

Such as where her so unexpected streak of wantonness hailed from . . . the sudden and disturbing surety that hers and Kenneth's mother had been their sire's *heart*-mate rather than his true and wedded hearth-mate.

A leman.

Mortification flamed Juliana's cheeks.

She would be no man's whore.

She would not suffer the years of pain and anguish she instinctively knew her mother must've endured.

No matter how much a braw, bonnie knight might quicken her blood!

Her pulse pounding, she whirled away from him and, heedless of her nakedness, hurried to the windows where she pulled in great, greedy gulps of the chill night air.

He was upon her before she could even exhale.

"Do not run from me, lass," he said, seemingly undaunted when she raised arching brows at him. "I'll tell you true—in all the realm, I have ne'er seen a more comely, fiery maid than you. And, aye, I want you—and *have* wanted you—from the first. But I would not make you my leman, that I swear to you."

"And what else is there?" She pulled back her shoulders, stared at him. "Would you take two wives?"

"I would—" He broke off, blew out a sharp breath. "Ach, see you," he said, ramming a hand through his hair, "I do not know how I shall resolve this—would that I did."

At his honesty, and her own distress, Juliana turned away. She couldn't bear to look at him.

Fire glow gleamed on his shoulder-length hair, making it shine like moonlight on black water until she *ached* to run her fingers through the silky-dark strands, burned to draw his face to hers to receive and give more melding kisses.

Knight's kisses.

Tantalizing beyond belief.

But guilt curled icy fingers round her heart, squeezing hard until her conscience pressed objections from her lips. "You should ne'er have come into this chamber, ne'er opened my bed curtains. We should not be standing here doing this—discussing such things," she said. "It is . . . folly without redemption."

"It is what is meant to be." He reached for her, wrenched her against him, the close space of the window embrasure making it seem as if they were alone, far removed from outside cares. "We were made for each other, my Juliana, and I do not think I need to tell you? Aye, you cannot deny it!"

"'Tis madness," she whispered, tilting back her head, *begging* his kiss.

Catching herself as quickly, she jerked away, stared blindly at the window shutters. "You do not know what you say. Our minds are muddled from weariness, the trials of our journey. . . ."

Robbie shook his head. "Nay, my sweet, I think not." He pulled her back against him, straining her to him. "You are sore mistaken," he added, his heart clutching on the words for he, at least, knew exactly what crackled between them.

'Twas passion in its purest form. Blatant need, and it vibrated in the air around them, vivid and alive.

It was anything but madness.

It was *rightness*.

But he understood her hesitation.

"Sweet, so sweet." He touched gentle fingers to her lips, kept them there until he could feel the resistance begin to slip from her. "You needn't carry a whit of care." He leaned down to trail kisses along the curve of her throat. "Betrothals can be broken, new paths laid for the future."

"But you are yet . . . your betrothed. . . ."

"I have been given in name since I was a beardless laddie, as is the way with most sons of great houses—only those fated for the church are spared such arrangements," he said, needing, wanting her to understand. "My heart has ne'er belonged to anyone . . . until now."

Juliana swallowed, looked past him to stare into the shadows. "You do not know what you are saying," she whispered. "Faith, you know nothing of me. . . ."

"I know your name is Juliana and I feel the warmth *here*." Robbie placed her hand over his heart. "Such is enough."

"And if—"

"And you rattle your tongue too much." He looked down at her, his very heart streaming through flesh and bone, into her palm. "The devil take ifs and buts."

He had no thought but for her, his very own flame-haired beauty.

Consumed, he took up a length of plaid from one of the window embrasure's twin-facing benches and swirled it round her shoulders, once again covering her nakedness.

"Since your dreams were troubled, I shall make myself a pallet just outside the chamber door," he said, brushing her hair back from her face, his fingers combing through the silky-cool strands. "Should you require aught—you need but call out."

She nodded, this time clutching the plaid quite firmly around her.

"Sleep well, then, sweet Juliana," Robbie wished her,

and kissed the tip of her nose. "Tomorrow I shall begin slaying dragons for you."

Then, before he could regret the ill-timed return of his knightly honor, he strode from the room, every chivalrous inch of him aware that he was taking her name with him and leaving his heart behind.

'Twas a meet bargain.

A most fair exchange.

And one he wasn't about to let any living soul undo.

Nor any devil.

Chapter Seven

✤

A FULL SENNIGHT LATER, Robbie paused inside the entrance arch to the great hall, and surveyed the scene before him. Not long before sunrise, it was a dreary morning of the sort that brought the mist sliding down the braes and kept a drizzly rain falling. Even so, the lightsome mood in the hall gave him fresh heart.

And brought the beginnings of a smile to his face.

His sundry edicts and blustering had not been entirely for naught.

Unlike the hall of gloom he'd encountered in the first few days after his homecoming, an air of comfortable routine presided over Eilean Creag once again and the relaxed faces and jesting laughs of his waking kinsmen reassured him the tedious days of ill ease were past.

Or soon would be.

If only his dragon-slaying measures had not proved so effective, the very devil-demons he'd most desired to conquer seemed to have retreated so deeply into their respective lairs that they were nowhere to be seen.

Nay, not quite true.

One presided at the high table, his dark-scowling eminence quite visible indeed.

But as on every morning this past sennight, the Black Stag's stony-faced mien and tight-lipped silence assured no one sought to disturb his brooding.

All else appeared as it e'er had and should: smoking torches flickered in every available iron bracket along the arras-and-weapon-hung walls, some even flaring in iron rings suspended from the groin-vaulted ceiling. Well pleased, Robbie inhaled deeply of air pleasantly laced with the darkly-sweet aroma of burning peat, his gaze noting the flagons, drinking cups, and platters of viands littering the long tables.

Aye, all was as it should be.

And thanks to his insistence, a thick and fine-smelling layer of fresh, new rushes covered the floor—excepting on the raised dais at the far end of the hall.

A dip-of-the-head courtesy to the lady Euphemia.

The bare-floored dais was a fair enough compromise should the lung-strengthening herbs mixed into the floor rushes prove less effective than Robbie's stepmother and Elspeth declared.

Both women insisted the addition of speedwell, lungwort, and a smattering of yarrow would cure the air in the hall, making its fumes agreeable enough for the cough-plagued young woman.

But Euphemia MacLeod's place at the high table loomed empty all the same—as it had every morning since Robbie's arrival.

A slight that proved both annoying and an unspeakable relief, for although he harbored no great desire to meet the young woman, neither could he explore possible ways to disentangle himself from their betrothal unless he was first granted the opportunity to speak to her face-to-face.

And at the soonest.

A thousand pities on her if she continued to thwart him, for he believed he'd found a mutually acceptable solution to their dilemma.

One that might persuade her to release him quite swiftly, and amicably.

But his burgeoning plan was by no means a possibility that would hold overlong—too many and fair were the maids clamoring for the hands of young, marriage-hungry Clan Douglas men in the south.

Knowing it, Robbie adjusted his plaid against a chill draught pouring in through one of the deep-set arrow slits and steeled himself to enter the hall and to face another round of his father's interpellations and protests.

Objections he refused to accept.

Indeed, his heart ran wild with possibilities, his hopeful mind refusing to see the lady Euphemia as an insurmountable obstacle. And he certainly wasn't of a mind to view his flame-haired beauty as a treacherous pit yawning open at his feet.

If the saints were kind, the lass would soon acknowledge the inevitability of their attraction, and if the fates were kinder still, the lady Euphemia's rumored love of prestige and position would be his blessing.

Just as his beauty's disdain for suchlike might prove his greatest challenge.

Lifting his shoulders, Robbie rolled them in preparation for the trials ahead. Ne'er had he encountered a more stubborn maid. At times, he'd almost believe she'd prefer sleeping in the damp vaults beneath the keep rather than set foot in the sumptuous chamber she'd been given.

Guidsakes, even after receiving an open-armed welcome from all save his father, she kept herself in the background, stubbornly sitting at the lowest end of the hall and going about in borrowed kirtles of fine, but plain-woven cloth, stoutly refusing the finer raiments he knew his stepmother repeatedly offered her.

She'd also shown herself quite skillful at secreting herself from view, ofttimes slipping out of the hall so soon as courtesy allowed, and always before Robbie could easily take his own leave of the high table.

A feat she seemed to have accomplished already this morn, for like his faceless bride-to-be, the fetching Juliana, so vital and warm, was nowhere in the hall.

Just to make certain, Robbie scanned the shadows one more time, scrunching up his eyes to peer through the haze of bluish peat smoke hanging in the air, its dark sweetness even permeating the entrance vestibule, reminding him anew that he was indeed home.

His days of traipsing the length and breadth of the realm, sometimes sleeping beneath the roofs of allied clan chieftains, sometimes sharing the bed of a comely, warmhearted tavern wench, more often making his pallet in a comfortable hollow amongst the heather, are now past.

But not forgotten—or useless.

He'd learned many skills in the years he'd been gone—and made numerous friends.

Some of whom he hoped would help relieve him of an unwanted bride. Others whose undoubted capacities as bedmates might now help him woo and win the bride he wanted.

If he again gained the opportunity to ply her with those skills!

Determined to confront her this very day, and to claim at least one sweet, full-on-the-mouth kiss, Robbie savored the thought of their encounter, wrapping round him all the sensual confidence he'd accrued in his time away.

The rough years.

But not so turbulent and lonesome as to have been unpalatable.

The corners of his mouth tilting upward again, he stretched his arms and flexed his fingers, for once not trying to quell the pleasurable tightening in his loins. Truth be told, a bed in the heather, his naked body wrapped in his plaid and sprawled beneath the stars, had ne'er displeased him.

Though not quite the bliss of lying unclothed with a toothsome, well-rounded lass, bodies intimately entwined, he'd found much wonder and gladness on such nights nevertheless. And he'd e'er consider each hour spent so close to the land, a blessing indeed.

Memories to be treasured for always.

But now new memories stood to be made—just as sure as old ones welcomed and embraced him. Some bore hard on his patience, testing his wits most severely, but others warmed him to the roots of his soul, made him feel a wee lad again.

One of those latterly memories, grizzle-headed Fergus, sat nearby on a three-legged stool, a clutch of young squires, fresh-faced and in high-spirits, gathered round him as he regaled them with ancient tales of valor and battle, Highland honor and bloodletting.

Robbie watched the old man for a time, his heart smiling as surely as the grin tugging at the corners of his mouth. The bandy-legged Fergus, Eilean Creag's long-time seneschal before he'd reluctantly relinquished his duties to his capable wife, Elspeth, appeared not to have aged a day.

Unchanged, but still older-looking than stone.

And silver-voiced as always.

A flaring pitch-pine torch hissed and smoked on the wall above the graybeard's head, and glancing up at it, he changed the tone of his storytelling from that of braw Highlandmen belting on broadsword and dirk to the more wrenching but oh-so beloved Celtic themes of lost and unrequited love.

Deep, heart-piercing tales dredged from the very warp and weft of the Gaelic soul.

Robbie winced, deliberately closing his ears.

He may be Highland to the bone, mayhap even more so than some, but at the moment he had no stomach for soppy sentimentality.

Pretending not to have seen Fergus, Robbie started forward, heading great-strided away from the old man and his audience of eager-eared youths as swiftly as he could. His mind set, he cut his way through the crush of the crowded hall, only breaking stride when he neared his father's hounds.

Large, gray, and shaggy-coated, they slumbered in the glow of the hearth fire, wee Mungo welcomed into their midst, unafraid and content-looking, snug as a flea in a pig's ear.

Once again, Robbie's body tensed, but not in a pleasurable manner. A light throbbing began at his temples, worsening the longer he stared at the sleeping dogs.

He did not want to know how many days, before his return, the loyal animals had been banished to curl together for warmth, huddling in the hall's darkest corners, damp and shivering with cold.

He shuddered, chilled by the thought.

Even Roag, his father's declared favorite and great-grandson of Robbie's own beloved childhood companion, Mauger, had suffered amongst the banned.

Yet now they roamed where they willed again—save on the dais.

A discipline the dogs accepted with usual canine grace.

Robbie's mouth curved in satisfaction. Aye, the passing of seven days and nights had made clear the successes of his admittedly untried skills as a dragon slayer.

But much more stood to be accomplished.

His most fearsome hindrance yet breathed fire and swung a razor-sharp tail, his black glowers even causing any hapless souls yet trapped at the high table to hang their heads and lower their glances in abject submission to the Black Stag's most virulent whims.

"God's eyes!" Robbie muttered, staring at the morose lot.

He quickened his pace, his own face grim-set, his shoulders squared—this was his father at his blackest.

A situation best settled at once before it could worsen and refoul the entire hall. But when he reached the high table, the words he'd meant to have with his father froze on his tongue.

He'd been sore mistaken.

It hadn't been the Black Stag's frown that had those sitting round the table looking downward. Nor did his father's renowned ill temper have aught to do with it.

Not at all.

Everyone present, including the Black Stag, was simply examining the array of oddities displayed on an opened length of sheepskin spread across the table.

Gog-eyed himself now, Robbie stared at the collection of peculiarities. Everything imaginable and *un*imaginable appeared to be on hand.

Bundles of dried herbs the dubious likes of which he'd ne'er seen, an assortment of vials, earthen jars, leather-wrapped flagons, and a few less than savory-looking objects, the origin and purpose of which he did not care to speculate on.

But someone had to.

Using two fingers, he picked up what he hoped to be no more sinister than a dried bat's wing and dangled the thing in the air.

He turned to his father. "What manner of nonsense is this?"

The Black Stag shot him a grieved look. "Have a care, laddie," he said. "You tread dangerous ground if you mishandle such things."

Robbie raised a brow, but the look on his father's face was enough to make him cease wriggling the thing in midair and let it drop from his fingers.

"I thought to find you breaking your fast on cold meats and slaked oatmeal . . . not contemplating a horde of . . ." He trailed off, suppressed a shudder.

Warning or no, he couldn't help drawing his dirk and

poking at what looked like a browned and withered finger.

"I hope that is a stick?" he asked of no one in particular, not really relishing an answer.

"A God's name, think you any of us can say you what it is? 'Tis *charms* they are, I suppose we could say," Duncan snapped in response, tossing down a swig of ale, then dragging his sleeve across his mouth. "Though for what purpose, I canna tell you."

Robbie raked a hand through his hair. "I am not sure I'd wish to know."

His father snorted. "You ought be interested for amongst these *enchantments* is a cure for your bride-to-be's ailing—or so we are told."

Ignoring that, Robbie dropped onto the trestle bench and demonstratively reached for a large wooden bowl of oatmeal. "And where did these . . . eh . . . treasures come from?"

"From old Devorgilla herself," Sir Marmaduke put in from the end of the table. "You would be wise not to rumple your nose too vigorously over that one's offerings. The crone sent them in honor of your wedding."

Robbie all but choked on his slaked oats.

"The Devorgilla?" He stared round. "Clan MacLean's fabled *cailleach*?"

Sir Marmaduke nodded.

"The very one—the most revered wisewoman in the Isles, or so it is claimed," he confirmed, smearing a thick layer of honey onto a bannock.

Looking up, he narrowed his good eye at Robbie. "Since you've heard tell of her, you will know that her gifts are not to be taken lightly . . . or shunned."

Unable to keep a tremor of humbled respect, or mayhap trepidation, from tumbling down his spine, Robbie eyed the bundled herbs and spelling goods with new esteem.

"And how did the cailleach learn that I am . . . er . . . *was* to wed? How did these things find their way here? The Isle of Doon lies far to the south and I've heard the crone seldom leaves its shores."

Sir Marmaduke held up a hand, washed down his bannock with a long swallow of frothy heather ale.

"'Tis said there is naught under the Hebridean skies that old Devorgilla is not aware of," he said, setting down the ale cup. "All the more reason to pay close heed to her attentions when she bestows them."

"But how did—"

"No mumbled magical nonsense sent those . . . *charms* a-sailing through the night and onto this high table, you can be sure," his father said, sending a hot glance at Sir Marmaduke as if to quell any rebuttals he might wish to make. "They came here delivered by fair and gentle hands. Your Aunt Caterine arrived from Doon late last night, and it was she who brought these healing herbs and suchlike from Devorgilla—the cailleach told Lady Caterine she knew that your bride-to-be is in need of special healing."

"Lady Caterine is here?" Robbie ignored the reference to his betrothed.

He glanced round the table, thinking he might have missed Lady Caterine, but his stepmother's sister and Sir Marmaduke's lady wife proved as glaringly absent as all the other womenfolk of the castle.

"Where is she then? And my stepmother?"

"They are in the herbarium, sorting through yet more such *gifts* old Devorgilla sent along to us." Duncan indicated the spelling goods with a not quite but almost derisive wave of his hand. "If I heard aright the cailleach explained to Lady Caterine which herbs and potions would best heal your bride-to-be's wheezing and ease her coughs—if such seizures can even be cured."

"If?" Sir Marmaduke looked down the table. "You would be well cautious not to doubt, my friend. I do not."

Leaning sideways to catch the light of a nearby torch, the Sassunach ran a finger down the scar seaming his once-handsome face. At one time angrily red and puckered, now naught but a faded silvery line marred his noble visage.

A remnant of a troubled time, beginning at his left temple and ending at the right corner of his mouth—the scar's worst legacy, its taking of his left eye.

Clearly at peace with his face, and his life, Sir Marmaduke gave his old friend his best comradely smile.

"Even you, with all your blusters and airs, cannot deny the improved appearance of my scar in recent years?" He placed the flat of his hand on the table, leaned forward to stare at Duncan. "To be sure, your lady wife's so kindly proffered jars of ragwort ointment have helped, but it was Devorgilla's special potion that truly made the difference."

Duncan gave a noncommittal shrug.

Sir Marmaduke's gaze sharpened. "Why do you think my Caterine makes the journey to Doon every spring?"

"H'mmm . . ." Duncan acknowledged with a gruff nod.

Even at his worst, he was unable to deny how much better the Sassunach's face appeared.

"She visits the crone every year?" Robbie glanced at his father, scarce able to believe it.

"Do not turn to me for an answer, lad." Duncan leaned back in his chair and folded his arms. "I do not ken why she goes to Doon, but I vow we are about to learn."

Sir Marmaduke nodded.

"And so you are," he said, looking smug. "She wishes to pay tribute, to thank the crone for all she's done for us at Balkenzie Castle. Caterine takes her provender ... plaiding, creels of cut peats, dried haunches of meat and suchlike, and—"

Duncan cocked a dark brow. "And she returns with ... dried bats' wings and fossilized toe of newt?"

"She—" Sir Marmaduke snapped his mouth shut as quickly as he'd opened it. Refilling his ale cup, he took a long, slow sip before he spoke again.

"We both have a touch of gray in our hair these days, my friend," he said, not looking at all distressed by the disclosure. "In most men, wisdom is thought to increase with the arrival of such signs of maturity. I like to think I am now sage enough to know better than to comment on such foolery as just left your li—"

"Sage? And only just now, you say?" Duncan grabbed the edge of the table, leaned forward. "Sakes, English, you were born sage. That, I vow!"

Sir Marmaduke shrugged. "Then mayhap you will heed your own advice to your son and not make jest at the crone's gifts."

"Bah! See you, I've another question for your aged and wise ears," Duncan said, settling back in his chair again. "Now that your Caterine is returned, when will you be returning to your own Balkenzie?"

Robbie frowned.

Their bickering, though good-natured, had gone on long enough.

"Have done behaving like mummers," he said and was rewarded by a sharp, unrepentant look from his father.

His uncle continued to stare fix-eyed down the table, calmly sipping his ale in that oh-so-slow way of his, a gesture designed solely to tread on his longtime friend's renowned impatience.

Determined, Robbie seized up his dirk and, raising it high, hammered its blunt-ended handle on the table, promptly catching their fullest attention.

He cleared his throat, laid down the dirk. "And I say, my uncle and the lady Caterine stay with us for as long as they desire—to be sure, until my wedding," he said, deciding the matter for them. "It would not be meet for them to leave the sooner."

His father's mien lightened at once.

"There speaks my lad," he said, sounding much appeased. Enough so to send a quick triumphant glance down the table. "So you have come to your senses at last?"

Borrowing his uncle's trick, Robbie took a long, slow sip of his ale.

"I have come to know my mind, aye," he said, putting down the cup with a *clack*. "And if I hadn't, the lady Euphemia's absence in the hall yet again would have set my purpose, that you can be sure of. I will not wed her."

His father's brows snapped together, his face coloring again.

"Dinna think you will take this . . . this *Juliana* to wife!" he rapped out, a muscle beneath his eye beginning to twitch and jump. "I will not allow such shame to befall this house—know it."

"The lady Euphemia need not be shamed," Robbie said, glad for the steadiness of his voice. "I have a plan I believe she will receive with favor."

His father hooted. "Saints cherish us—a plan to humiliate her and you say she will be joyed to hear it!"

He glared down the table at Sir Marmaduke, jabbed a finger at him. "English, I will personally see you off to Balkenzie if this nonsense comes from you—aye, I'll see you set sail in a storm—and in a galley with holes bored in its hull!"

"And mayhap I aught take my leave indeed," Sir Marmaduke countered, lifting his cup in mocking toast, "since staying might drive my good temper past its limits."

"Your good temper," Duncan grumbled, swinging back on Robbie. "Whate'er fool plans you are hashing, lad, you must give the MacLeod lass a chance," he said, a strange note of tight-stretched nervousness in his usually so authoritative voice.

"She ails, I tell you—wait till you see her," he went on, the tinge of ill ease quite plain now. "A blind mole could see she fares poorly. A wee teensy bit, she is. Fragile. I pray you, wait before you do aught that will bear grievously on this household."

Robbie sat up straighter. "So ever you say, Father. But you mistake if you believe I wish to bring grief on this or any good house—such is not the knightly way."

"And neither is rejecting a bride—last I heard!" Duncan snapped.

A decided clearing of throats and muffled snorts rose at that, Sir Marmaduke and some of the other kinsmen within hearing range not quite able to smother their guffaws.

Those old enough to remember knew well how vehemently the Black Stag had objected to wedding his own much beloved lady wife.

Robbie raised a hand, waving his father to silence when he looked to spout more objections—or rain darkest epithets on his smirking kinsmen.

"Be assured, I only desire what is good for the lass, mayhap even better for her—a possible alliance to one of the many marriageable Douglas lads I met in the south," he said, warming to the notion. "Clan Douglas is great in number and mayhap the most powerful family in all the realm. And their lands are in the fair south, a climate where Lady Euphemia's ailments will surely not trouble her so sorely as here, in Highland, with our continual rain and cold."

"You have thought this out." His father frowned. "Have you sent a gillie south already? Dared to begin negotiating such foolhardiness?"

Robbie stiffened, but he held his father's gaze.

"Nay, the idea has only just come to me in recent days," he admitted. "But I am on friendly enough terms with the Douglases, both the Blacks and the Reds—they even took me hunting wild bulls in Ettrick Forest. They are hard and able men, capable of holding their own against any Highlander, and they are e'er in need of young wives. There could be no shame for the lady Euphemia in becoming a Douglas bride."

"Think you such a high-born family would accept the daughter of a bit laird the likes of Hugh Out-with-the-Sword?" That from Sir Marmaduke.

"To be sure." Robbie helped himself to a fresh cup of ale, his spirits lifting. "They'd jump at gaining a foothold above the Highland line—a lass of good enough house and standing who could make that possible would be greeted with much favor—"

"Och, well and I believe it," the Black Stag said, swinging around to quell the chatter breaking forth at a few of the nearer long tables. "But it matters not, for it is you the lass shall wed."

Pushing back from the table, he stood, rising to his full, imposing height.

"I will not have her shunned," he said, his voice edged with authority. "Not beneath my roof. She has not wronged you—and she's sent you her regrets at being bed-bound, as you well ken. There will be nothing of it, but that you do right by her. And honor your vows."

Robbie shot to his feet as well, glad for the chill air pouring in on them through the small high windows. "The lady Euphemia has my greatest sympathies that she is . . . of frail health. Would God I had the means to spare her such trials and I do regret she must suffer her days abed—"

"Some say she lies."

Gelis, Robbie's saucy-eyed youngest sister, came flouncing out of the shadows at the back of the dais, her older sister, the raven-haired Arabella, close on her heels.

Looking pleased to have drawn all gazes with her impudence, Gelis flipped a bright-gleaming braid over her shoulder and raised a cheeky voice.

"Do not gape so," she said, jutting her chin. "She does lie—and if she doesn't, then she twists things to suit her."

All round the high table, jaws dropped and eyes stared. And at the long tables close by, the excited buzz of speculation stopped abruptly.

"Who would dare spout such nonsense?" The Black Stag wheeled on his daughter, his expression fierce. "The lady Euphemia ne'er leaves her room—all know it. There is nary a one amongst us who has been in her company long enough to make such an unfounded accusation. Tell me true, lass, who would speak so unfairly?"

Gelis shrugged, the cheekiness of her dimpled smile not diminishing a jot under her father's narrow-eyed stare. "Mayhap the laundresses?"

"Sssssshhh you," Arabella sought to silence her. "We cannot know if what they say is true."

"So they did say something?" Robbie strode over to his sisters, his interest arrested. "What did they say, Gelis?" He fixed his attention on his younger sister, the one most likely to babble forth whate'er weighted her tongue.

But to his surprise, she blushed, her smooth cheeks turning nigh as bright a red as her hair.

She glanced round, her gaze lighting first on her father and uncle, then flicking over to the lady Euphemia's own guardsmen filling nearby trestle tables.

"'Tis not fit to be spoken in front of menfolk," she said, her flush deepening. She sent a sidelong look at her sister. "Tell him, Arabella—we ought not talk of it."

Arabella said not a word.

Indeed, she tried slinking back into the shadows whence the two young women had come.

"Och, nay, lass. Too late—you already have spoken of it." Robbie snagged her arm. "You—and your sister—are not leaving this dais until you tell us what demons have perched on your shoulders."

In sorry plight indeed, Arabella bit her lower lip. "'Tis only that we do not wish to see you cozened," she said at last, and immediately lowered her dark gaze to the stone-flagged floor. "Is it not enough to know that the kitchens are agog with rumors—and have been ever since she came here from Castle Uisdean?"

"Then I would know what you have heard." Robbie hooked a finger beneath her chin, lifted her pretty face. "Every word of it—kitchen gossip or no."

Arabella pressed her lips together, looked to Gelis.

"Ach, leave her be," that one declared, sashaying up to them and knocking Robbie's fingers from Arabella's chin. "With surety, we canna vouchsafe for the prattlings of laundresses, but we can promise you that the lady Euphemia leaves her chamber!" Gelis cried, her eyes flashing triumph. "'Tis addlepated she is, I tell you. We have seen her slinking about where she had no right to be . . . a-talking to herself about nonsense."

"And just where have you seen her *slinking about*?" Duncan wanted to know, lowering himself into his laird's chair, his expression no longer wrathful, but weary.

"Since no one else has glimpsed the maid, mayhap it interests me, as your father, to learn where the two of you have been keeping yourselves?"

They all waited, but Gelis kept her rosy lips sealed and Arabella fixed her gaze on the windows.

Getting up again, the Black Stag moved round the high table and laid his hands on his eldest daughter's shoulders. "If you do not wish to reveal where you were when you saw her, then tell us where the lady Euphemia was when you saw her," he suggested, his tone incredibly reasonable for so hot-blooded a chieftain.

Arabella slid an uncomfortable glance at her sister. "S-she was in the passages of the tower where her chamber is, and—and . . . in her room."

"So-o-o—that is how the cat jumps. Now we come to the bit, eh, lassie?" Releasing her, the Black Stag stroked his knuckles down her blushing cheek, then slid a telling glance at Sir Marmaduke before looking back at his daughter. "Now tell me—did the lady Euphemia see *you*?"

Her face running red as a sunset, Arabella shook her head.

Duncan jerked a much-telling glance back toward the deepest shadows of the dais—to a wedge of blackness where a little-used door stood cracked open.

His expression spoke volumes. "Can it be that you and your sister have been skulking about in secret wall passages that ought to have been sealed off many long years ago?"

Switching his gaze between his flush-faced eldest daughter and the silent Sir Marmaduke, he let his most penetrating stare settle on the latter.

"Is it possible, English, that not all such passages and hidden stairwells were tended to . . . back then, long years ago, when it fell to you to oversee such measures?"

Sir Marmaduke had the good grace to appear chagrined.

But he caught himself as quickly, and rather than splutter a retort, he, too, pushed to his feet. Stepping forward, he took Arabella's hand and raised it lightly to his lips.

"If you do not wish to tell us what you heard being bandied about by the servitors, perhaps you can tell us what you heard the lady Euphemia saying?" He slanted a warning glance at Duncan. "Regardless of how you came to be close enough to her privy quarters to observe her . . . thusly?"

"I—I . . ." Arabella began, shuffling her feet. "W-we were—"

"We were in the squint above her chamber," Gelis blurted, her eyes sparking indignation. She glanced about, her hot amber-eyed gaze pinning anyone who dared to crook a brow at her.

"We were bored if you would know the truth of it!" she blurted, not a thread of remorse in her voice. "We meant the lady no harm. We were only curious why she hides herself up there. And so we saw her—prancing mother-naked round her chamber, not a-coughing at all, and talking up a storm about Fladda Chuan, beyond Duntulm Bay on Skye, and how she was certain it is in truth the fabled Tir-nan-Og, the Isle of Perpetual Youth!"

At the ensuing silence, she sketched a mocking curtsy.

"And that, my lords," she finished, beaming, "is why we are certain she is daft—all ken Tir-nan-Og is but a myth . . . yet she was prattling on about sending men there."

Ignoring his father's snort, Robbie raised arching brows at his sister, looked deep into her outraged eyes. "Can it be she was drink-taken?"

"Mayhap." Gelis shrugged. "All ken her father is e'er deep in his cups and she is delivered an ample supply of heather ale each morn—more than enough to last her through the day."

"Walking around her privy chamber unclothed does not make her addled," Sir Marmaduke said, rubbing his chin. "Nor do I believe she partakes of more ale than she ought—so slight as she is, like as not, she'd fall asleep if she did."

He began pacing the length of the dais, his hands clasped behind his back. "It could be, though, that she takes after her sire in other ways," he said, dropping his voice so it would not carry to where the MacLeod men-at-arms sat at a long table some ways into the hall.

Moving closer to the high table, he explained, "Hugh MacLeod had some very strange things to say during my visits to Castle Uisdean to arrange his daughter's journey here. If the lady Euphemia is prone to nonsensical blether mayhap she learned the habit from her father?"

"Hah!" Duncan snorted again. "Old Hugh cannot help but speak foolery—his wits are e'er pickled by ale or befuddled by women. The man is a notable wencher," he said, reclaiming his seat. "You cannot trust what'er babble slides off his tongue—and I'd think you would ken as much!"

"Still. . . ." Sir Marmaduke lowered himself onto the trestle bench, shot a glance at Gelis and Arabella before adding in a near-inaudible whisper, "The Hugh *I* saw and spoke with did not appear capable of undressing a woman, much less bedding one. The man is sore ill, I'd swear it. And he either speaks twaddle—or he lies."

Robbie turned to his uncle. "And what makes you

think he might lie? That Hugh is a man not much esteemed, a great skirt-chaser, is well known in these hills, but that he speaks untruths?"

Shaking his head, Robbie puzzled. "He ne'er denied having a different lass in his bed nigh every e'en, even when his wife yet lived. Indeed, as I remember the man, he enjoyed boasting of his . . . er . . . accomplishments."

Sir Marmaduke hesitated, shrugged his wide-set shoulders.

"For truth, lad, he may well have been in his cups or perhaps dazed from a too-deep slumber, but when I mentioned the most crucial part of your marriage treaty—that he no longer lower his treacherous Girt of Strength, that foul chain the MacLeods have e'er been so fond of stretching across the narrows, the man swore the chain hadn't been used in years."

His piece spoken, Sir Marmaduke fortified himself with a gulp of ale. "And such blather, my friends, can only be a lie or an indication his wits have flown, for we all know how often the wretched chain has been put to use—including in very recent times."

Robbie glanced at his father, not trusting himself to speak.

His uncle looked at the Black Stag, too.

As did all present.

But Duncan only shrugged his own great shoulders and, like his friend, snatched up his ale cup and downed the contents in one long swallow.

"You are the wise one," he spoke at last, jerking a nod at Sir Marmaduke. "What say you we ought do? Faced as we are with a maid who coughs but supposedly doesn't, and who hides herself in her room—yet is seen darting about in darkness, talking to herself whilst walking naked circles in her bedchamber?"

"What do *you* say?" Sir Marmaduke gave back, for once offering no sage gems of wisdom.

"I say none of it makes a whit of sense and my head aches too sorely this morn for me to attempt to find reason behind any of it—should suchlike prove grounded," Duncan said, half turning away to stare at the wet, gray murk visible through the tall, arched windows lining the back of the dais.

"And you, lad?" Sir Marmaduke turned to Robbie.

Robbie drew a long breath. "I would know the truth howe'er it may fall," he said, slowly sipping his own ale.

Sir Marmaduke lifted steepled fingers, tapped them against his chin.

"Mayhap we should take whiche'er of the laundresses spoke poorly of the lady Euphemia to Trumpan on Skye? To Clach Deuchainn, the Trial Stone that is kept there?" he suggested, arching his good brow. "Mayhap we should take the lady Euphemia along as well? 'Tis said the stone does not lie."

Gelis and Arabella exchanged glances again. "The *Trial Stone?*"

"You have not heard of it?" Robbie looked at them. "'Tis a truth stone," he told them before his father could hoot with derision. "A pillar stone at Kilconan Church on the far side of Skye, on the Waternish Peninsula. It stands about four feet high and has a finger-sized hole near its top. 'Tis said the stone unmasks liars and unveils the truth by—"

" . . . declaring anyone a liar who, blindfolded, has the misfortune of not being able to thrust their finger into the hole," Duncan said, lowering himself back into his elaborately-carved laird's chair.

He looked round, his dark gaze lighting in turn on everyone lining the high table or standing close by.

"I see no need to take hapless young women clear to the far side of Skye only to expect them to perform such silliness," he declared, his voice ringing with finality. "Finding out liars by poking fingers into holes is as great a folly as believing the tongue-wagging twaddle of kitchen lads and laundry maids."

"Yet you do not doubt your own good wife's *taibh-searachd,* her gift of second sight?" Sir Marmaduke slid a pointed glance at Robbie, then looked back at Duncan. "You have seen the proof of such wonders as we cannot explain."

Duncan huffed.

"That is different—and you know it."

"As you say," Sir Marmaduke agreed with a carefree-seeming lift of his broad shoulders. "Yet you believe in the blessings bestowed by your own clan's famed Marriage Stone," he persisted, now examining his fingernails. "Surely a journey to Skye's Clach Deuchainn cannot do harm and if—"

"Euphemia MacLeod is not lying," Duncan insisted, his voice underlaid with steel. "Not about her ailments nor concerning whate'er mysterious matters my two flap-eared daughters think they heard someone say." He paused to give the girls a stern look. "The blether of servitors cannot be trusted."

"But we can be trusted, aye, Papa?" Gelis tilted her bright head, flashed Duncan her most disarming smile.

"Aye, and to be sure I believe you—with all my

heart," the Black Stag capitulated, his voice not near so gruff, but his eyes still full of wariness.

"Then you believe us when we tell you she is a liar? That we saw her . . . acting strangely?"

"I believe you *think* she speaks untruths," Duncan said, speaking to his daughter but slanting a glance at Robbie. "As for the rest—there are many who would not condemn a maid for enjoying herself within her own chamber walls, lass."

"Naked . . . alone?" Gelis sniffed.

The Black Stag looked . . . thoughtful.

Robbie reached for the ale jug, replenishing his cup and downing the contents. A fool would know where his father was heading and he, for one, wanted none of it.

Especially after he'd had a taste of his beauty's undoubted charms.

Sure enough, he'd no sooner set down the ale cup then the Black Stag leaned forward in his chair, the hear-me-well look spreading across his face boding imminent trouble.

"If the lass favors walking round her chamber bare-skinned as the day she was born—you ought consider yourself fortunate, son," he said, pinning Robbie with a stare. "Many are the men whose wives are not so . . . generous."

"I am not interested in Lady Euphemia's generosity." Robbie kept his own stare as fixed and level as his father's. "I would rather see her . . . er . . . *wealth,* preserved for expenditure elsewhere, where it'd be more appreciated."

"I wager!" The Black Stag leaned back in his chair

again. "Even so, you might surprise yourself by finding her pleasing."

Robbie shrugged, his mind set.

"I will not make cause with you on this," he said, his voice calm, but his heart already pounding a fast beat. "I wish to take my pleasure elsewhere . . . and I shall."

Standing, Robbie sketched a quick bow to his wide-eyed sisters, then strode from the dais before steam could shoot out his father's ears.

He felt good.

In fact, if he weren't certain someone might see and deem it outrageously inappropriate after the heated discourse on the dais, he'd give in to the grin trying to spread across his face.

The notion of Lady Euphemia's naked pacing *did* please him.

But not for reasons his father would approve of.

Truth be told, the maid's strange behavior might just prove to be the best thing that had happened to him in days.

Having gained the end of the hall, Robbie smiled openly now. And his smile broadened even more when he started mounting the turnpike stair that would take him to a particularly fine tower chamber presently occupied by a certain comely lass.

One that well pleased him.

And if the lady Euphemia truly were weaving some sinister web of duplicity as his sisters believed, or if she was indeed possessed of addled wits—all the better.

He would then have fullest grounds to break their betrothal and none could look askance at him, or his house.

To knowingly bind himself to such a lass would have him laughed to the winds.

A fate even the Black Stag would not condone.

And, saints above, but that was an uplifting prospect.

Chapter Eight

❧

H E SHOULD HAVE KNOWN she'd not be there.

Hope and expectation frozen on his face, Robbie stood on the threshold of his beauty's bedchamber, the fast pounding of his heart dwindling to a slow, disappointed beat as the room's silence confirmed what he ought to have realized when his knocking received no response.

She'd slipped away again, sight unseen, and the sharp bite of his disgruntlement shocked him.

Stepping into the room, his gaze still searched, hoped.

But she was well and truly gone.

As was the wee pricking of guilt he'd experienced upon opening the door without invitation—that quibble soundly wiped away by the stronger lure of her presence.

An irresistible *pulling* that drew him ever deeper into the empty bedchamber. A vivid, almost tangible potency claiming bold sovereignty over any knightly codes of honor that might frown on such an intrusion into an innocent maid's privy quarters.

Saints, but the chamber reeked with the essence of her!

It was sheerest possession, the truth of her claim reflecting back to him from the furnishings and even the walls.

"Possession, indeed," Robbie chided himself, the two words overloud in the empty room.

He frowned.

Nonsensical or nay, the chamber *did* look like her.

He doubted he'd e'er own to having courted such a fool notion, but he did feel surrounded by her . . . caressed and welcomed by every inch and corner of the room, each sensuously wavering flicker of light and shadow.

Even the air vibrated with her presence, wrapping round him and filling him with such a shock of unfettered *need* he could no sooner take his leave of her quarters than he could fly to the moon.

Too many enticements lay scattered about, and Sir Robert MacKenzie, proud knight of the Scottish realm and heir to the vast and majestic lands of Kintail, suddenly found himself more long-nosed than the most intrepid prattle-mongers of the glens.

His heart thumping, he drew slow, deep breaths of the room's chill, peat-tanged air, his senses smiling at the subtle hints of lavender and warm, vital *femininity* accompanying each indrawn breath.

He moved to the great four-poster bed, noting the carefully drawn-back bed curtains and how neatly the bedclothes were arranged: the linens and coverlet smooth and tidy, the sea of lavishly-embroidered cushions arranged just so against the oaken headboard, the plaiding meticulously folded at the bed's foot.

A smile touched the corners of his mouth, something deep inside him warming as he slid his hands down the cool, richly-worked folds of the brocaded bed curtains, dark and heated images flashing through his mind with each glide of his fingers.

But more than recalling his beauty's warm, voluptuous nakedness or her splendorous, hard-tipped breasts gleaming in the fire glow, the bed's very neatness spoke of her unbending Highland pride.

Her refusal to be compromised in circumstances not to her liking.

A stubborn, chin-held-high dignity Robbie found both admirable and refreshing, for unlike any of the gentleborn ladies he'd known, including his own well-loved sisters, castle tongue-waggers claimed his beauty repeatedly shooed away any and all servitors who came to straighten her chamber.

Rumor was, she'd steadfastly insist that so long as she possessed two good arms, she would not allow others to do for her what she herself could easily manage.

Another glimpse of her stared back at him from near the little red-glowing brazier hissing away not far from the window. There, within the brazier's circle of warmth, she'd gathered a lovingly-plumped mound of soft plaiding and furs, a luxurious resting place that could only be wee Mungo's bed. A wooden bowl of fresh water stood close by, as did a juicy marrow bone, lying in wait upon the rushes.

And only a pace or two away from the mite's water bowl loomed the greatest temptation Robbie'd encountered since ripping open the bed curtains to find his beauty kneeling full naked before him, all sunfire hair, welling breasts, and smelling of lavender and woman.

A blazing-eyed delight, every dip and curve of her undoing him—just as this new temptation undid the last threads of his compunction and propelled him forward. And dropping to his knees before it made him feel more like a prying, interfering old woman than he would have believed.

For a long moment he stared at the two travel satchels, both looking painfully thin and whiling so innocently beside her suspicious pouch of good Scottish sillers.

He carefully opened the first satchel, then the other, holding his breath as his hands plunged and searched. But when his breach of her privacy rendered naught but a few bits of worn and rough-spun garments, he almost snorted a mirthless laugh.

His own outraged conscience revolted against such despicably intrusive behavior.

Certain he'd never sink any lower, he attempted to restore some semblance of order to her meager possessions.

But before he could, something oddly familiar caught his eye and made his heart slam hard against his ribs.

Quite sure his eyes were tricking him, he shoved aside a patched kirtle and peered deeper into the first satchel's depths at the folded plaid every MacKenzie with even a sliver of heart would recognize at once.

Moth-bitten, faded, and smelling of age, just looking down at it plunged Robbie back to a long ago day in his boyhood when, at his father's wedding feast ceremony to Lady Linnet, his thin chest had swelled with pride as he'd proudly recited to her the meaning of the MacKenzie colors.

'Tis green for the forest and fields, and blue for the sky and sea, drawn through with white for . . . for— there he'd faltered, stumbling, until his father had taken heart

and supplied the parts he'd forgotten, *white for purity, red for blood and bold warriors . . .*

. . . and all mean freedom, fairness, honor, and courage, he'd finished the verse on his own, his youthful heart bursting with hero worship and love for his formidable sire.

His heart near burst now, too.

How the ancient MacKenzie plaid came to be in her possession was a mystery he'd solve later—so soon as he could breathe again.

For the nonce, he decided to examine the plaid, for some elusive trace of poignant nostalgia clung to the brittle-looking cloth, compelling him to lift it from the satchel.

Much larger than he'd originally thought, it proved to be a *breacan an fheilidh,* a man's great belted plaid. And every bit as old as he'd originally assessed. Clearly some lonely relic of her past and his own, its hoary wool smelled of peat smoke, wind and rain, and the good rich earth.

And within the center of its worn and aged folds rested something lumpy.

Something that was none of his business.

At once, Robbie's conscience rebelled again, smiting him with livid reproach. But even as his chivalry upbraided him, his hands were carefully opening the plaid, the hard thudding of his heart urging him on and speeding his fingers until their questing revealed the treasure within . . . a thick coil of glossy braid plaited of his beauty's flame-bright hair and someone else's.

Someone's blue-black hair, shiny as a raven's wing, and so like Robbie's own, his stomach dropped and his mouth went ash dry.

Pushing to his feet, he went to the window embrasure where he lowered himself onto one of the padded stone benches, his beauty's keepsakes nestled reverently on his lap.

In the gray morning light, the braid's age became apparent. Someone had woven sprigs of heather throughout the plaited hair and cross-guarded the whole with a fine blue ribbon. But the heather had long withered to brown and near crumbled beneath his fingers.

And the unforgiving passage of time had faded the ribbon's blue to the merest hint of the shade.

More intriguing still, closer inspection showed the sunfire strands were not quite as bright as his beauty's.

The flame-bright half of the braid was not hers.

Lovely it was, to be sure. Even with the same coppery gleam, but a *softer* shade somehow, and indefinably . . . different.

His brow furrowing, Robbie touched a reluctant finger to the black strands. Something about them chilled his blood and tightened his innards. Uneasy, he blinked, tried to clear wits that, of a sudden, seemed muddled and slow.

The plaid and the braid held the answers he sought . . . the key to her identity.

Yet now that such riches rested in his hands, he could scarce think beyond the miasma in his head.

But then, having enough, he got to his feet and placed the braid atop the table as gently as his mood allowed. He draped the plaid over his arm with equal reverence.

Setting his jaw, he strove to ignore the ill ease sweeping through him, told himself he was needlessly seeing shadows where there were none. His skittish nerves and queasy gut were surely of no more sinister origin than his earlier battling with his father. Mayhap, too, from having not properly filled his belly because of that less than affable encounter.

He cast a glance at the table, shook his head at his foolhardiness.

The braid was old and clearly not clipped from his beauty's tresses.

The plaid was older still.

Ancient.

Many were the ways it could have happened into her hands. No matter how deep in the heather she'd made her home.

For, like it or no, hard cold brutality went along with the wonder and magic of Highland life. Just as so much more colored a seannachie's fireside tales than the inimitable beauty of soft mist and purple moors.

Since time immemorial, as much blood as tradition had soaked into the soil of these hills, and though peaceable enough now, more than a few MacKenzies had enjoyed their day of looting and rampaging up and down the glens.

Such was e'er the way of the Gael, and his beauty's moth-eaten MacKenzie plaid was surely a remnant of marauding, cattle-thieving times—mayhap snatched by her father or grandsire, a trophy of a skirmish won.

Certain that would be the way of it, Robbie exited the bedchamber and hastened back down the winding turnpike stairs, his thoughts on naught but finding his flame-haired beauty and probing her secrets.

And not just the sort that had to do with locks of ribbon-and-heather-twined hair and tatty old lengths of plaid.

�֍

Over the hills and far away, across the cold swells of the northern seas, Kenneth MacKenzie sat counting his coin in the common room of The Golden Puffin, a dimly-lit tavern in the Orcadian seaport of Stromness.

A stiff wind, cold and rife with the smell of the sea, blew in through the window shuttering, guttering candles and riffling the edges of the blue-and-green plaid casually slung over Kenneth's wide-set shoulders.

The MacKenzie plaid . . . his only reminder of the man who'd sired him and, generously some would say, allowed his mother to give him the name—even though the reputed womanizer saw no need to diminish her shame by wedding her.

At the thought, the hard line of Kenneth's mouth grew even more uncompromising and a nervous twitch began just beneath his left eye. From long habit, he reached up and smoothed the plaid's woolen folds, silently vowing to banish the cares from his mother's brow.

And if undoing her burdens cost him his last breath, it was an accomplishment he was certain he'd soon achieve.

So soon as he could hie himself off this cold isle of wind and stone at the veriest end of the world.

Already he'd spent so many long weeks trapped in Stromness, the Orcades's most important port, he half believed he'd disgrace himself by swooning the first time he encountered anyone who greeted him with the gently lilting burr of the West Highlands.

Not that his time in the Orcades had been ill spent.

And 'twas well he knew there were worse places.

Years at sea, chasing the dreams of wealthier men, had shown him that truth. And, too often as well, he'd risked his life being lowered on ropes down perilous sea cliffs alive with nesting sea fowl—for the greed of other men, braving icy white spray thrown high on the razor-sharp rocks of the stacs to gather *bird oil*.

A much-prized commodity for the Hansa traders and merchants of the Baltic seaboard.

Such traders dealt with wealthy churchmen, men who demanded an endless supply of the oil for their church lamps and anointing practices. They also coveted the precious oil because of its purported medicinal properties.

He shuddered, not quite able to close his mind to the memory of the birds' angry screeching. Shrill, ear-piercing cries nigh loud enough to drown the roar of the crashing swells.

His gut clenching, Kenneth tightened his fingers on his ale cup. Indeed, he had seen the best and worst of men . . . and of the world.

But his own coffers were now well filled—thanks to the hunger and cupidity of those other men, good and bad.

Now running a finger around the edge of the cup, he forced himself to recall the beauty of the delicate sea thrift blossoms, sweet rose-colored glimpses of sanity that e'er bloomed in the niches and crevices of the dark, wet-gleaming cliffs.

Then, drawing a deep breath of the tavern's smoky-moist fug, he lifted the ale cup to his lips, took a long swallow, and counted his blessings as well as his coin.

Aye, the Orcades had treated him fine.

Stromness, in particular.

A veritable labyrinth of gray stone houses, taverns, and warehouses pressing against the steep hillside overlooking Hamnavoe Bay, the bustling harbor town made its fame by being the first port of call for any sailing vessel leaving mainland Scotland and bound for the north.

Or, as he so greatly wished it, the *last* port of call before sailing into the waters of home.

And Kenneth MacKenzie wanted naught under the heavens more than to return home.

It was his most fervent wish.

His heart's only desire.

To go back to Kintail, the wildest, most stunning country in all Scotland. In especial, the place that gripped him most, the quiet peace of Glenelg where he'd been born.

Just the name let soul-searing images flood Kenneth's mind . . . sweet glimpses of a hard but well-loved life in the narrow, sheltered glen where even the emptiest hour held some redeeming beauty to cheer the heart and where little more than deer, boar, and wildfowl kept a man company.

And, above all, where he hoped, with the riches spread across the tavern table, he'd soon be able to carve out a modest holding. A better, more substantial home for himself and those who depended on him.

His heart swelling at the notion, he scooped up a handful of siller from the pile on the table, let the coins spill like sand through his fingers—and thought not of the monetary value but of how much he'd relish living quiet by day and by night, counting his wealth not in coin and plundered seabird nests, but in the richness of the blue darkness sliding down the braes each e'en.

A bliss that seemed distant as the stars in this loud, full-to-the-lintels tavern, clogged with choking, eye-stinging cook smoke, ale fumes, and the sweetly-sharp tang of too many unwashed ladies of dubious virtue.

Bold-eyed bawds who, despite the repeated offering of their full-breasted, sway-hipped wares, left him colder than Saint Columba's grave.

Determined to repel the gap-toothed blond one sashaying his way again, he was spared the trouble when the door burst open and a great, burly bear of a man strode in, a blast of chill, rain-laden wind with him.

"Ho! There you are, MacKenzie! Good fortune is yours—if you are still wont to call it so!" the man boomed, spotting Kenneth at once.

He came forward, swiping raindrops from his bristling blond beard, a self-pleased grin splitting his broad, Nordic face. *Orkney Will,* he went by, claiming the name as good as any, and boasting that not only did he have the blood of Norse kings running in his veins, he could also procure the starlight from the heavens.

If the price were to his liking.

Kenneth cared naught for the stars or even less for the moon—he only wanted passage to Glenelg Bay and home.

And he'd gladly give the man the entirety of his savings to get there—did he not need the coin to help his mother and to fund the rebuilding of his own life in their peaceful glen.

His dreams close in his heart, he reached for a small pouch of siller, an almost gnawing hunger spreading through him as the burly giant took a seat on the opposite trestle.

Kenneth met the man's startling blue gaze. "Good fortune, aye—for you, my friend, if you've located a southbound galley willing to take on an extra hand," he said, nodding thanks when, unasked, the ale-wife plunked down a fresh ewer.

"My own endeavors have availed naught," he admitted, his fingers kneading the soft leather of the well-filled money purse.

"I told you it would not be a roll in the spring grass— finding favors without you being an Orkneyman. But let us be at it." Orkney Will settled his bulk on the trestle, poured himself a brimming cup of ale. "*The Nordic Maid* sets sail at first light, bound south, clear down to the Isle of Mann, 'twas claimed," he added, and quaffed his ale.

Kenneth's chest tightened on the words, a thousand images, long-seared on his heart, breaking free to thicken his tongue and scald the backs of his eyes. "They ken I must be . . . need to . . ."

Saints!

He could not speak past the burning lump in his throat. Frowning, he snatched up his ale cup, draining its contents—and hoping the blond-bearded Orcadian didn't notice that his fool hand trembled.

Merciful saints, in the name of God's holy breakfast, it wasn't just hands—his entire body shook.

"Ho! Never you worry," Orkney Will assured him, his shrewd gaze measuring, "they know well enough where you wish to go—though they think you a fool for turning your back on a trade so rich in compensation. 'Tis no secret in these waters that all Christendom prizes bird oil," he added, his expression declaring beyond doubt that he, too, held Kenneth for a loon.

But then he slammed a meaty fist on the table and a triumphant twinkle lit his sky-blue eyes. "I have it on good word that unless the Blue Men of the Minch rise up from the depths and cause havoc with the tides, the shipmaster is willing to sail east round Skye and Raasay, setting you ashore at Kyle of Lochalsh."

"You are certain?" Kenneth's brows shot heavenward. He could scarce believe his good fortune—Kyle of Lochalsh was far closer than he'd dared to hope.

Looking mightily pleased with himself, the Orcadian slid an appreciative glance at a toothsome tavern wench whiling nearby, artfully displaying her debatable charms for any who cared to gawk at her.

And, grinning as he now was, Orkney Will appeared more than eager to gawk. "Be that my wages?" he asked suddenly, cocking a brow at the bag of coins still clutched in Kenneth's hand. "If it is, I'd have a coin of it now—for the lady."

Biting back any comment about the *lady*, Kenneth gave the man a curt nod and slid the money bag across the table. He looked on as the Orcadian giant opened the bag's drawstring and, retrieving a coin, wagged it in the whore's direction.

Catching the glint of silver, she obliged at once, deftly tugging down her bodice just enough to expose her heavily-rouged nipples. Though relaxed and quite puffy as they popped into view, they began tightening immediately, the unusually large rounds of her aureole becoming exceptionally crinkly under the appreciative stares and encouraging hoots of the tavern patrons.

"Tush! Do you see those sweet teats, lads?" A bald-pated man roared at the next table, dropping his hand to his crotch in obvious intent. "Gods o' thunder, save me before my tarse snaps off!"

"'Tis how fine and pinky-red another *crinkly* part of her looks is what I be a-wanting to see," another cried, hand pressed on his heart.

"'Tis how that part of her *tastes* is what interests me," someone else yelled from the lower end of the common room, his cheek earning bursts of guffaws from all around.

Even Orkney Will shifted on the trestle. Grinning, he reached down to hitch his sword belt a bit upward, a certain not-to-be-overlooked bulge at his groin making clear the need for the adjustment.

Only Kenneth did not smile, did not feel any grip of the letch whatsoever.

Though he did *look*.

With the same fascination one might watch two adders mating if one e'er happened to chance upon the snakes engaged in their repulsive yet hotly-sensual coupling dance.

"Another coin if you squeeze 'em," a new voice rose above the ruckus, and the light-skirt complied again, taking her now thrusting nipples between thumb and middle finger and giving the hardened peaks a fast pinch—much to the pleasure of her tongue-lolling audience.

Not to be bested, Orkney Will thrust his fingers into the coin purse again. "I'll up my offing to *two* sillers if you rub 'em nice and easy," he called out, slapping the coins on the end of the table. "And a third coin if you pluck and pull on 'em a bit—but s-l-o-w-l-y, if you will!"

"As you wish," the whore purred, easing down her bodice until her full breasts sprang completely free. Her sultry-eyed gaze fixed on the Orcadian, she sauntered over to their table and retrieved the coins, slipping them into a small money pouch tied to her low-sitting belt of red braid.

"Here," Orkney Will said, his voice thick with rut. "Rub those teats here," he added, perspiration beginning to glisten on his brow. "Pull on those sweet nipples for me—here, where I can see and smell you."

"Nay, *there*, where I cannot," Kenneth amended, jerking his head toward the corner where she'd performed earlier. The muscle beneath his eye leaping beyond containment, he scooped up a loose handful of coins and thrust them at her. "Do what you will to entertain my friend, but hie yourself back into the shadows if you'd please me."

The whore pouted lips rouged as deep a red as her nipples, and shrugged—but she did take the coins and disappear.

"You are passing strange, MacKenzie," the Orcadian said the moment the light-skirt melted into the shadows. He mopped his damp brow with his sleeve. "What harm is there in watching a buxom wench a-toying with her teats?"

"No harm at all so long as they keep their taint from me," Kenneth said, regretting the harsh coldness of the words the moment they'd passed his lips.

Too private were his reasons for not being able to abide whores—but the bawd's actions had somehow reached deep inside him, ripping open the place where he kept his anger over his long-dead sire's passion for a wanton-hearted woman.

A licentious obsession that had set his own mother's life on a turbulent slide to destruction.

"Forget my words," he said, and rubbed a hand down over his face. "I am weary and tired, naught else."

Orkney Will shook his shaggy-maned head, took a long swill of ale. "Then you have me even more befuddled than before," he said, clearly puzzled indeed. "I' faith, a lusty tumble with the wench or one of her like would've eased your taut . . . *nerves*. Mayhap even helped you sleep tonight—long as you've been a-waiting—"

"There are other succors to lend a man ease," Kenneth said, well aware the blond giant would mishear him, would not realize he spoke of the solace found in such simple pleasures as breathing air that smelled of soft Highland mist, damp earth, and gorse.

Misunderstanding indeed, Orkney Will leaned forward and stared penetratingly at the three vertical scars marring Kenneth's left cheek. Glancing round, he lowered his voice to a conspiratorial whisper.

"Ah-h-h, so you've not gone monk, after all? Now I see. 'Twas a fiery-blooded minx who marked your face and she is the true reason you've no taste for whores, eh, MacKenzie?" He cocked a bushy blond brow. "I'll wager the urge to sink yourself into that one's fine warmth is why you burn to have done with the bird-oil trade and get yourself back to your precious *Hielands*, am I right?"

Nay, you could not be more off course.

The words itched to spring off Kenneth's tongue, but

he kept them to himself. He'd already said more than he'd wished. So he simply gave a noncommittal grunt and plucked a nonexistent piece of lint off his plaid.

Truth be told, the bristly-bearded knave sitting opposite him was partly right.

He did have a blaze inside him to get back to the Highlands and there *was* a hot-blooded vixen awaiting him.

And, to be sure, he ached to see her, wanted especially to gather her in his arms, hold her close, and know her safe and well.

But the fiery minx he ached to see again was his sister, not his paramour.

And she'd had naught whatsoever to do with the three scars lining the left side of his face.

No lass had caused his scars—even if they did look as if they'd been slashed down his cheek by a furious woman's raking talons.

He'd simply earned the scars when he'd lost his footing on a narrow rock ledge and plunged down the perpendicular sea cliffs of Hirta, St. Girta's Isle. The most favored harvesting ground for the petrels, fulmars, and other seafowl whose innocent young provided the richest source of bird oil to be gleaned in all the Hebridean Isles.

A moment's concentration lost whilst clinging to the rope lowering him down the treacherous cliff side, the whole of him surrounded by screaming, swooping seabirds, and he'd near lost his life.

Or should have.

But the jagged rock face had only sliced open his left cheek, leaving three perfectly vertical scars—an almost eerily fitting tribute to Hirta's stac-like cliffs and a trade he'd grown to revile more vehemently each time he'd joined such a bird oil gathering expedition.

Aye, he wanted naught more to do with it.

Already his sleep was plagued with dreams of teeming clouds of angry, screeching seabirds, gliding and wheeling above and all around him, diving in to scold and attack him—as well they should challenge any danger about to plunge thieving hands into their great nests of seaweed, filled with frightened, squawking chicks.

Swallowing the hot bile rising in his throat, Kenneth abandoned the disturbing images to the dark place inside his mind where he preferred to keep such terrors. Then he blinked hard and reached for his ale cup, draining it.

An overwhelming wish to be gone from Stromness surging through him, he looked hard at the giant of an Orkneyman who still watched him as if he'd grown the devil's own horns.

"You are certain the shipmaster of *The Nordic Maid* has agreed to set me onshore at Kyle of Lochalsh?" He had to know. His heart needed the surety. "And can you take me to the ship now . . . this very e'en?"

At last Orkney Will's face cracked in another smile.

A broad one.

"To be sure, and I can," he declared, hooting a laugh before he leaned across the table, coming close.

"See you, MacKenzie," he said, grinning again, "here is a surprise for you. Do not tell him I told you, but the shipmaster even implied he might see you clear through to your own Glenelg Bay—if you weight his palm with an extra coin or two."

"Saints of mercy! You tell me this only now?" Kenneth jumped up so quickly, he knocked over the trestle bench. "Come, man! Let us be on our way."

"Now?"

"Aye, now," Kenneth said, feeling very much as if the heart and soul that had been lost to him was about to be restored. "The shipmaster can have all the coin he requires—anything to get me home again."

Home.

Juliana's heart lurched on the word, molten intensity swirling into her breast, squeezing the breath from her. At once, she stopped sifting through the herbs and oddities scattered across the herbarium's sturdy worktable, recognizing the pangs for the homesickness and frustration they were and knowing she could do naught until the moment passed.

She touched a finger to the little stoneware jar of healing ointment she'd been rubbing on her forehead earlier, wondered if her increasingly sharp-cut images of home could somehow be linked to the unguent.

Just one of the many medicinal goods sent to Eilean Creag by Doon's famed wisewoman, Devorgilla. But for that reason, Juliana suspected a connection.

Indeed, suspicion tingled all through her, increasing the longer she held her fingers to the jar's smooth-wood stopper, almost as if the container itself held . . . magic.

But if so, the magic hadn't been intended for her.

Unable to hold back a twinge of resentment, she took her hand from the jar and reached up to rub the nape of her neck. Like her shoulders and back, her neck ached from long hours of work—desired tasks or nay.

The ladies Linnet and Caterine had given her a supply of the ointment, supposedly a cure-all intended for her knight's lady betrothed.

That one, she'd heard, had refused the offering.

Juliana knew better than to dare.

Besides, the two ladies of the castle had insisted frequent application of the unguent would help heal her forehead. And, to be sure, the dull aching pain had all but vanished and the gash at her hairline no longer appeared even the least swollen or reddened.

Yet, the healing salve also seemed to shine clarity and light into the darkness clouding her mind, and at the least anticipated moments.

Wishing she knew why, Juliana went to the herbarium's one small window and drew a deep breath of the chill, damp air.

Faith, even that simple act, breathing in the soft, moist air, brought echoes—faint and distant. Some frightening, some . . . incredibly alluring.

She shivered, drew her borrowed *arisaid* closer around her shoulders, welcoming the warmth of its soft woolen folds. She glanced at Mungo, took strength in watching him circle the herbarium on his stubby little legs, snuffling dust motes and fallen bits of dried herbs on the hard-packed earthen floor.

Leaving him to his explorations, she strove to ignore the tight knot forming in her throat. If only the shadows of her past that swirled round her each time she used the ointment were happily innocent images, she'd be far less unsettled, might even reach for the little jar with smiling anticipation.

But the emotion crashing through her came from more than the unguent.

It was the herbarium, too.

Not that she could say why the little stone building nestled against Eilean Creag's seaward wall so reminded her of home—where'er that might be.

But it did.

Each time she stepped into the low-ceilinged work-shop with its age-and-smoke-blackened rafters, soothing warmth slid round her, precious and intimate, and for whate'er space of time she worked there, the rarest peace was hers.

Until that elusive something else gilded the pungent air and her sweet haven would suddenly seem crowded with unseen whispers and rustlings.

Fragmented images.

Deep memories trying to surface—the waves and ripples of her life, all that had e'er touched her in joy and laughter, pain and grief.

Like knowing her mother had been someone's leman.

A fate she would not endure—and for all her foolish yearning!

She looked down, brushed at the wee bits of dried herbs clinging to her skirts. Faith, a rush of longing for her knight seized her even now. Wantonness she'd perhaps carried in her blood since birth, ignited to flame by simply *thinking* of him.

Recalling his touch and kiss . . . his scorching gaze on her quivering, naked flesh.

The rigid press of *that part of him* rubbing so sinuously against the softness of her belly as he'd held her in tight embrace.

Hot little flames of want licking at her, she turned from the window, appalled but not surprised that the cold draughts and gusty spatters of rain hadn't cooled the heat inside her.

"Nay," she said, willing the tingles to cease, gulping back another wave of fast-rising . . . need. "I-will-be-no-man's-concubine," she ground out the words between her teeth as she strode about the herbarium, wee Mungo chasing at her skirts, clearly thinking her quickened steps a game.

After enough agitated sails around the worktable to wear a track in the dirt floor and still no cessation to the maddening tingles, the cravings and *chaos* he'd awakened in her, she finally paused at one end of the heavy oaken table. Pulses pounding, she gripped its edge for support, her breasts rising and falling with the exertion.

Exertion brought on by a foolhardy and useless endeavor, for the tingles still raged . . . coming now in waves of apparent endless succession.

She bit her lower lip, glanced at the cailleach's little jar of cure-all ointment and then away.

Devorgilla was a known meddler to be sure—but in a good way. She'd ne'er stoop to darker sorceries or devilish tricks to make an innocent lass . . . *uncomfortable.*

Nay . . . such a notion Juliana dismissed at once.

She looked at the tidy shelves lining the thick walls, seeking something to do . . . if only straightening or dusting.

Each shelf held flagons, jars, and earthenware pots, and the large worktable was covered with Devorgilla's offerings. A second table, a smaller one in a corner, boasted a fine collection of pestles, mortars, and wooden bowls.

Everything a goodwife or a self-respecting leech might desire.

Wondrous luxuries that made any and all tasks fall light from hand.

And that truth, in a sad, faintly mocking way, reminded her of her mother's hands.

Hands far more marked by a hard life than Juliana's own, and oh-so-deserving of the easements so evident throughout the well-stocked herbarium. Hands that, Juliana now knew, had ne'er enjoyed even the simplest comfort.

In great part, because she'd succumbed to the lure of illicit love, believing it to be true-hearted. She'd closed her ears to the spiteful natterings of glen gossipmongers and had given her all, trusting a man who only used her.

Juliana stiffened, the heat of anger creeping up her throat and onto her face. Dark memories assailed her, rising up like fog lifting in sunlight.

The most damning, wrenching flashes of her mother's eyes, always so calm and loving, yet e'er tinged with a trace of sorrow, did what all Juliana's furious pacing had failed to do.

The tingles were gone.

Banished and replaced by the dull-edged resentment she now knew had e'er fermented in her soul. Names were all she needed . . . her own full one and the name of the man who'd ruined her mother's life.

Only then could she avenge its loss—face her own deep sorrows.

As if wishing to cheer her, wee Mungo gamboled around her, jumping at her skirts until she reached down to rub his warm, floppy ears. He responded at once, rolling onto his back for tummy rubs. She took comfort in his adoring gaze, the enthusiastic swipes of his little puppy tongue across the back of her hand.

Straightening, she went to a corner aumbry, a masoned storage cupboard set into the wall and containing a precious set of metal measuring scales, carefully-rolled lengths of bandaging linen, and a handful of snake stones.

Special curing stones they were, precious and rare.

To the untrained eye, just a small round stone with a hole through it, but to those who knew, such a marvel possessed great powers because snakes were believed to slither through the hole to slough off their old skins.

Juliana's pulse began to race as she took one of the stones in her hand, rolled it around on her palm. Some even claimed that, just as such stones could help an adder shed its unwanted skin, so, too, could a snake stone rid a person of whate'er troublesome burdens a soul carried.

One had only to drink of heated water containing such a stone. Then, it was said, a purging would quickly follow.

If one's heart was pure.

Her cheeks flaming, Juliana returned the curing stone to the aumbry at once.

It was said, too, that great ill would befall any unworthy soul who'd dare attempt undeserved use of a curing stone's magic.

"There are more ways than trusting on snake stones to banish one's cares, my lady," said a deep voice at her ear.

Juliana's heart stopped.

She whirled around, the curing stones forgotten.

And her resolve not to . . . tingle.

Saints of mercy, just breathing the same air as her knight set the tingles to resurging with a vengeance.

"I am certain there are many . . . *ways,* aye. And I am sure, too, that you would be nothing loath to show them to me," she said, hardening her heart—if she couldn't extinguish the heat.

"And I have told you as well that I am not a lady," she added, just to be belligerent. "From what I have seen of most—I praise the heavens I have ne'er aspired to be one."

To her surprise, he looked . . . amused.

He even smiled, and his dimples did funny things to her knees.

"And if I tell you it matters not a whit to me whether you are a lady or nay?" He watched her closely, definite mirth brimming in his dark blue eyes.

Mirth, and something infinitely dangerous.

Something that made the floor dip and sway beneath her feet.

"If the circumstances of my birth are of no consequence to you, good sir, there can only be one reason," she said, letting her own snapping-eyed stare challenge him to deny it.

And, of course, he did.

By shaking his head and smiling some more.

Juliana began to melt, the deepening of his dimples disarming her—much as she tried to ignore their effect.

Ignore . . . *him.*

In especial, how his mere presence turned the herbarium's musty dimness into the brilliant warmth of a thousand bursting suns.

Suns that, no matter how bright they shone, could not chase the shadows of foreboding from the faded MacKenzie plaid draped over his arm.

Juliana shivered. Just seeing the plaid in his possession turned the molten heat inside her to rivers of ice.

"You were in my chamber," she said, the words rusty-sounding, her voice someone else's—someone who knew her past and was keeping its secrets from her. "You pillaged my travel bags."

He had the good graces to look chagrined—but not remorseful.

"I am trying to help you," he said, laying the folded plaid on the worktable, then pulling her into his arms, dragging her close before she could scoot away.

"See you," he said, giving her a reassuring squeeze, "it matters naught what I have seen or who or what you are. All that matters is that we . . . are."

"And how can we . . . *be,* when you—" she broke off, her body acquiescing, some brazen part of her rejecting any objections her tongue might form.

With a sigh, she melted against him, welcoming the way he lowered his head to nuzzle her neck, her heart flipping when he used the tip of his tongue to gently tease the soft, tender flesh beneath her ear.

But even as the tingles rampaged anew, some even more stubborn part of her rebelled.

A determined rock-hard kernel of will deep inside her that kept sending her gaze to the tatty-edged plaid.

The wretched thing fair glared contempt at her.

"Come, sweetness—let me kiss you," her knight was murmuring, his hands now sweeping down her back, over the curves of her hips and lower as he urged her to him. "One kiss, no more—there can be no harm in sharing what we have already known."

But there was, and every inch of her screamed the danger.

As did the damnable plaid.

"No," Juliana said, her voice firm. Unbending. "Not even one kiss."

On the words, he released her, his expression darkening with some unnamed emotion.

"As you wish, my lady, but be well warned—I desist only this once," he said, the true measure of his vexation showing in his tightly clenched hands. "Do not underestimate me and falsely believe I shall let you keep yourself from me forever."

He tucked a wispy curl behind her ear. "Hear me well, sweetness, for I say you again, there can be naught but joy in our kisses—in all else I would see us share."

But Juliana said nothing.

Truth be told, she found herself too disconcerted by the regret welling inside her to do more than briskly dust her skirts, for once not able to parry with a sharp retort or even meet his eyes.

. . . there can be naught but joy in our kisses . . .

The words coiled through her, spiraling upward and down, twisting her innards in knots, slicing her heart.

. . . naught but joy . . .

Juliana bit the inside of her cheek until she tasted

blood, wished desperately she could have agreed with those words.

But she couldn't.

And the sooner she made that clear, the better for the both of them.

Chapter Nine

❧

JULIANA PACED THE HERBARIUM'S trampled earth floor, stopping at the worktable just long enough to trail her fingers along its thick edge and compose her wits before she swung back round to face the man she was beginning to think of as both her light and her darkness.

Her *light* because ne'er had any man stirred such deep feelings in her, awakened such a keen sense of inner knowing. Faith, his very smile or just one twinkling glance melted her and filled her with such sweet golden warmth she wondered she could contain its brilliance and not glow like a roomful of candle shine.

Darkness because no other man held the power to unleash true calamities on her heart. This one, she knew, could shred her soul if she weren't cautious. She shivered, did not even want to consider the yawning abysmal void he could plunge her into so easily.

She recognized that threat with absolute surety.

Ne'er could any affection between them bloom into aught more than a fiery physical conflagration—even if she were willing to step over such bounds as his betrothed whiling beneath this very roof.

Or a sire who not only lairded it with an iron fist, but who also appeared ever so wont to smash down that balled might right onto her head!

"Yon plaid is a MacKenzie plaid."

The deep voice came so close by her ear, her fingertips stilled on the table edge.

"Aye, and well I know it," she said, her back still to him.

She took a deep breath, wished he hadn't come up so close behind her. Sensual heat, both seductive and annoying, poured off him, warming and unsettling her to such a degree even the tops of her ears began to tingle and burn.

His scent beguiled her as well.

A heady blend of clean linen, leather, and pure masculine musk laced with a faint trace of peat, the scent swirled around her, thrilling her, and almost making her forget her purpose.

But not quite.

Bracing herself, she whirled to face him, tried to pretend he wasn't standing so maddeningly near, arms folded across his chest, and looking at her as if he held some irrefutable and unspoken claim on her soul.

Her soul, her heart, her body and mind—her very life, each indrawn breath of it, every exhale.

Not about to admit any such dependency, she tilted her head and regarded him as solemnly as she could.

Fearing she'd embarked on a losing battle, she began to fidget—a demeaning trait she'd ne'er been bothered with until this very moment. But somehow it proved easier to meet his perusal if her booted toe worried a pebble in the hard-packed dirt floor and if her fingers repeatedly tested the texture of woolen *arisaid* slung round her shoulders.

A borrowed *arisaid*, she minded herself.

Loaned to her by his lady stepmother—as was everything else she wore . . . including the buttery-soft kid boots on her feet, a luxury so unlike the rough-leathered brogues she was accustomed to wearing.

A kindness she sought to repay by making herself useful in the herbarium and where'er else she could find some task in need of doing.

But any MacKenzie largesse shown her by the lady of the keep and others at Eilean Creag would not be repaid to the son of the house.

And with surety, not on her back.

No matter how penetratingly he stared at her.

Nor how much he . . . excited her.

And, to be sure, he did.

Enough so to make her knees jelly and to set waves of giddy excitement washing through her—even at moments like these when she was doing her very best to remain soundly . . . *unaffected*.

Resolute and aloof.

Yet he'd caught her so unawares, looming up behind her as she'd examined the snake stones, then taking her in his arms and . . . nibbling on her neck!

Mercy, but she could feel his mouth on her still, the light flicking of his tongue against the oh-so-sensitive spot beneath her ear, the deliciously pleasing hush of his warm breath on her skin.

Sensual delights designed to intoxicate her—as well they had.

Making her needy—desirous of more.

And just remembering sent floodtides of sensation crashing through her. Molten, intoxicating heat that pooled deep in her belly, low by her thighs . . . there, where the tingles whirled across her most sensitive flesh until she had to lock her leg muscles lest she sag against the edge of the worktable.

So thoroughly had he laid siege to her, staked his *claim* on her.

A claim she knew with her heart and her soul that he meant to redeem to the fullest.

And soon . . . if the smoldering heat banking in his eyes and his confident stance were any indication.

A possibility she could not allow.

Especially since even just standing so close to him, them both fully clothed, proved so overwhelmingly titillating, she could scarce draw breath for wanting more—a deeper, utterly lascivious closeness the sinuous likes of which she suspected only flared so hotly between paramours and their lemans.

Leman.

The word and all its illicit meaning gave her the strength she needed to put an end to whate'er crackled and sizzled between them before the blaze raged out of control.

Drawing herself up as straight as she could, she dragged in a tight breath and surrendered to the inevitable.

"Aye, 'tis well and I am knowing the plaid comes from this house, Sir *Robert*," she said, emphasizing the name she knew he did not wish her to use, secretly amazed she could get any words at all past the knots in her tongue. "And if you sought me out to inquire why I have suchlike in my possession, you will be sorely disappointed because I cannot tell you."

"Cannot or will not, my lady?"

Juliana bristled at the title, but she said nothing. After all, he had repeatedly told her to call him Robbie—and she'd just deliberately used *Robert* for the sheer pleasure of annoying him.

"Well?" He leaned against the worktable, his feet crossed at the ankles, and simply . . . eyed her.

Eyed her and, Juliana suspected, seeing much more than the agitated flush she knew stained her cheeks and the furrowed brow that could ne'er seem to stay smooth in his presence.

"Must I ask you again?" He picked up one of the little earthen medicinal jars, a fat, globular one, and began circling its rim with his middle finger.

A decidedly slow-moving middle finger whose leisurely explorations of the round jar lid annoyed her beyond all bounds of reason.

"Cannot or will not? Answer me and I shall set down the jar," he said, a triumphant gleam in his eye.

Sheer indignation kept her from spluttering.

"Ne'er *will not,* good sir, for I do not lie," she said so soon as she was sure her voice would not quiver. "I will ne'er hide the truth from you or any man. *Cannot* is your answer."

She flicked a hand at the ancient plaid. "I cannot tell you the origin of the *breacan an fheilidh* because I do not know."

He set down the jar, followed her gaze. "Lady, forgive me—I would not see you distressed."

Juliana shrugged. "In truth, sir, I am glad-hearted I can tell you aught at all. In especial, a good deal about the woman who owned the *breacan*—and I do wish to speak of her. Indeed, I must."

"The woman who owned it?"

He stared at her, the stiffness of his son-of-the-laird-leaning-against-the-table posture falling away as quickly as he'd struck the pose.

"So you have been remembering?"

"I have been regaining my memory, aye. Though not as much as I'd prefer—bits and pieces only."

"Praise the saints," he said, and turned all his smiling-eyed good humor on her. "Here is news to lift my spirit!"

Juliana's heart began to thump.

He would think otherwise once he'd heard what she had to say. She turned back to the worktable, rested a hand on the plaid's brittle folds.

His gaze, too, slanted back to the aged lump of fray-edged wool. "If the memories pain you, you needn't tell me. I should have left the thing where I found it . . . 'tis hoary old, anyway. I ought not have been looking in—"

"Nay, you should not have, but I am well pleased that you brought it here."

He lifted a brow at that, looked doubtful.

Juliana rubbed her fingers over the plaid's moth-eaten wool, an entirely different kind of heat now constricting her chest.

"The plaid was my mother's," she said after a moment. "By bringing it here, you have given me good reason to tell you about her—about things I should have told you when the memories first started coming back to me."

"You are crying, Juliana." He took a small length of linen bandaging from the table, used it to dab at her cheeks.

"I never cry." She reached up to ease his hand from her face, stunning herself when her fingers brushed against the wetness there. "My mother prized the plaid, although I cannot say why it meant so much to her. She is dead, see you? I—... she ..."

He reached for her when her voice broke, tried to put his hands on her shoulders, but she sidestepped him.

"I am sorry, lass," he said, soft-voiced. "Losing a mother is one of life's deepest sorrows." He paused, looking at her as if expecting her to say something more. "You say she cherished the plaid?" he asked finally, his tone and expression soothing.

Too soothing.

Blinking, Juliana dashed the moisture from her cheek. Scalding heat squeezed her chest and thickened her throat, making it difficult to wrap her tongue around the words she wished to say.

"Aye, she cherished the plaid. And highly, that I know," she admitted at last, glancing around the herbarium.

She needed to get away from him—even a handbreadth would suffice.

Her gaze lit on the snake stones in the still-opened aumbry and she went there, taking up position in front of the little wall cupboard, and hoping he would not follow her.

But he did—looming over her in an even more intimate way than he'd dared at the worktable.

"You were telling me your mother was fond of the plaid?"

She nodded. "I cannot recall a day I did not catch her taking the plaid from its place of honor on her special shelf and holding it close to her heart, or simply smoothing her hands over it. But unless her attachment had aught to do with the treasure she kept wrapped within its folds, I do not understand why she felt as she did."

"Nay?"

"Nay, indeed. To me, the reverence she showed the *breacan* wasn't . . . seemly," she said, regretting the coldness of her words, but the gentle caring in his own thick-voiced *"nay"* had struck uncomfortably close.

"It is a MacKenzie plaid," she said, smoothing her skirts.

"There could be worse colors to sling round your shoulders in these parts."

He gave her an all-too-endearing smile. A slightly lopsided one the likes of which she'd not yet seen on him—and didn't want to again.

The boyish charm of it . . . bothered her.

So she pulled another weapon from her dwindling supply, a bright-shining new one she was only just beginning to form and mold back into the cherished place she now knew he'd e'er held in her heart: her brother, Kenneth.

"The MacKenzies may rule Kintail, but they are by no means seen with grace by everyone." She lifted her chin at him. "My own brother could ne'er abide them."

"And would your brother be this . . . *Kenneth,* you've mentioned?"

Juliana nodded, thoughts of her well-loved brother making her eyes threaten to well again.

Her knight smiled again, even possessed the bold-heartedness to gentle his knuckles down her cheek.

"Then I should give much to meet your brother," he said, his dimples coming out to further annoy her. "I'd like the opportunity to set his mind aright."

"I doubt you could." The surety of that was writ in stone. "Kenneth is man of his own mind and heart. A man unbending in his beliefs . . . his principles."

"All the more reason I should value the honor of his friendship—if e'er I have the chance to win it," he said, a barely noticeable shadow crossing his face. "See you, I, too, am a man of strong principles, my lady. For all my behavior may look otherwise to those who do not know me."

Juliana stiffened, pretended to focus her attention on the assortment of small wooden storage boxes arranged so neatly within the deep recess of the aumbry.

"Do you mean, perchance, pursuing me whilst your own bride-to-be sleeps beneath your roof . . . mayhap awaiting you even now, in these very moments?"

She glanced at him, saw his set-faced expression, the displeasure in his dark blue eyes. Eyes so deep a blue, at times, she'd swear they were black as fresh-cut peat.

"You do not know of what you speak," he said, tight-voiced. "I have taken measures, made arrang—"

"She has agreed to become your lady wife." Juliana took one of the tiny wooden boxes from the aumbry, began dusting it with a fold of her *arisaid*. "Mind you well—I have not and ne'er will assent to being your . . . leman."

"My leman?"

"Your concubine," she said, returning the wooden box to the aumbry. "Since you have the *breacan an fheilidh*, you surely saw the coiled braid that was wrapped within its folds?"

"Aye, but I do not see what that has to do with such a fool notion. I would ne'er—"

Juliana raised a hand, silencing him. "The braid was plaited of my mother's hair—hers, and her paramour's," she explained. "He was her heart's treasure, the only man she e'er loved. But he shunned her, leaving her alone to eke out an existence from the harshest soil when another, more pleasing attraction caught his roving eye."

"This man was your father?"

"He was, aye," Juliana admitted. There seemed nothing more to be said.

He was watching her carefully, the only outward sign of emotion, the whitening of his knuckles as he clenched his hands round his sword belt.

"Tell me who he is, and I shall sort him for you."

Juliana looked aside. "His name, as my mother's, refuses to surface long enough for me to grasp—I only know they are both dead. Him, many years ago . . . I do not even recall his face, and my mother, more recently—as I told you."

"I am sore grieved to hear this, lass . . ." He raked a hand through his hair. "You have borne much, I see. Would that I . . . that your life's path could have been . . . otherwise."

Biting back the hot fury rising inside him, he struggled to school his features lest she misread his outrage, and become even more distressed.

"I truly am sorry," he said, aiming a pointed glance at the folded plaid, furious at himself for having succumbed to the temptation of rummaging through her belongings.

He lifted a hand, let it fall as quickly. "Hear me, lass, ne'er would I have willfully deepened your sorrow. I regret—" he broke off, his gaze narrowing on the faded colors of the plaid.

"If your family held such a poor opinion of MacKenzies—our clans were surely at feud with each other at some time," he said, voicing the only explanation.

All knew such conditions ran rampant between most clans at some point down the long centuries of Highland existence.

He moved to the table, placed his own hand on the frayed cloth. "Considering the age of this great plaid, clearly a man's—can it not be that some male kin of yours snatched the *breacan* as a war trophy? Mayhap during some skirmish or raid o'er the years?"

"That well could be," she said, not sounding entirely convinced. "To be sure, I have seen enough such relics adorning the walls of your great hall—I ken such *badges of honor* are often taken. Still, my mother cherished the plaid—more so than she would have a mere battle trophy."

She looked at him. "But since I cannot know for surety, your explanation seems as sound an answer as any."

Her motions slow and deliberate, she turned away from him, selected a peat brick from a small creel in the corner, and placed it on the brazier's grate.

"Of more importance to me than the *breacan*'s origin are the hazy snatches I recall of my mother's last hours," she said, using a small pine bough to brush aside a scatter of peat ash from the dirt floor in front of the red-glowing brazier.

"See you," she said, putting away the pine bough, "I now know why I had the pouch of siller with me when you rescued me from the lochan—the coin belonged to my mother and her last wish was that I deliver it somewhere in recompense for aid given her o'er the years."

Robbie's brow furrowed. "Aid?"

She nodded. "I am certain of it—such was my mother's way, her heart. Ne'er would she accept the merest help, freely given or nay, without making due repayment."

"So someone helped her in the years after your father abandoned her?"

"I believe so." She turned away from him again, her gaze seeming to settle on the snake stones in the aumbry. "To be sure, we ne'er had much—but someone regularly sent enough coin to supply us with the most basic provender, and, as need arose, a creel of cut peats, or a few good laying chickens."

Looking back at him, she smoothed a curling wisp of hair from her face. "Once, at Christmastide, we awoke to find a side of venison, several rounds of fine green cheese, and two creels of salt herring on our door stoop."

Robbie studied her. "'Twould seem this someone cared about your mother?"

Juliana shrugged, long-forgotten memories rising in her mind like a freshening wind.

"Whoe'er he was, he once sent us the sweetest milch cow," she went on, some hard place deep inside her softening upon remembering. "Nigh loving as a dog she was, e'er putting down her head to be stroked whene'er any-one approached her. And her milk . . ."

She glanced toward the window, for a very brief moment seeing not the misting rain but the dear little brown cow she'd so loved as a girl.

"Her milk," she said, looking back at him, ignoring the lump in her throat, "was the finest I have e'er known. A cup of it had but a wee measure of milk at the bottom . . . all the rest was thick, sweet cream and tasted of peat smoke."

"I ken such milk," her knight said, warmth flooding his eyes. "When I was small, we had a cowherd from the far north, and he had a tender hand with the beasts. He claimed there were fairy cows mixed in with our herd and that was the reason for the richness of the milk, and though I believed him at the time, I now suspect it was the way he gentled them."

The warmth in his expression began . . . disturbing her. Like fine wisps of peat smoke or soft, Highland mist, his appeal seemed to slip inside her, making her breath catch and curling itself ever more insistently round her heart.

"So-o-o," he said suddenly, the new brisk note in his tone breaking the spell, "your mother was appreciative—wished you to deliver repayment to her . . . benefactor?"

"I believe that to be the way of, aye," Juliana agreed, the truth seeming clearer by the moment. "See you, without this person's largesse, whate'er coin she may have had when my father set her aside would've swiftly diminished, especially with two hungry bairns clambering at her skirts."

"And so you set off on this journey after she died?"

"Nay—before," she remembered, her throat almost closing on the admission. "She swore she could only pass in peace if she saw me away to see her wishes done. And so . . . I left, surrendering her to the care of the glen goodwife and whate'er mercy the saints cared to bestow on her."

The pain of her acquiescence weighing on her, Juliana fixed him with her most level-eyed stare. "And that is where the coin hailed from—I told you on the day that I had not used ill means to come by such wealth."

His brow darkening, Robbie closed the small distance between them in two long strides, drew her tight against the warmth of his hard-muscled chest.

"I ne'er believed you to be a thief, sweetness," he reassured her, kissing her brow. "I only wondered how—"

"—how a humble-born maid could have so much coin?"

"I puzzled, aye," he told her true, setting her from him just enough to see into her eyes. "But it concerned me more that you might be running from a husband or—"

"Or a paramour?"

He nodded, shamed for the thoughts, but he'd harbored them for other reasons than she believed.

"Such thoughts were more noble than had I mistook you for a sticky-fingered tavern wench on the loose with ill-gotten goods."

She pressed her lips together, a hint of her usual fire creeping back into her—its heat warming and delighting him.

"Mayhap, to me, a life as a common thief might be the lesser evil than falling prey to a man who would only use my body and then discard me when his gaze fell upon a sweeter harvest?"

Robbie arched a brow at that. "Know this," he said, smoothing his knuckles down her cheek, "it did not and would not have mattered to me what problems or mischances of the past burdened you." He leaned forward, kissed the tip of her nose. "I was only enchanted by you and dreaded the possibility some other man may already have had his claim on you. I—"

"You wanted me for your own . . . pleasures."

"Aye!" The word burst from him, his patience flown. "And I *burn* for those pleasures, aye, I do. Ne'er doubt that I wanted you, then and there," he said, his eyes blazing. "And I want you still—but not as my leman . . . as my wife!"

"Your wife?"

"So I just said."

Juliana could not speak. She lifted a hand to her throat, stared at him. "But you—"

"By all the saints, but you chatter like birds in a wood." He snatched her hand, upturning it to place a smacking kiss on her palm. "Quiet you, and hear me well—already I have faced down the devil for you, told my father I shall not wed the lady Euphemia. God's bones, the maid hides herself from me . . . and unlike you, false thinking on your part or nay, she has nary a reason to secret herself from my view."

At his words, the dark uncertainties about her future began to slide away, but his father's black-scowling visage loomed up in her mind as quickly—his displeasure in her, calling them back again.

"Your father will ne'er condone a union with me," she

said, looking him full in the face. "And I, good knight, am no starry-eyed maid to believe you can convince him otherwise."

He hesitated but a sliver of a heartbeat. "Then he shall lose not only a fine and meet good-daughter, but the only son and heir he has," he said, the commitment behind his words streaming off him in hot palpable waves.

Each one crashing over her with the sweetest allure, the portent of his avowal searing her to the bone, sweeping away the last knots of her resistance, and drawing her closer to him until she was . . . lost.

Lost, drowning, and so wanting to believe him . . .

Chapter Ten

❦

SHE WAS GOING TO DROWN.

Nothing was surer.

Juliana-of-the-glen, rescuer of floundering sheep and known to have the keenest wits of any lass this side of Loch Ness, had lost all her confident possession, abandoning her well-peppered steel for the deliciously languorous heat ignited by the devil's own spawn.

He sensed her quickening, too, recognized with a man's deepest instincts the surrender sweeping through her.

She shivered, her breath catching as his expression changed and a new, more dangerous potency spun out from him to enfold her, the simmering intensity of him making her both wary and . . . exhilarated.

And though she was loath to admit it . . . making her tingle again.

Even so, some bastion of grit deep inside her sturdy, glen-raised soul made her lift a staying hand in a half-hearted attempt to sway the inevitable.

But he merely seized her protesting fingers, bringing

them to his lips to gentle the sweetest, most searing kiss from their tips to the flickering pulse at her wrist.

His pulse fluttered, too. Its rapid beat throbbed at the base of his neck, the undeniable testament of his desire sending jolts of pure female triumph shooting through her.

My precious, Juliana thought she heard him say, the words, true-spoken or nay, spiraling round her heart and . . . allowing her to hope.

Believe that one such as he might cherish her—even if only for a night.

"My very own."

That, she heard, the three huskily murmured words setting her senses spinning and reminding her that she could ne'er be . . . his own.

Not when, in the estimation of his world, her best recommendation was not a stout-walled strength to rival his own but a birthplace so humble it was little more than a patch of green turf amongst the heather.

Even if *she* would wager the riches of one gilded moment passed in Glenelg against a thousand nights of glory spent in a castle's thronging, arras-hung hall.

"You should not . . . we ought not do this," she said, hoping only she'd heard the hitch in her voice. "'Tis folly and—"

"—and the sweetest of heavens," he disagreed, dragging her to him, slanting his mouth over hers in a hot, claiming kiss.

A deliciousness she neither returned nor resisted, her stubbornness not allowing her to acknowledge the pulsing heat building inside her, the thrilling pleasure of every swirling slide of his tongue against hers.

"Come you . . . give," he murmured, pulling back just enough to breathe the plea against her cheek, "have done withholding yourself."

She shook her head, but a persistent little sigh slipped past her resistance, telling enough for his lips to curve in a knowing smile—just before he trailed a flurry of soft, wet kisses across her face, down her throat, and pushing aside her *arisaid*, along the sloping curve of her shoulders.

Anywhere her flushed skin was exposed to him.

"'Tis *you* I want, my Juliana," he breathed, his voice husky with desire. "You, and only you—since the first moment I saw you."

He looked at her, his gaze capturing hers, breaking her resistance. "Ne'er have I seen a lass who pleased me more—you must know it!" he vowed, thick-voiced. "Speak true—you canna deny it."

And she couldn't.

She'd seen the thrall in his eyes at the lochan. So she looked aside—and said nothing.

Clearly scenting victory, he took hold of her shoulders again, pressed his fingers into her flesh just enough to make her flash an irritated look at him—as well he'd known she would.

He read her that surely.

Or else she'd grown pitifully transparent.

Her lifelong resilience ripped to shreds by a bold-eyed knight's dimpled smile and heated glances.

"See you, lass, it matters not if you do not tell me," he said, letting go of her. "You do not need words for your eyes speak more than plain—as does your body."

Juliana squirmed. Her heart thundering, she cleared

her throat. "You believe yourself well skilled at reading women, Sir Knight," she said, some hot-pulsing thrill in the lowest part of her belly making her taunt him.

He lifted a brow, the darkening glint in his eyes wickedly seductive. "And am I?"

"If you are so *gifted,* mayhap you ought tell me?" she challenged. "What do you think my eyes and my body are saying?"

He rubbed his chin, appeared to consider.

"H'mmm . . ." he said, clearly enjoying a reason to let his gaze travel up and down the length of her. "I would say they tell me that you know we were meant to meet— that we were made for each other. And that we will find much joy and deep contentment together."

Juliana made a noncommittal sound and looked down to fluff her skirts, not wanting him to see how much the sweetness of his proclamation affected her.

Nor guess how many girlhood nights she'd spent assailing the mercy of all the saints that she'd someday find a braw and dashing man who'd love, want, and cherish her—a *good-hearted* man, loyal and true, who'd face down dragons for her, battle the wind, and, aye, fill her with breathless anticipation, longing, and . . . hope.

The very kind of bright-shimmering strands of hope winding all through her now, this very moment.

"Come you," he said, devouring her with his eyes, "deny what blazes between us and I shall leave this herbarium and ne'er come seeking you again—but deny it not, and know that you are mine . . . wholly and irrevocably."

Juliana bit her lip, her heart pounding desperately.

His gaze narrowed ever so slightly. "Is your silence a denial, lady?"

"I am not a lady," she blurted, evading his question. "You know that truth better now than before."

"I know you are *my* lady . . . naught else matters."

"Everything matt—"

"*We* matter," he corrected, watching her with eyes that looked into her soul. "Now, come . . . please me. Admit there is a we."

Juliana ground her teeth together.

She burned to please him, was ever so warmed to think he wanted her . . . and enough to defy the constraints and strictures of his own world to have her.

She even swooned with pleasure that he called her his *lady*.

Indeed, heat suffused her cheeks upon his words—but ne'er would she allow how much his insistence about the silly title meant to her.

Not because she yearned for such frivol, but because he used the word to please her.

But admitting such was to walk a perilous precipice, one that still boded caution.

"Well?" He reached to smooth a few strands of hair from her face. "I am waiting."

"I cannot say the words . . . but neither will I deny them—aye, there is something."

Not a true avowal, but the best she could do.

The words out, she jutted her chin, let her lips curve into the smile she'd been fighting.

"Are you now satisfied, my lord?"

"I am well enough content, aye," he said. "But I shall be more pleased after I've convinced you that I ne'er once considered taking you as my leman—that my intentions were noble from the start, even at my very first glimpse of you."

"Oh, I believe you," Juliana said, the prickling at her nape warning that more hid behind his words than was on the surface.

He looked to the side, a distant look clouding his eyes. "See you, ne'er would I condone suchlike—not for myself, nor would I visit the fate on any woman."

"Then you . . . like my brother, are a man apart." Juliana took one of the snake stones from the aumbry, closed her fingers over its cold roundness. "Kenneth, too, vows he would sooner cut his flesh than suffer a woman to our mother's fate—faith, he is so embittered by the tragedy of her life, he does not believe in love at all. Illicit or otherwise."

Pacing now, her knight shot a glance at her, his gaze sharp. "Faugh, I say to that folly," he said, incredulity in his voice. "Now I know I must meet your brother—he *does* need his head turned around. I have e'er believed in love and e'er desired it, though I ken only too well how precious and rare its blessing can be."

He spoke the last words with a rich smoothness that slid through her like molten honey, turning her knees to water, and doing unspeakable things to . . . other parts of her.

Her breath catching, she began rolling the snake stone around in her hand, excitement whirling through her as the round little stone passed over the very parts of her palm he'd kissed, the places he'd licked with the tip of his tongue.

Juliana frowned, stopped playing with the stone at once.

Aye, the man brought out the worst in her.

But he also filled her with a great desire to . . . delight him. Win his regard and affection. Mayhap even his love. She followed his progress about the herbarium, a delicious warmth spooling through her just watching him.

Without doubt, she'd ne'er seen a more dashing man . . . save perhaps her brother. He, too, was darkly handsome, despite his scarred cheek. And his eyes were of the same deep sea-blue.

Even her knight's formidable father was a handsome man, she grudgingly admitted, his dark-brooding face rising up from nowhere to bedevil her.

Truth be told, with the exception of his ill humor and scowls, there was little bad that could be said about the man. With surety, he appeared almost ageless . . . raven-haired save a wee sprinkling of silver, he shared the same strapping build and great height as his son and her brother, looked every bit as hard-trained as the two younger men.

Aye, she'd find him striking indeed, his face most bonny if e'er he'd smile.

But she doubted he knew how, so she drew her *arisaid* closer against a sudden chill wind knifing through the window and returned her attention to a MacKenzie who did smile.

And with the most delightfully dimpled smiles—reason enough to fill her mind with him and forget his grim-bitten sire.

"*. . . many kinds . . . though the true-hearted love of a*

man and a woman is surely the greatest blessing under the heavens."

Juliana blinked, her knight's deep voice startling her. He'd ceased his prowling, and stood not two feet away from her, his dark blue gaze locked on her face, studying her.

"You did not hear me."

"I am sorry," she said, meaning it sincerely, for he was looking at her from beneath black, down-drawn brows, and with an earnestness to almost match the darkness of his sire's stone-cast visage. "Will you tell me again what you wished me to know?"

"I only said that we have more in common than you suspect, and that this herbarium is a meet setting for me to share this . . . *secret* with you," he told her. "For it was here that I spent much of my boyhood yearning for the love of a mother who cared more for her paramour than her son, and crying o'er a father who'd stopped loving me because he'd been told, albeit falsely, that I was not his."

Juliana stared at him, her own cares forgotten. "Dear sweet saints, what are you saying?"

"Ach," he said, lifting his shoulders in a shrug that fell just short of appearing casual. "'Tis all long past, and best left there. I am only telling you so you believe me when I assure you that I ne'er meant to offer you an illicit liaison . . . although I know many men enjoy them."

Pausing, he scooped Mungo off the floor, nestling him in the crook of his arm before he resumed his pacing.

"See you, both our mothers lost their hearts to dastards," he said, kneading Mungo's floppy ears. "Though it would seem yours was a truly good woman who merely gave her love unwisely. My own mother, I regret to tell you, was as black-hearted and evil as her lover."

"Evil?" Juliana gasped, the curing stone so cold now it nigh burned the flesh of her palm. "Black-hearted?"

"To the bone and deeper. Their passion was not only immoral, but innocent lives were ruined or lost before they met their own respective ends," he said, glancing at her.

"Castlefolk knew. They e'er hovered about, prattling and shaming my father even if, at that point, he wasn't aware of the treachery. Uncle Marmaduke learned of it swiftly. Crusader of goodness and virtue that he is, he confronted my mother's lover, demanding they be gone from our lands, ne'er to return."

"They fought—and Sir Marmaduke lost," Juliana guessed, recalling snatches of kitchen babble. "'Tis how he was scarred?"

"Aye, but not quite then," he said. "That day Marmaduke only issued a warning. He even suggested they journey to the sanctuary of the wee Isle of Oronsay where, if they remained for a year and a day, they'd be cleansed of all sins, might even return to these parts, un-molested—but his advice went ignored and worse was yet to come."

"Worse?"

"Much blacker, aye." He looked at her, a shadow crossing his face. "My father's sister, Arabella, who was married to Sir Marmaduke, overheard the lovers plotting to kill my father. They found out and had done with her before she could warn him."

"Dear sweet saints." Juliana shook her head, her pulse roaring in her ears. "I am beginning to see why your father is so grim. Merciful heavens, I have ne'er heard of such villainy."

"Ach, mercy came of it in the end," he said, setting down Mungo. "But the darkness was a long time in healing." He fixed his gaze on the window, his face hardening with a stoniness to match his father's.

"Such is the reason I spent so many years away—even though, in time, I came to have faith in my father's affections again."

He turned to face her. "I'd lost too much heart as a wee laddie, see you? I needed distance and time . . . hard deeds to rebuild and prove my faith not only in my father but in the worthiness of my own good self."

Juliana cleared her throat, hoped her voice would not betray her outrage. "Your father's reputation harkens from those dark days, doesn't it?"

He gave her a wry smile. "In great part, to be sure, but, God kens, he's earned it in other ways as well—do not be fooled. He is a hard man, as the notches in the haft of his war ax will prove, but he possesses a softer heart than most people allow."

"And he knew of these goings-on?"

Her knight took one of the bunches of bundled herbs from the table, lifted it, then replaced it again as quickly, his expression inscrutable.

"At the latest, he knew the day his world smashed down around him," he said, not looking at her. "The day his sister, Sir Marmaduke's first wife, was murdered. The whole treachery came out then, and he confronted my mother."

"As well he should have," Juliana said, worrying the

snake stone, twirling it round her palm with her thumb. "I imagine she begged for forgiveness?"

He cocked a cynical brow. "Nay, I do not believe so," he said, moving to the window to stare at the darkening sky.

" 'Tis said she fled to the battlements, him chasing after her. Kintail's clattermouths will tell you she taunted him as she ran up the stairs, boasting to the last that I was not his . . . that I'd been sired by her lover."

"And she fell from the tower—plunging to her death?" The words just came to her, some deep-buried *knowing* she must have heard somewhere, dredged from her memory like gravel stone from the bottom of a river.

She stared at his back, her stomach clenching. "Your father was blamed for her death."

"That was the way of it," he said, his raven-dark hair riffled by the damp wind blowing through the window. "But I swear to you, he had naught to do with her death. Of that, I am certain—as is anyone who knows him. My mother tripped on her skirts, caused her own fall to doom. But, aye, my father was blamed, and shunned, for many a year."

"And Sir Marmaduke's scarring? Your mother's lover?" Juliana sank onto a three-legged stool near the brazier. "What happened to them?"

He was silent for a moment, considering.

"What happens so oft in life," he finally said, rubbing the back of his neck. "Uncle Marmaduke caught my mother's lover trying to flee. They fought, and Marmaduke lost. Both men were excellent sworders, but Marmaduke's rage made him clumsy . . . a weakness that cost him much. My other uncle escaped, but lived to rue the day—he died by Marmaduke's sword some years later."

"Your other uncle?"

"My other uncle, aye." Her knight looked down, flicked a speck of lint off his plaid. "He and my mother were lovers for several years—their liaison is why my father believed the taunts about me not being his."

The damning words glittered between them like splitters of ice.

"That was the bitterest bile of the scandal—my father's own brother seducing my mother."

"Of a mercy!" Juliana pushed to her feet, unable to remain seated. "Ne'er have I heard suchlike."

"Believe it or no, lass, there are some who would not pour scorn on such a one as my late uncle," her knight said, surprisingly level-voiced. "Much blacker deeds than his came to ears during my journeying . . . trust me, there are enough dastards scattered about these hills—and elsewhere!"

"But your father's own brother—and at such cost!"

"Ach, in truth, he was my father's bastard half brother," he revealed, a brief flash of long-ago pain in his eyes. "But, in youth, my father loved him as a true brother—or so it is said. My father will not speak of the man, even pretends he ne'er existed."

"But he did, and what a dark legacy he left of himself." Juliana frowned. "I am sorry . . . for all of you."

He came forward, rested his hands on her shoulders. "'Twas a baring of the soul I felt you should hear, but remember—we were blessed with much mercy in the end."

"Mercy?" Juliana could not believe it.

But he apparently did, for a slow smile spread across his handsome face. "So I have said, sweetness. Come, I will show you."

Juliana made a doubtful sound in her throat, but before she could form a true response, he linked her arm through his and drew her to the door, easing it open with his foot.

"Do you see yon walls of the keep?" he asked, gesturing toward the gray stonework barely visible through the sheets of gusting rain and mist. "Those stones have withstood the storms of centuries—and flourished," he said, slipping his arm around her shoulders.

"When darkness spreads o'er them each night, those within endure—and have endured, each new generation in their time. Some may see malice and scheming, 'tis true, but they will also know joy, happiness, and triumph along with the sorrow and pain."

He smiled at her, squeezed her arm. "See you, Juliana, we should ne'er forget that even the blackest night is greeted by the morn. So even though bitterest tragedy may stain my home, the blessings that followed were perhaps all the more dear."

"What blessings do you mean? I would hear them."

"Och, mayhap the kinds of blessings I would teach your brother," he said, leading her back into the herbarium, away from the rain. "For one, I have learned that true-hearted love is ever worth the journey to reach it, no matter how long or fraught with hardships."

"True-hearted love?"

A jolt of sharp-edged envy shot through Juliana at the thought of him loving, or even having loved, some other woman with the deep emotion he'd just described.

"Have you—have you known suchlike?" She had to know.

He gave her another of his disarming smiles and reached to swipe his thumbs across her cheeks, before dropping a kiss to the tip of her nose.

"So you would hear of love, would you?" His eyes twinkling again, he held up a hand, began counting on his fingers. "Let us see . . . I have known the love of a father, lost and regained," he said, indicating one finger, then moving on. "Then there is the love of a faithful four-legged friend; the love between friends—even when they bicker constantly."

Juliana smiled at that for she knew he meant his father and his uncle, the good Sir Marmaduke of the fabled even temper.

"And . . ." her knight continued, leaning so near his breath warmed her cheek, "I have witnessed the soul-deep contentment of men who are blessed to win love with the woman of their heart . . . most times when they'd long surrendered any hope of experiencing such bliss."

His explanation finished, another lazy, deep-dimpled smile lit his face. "So-o-o, have I answered your question?"

"Nay, to be sure, you have not. I asked about *you* loving a woman."

"Och, but if you do not know the answer to that, I am thinking I will not be telling you," he said, and winked at her. "But, later this e'en, I might be of a mind to show you."

"Show me?"

He nodded.

The look on his face, and its portent, heated her in all her dark and secret places—awakening the sparkling tingles, so sweetly tantalizing, an echo of delicious prickliness right at her neediest, most feminine core.

"Then, mayhap, good sir, I shall look forward to being . . . *educated*."

"I am sure you will be most adept at learning, Juliana."

Caught in his knowing gaze, she could only nod her agreement.

Faith, just having him so near, looking at her as he was, she would've sworn she could feel his hands on her body as if he were touching her again—smoothing and probing her naked flesh, his skilled fingers taking sensual measure of her every curve, dip, and hollow.

"Be assured it shall be my greatest pleasure to instruct you," he said, his voice dropping to a murmur, husky and low.

He touched her face.

"I've a feeling you shall be teaching me a thing or two as well, and that notion delights me," he added, those knee-melting dimples flashing again. "I rather favor a lass who knows her mind."

Juliana kept her face blank of expression, not wanting regret to color this moment, the closeness forming between them. For while she might give him her passion, *knowing her mind* seemed an obstacle determined to cast shadows on her happiness.

He touched two fingers to her mouth, rubbed her lower lip. "We at Eilean Creag ne'er speak of past sorrows, lass," he said, perhaps seeing her hesitation and sensing the reason for it. "'Tis e'er best to look only to the brighter path ahead," he added, laying a note of finality onto the words.

"But—"

"You need only trust that I desire to have you as naught but wholly and truly mine . . . in the good graces of God and man," he said, deliberately steering her away from hurtful places and into waters requiring equal but decidedly more agreeable navigation.

"And I *do* want you," he added, placing his hands on her shoulders again, kneading them.

"But," she said, "how can you make me yours *before God and man* with your own soon-to-be bride beneath your roof, even if she is not . . . *underfoot*?"

That last made her cheeks flame, but thoughts of the other woman did not put her in good fettle and she'd not been able to bite back the wee jab at the gentleborn lady she now viewed as her rival, fair or no.

Besides, she had spoken true.

Euphemia MacLeod did hold herself invisible as a castle ghost.

Keeping her head high—her best defense against the stabbing resentment seizing her, she asked, "Well?"

"To be sure, you have it rightly," he said, glancing at the chill drizzle blowing past the window square. "The maid is not *underfoot*. But I know in my heart that she will be happier, mayhap even flourish, if given to another."

"Given to another?" Juliana echoed, her heart jumping. "What do you mean—another? Who?"

"A Douglas." He spoke low and gently, the certainty in his voice making her pulse leap. "There are enough of them and I ken a goodly number. There will be one amongst them willing enough to accept a Highland bride—in especial if I send along enough coin to fill a coffer or two for the favor."

"You would do this?" She looked at him, scarce able to breathe, his words going to her head like wine. "For me?"

"With surety." A hint of his dimpled smile curved his lips. "But also for myself—and for the lady Euphemia. See you, I would be seeking to find . . . other arrangements for her whether I'd happened across you trying to save that fool ewe or nay."

Juliana's heart began to beat hard. "Truth tell?"

"You can be sure of it, sweetness," he said, the hint of his dimpled smile now spreading into one of his slow, lazy ones.

The kind that melted her bones and made her forget to pepper her tongue.

"And why can I be so sure?" she asked, warmth already spooling through her.

"Because having believed myself unloved as a wee laddie, I long ago vowed ne'er to take a woman to wife who did not truly want me."

For a long moment, Juliana could only stare at him, unable to speak past the hot lump burning in her throat, the swell of hope and possibilities tightening her chest.

Her knight wished a bride who wanted him.

Her want for him reverberated all through her.

"And you do not think the lady Euphemia wants you?" she asked, her voice sounding strange in ears . . . breathy and *expectant*.

"Wants me?" He shook his dark head, gave a mirthless

snort. "The wooden sword I played with as a lad would sooner become a tree again."

"I believe you err," Juliana said, her stomach knotting on the admission, the tingling up and down her spine making it difficult to trust such a bright promise. "She would be a fool to reject the match."

Nor would her presence, seen or nay, haunt Juliana so thoroughly did the other not greatly desire the marriage.

"Aye," she added, her heart sinking, "she will surely want this union."

"I mean *me,* sweetness," her knight corrected, his words almost drowned out by the sudden tolling of the bell for Vespers, its pealing carrying across the bailey to echo round the herbarium's garden walls.

He waited until the clanging died away. "I've no doubt Euphemia MacLeod relishes the match—from what I hear of her. But of me? Och, to be sure and I promise you, she desires naught."

"Yet you believe she will favor a Douglas?"

He nodded. "They are powerful and wealthy—their lands in the south where her health will benefit."

"And if she does not agree?"

"Then I shall have to convince her," he said, catching her to him and kissing her full on the lips, making her burn.

"'Tis an endeavor I mean to begin now," he added, lighting a welter of softer, more gentle kisses across her brow, just below her scar.

"*You,* I should like to visit later . . . if you will have me?"

The words out, he lifted a brow at her, his meaning unmistakable.

"H'mmm, sweetness?" He quirked his brow a notch higher. "Will you leave your door unbarred?"

Juliana nodded without hesitation.

If the lady Euphemia did not want him, she certainly knew someone who did.

Chapter Eleven

❧

"*GOD ROT SIR ROBERT MACKENZIE.*"

Lady Euphemia consigned her little jar of self-mixed skin-smoothing cream to the table and fixed the naked man on her bed with a penetrating stare.

She did not require the dubious ointments and potions of a cailleach many claimed was older than time and, like as not, blind as a mole . . . unable to see what simmered in her brew pot!

Nor did Devorgilla of Doon's apparent good foot with the MacKenzies make her particularly endearing.

Sniffing, Euphemia patted the dark, tightly-coiled braids wound above her ears and narrowed her gaze on a much more appealing prospect—the golden magnificence of Big Red MacAlister's full nakedness.

"Hear me well . . . I do not want him," she said with chilling contempt, her hands balled to tight fists. "I shall wed him, to be sure, but I have ne'er been able to abide even the thought of him . . . and I shall not suffer his presence until I have the surety and means I need to ruin him."

Big Red listened to her from the sparsely-dressed four-poster, his expression doubtful.

"You canna keep yourself from him much longer, whether you wish to or nay," he said, raising his deep voice above the clanging of the Vespers bell.

Pushing up on his elbows, he cocked a brow and eyed her closely, his light blue gaze passing over her nakedness with heated interest.

"'Tis rumored the man is a lusty sort," he ventured, a suggestive smile touching his mouth. "You might find him more palatable than you think?"

Euphemia pursed her lips, tossed her dark head. "I would sooner diddle the devil—and I do not mean his father!"

"Tush, lass! Robbie MacKenzie is a landed knight . . . well-beloved son and heir of Kintail," her lover pointed out. "He will someday laird it o'er the whole of these hills. You ken I am not one for styles and titles, nor the man's friend, but he is not the thrice-cursed fiend you make him."

"You speak as his friend—even if you proclaim not to be," Euphemia huffed, annoyed by the hot tightness clamping round her rib cage . . . her dread shortness of breath.

"I am *your* man, as you well ken," Big Red assured her. "'Tis only that your face is dark as a rain-laden sky and I would but give you solace by sharing what I have observed of him: that, unlike his father, he goes about in high spirits, is e'er a fount of good cheer."

He paused, shook back the thick mane of his bronze-colored hair. "Guidsakes, you ought hear the kitchen lasses babbling about him—it would seem they hold him for a very paladin, a man to ignite a maid's lust."

Euphemia pressed her fingers to her temples, irritability coursing through her on his pronouncement, his mention of the kitchen wenches only serving to remind her of their well-made, ripe-curved bodies . . . the rake-handle thinness of her own.

"The fair kitchen wenches with their milch cow bosoms can have him every morn for breakfast for all I care," she snapped in an even chillier tone than before. "For the nonce, 'tis *you* who suits my tastes—and my needs."

Her expression tight, she rubbed her arms, the whole of her shuddering at the mere thought of having to endure physical importunities with Sir Robert.

The man who'd destroyed her life—a thief who'd stolen her heart's joy and shredded her soul, and at her tenderest age and vulnerability.

"For the nonce?" Big Red was saying, his gaze lowering to the juncture of her thighs, settling there with the concentrated attention that e'er excited her.

Made her forget her ailments and . . . lackings.

"I am *e'er* at your service, Phemie," he added, his deep voice dropping to a husky note that made her tender parts grow heavy and moisten—despite her agitation.

"Or," he added, lifting an auburn brow to stare at the sparse brown curls topping her femininity, "have I misread your . . . need of me?"

"Nay, you have misread naught," she conceded, both willing him to keep his hot, deep-lidded gaze pinned to her exposed woman's parts, yet also fuming that she'd allowed herself to become so dependent of his particular brand of . . . attentions.

For truth, no other man had e'er excited her as wildly, satisfied her as deeply . . . or posed a greater threat to the attainment of her *non*lascivious needs as Big Red MacAlister.

Already she'd wasted far too many hours lying on her back, spread-legged and letting him *lick* her . . . precious time that would have been better spent assuring her stalwarts back home at Castle Uisdean yet bowed to her wishes.

"I would see more of you, Phemie," her *special* stalwart said then, the smooth deepness of his musical Highland voice pouring through her, melting her, and triumphing yet again over her every other concern.

The need to keep her laggard servants at Castle Uisdean glutted with enough coin and promises to ensure they not only held their tongues, but continued to ply her father with sleeping draughts.

And the equally pressing need to garner enough riches to implement her plans—to use greed to turn the heart of every man, common or lairdly, who e'er thought to call himself a friend to Clan MacKenzie.

"Ah-h-h, sweet lass," Big Red coaxed, clearly seeing the displeasure knitting her brow, "let me gaze on you rightly—if I indeed serve you so well?"

Anger at her weakness welling inside her, Euphemia shut her mind to her plans for revenge and drew a quivering breath, the best she could do without risking a coughing seizure.

Then, steadily as she could, she placed a delicate foot onto a three-legged stool, the pose opening her to Big Red's fullest view—and, hopefully, appeasing his voracious appetites enough to make him more . . . biddable.

"Aye, you serve me . . . *well*," she admitted, the urgent pulsing between her legs almost unbearable, so sweet was it to have his hot blue gaze latching on to her, *examining* her.

Looking at her, there, where she pulsed and burned, and doing so as if he found her truly desirable—despite her near lack of intimate hair and the slightness of her tiny, curveless body.

"I would find even more ways to please you if you use the cream again, my lady." Big Red's gaze flickered to the little jar she'd just set aside. "You know how *smooth* it makes you . . . how much I enjoy watching you apply it," he cajoled, the heat of his gaze damping her. "I would test the smoothness for you, Phemie . . . with my tongue. Tasting and savoring until I am full-sated . . ."

Euphemia shivered . . . then damned her ailments for, in her mounting excitement, the cough building in her chest and its itchy, breath-stealing heat rose to constrict her throat before she could even close her fingers round the little earthenware pot of cream.

Willing the discomfort to recede, she swept her own hot gaze over Big Red's sprawled form, nodding in approval when, under her perusal, he opened his muscular legs for her, spreading them without being asked, to the exact width he knew she e'er desired of him.

As she stared, admiring the lines of his hard-muscled body, he settled back onto the pillows, and folded his powerful arms behind his head, his considerable *pride* relaxed and resting against the thick nest of springy, cinnamon-colored curls at his groin.

"So-o-o, my sweetmeat," he said, sliding another glance at the little oaken table, "the cream . . . ?"

"We must speak first." Euphemia's brows snapped together in irritation at the wheeze in her voice. Flustered, she looked down at her nakedness, her almost-but-not-quite-flat stomach. "I—I . . . need more time . . ."

When she looked up again, a knowing smile had spread across Big Red's broad, ruddy face.

"More time for our . . . pleasures, or more time to weave Robbie MacKenzie's doom?"

"Sir *Robert's* destruction, of course," she hissed, her wrathful glare scalding the hapless little jar of skin-smoothing cream she'd been applying to her small breasts earlier—before the annoying peal of the Vespers bell interrupted their entertainments.

No longer frowning quite so vehemently, she considered reaching for the jar. She mixed the cream herself— blending deer milk, honey, and roots of silverweed into a generous portion of goose grease.

The resulting ointment·not only kept her white skin flawless, but greatly eased the in-and-out glide of Big Red's sizable tarse whene'er their ofttimes rigorous couplings proved too much for her.

Better still, her great stirk of a red-haired Highlander craved the taste of the cream—his unquenchable appetite being the most pressing reason she enjoyed rubbing a goodly portion of the goose grease mixture betwixt her legs, always taking especial care to assure that enough vestiges remained inside the pouty folds of her woman's flesh.

White-hot bolts of excitement streaked through her just thinking of how skillfully he licked her. She shifted her foot on the stool, opening herself just a teensy bit more, the deep-tingling thrill of being even more fully exposed to him, well compensating the fury roiling inside her.

"On my soul, lass, I will ne'er completely understand your spleen toward the man," Big Red said, reaching down to scratch the wiry, red-gold bush of his nether hair.

"If he displeases you so, 'tis valid enough reason you now have to walk away . . . return with me to Castle Uisdean and your plans there."

Euphemia scowled, jerking her attention from his *scratchings,* only to frown all the deeper when her gaze lit upon the glistening bronze hairs of his chest. Saints, but he distracted her! She swallowed, did her best to tamp down another persistent cough.

Her control slipping fast, she glanced around the bleak little bedchamber, her vexation rising.

"I will not go back to Uisdean—my place is here," she said, tight-voiced. "My plans and all that we have arranged, everything that has transpired, was done with Sir Robert's ruin in mind—as I thought you knew?"

"Och, I knew," Big Red acceded, now leisurely rubbing his ballocks, "and I suppose 'tis well enough I ken why you despise him, but I thought certain circumstances of late might have colored your . . . wishes?"

"Naught has changed—not yet for surety," she said, her blood now stirring with an entirely different kind of heat. "But I am disturbed by this . . . this slattern of a byre-maid Sir Robert brought home with him."

"The maid Juliana?"

"Whate'er her name is—I scarce believe she is a maid!" Euphemia's voice rose high and indignant. "She has a bold eye and is bonnie in a common, blowsy fashion. I have watched her from the secret passages and—"

"Hah!" Big Red hooted, lifting his heavy ballocks with one hand to scratch vigorously beneath them with the other, "just as old Out-with-the-Sword's daughter can outdevil the devil, so, too, can she do as she would with a mere rival—"

"She is too far beneath me to merit more than passing concern." Euphemia glared at him, wished he'd stop rubbing round at his male parts . . . even riled and vexatious, watching him touch himself roused her too much for her to think clearly.

"If you believe her too lowborn to earn your consideration, then why does she bother you?" Big Red countered, taking his still-flaccid shaft in his hand and letting his thumb glide back and forth over its limp thickness with a studied slowness surely designed to drive her from her wits. "Let him keep her as his lust-mate if she pleases him . . . as you have me to see to your own needs and desires."

Euphemia flushed.

'Twas well she knew neither Sir Robert nor any other man could e'er come close to slaking her *unusual* pleasures so roundly as did Big Red MacAlister . . . one-time leader of the band of broken clansmen and other assorted miscreants who dwelled deep within the thickly-wooded reaches of the Isle of Pabay, not far from her own Castle Uisdean.

Her man now, Big Red satisfied her darkest cravings.

Blessed with notable patience and stamina, he'd remain poised in place for hours if it pleased her, untiring, and keeping his tarse wholly relaxed for her so that if she positioned herself beneath him, the long, thick shaft and his good-sized ballocks simply dangled loosely above her face as so excited her.

And he ne'er once complained when she'd repeatedly flick a finger at the swinging weight of his musky-scented male parts, her light touches setting the free-hanging shaft into motion so that it would delight her by swaying to and fro . . . again and again and again.

Nor did he balk at her blacker requirements, her less pleasurable requests . . . tending without questions or a raised eyebrow to any deed she asked of him.

Until recent days.

Of late, he'd been countering her plans . . . constantly voicing concerns and objections and, most annoying of all, pressing her to break her betrothal and become *his bride*.

Another shift in her life she attributed, if indirectly, to the arrival of the voluptuous, flame-haired whore who had every man between eight summers and eighty years either addlepated or running full-stretch at the merest glimpse of her.

"Dinna fret so o'er the lass—I will keep you too oc-cupied to think on her." Big Red's deep voice penetrated the red haze of her hot-whirling ire. "What harm can she—"

"The wench cannot harm me at all—and I care naught who sniffs betwixt her fat thighs or occupies their time making moon eyes at her," Euphemia snipped, well aware her eyes flashed meanness and jealousy yet unable to quell her perturbation. "'Tis only how her very pres-ence can lessen the jolt of my plan that vexes me."

Her heart racing, she snatched up the little pot of skin-smoothing cream and thrust her fingers into its depths, retrieving a generous scoop of the icy-cold ointment.

It was time to push Big Red MacAlister beyond his endurance.

Her purpose set, she flopped down onto the stool, spread her legs, and slapped the cream onto the quivering flesh of her womanhood.

"'Tis overdue for Sir Robert to learn that I am not some soppy milk-and-water maid to be trifled with. We must send him crawling on his belly through the darkling hills—and, anon . . . before his lusty-looking whore becomes such a comfit that he cares about naught else," she said, hovering her fingers just close enough to the gleaming dollop of cream to make perspiration bead Big Red's brow.

He moistened his lips, his breath coming fast and hard as he nodded in mute agreement, his light blue eyes nigh glazed with letch.

Her own breath catching, Euphemia wriggled her fingers—just enough to make Big Red groan and squirm.

"The MacLeods' Girt of Strength must be lowered again," she said, pleased when her voice came smooth and firm, unmarred by her usual wheeze.

"The Girt . . . again?" Big Red blinked, the words a dry whisper.

Euphemia nodded.

"If we cannot persuade Clan MacKenzie's allies to change their allegiances through the coin we've already spent, then another MacKenzie friend must lose a vessel. And more than one!" she declared, her temper heating her blood.

"Let a full score of outraged allies come in complaint

to this castle gate, demanding recompense and protection lest they disavow their loyalties," she ranted on, drifting her fingers just a teensy bit closer to the cream. "I want Sir Robert and his father vexed . . . and we need the coin we can glean through another wrecking to fund the expedition to Fladda Chuan."

To pillage that sacred isle's treasures and use them to hammer the final, laming blow to Sir Robert MacKenzie.

Sir Robert, his black-hearted sire, and her own drink-taken fool of a father . . . the three men she hated most in the world.

Men she was determined to teach the meaning of vengeance.

As she would Big Red MacAlister as well if he did not stop looking as if he were about to naysay her.

Or, just as irritating, wasn't paying attention to her words at all.

His open features working, his hand pumping steadily on his finally-hardened shaft, he kept his gaze centered on the dollop of cream—and said nothing.

"Did you not hear me, MacAlister?" Euphemia swirled the tip of one finger in the dollop of cream, careful to touch only the cream and not herself. "I have not come on this long road not to prove that I am a foe who strikes first and talks thereafter! The chain must be lowered again—and at the soonest."

"Och, I heard you right enough," the Highlander responded at last, stroking rhythmically now. Faster, and harder. "But I vow my ears must have wax in 'em—mayhap I'll hear better if you start rubbing in that cream?"

On his words, a surge of sheer female elation shot through Euphemia, the raggedness of his lust-hazed breath and the heat in his gaze exciting her and increasing her own arousal, but then his underlying belligerence seeped through her own tingling needs, and she frowned, the heat flowing out of her until she felt cold as a slimy, fresh-caught herring.

Gritting her teeth, she lowered her hand and used a deliberate slow circling of her fingers to begin spreading and rubbing the cream into her throbbing flesh.

But, unlike most times, her base ministrations left her unfulfilled—throbbing, aye, but only with the burning desire for revenge.

"You, too, will benefit from my felicity if a successful journey can be made to Fladda Chuan," she said, applying the cream with the greatest of care, but speaking with the kind of chilly menace that served her best when all else failed.

Narrowing her eyes, she let her high blood show in a calculated stare of gentle-born hauteur. "God curse the lot of any who refuse you aid in setting sail on this venture."

To her annoyance, Big Red did not appear impressed.

Far from it, he even ceased stroking his tarse and, reaching for the wine flagon on the bedside table, poured himself a generous measure, and drank, sipping leisurely.

"I ought tell you," he finally said, setting down the emptied wine goblet, "the reach of my influence amongst the men of Castle Uisdean and even my good friends on the Isle of Pabay is fading . . . lest you procure more coin to sweeten their willingness to dirty their hands for you."

"More coin?" Euphemia's fingers stilled, heat suffusing her face. "Have you run mad, MacAlister?"

The last vestiges of her letch spinning away, she sprang to her feet and stalked across the bare-wood floor to her largest strongbox, the one that had brimmed with treasures and ample monies upon her arrival at Eilean Creag.

Funds drained away to secure assistance and silence in keeping her dim-witted sire so deep in his cups and . . . otherwise occupied that he scarce noted the rising and setting of the sun, much less the lowering of the MacLeods' chain, the exacting of tolls, or the wrecking of those galleys whose shipmasters refused to pay them.

"My coffers are nigh empty—all of them!" she railed, shaking the iron-bound chest with a surprising burst of strength, gall rising in her at the pathetic rattle of the few coins and bits of bejeweled gewgaws that remained within. "Why do you think we need to sail to Fladda Chuan?"

She let go of the strongbox, thrust balled fists against her slim hips. "That fabled isle's riches will enable us to lure away even the staunchest MacKenzie sympathizers. We must—"

"*We?*" Big Red sat up, stretching his well-muscled arms high above his shaggy-maned head before lowering them to briskly rub his broad, hair-roughened chest.

"I have no need to journey to Fladda Chuan," he said, as if dismissing the notion, "even if the isle is the purported Tir-nan-Og of Celtic fame. 'Tis well content I'd be to spend the rest of my days with you on a small holding far from here where no one kens who we are or whence we came."

Euphemia made a sharp, dismissive gesture with her hand. "And I say that if the famed Weeping Stone can be recovered from Saint Columba's ruined chapel on Fladda Chuan, untold riches will be ours," she contended, ignoring his own fool suggestion. "The stone can perform wonders. All know it. We must get there . . ."

Even if the saint's sacred Weeping Stone could not be found, the fabled isle surely held enough other riches to wrap a stranglehold round Kintail and crush Sir Robert and his ilk for all time and eternity.

Stifling a cough, she drew herself as high as her diminutive stature would allow and, heedless of her nakedness, crossed the small room to the hearth where she prodded the fire with an iron poker until sparks flew and new flames curled up around the peats.

Hot words and losing her temper would avail nothing with Big Red MacAlister.

He required other forms of persuasion.

"You err if you believe I desire to leave here," she said, setting aside the poker, furious to hear the wheeze back in her voice. "I thought you understood my sole wish is to *stay* here . . . not ever to return to Castle Uisdean?"

"Aye, well." Big Red shot a glance toward the door, his open face a bit wary as if he'd heard something on the draughty stair landing beyond. "I thought you only sought Robbie MacKenzie's ruination . . . not chatelainely duties of his devil-damned house?"

"Heaven grant that I achieve both, for I desire nothing less," Euphemia said, her resolve stiffening on each word. "Only so will fullest revenge be mine."

She paused to look up at the ceiling, her brow knitting at a sudden sound that could only be rats scooting about inside the tower's wretchedly damp walling.

"Heed my words, MacAlister, I live to be the bane of

Sir Robert's existence—if he were wise and sagacious, he would have sensed my wrath and ne'er returned."

Then, with a sharp twisting at the heart that rose up and seized her from the deepest, darkest pit of her past, she moved to the window so the wall sconce flickering there might better illuminate her nakedness and so that the evening's chill, though bad for her lungs, might tighten and perk her tiny dark-colored nipples.

And, in especial, so that the night breeze could speed away the annoying remnants of the innocent lass she'd once been and whose life had been so thoroughly shattered when, against all her protestations, she'd been given in betrothal to the MacKenzie heir.

"You revile him that much?" Big Red's deep voice came from years and years away.

"More than there are sands on the shore," Euphemia said through tightly clenched teeth as she looked out through the opened shutters, some long-withered part of her wrenching at the softness of the evening light on land and sea, the beauty of the spent day rising gently to the quiet sky.

Kintail *was* beautiful.

But its splendor had naught to do with her refusal to leave. Nor her steadfast determination to become Sir Robert's bride.

She wanted to ruin him, aye.

To humiliate and shame him so deeply that he'd ne'er be able to stride o'er the heather again without knowing any and all who saw him pass were twittering behind their hands, laughing, and calling him for a fool.

Aye, such were her reasons.

But above all, she wanted to wrest from him that

which he held most dear, his land, and then use that loss to teach him how it feels to have one's hopes and dreams ripped from one's heart and be plunged into darkness unending, without any hope of resurrection.

❧

The Vespers bell still echoing in his ears, Robbie paused near his old tower's stair foot and observed the approach of a harried-looking kitchen lass. He made a silent note to light a candle and say a prayer of thanks to the saints for yet another small blessing.

Later. At the moment, he chose to only smile and savor his unexpected fortuity.

His timing could not have been more propitious.

Indeed, bolstered by the most expansive mood to seize him in some time, he looked on as the maid darted past him, swift as the wind, a large dinner tray balanced against the curve of her hip.

A tray well-dressed with a generously-piled trencher, a good-sized wine flagon, and not one but *two* surprisingly fine silver-gilt goblets.

But of even more interest, the maid's hurrying feet were carrying her toward the same turnpike stair he'd been about to ascend.

The little-used stair whose tight-winding stone steps led directly to Robbie's boyhood bedchamber . . . quarters now occupied by his betrothed.

His soon-to-be *un*betrothed if, as he so dearly wished, he'd managed to acquire even the barest touch of a silver tongue in his years away.

A wee trace of knightly . . . charm and persuasion.

And if not—well, there were alternatives. . . .

More than eager to begin testing his abilities, he strode forward, closing the distance between himself and the scurrying kitchen lass in quick, long-striking strides.

"Ho, maid!" he called, catching up with her on the stairwell's first landing, relieving her of the tray before she could even think to splutter him a fine *good e'en*.

Feeling a jab of guilt for startling her, he flashed his best smile. "I see you are taking the lady Euphemia her dinner? Or"—he aimed a glance at the two wine chalices—"are these viands meant for elsewhere since there are two goblets?"

Two *strange* goblets, for although Eilean Creag possessed enough such fancily-worked drink-ware to line the shores of Loch Duich once, mayhap even twice round the sea loch's impressive circumference, most within the castle's walls, including the Black Stag hisself, favored simple ale or wine cups save on the most festive occasions.

Stranger still was the furiously bright flush staining the kitchen maid's cheeks and her seeming difficulty in meeting Robbie's eye.

"Ach . . . 'tis your lady's supper to be sure and it is," she stammered, blinking furiously. "If my lord will excuse me, I will just be a-taking it to her." She bobbed a wobbly, off-balance curtsy and held out her hands for the tray. "Please, sir, the lady has a temp— . . . I mean, she will be much displeased if she must wait."

"Then mayhap the surprise of having me deliver the tray will sweeten its tardy arrival?" Robbie suggested, ignoring the maid's outstretched hands.

His curiosity piqued, he eyed the mound of steaming meats and oversize portion of honeyed almond cakes.

"The lady appears to have a man-sized appetite," he said, lifting a brow. "And . . . two goblets? Are you certain you did not snatch the wrong tray . . . in your haste?"

Looking miserable, the lass gulped audibly and shook her head. "Nay, sir," she admitted, "the lady Euphemia e'er eats so well . . . her appetite astounds us all."

"And the two goblets?" Robbie lifted one, held it up to the fading evening light falling through a narrow window slit above where they stood.

" 'Tis her own goblets they be, sir," the lass revealed, the color in her cheeks deepening. "She brought them with her from Castle Uisdean. Part o' her dowry, just like the guardsmen what came along with her. She—"

"I do not care whose goblet she drinks from, nor whence such a piece of frippery came," Robbie said, returning the goblet to the tray. "But I will swing from the next crescent moon if I can fathom why she requires *two*?"

"By your leave, sir, but the lady says . . . she claims her wine becomes her better if she drinks each measure from a fresh goblet."

"I see," Robbie said, nodding as if he did, but not seeing at all.

Save that the MacLeod lass now struck him as more odd-minded than he'd realized.

A notion that accompanied him up the remainder of the spiraling stairs, troubling him more with each mounted step—until his winding ascent was arrested by a huge, low-slinking shadow.

A shaggy-haired shadow, yellow-eyed, dark as a winter's night, loped right at him, ready to pounce, its fast-moving bulk chased by two screaming *beanshiths,* the

first banshee wreathed in fire, the other cloaked in blackness.

Or so he thought until Roag, his father's favorite mon-
grel spotted and leapt at him, the great rough-coated beast
flattening him against the dank, cold-stoned wall. Before
Robbie could do aught to prevent it, the lady Euphemia's
dinner tray sailed into the air and clattered down the curving stairs.

Roasted meats, honeyed almond cakes, two silver-gilt
wine goblets and all.

Only the shattered ewer of wine remained where it'd
fallen on the landing, its spilled contents forming a
blood-red pool across the stone flags . . . the rich Gascon
wine blessedly proving a greater temptation to Roag's se-
lect taste buds than Robbie's startled, well-licked face.

Blinking, he used a fold of his plaid to wipe away the
remains of the dog's sloppy-wet *enthusiasm*, regaining
his wits as quickly as the encounter with Roag had
plunged him into momentary madness.

He stared at the dog, deeming the beast much more
agile than he would have believed—and noting at once
that the two wailing banshees trailing in Roag's wake
were not dread *beanshiths* at all, but his two younger
sisters.

They stood panting before him, their unbound hair in
a tangle from running, their faces flushed with excitement, and their night-rending cries not screams of doom
but . . . *teeters*.

Nay, worse than teeters.

The two young lasses were nigh convulsing with ringing, rib-splitting laughter.

And not, Robbie was certain, because he'd been set

upon by a huge, hairy beast of a dog, the wind nigh knocked out of him, only to be smothered with over-affectionate canine kisses.

Nor even because he'd let loose of Euphemia MacLeod's well-laden dinner tray.

Nay, whate'er cause for amusement sent rivers of tears coursing down Gelis's and Arabella's cheeks had naught to do with him—and mayhap everything to do with his *not*-soon-to-be bride.

Of that he was fairly certain.

"So-o-o," he said, pushing away from the clammy wall and straightening his plaid with the stoutest dignity he could muster. "What have you to say for yourselves?"

The two girls exchanged glances.

Arabella blushed and dashed the tears from her cheeks with the backs of her fingers.

Gelis, looking nigh to bursting with jollity, bit down hard on her lower lip and wrapped her arms round her ribs, then leaned forward as if only so she could suppress the peals of laughter welling in her belly.

Roag ignored them all and simply kept lapping at the pool of fine Gascon wine.

Seeing no other way around the matter, Robbie positioned himself so that the sheer mass of his body blocked the downward-spiraling stairs. That move accomplished, he drew himself up to his full height, spread his powerful legs, and planted his hands on his hips.

His two squirm-footed, wriggly-hipped sisters would not endure more than a few minutes trapped thus on the dark, dank-smelling landing—especially once he'd fixed them with his most thunderous, censorious stare.

"So-o-o," he began again, drawing himself up yet another half inch and laying as much authority onto the word as he dared without risking sending them into further gales of out-of-control feminine ribaldry.

"I can scarce think what it might be, but I vow you do have a good explanation for careening down these stairs hallooing and screeching like two witless hens?"

Silence, and more giggles rewarded his attempt at gently impressing an answer from them.

Robbie frowned.

A more drastic approach was needed.

"Gelis—I have heard whispers that a certain soft-eyed squire sings you Gaelic love songs of especial yearning at table every e'en—and sometimes in darkened window embrasures," he declared, curling his hands round his sword belt and rocking back on his heels.

"And, you, Arabella . . . I am told there is a young newly-dubbed knight amongst our Uncle Marmaduke's men who e'er requests your singular attentions whene'er he visits and the courtesy of a warm bath is offered him?"

He took a step toward them and let his brow darken a bit. "Is this so, my sisters?"

The girls did not deny it.

But neither did they meet his eye . . . or completely stop sniggering.

"Then, since your blushing faces and laughter say as much as any words," Robbie informed them, "I shall assure that neither of you venture forth from your bedchamber for a full sennight lest you loosen your tongues—and tell me, too, if you were skulking about in this tower's secret passage again?"

Gelis straightened at once. "We were not . . . skulking."

"But you were *in* the passage?" Robbie pounced on her slip of tongue.

Gelis clamped her lips demonstratively tight . . . her elder sister sketched a noncommittal, wholly unconvincing shrug.

"And if you were sneaking about in the secret way— I vow you also crept into the squint above my old bedchamber? Again?" He narrowed his eyes at them, already well aware of what they'd been up to whether they chose to speak true or nay.

Lifting a hand, he pretended to examine his fingernails. "Admit your foolery and you shall only be sequestered in your room for seven days—continue to deny your mummery, and I shall increase your penance to a fortnight."

"Bah . . . Robbie!" Gelis protested with a toss of her flame-bright head. "Aye, we had good reason to be a-flying down the stairs," she admitted, her eyes still streaming. "Though I canna say why we're a-laughing—truth tell, what we saw was frightful enough to scare the devil into drawing in his horns!"

She whirled on her sister, grabbed the other girl's arm, shaking it. "Tell him, Arabella," she pleaded, "I-canna-speak-for-the-stitch-in-my-ribs . . ."

"God's blood, think you I can speak of it?" Arabella wailed, her cry half a laugh and half a sob. "My very tongue would fall out if I tried," she added, her blush flaming brighter as she swept a loose-spilling swath of raven hair over one shoulder, using the gesture to glance up the stairwell behind her.

Almost as if she expected someone to come winding their way down out of the torch-lit gloom.

But when the shadows failed to stir and no sound save Roag's slurp-slurping of the spilled wine came to their ears, she turned back round, glancing up at Robbie through wet, spiky lashes, her pretty face as sore-stricken as her younger sister's bloomed with mirth.

"I am sorry, Robbie—I fear . . . 'tis only . . . you have ridden hard and far to return to us, and—" she faltered, looked down to fiddle with a loose thread on her *arisaid*.

An *arisaid* whose soft, woolen folds were more disheveled and askew than Robbie had e'er seen on the most-times fastidious Arabella. Unlike her carefree younger sister, the giddy-eyed, fiery-topped Gelis, Arabella ne'er greeted the day without first assuring she was impeccably clad, her every hair sleeked into place and nary a speck of dust clinging to her skirts or even her calfskin boots.

"And?" Robbie prodded, rubbing his chin. "What if I have . . . ridden hard and far?"

"Then," Arabella said, clearly breaking at last, "unless your purpose was to merely see us and walk Kintail's heather slopes again, Gelis and I fear you have returned to wed a madwoman."

"A madwoman?"

"Crazed as a loon!" Gelis answered for her sister. "She was prancing about her chamber again—naked as a newborn bird."

"And talking up a blue wind about Fladda Chuan . . . just like she was last time we watched her from the squint," Arabella exclaimed with a shudder. "Mind you, she—"

"The last time you *spied* on her," Robbie intoned, his chivalry insisting he correct the term even if he was half a mind to do some spying himself—not to ogle the lady's doubtful charms, but to judge his sisters' troubling concern about the maid's wits.

Or lack of them.

Even so, fairness made him defend her one more time.

"See you, lasses, as you have already heard from more experienced lips than mine, simply moving about one's privy quarters unclothed does not make a person crazy-mad," he said, wishing he could put more conviction into his voice.

"And many have been the days I've happened on the two of you reciting bardic epics or love verses while working at your stitching," he added, watching them closely. "Speaking to oneself does not always mean someone's brain has gone to mush."

"And playing with oneself?"

Robbie's eyes flew wide.

Surely Gelis meant something entirely different from the image that leapt into his mind.

"What do you mean . . . *playing with oneself?*"

Arabella clapped a hand to her mouth, wheeled away from them both, her shoulders shaking.

Gelis thrust out her chin, her eyes flashing challenge. "I believe the vulgar term is diddle," she said, plain as day, her meaning unmistakable. "She was sitting spread-legged on a stool and . . . diddling herself."

"Di—" Robbie broke off, unable to say the word.

Not in the presence of his sisters.

"You saw her doing this?" he asked instead.

"We did," they answered in unison.

"If you hurry to the squint," Gelis suggested, "you

might catch her doing it still . . . she did not appear in any hurry."

And neither did she just a scant few minutes later, when Robbie emerged from the narrow secret way cut between the thickness of the tower's walls and maneuvered himself into the slight widening in the passage that formed the squint above his boyhood bedchamber.

But, although certainly at her leisure, as one peek through the small, down-slanted spy hole revealed, the tiny, dark-haired wisp of a woman he knew to be his betrothed was not sitting naked on a stool but merely *standing* unclothed before the little bedchamber's one arch-topped window.

And the gray watery light silhouetting her nakedness afforded him a much greater shock than if he'd caught her practicing unmentionable acts of lewdness upon her surprisingly girlish-looking female parts.

A wholly unexpected and stunning shock but also, mayhap, another blessing in disguise.

One his chivalry made him hope he would not have to exploit.

For, unless his knowledge of women was much less considerable than he hoped, the lady Euphemia appeared to be enceinte—a distinct thickening at her waist and the slight swelling of her childishly small breasts softening her otherwise thin, sharp-angled body into gently rounded bloom.

And the longer he peered down at her through the square-cut spy hole, the more convinced he became.

His sisters' jib-jabbering chatter held truth.

The lady Euphemia, proud daughter of the great race of MacLeod, if only sired by a drink-taken lesser laird who styled himself *Out-with-the-Sword*, was anything but a virtuous maid.

Where'er she'd kept herself in recent months, and with whome'er she'd dallied, did not interest Robbie.

All that mattered was what any practiced eye could not deny.

His unwanted betrothed was in the earliest swells of her confinement.

Beyond all doubt with child.

Chapter Twelve

❦

$\mathcal{O}$N THE OPPOSITE SIDE of Eilean Creag from Robbie's boyhood bedchamber and the wee squint he'd ne'er known existed in those long ago days, the lady Linnet sat beside the hearth fire of the castle's sumptuous Lady's Solar, and made slow, tedious stitches on her embroidery, a fine gentlewomanly task her somewhat clumsy fingers ne'er truly allowed her to master.

She did, though, possess the ability to listen with only half an ear to her sister's quiet ramblings.

"Battles, blood feuds, and usurpations," Lady Caterine was saying this time, murmuring the words from her own hearth chair as she, too, plied her needle, but with more skill and grace than Linnet could e'er dream to achieve.

Or, truth be told, cared to attempt.

Caterine glanced at her, shook her head as if to rid all thought of foolish men and their warring ways.

"'Tis glad my heart is that you've work a-plenty, for I weary of sitting in the hall and listening to the men recount the same vainglorious tales," she declared, stitching away. "You would think they are all born with a sword in their hands and bloodlust in their eyes."

"And are they not?" Linnet could not help the smile that curved her lips.

"But," she added, setting aside her needlework to stretch her arms and flex her aching fingers, "full of steel and muscle or nay, oft enough are the nights old Fergus brings tears to their eyes with his fireside tales of heart-piercing love and yearning—or delights us with his knowledge of where the fairies dance of a night and in which lochs water kelpies can be seen."

Linnet sighed, helped herself to a restorative sip of heather ale.

Truth be told, at the moment, much more interesting things than the Wee Folk were to be seen in Eilean Creag's Lady's Solar, and although she'd taken great pains to keep her head bent dutifully to her task e'er since her sister had joined her, too much candle shine and fire glow illuminated the chamber for her not to note what a less observant eye might miss.

Indeed, unless her vision was failing her, there appeared to be a great deal more of her sister than there had been at Christmastide, the last time they'd seen each other.

Unable to hold back her suspicions any longer, Linnet pushed to her feet and pressed her hands against the small of her tired back.

"Tell me," she began, sliding a sidelong glance at Caterine although she pretended to be peering into the hearth, her gaze seemingly fixed on the softly-glowing bricks of peat, "was your sole purpose in visiting Doon truly to take provender to old Devorgilla . . . or could you be secreting another, more *vital* reason for having sought out the crone?"

To Linnet's surprise, Caterine hooted a laugh.

A *chuckle* by anyone else's measure, but for the splendidly elegant Lady Caterine, more prone to pensive musings than boisterous jollity, a good and hearty laugh.

"You can stop trying to pretend you are not staring," Caterine said, looking at Linnet with amused affection. "The kitchen lasses and laundresses have been much less discreet—you, as my sister, have no need for such cantrips . . . aye, there was another reason for visiting the cailleach."

"A wee sweet reason?" Linnet couldn't resist teasing her.

In answer, Caterine put down her own stitchwork and flattened her gown over her middle, letting the taut-drawn linen reveal the swell her full skirts could no longer quite hide . . . the blessed bulge of a new, quickening life inside her.

"'Tis true, as you can see," she said, her eyes filling with warmth and pleasure, "but although after four nearly-grown daughters, we have surely missed the joy of a son, my dear Marmaduke was beside himself with concern. He was troubled and fretting because of my age. So he made me promise to beg Devorgilla for a boon . . . a charm or blessing to assure a safe confinement and delivery."

"Oh, Caterine!" Linnet rushed forward to embrace her, placed a gentle, wondering hand on her sister's swollen belly. "What joy, I say! And your great lumbering lout of a husband ought to have told us," she added, her voice choked with emotion. "'Tis fair glowing with good health you are, though I understand his concern for you and the child."

Stepping back, she smoothed Caterine's hair. "Had aught been amiss, you know I would have . . . felt something."

Linnet looked hard at her sister, pleased by the fine color of her skin, the luminosity of her smiling eyes, and, above all, the wonder and awe of the wee, growing life Linnet's special gift had let her sense so strongly when she'd hugged her.

A healthy, strapping life—of that she was certain.

Mayhap even the son and heir she knew her sister and Sir Marmaduke had e'er desired but no longer dared to hope would bless them.

"All will be well—I am sure of it," she added with all the joy swelling her heart.

"I am confident as well," Caterine said, nodding agreement. "And Devorgilla claimed so, too. Though she did wave a rowan branch o'er my head and mutter some unintelligible blessing before giving me her reassurances. Strange, though . . . I cannot help but wonder if . . ."

"If . . . ?" A sudden flurry of prickly warmth on Linnet's nape dampened her bliss, the shivery chills warning she ought hear her sister's unspoken words.

As did the faint but unmistakable droning of bees.

A dread sound rising and falling with growing persistence and coming from the direction of the hearth fire.

"If . . . *what?*" Linnet coaxed again, sliding a quick glance at the hearth and its innocently glowing peats.

"If," Caterine capitulated, jabbing her needle into the embroidery cloth, "I went there armed with provender

and seeking Devorgilla's sage wisdom and counsel—or if she summoned me."

"Summoned you?"

Catherine shrugged, flicked a speck of lint from her skirts.

"The cailleach is known to do so," she said, her gaze on her stitching. "I considered the possibility because although she was pleased as always to receive supplies from us, and especially delighted at my own tender condition, she seemed more interested in impressing me to deliver her special healing ointment into the hands of Robbie's soon-to-be bride, claiming the lass would need its curing."

"So?" Linnet's heart thudded, her nerves beginning to twitch and prickle.

She set aside her embroidery for good, tried her best to unobtrusively rub away the gooseflesh rising on her arms.

"Any worthy wise woman will have seen that the MacLeod lass is frail . . . *ailing*," she said, not wanting to trouble Caterine with her own convictions about which lass beneath Eilean Creag's roof would prove her stepson's own true bride.

"'Twas kindhearted of the crone to send along a charmed potion for the maid," she added, assuming her most calming tone.

"But that is what unsettles me," Caterine explained, "do you not see?"

Linnet lifted a brow, not seeing at all, but well aware the explanation would soon bubble forth like a burn in spate.

Caterine stood again, moved to the opened windows

where the evening chill stole up from the loch. With a small sigh, she looked out at the darkening sky.

"See you," she began, "o'er the years Devorgilla has oft sent us potions or charms—she has ways of getting suchlike into the right hands. And whene'er she blessed us with such a remedy, she ne'er failed to specify who she felt might be most needful of her cure . . . and the cure's purpose."

Linnet took a deep breath, struggled to ignore how, in addition to the prickling of her nape, her stomach was now beginning to twist into knots.

"I have heard the crone can be a bit . . . *mischievous* about revealing the true purpose of her spells and potions."

"Oh, 'tis not that." Caterine turned away from the window, waved a dismissive hand. "She prattled on and on about the wonders of her healing ointment, even declaring it her best triumph because she'd imbued the cream with the magic of adapting a cure to suit the needs of whoe'er used it."

"A cure to suit one's needs?"

Caterine nodded, her beautiful face uplit by a nearby branch of softly-burning candles. "She minded me of the special bronze cook-pot she once sent to my lord husband, claiming his good-heartedness might, at times, make him a poor judge of men."

"A charmed cook-pot?" Linnet blinked, her ill ease and even the drone of the dread bees momentarily besieged by her surprise. "How can a bronze cook-pot aid a man in assessing another man's character?"

"I would have thought you, with your own special gift of *taibhsearachd,* would have known of such wonders?"

Caterine's face lit with teasing affection. "'Tis simple enough magic . . . perhaps not as infallible as your second sight, but effective all the same—as we have seen often enough whene'er we've had cause to use Devorgilla's special cauldron."

In a swish of skirts, Caterine returned to her stool by the fireside. "See you," she said, settling herself, "the cook-pot has the virtue of yielding up to each guest the piece of meat to which his character entitles him. If my lord husband is unsure of someone's heart, we invite them to table and then we wait . . . if the cook-pot produces a fine morsel for the guest, we know that person can be trusted—"

"—and if a less than savory portion is fished from the cauldron, wariness is in order?" Linnet finished for her, realizing she should have known at once for she had indeed heard of such charmed cook-pots.

Though, as best she could recall, such bronze cauldrons more often boasted the magic of offering up the choicest pieces according to a person's status and not the goodness, or darkness, of one's heart.

Scarce that it mattered with the feeling of fast-encroaching dread beginning to swirl round her again, a darkness that lapped at the edges of her consciousness and even along the carefully-smoothed folds of her sister's deep blue skirts.

"Even so, I do not see why Devorgilla's ointment and its magical powers ought trouble you," she managed, the words coming to her ears as if from far away, faint pulses of scarcely audible sound, lost in a renewed surge of buzzing, whirling bees.

"Or"—she forced herself to hold her sister's gaze—

"are you bothered because she wished you to deliver the cream to Robbie's betrothed? You have seen the maid is not well-loved here."

"Nay, 'twas not the delivery of the ointment that troubled me, but the way Devorgilla *spoke* of Robbie's intended," Caterine explained, her voice little more than an echo.

Linnet touched her brow, tried to concentrate past the droning sound pressing ever closer.

"I do not understand," she said, repressing a near overwhelming urge to glance at the hearth fire, the usual source of her torments.

"Ach, I am making a muddle of it," Catherine said, fluffing her skirts, the dark blue folds reminding Linnet of the deep blueness of the hills, an endless rolling expanse of them rising steeply from the sea.

But her sister was still speaking. "'Twas the crone's references to Robbie's bride as being 'of a great beauty' that bothers me," she said, her voice so distant now, the words sounded more like the low murmur of ceaseless, lapping waves.

"*She is of a great beauty,* she'd exclaim, then give me that sly-eyed look of hers," Caterine went on, shifting on her stool. "I'd dismissed the words as an old woman's fancy until I arrived here and caught my first glimpse of the maid."

"The maid?"

"The lady Euphemia." Caterine's voice came surprisingly clear, breaking with startling ease through the countless peaks rising dark against the deep blue of the sea. "Mischievous or nay, even at her most charitable,

Devorgilla is too all-seeing to mistake one such as Euphemia MacLeod for a *great beauty*."

Nay, but Robbie's intended bride—is—a great beauty.

Linnet shook her head, not certain if she'd spoken the words or if they only rang so loud in her ears.

For truth, each one came almost as deafening as the thundering hoofbeats of the lathered horse hurtling ever faster toward the distant horizon—pounding at full gallop through a world of blueness that now surrounded Linnet, filling her vision with the deep blues of the hills and the sea, the water even reflecting the blue of the sky.

Her heart racing, its thunder joining the drumming beat of the horse's hooves, Linnet gripped the seat of her stool, tried not to see the horse or even the dark flurries of wind on the water now showing between the broken cliffs of a strange coast.

Cold, tossing water that should have been the skirts of her sister's blue-colored gown.

But Caterine's skirts were nowhere to be seen.

The voluminous folds were ululating and expanding to blot out the Lady's Solar and plunge Linnet into a landscape she knew she'd ne'er glimpsed, where for mile upon lonely mile not even the humblest cot-house could be seen.

Only the sea and the sky.

The great hills stretching away in endless succession.

And a flame-haired lass riding pillion behind a man who looked like Robbie but was not. The maid sat rigid, her arms wrapped tight around the man, her endlessly flowing tears copious enough to fill an ocean.

The man's face appeared to be sculpted of granite, his tight-checked fury icy enough to freeze Linnet's heart.

Lady . . . 'tis long I have waited . . .

The strange words echoed from the blue darkness swirling round her, an ever deepening blue, its edges now tinged with soft-glowing gold . . . a pulsating red-gold that crept outward across the blue land, swallowing the galloping horse and its two riders, then embracing and engulfing Linnet herself until she stood alone surrounded by a sheet of ringing flames.

Nay, not quite alone for the male rider was returning on foot.

Linnet straightened her back at his approach, even squared her shoulders in preparation for a confrontation— her fear chased by a burning need to hurl challenges at the man for the cold mien and stony silence he'd turned to the flame-haired maid's proud anguish, her river of tears.

But then he came closer and Linnet's heart plummeted.

At once, a new terror iced her skin and froze her marrow, filling her with a numbing cold such as she'd ne'er dreamed existed . . . despite the heat of the raging inferno blazing all around the fiend coming so sure-strided toward her.

Not the rider at all, she now realized, but a magnificent-looking man whose heart-stoppingly handsome face she'd ne'er once seen without a roguish grin, his wickedness shimmering all around him—a sickly greenish black glow that marred his beauty and marked him as a truly evil man.

A man who, in life, had been her lord husband's bastard half brother, Kenneth MacKenzie.

A dead man . . . a *ghost* . . . whose flashing smile and glimmering aura of evil-green were no more, the wrenching sadness replacing them, scattering her terror and twisting her heart as none of his e'er so silkily spoken words and false chivalry could have done.

"You!" she cried, some small part of her blessedly aware of the hard stool beneath her, someone's tender hands pressing a cooling cloth to her forehead.

Gentle hands that held her steady in place on the three-legged stool when her body's own limpness threatened to send her sliding onto the floor rushes.

"Kenneth. . . ."

"Aye, fair lady," said the apparition as he sketched her a gallant bow—just as he'd done so often in the past, using his undoubted charm to spew his darkness on whoe'er was fool enough to be blinded by his smooth tongue and high looks.

"You are dead," Linnet stammered. "Run through by Sir Marmaduke's sword—"

"Aye, and a well-deserved end it was," Kenneth owned, his deep voice . . . accepting.

His gaze pinning her, he came closer, the flames licking round him scorching her, the intensity of his heat scalding the breath in her lungs.

He reached a hand toward her, let it fall as quickly.

"Ach . . . dinna cringe, my dear lady," he said, a shadow crossing his still-handsome face, the ne'er forgotten richness of his voice curdling her blood.

"I told you once that you had not seen the last of me . . . that we would meet again," he said, the sad echo behind his words undermining her best efforts to shield herself . . . to hide from whate'er vileness he desired of her.

"You are a ghost," Linnet protested, her fingers clamping round the edge of her stool. "I am not . . . seeing you."

"Alas . . . I am here all the same, fair lady." He shrugged, flashed her a travesty of his old smile, his voice so close by her ear she feared his sulfurous breath would singe her hair.

"But ne'er you worry . . . 'tis not forgiveness for long-ago sins that I ask of you." He made an expansive gesture with his hand. "You can see I am doing ample penance, am slowly losing the taint of deeds, a life I truly repent."

Linnet tried to look away from him, struggled to leap from her stool and run from the solar . . . escape *him*.

But her limbs had turned to lead, holding her soundly in place and damning her to the whims of her *gift's* latest nightmare.

Not that her heart would have allowed her to flee if even she could, for something in Kenneth's eyes held her captive and made some small part of her heart melt for him . . . let her almost believe his anguish.

The depth of his pain . . . the soul-wrenching plea her fright-filled ears refused to hear.

"A boon, naught more. . . ."

That, she heard, and her eyes rounded with terror.

Sakes, she could even feel her own heartbeat pulsing through her body, tickling fingers of ice creeping up and down her spine.

"A boon?" The two words left her tongue of their own

volition, scarce more than a squeak but the specter heard them . . . and smiled satisfaction.

He nodded at her, his smile deepening, but unlike his earthly smiles, this one held warmth and hope. "Naught that you cannot give without pain . . . so as I have e'er observed you."

Linnet swallowed, her heart falling open just a wee bit more when he crossed his arms in a gesture so like the Black Stag's her breath snagged in her throat.

For one full crazed moment, she glimpsed his once-pulsating handsomeness, the spent and wasted vitality, and . . . sorrowed for their loss.

And her husband's loss, for she knew that once, in another time and place, he'd trusted and loved this man to the last inch of his soul.

Her Duncan's only brother.

Bastard, blackguard, or nay.

"The boon, milady . . . I ask not for myself, but for them."

"Them?"

Nodding, he pointed to a fluttering tear in the sheets of flame surrounding them . . . a narrow, vertical opening that showed thronging clouds of blue and bright-glinting water, a tiny speeding horse with two riders streaking at a pace across the high moors toward the horizon, soon to vanish from view.

"I do not understand." Linnet pushed the words past the dryness in her throat. "You must tell me more."

But the specter was retreating now, his every backward step taking him deeper into the wall of crackling flames and letting her catch sweet, reassuring glimpses of the Lady's Solar's own tapestry-hung surrounds.

"I made many wrong choices in my life, milady, e'er took the darkest path or walked in the bitterest winds," he said, his voice fainter now, the flames fading with his image.

Would that I could undo my misdeeds. . . .

Linnet blinked, scarce hearing him for he was now little more than a shadow before the hearth, his once-proud form only visible at all because of the flickering vermilion edging his fast-fading silhouette.

His last words no longer spoken but borne on the night breeze circling round the solar.

Pray, dear lady, have mercy on one who repents and do not let innocents pay for my ill doings . . .

Do not allow her to flee . . . be gentle to him when he comes . . .

I beg you on your soul . . .

And then he was gone, leaving only a still, sepulchral darkness behind.

Linnet shuddered, hugged herself against the sudden biting cold. She glanced round, not yet convinced he had vanished—not truly certain he'd come at all.

For the only flames now crackling in the Lady's Solar were the smoky-sweet ones licking quietly at the red-glowing peat bricks on the hearthstone.

And the only blue in good glimpsing distance proved Lady Caterine's skirts and the deep late-night blue pressing hard against the tall, arch-topped windows.

Kenneth's emptiness and sadness did remain behind, the essence of unspoken what-ifs and might-have-beens, the sorrowful vestiges of an ill-spent and broken life, lingering in the air to squeeze her heart, haunt her, and fill her with a fierce and burning determination to fulfill her late good-brother's sole request.

Not that she knew what exactly would be required of her—or why her husband's long-dead nemesis would take interest in Robbie's flame-haired lass.

The maid she'd glimpsed on the horse could be no other.

The fury-bitten man she'd not worry about—for the nonce.

She would do all in her power to keep the maid from fleeing, would thwart any and all attempts . . . be they with Robbie if he'd indeed been the grim-faced rider.

Or, if not, with any other unfortunate soul who might attempt to waylay the lass.

That much she could do.

So soon as she'd regained her composure and convinced her sister she'd only swooned o'er that one's startling but jubilant news.

Drawing on a well of strength that ne'er failed to astound her, Linnet sat up straighter on her stool and grabbed her stitching cloth, using its clumsily-embroidered length to mop the dampness from her brow.

She'd been warned and such warnings were oft blessings in disguise, so she'd take good heed and mayhap even attempt to soften her lord husband's bitterness toward his long-reviled late brother and foe.

She had no need of magical bronze cauldrons to judge a man's character.

Though a charm or a spell to help her turn her husband's mind might be most welcome indeed.

But slip past his shields she would.

And with such stealth he'd ne'er know what had hap-

pened to him until she stood quietly before the deepest,
darkest corners of his heart and shone light into them all.

❧

Robbie stood before the single window in his old bedchamber and breathed deep of the chill night air. Blessedly *fresh* air tinged only with the damp of the rain and
the cold-gritty smell of wet stone.

Air not tainted by the faint but pervasive bite of roused
female and musky masculine lust.

Two odors that pulsed like a raw throb throughout the
immaculate, sparsely furnished little chamber whether
his teensy, flashing-eyed betrothed chose to ignore the
smells or nay.

He noted them well.

As he'd also spotted the opened jar of some kind of
glistening whitish ointment . . . and the jar's telltale proximity to a small, three-legged stool.

A stool he knew stood in a direct viewing line beneath
the little room's well-hidden squint hole.

Confirmation enough that his giggling sisters had spoken true.

He looked down, examined the shard of the broken
ewer in his hands. A jagged piece that included the ill-
fated ewer's handle—brought along as evidence and explanation for the lady's missing dinner tray.

And to keep his hands busy so fidgeting fingers would
not reveal his nervousness, the maddening importance of
persuading the lady Euphemia to heed his proposal with
goodness and grace.

Attributes he doubted she possessed . . . even if she did appear to be inordinately adept at *speed.*

Frail and ailing as she purportedly was, ripening with child or no, how she'd managed to dress so quickly, and secret away whoe'er must've been in here, proved a puzzle too great for Robbie's cudgeled wits.

Stunned disbelief still knotted his tongue, but he supposed he ought be grateful that someone relished the maid's *enchantments.*

He, for one, thought it best to admire her from a distance.

For the nonce, the scant breadth of his boyhood chamber would suffice.

Later, so soon as he'd made her more amenable to his suggestions and settled certain matters, as far apart and miles distant as he could arrange.

With hope, a Douglas would savor her enticements as a Highland heiress enough to accept her with a swelling belly.

"Ah, well," he said at last, twirling the ewer shard round his thumb, "mayhap if I'd not dropped your dinner tray and you'd been able to stave your hunger, you would not find the notion of wedding a Douglas so unpalatable?"

She colored—and held her perturbed silence. Save for a quick, harsh cough and a barely audible imprecation she could not quite keep from slipping out with the cough.

A low-muttered spot of insult that had sounded suspiciously like . . . hen piddle.

Hen piddle on the Douglases.

Ignoring the slur, Robbie glanced at the still-opened

door. "Shall I order more victuals?" he asked, giving her his most solicitous smile. "Another dinner tray . . . and with two goblets?"

Not to be intimidated, however peaceably, she squared her shoulders and frowned.

"I am not a plump-bottomed and complaisant byre-wench to be cast off to another, shoved aside as carelessly as the people of this castle toss bones to your hounds," she said in a tone of angry hauteur.

"God aiding me, I could wish it otherwise," she added, "but I require two chalices because I must guard my health, Sir Robert." She fixed him with a tight-lidded stare. "Wine becomes me better if imbibed from a fresh goblet."

"To be sure, and I stand rebuked, my lady," Robbie said, summoning a look of due contrition and praying his lips wouldn't twitch at the lie.

Pure deceit rolled off her in waves—her heckling indignation icy, but unconvincing.

She gave him a frosty little smile, flicked a speck of dust from the table's well-scrubbed surface. "I will not be bargained off to a Douglas—and if they do consider themselves one of the proudest houses of Scotland."

"They *are* a great and noble house," Robbie amended.

She said nothing more, but did not have to, for the arch-browed look she aimed at him was defiance personified.

Brandishing a sword or even shaking her fists at him would not have been a more effective measure of her refusal to listen to reason.

Robbie heaved a great sigh and folded his arms over his chest.

Alas for his hopes.

She was leaving him little alternative but to prove how little of the faint-heart dwelt in a MacKenzie.

So he crossed the room and stood before her, doing his best to imitate the look his father and uncle e'er bestowed on unruly squires caught slacking off at their swordery training.

"For truth, my lady," he said, rubbing his chin, "Douglas men are the stuff of heroes—valiants every one of them. And since you have not deigned to even once come down to the hall to greet me since my return, I would have thought the prospect of a potential husband of such stature and worth would have you going to sleep well content and rising happy?"

"I sleep well enough here," she said, reaching round him to close the window shutters against the night's chill and windy drizzle.

Straightening, she wiped her hands on her skirts and fixed him with her dark-eyed stare.

"I did not leave my quarters this long time because I have not been well—no other reason. I am pleased with our alliance and have no interest in marriage to a Douglas or any other man in the south—great lord or otherwise," she informed him, smug satisfaction glowing all over her.

Stepping closer to the table, she trailed her small fingers over a platter of half-eaten honeyed cakes. "I have heard the folk of the south are horned and tailed."

Robbie stifled a snort of laughter.

"There are enough who say the same of my father as you will ken," he said instead, eyeing her with a gaze as direct as her own . . . and praying the saints to wipe the image of her nakedness from his mind.

A memory that made his throat burn to guzzle an entire flagon of good Highland *uisge-beatha*.

Mayhap even two flagons.

Enough of the fine and fiery *water-of-life* to banish the image as easily as waking ended a fearing dream.

Crossing his arms again, he waited until she'd finished a honey cake before he spoke.

"The deepest pits of hell and the sweetest of heavens can be found anywhere, my lady," he said, assuming a tone he hoped was eloquent but laced with well-meaning authority.

"Just as my father is no true devil," he went on, "neither do the men of south walk on cloven feet. Indeed, you might find the south much to your favor . . . the gentler air ought prove kindly to your health."

Ignoring him, she lit the night candle on its iron pricket beside the bed, then came back to the table to open a little wooden casket. Her face set, she scooped up a handful of aromatic herbs and tossed them onto the hearth fire.

"The herbs help my cough," she explained, dusting her hands. "They suffice. I have no need to venture—"

"Your cough, my lady, is all the more reason to at least consider the south—the possibilities I am offering you."

Her eyes flashed. "So you might be free to indulge in more than a dalliance with . . . with your flaunting, flame-haired peasant?"

Robbie frowned, raised a silencing hand.

"You misjudge," he said, his voice allowing no rebuttal. "The maid Juliana might not be of high blood, but she has a more pure heart and mind than many who are, and I will not hear any ill spoken of her."

He set down the ewer shard, held her gaze.

"'Twas I who brought her here . . . not her own contrive. She neither desired nor asked to come with me," he added, remembering. "And I would meet any man to his beard who treats her without courtesy. You would be well counseled to greet her fairly as well."

Lady Euphemia made an annoyed *cluck-clucking* sound with her tongue, but refrained from comment.

"I am pleased you understand," he said, not missing how her eyes narrowed with resentment.

He was not going to let her maneuver him into a discussion about his beauty . . . in especial, Juliana's virtue.

Not when the reek of the lady's own flagrant indiscretions yet drenched the air, filling his nostrils. The sharp scent of a female stirred, in this instance, repulsing rather than arousing him.

"Nor am I the ogre you allude," he minded her, not quite able to keep the scowl from his brow, but amazed at the calm of his tone.

He drew a deep breath—badly needing its steadying brace despite the penetrating odor.

"Be assured," he said, picking his words carefully, "my proposals, including my offer to return your dowry and top it with a prodigious boon, are well meant and presented only with our best interests in heart."

"This time you err, Sir Robert," Lady Euphemia huffed, throwing back her thin shoulders. "*My* best interests lie here, and have since the windy morning I arrived."

She lifted her chin, turned a withering gaze on him.

"I will not be bundled off to wed another and nor shall

I return to Castle Uisdean *un*wed—even if you were a man only fit to catch whelks!"

"Think hard on what I have offered you, my lady," Robbie said, in a different voice than he'd yet used on her.

He flicked a hand at the walls. "You might be wise to mind that the very stones of this keep watch and whisper. I think you can consider yourself treated none so poorly by either suggestion I've made?"

It was the closest to a warning he intended to give her.

She nodded, wordless, a faint tinge of hostility glimmering in her eyes.

A temporary victory . . . but only of a small skirmish.

Still frowning, Robbie drew another great breath, then, without so much as glancing at her, strode to the window. Needful of air, he reopened the shuttering.

Not enough to further incite the lady's ire.

But enough to allow a rush of chill night wind to cool the heat pulsing up his throat before he forgot his wits and challenged her outright, risked making a crack-pated fool of himself.

Much better for them both if he could *reason* her away rather than stoop to the ruination of her name.

An alternative with consequences that did not bear dwelling on.

So he gritted his teeth and stared out the window, his mind and emotions in a whirl, and let the beloved panorama soothe him. As always, his frustration drained away, receding and lessening the longer he looked down at the night-silvered waters of the loch, the familiar hills rising beyond. Each well-cherished peak, a dark mass against the scudding rain clouds, every rugged contour softened by drifting curtains of mist.

A perfect night to his mind and heart.

A blessed one marred only by the renewed fulminations of the wee slip of a dark-eyed lass harping at him from somewhere across the room, doing her worst to vex him.

". . . may as well toss me into a quaking bog and suffer me to drown on peat-broth," she snipped, her agitation plain in the sharp rasp of her voice, the *wheeze* that gave Robbie a distinct jab of guilt . . . despite what he suspected and knew of her.

She appeared at his elbow then, leaned against the cold, damp stone of the window's edge to peer up at him with glittering eyes, one hand pressed hard to her smallish breasts, her displeasure palpable.

"I will not accept such shame, Sir Robert, I—"

"There is no shame in becoming the wife of any good and worthy man," Robbie said dryly, his gaze on the dark rippling surface of the loch. "The Douglases are—"

"No loftier than my own race."

Turning aside, she pressed her lips together and shot an irritated glance at a nearby wall sconce as its candle hissed and sputtered in a sudden gust of cold wind.

"The MacLeods descend from the Norse god Odin," she informed him, swatting at the drift of smoke billowing out from the guttered candle.

As soon as the smoke began to dissipate, she turned back to him, pinned him with another haughty stare. "A good seannachie needs a full five nights to recount our lineage."

"And I, my lady, shall give you longer . . . a full sennight, to consider what I have proposed," Robbie said, more than conscious of the sharp female scent still clinging to her—even here by the opened window.

Even with the heavy smell of burning tallow lingering in the chill, damp air.

"Think on what I have said, lady," he bid her, repressing a shudder.

Then he schooled his features into blandness, gave her a curt nod, and strode from the chamber.

Swiftly, before he was tempted to toss her o'er his shoulder and return her to Castle Uisdean . . . now, this very night.

Dark-flashing eyes, tight-pursed lips, protestations, and all.

Indeed, for less than the scantiest wager, he'd seriously consider the pleasure.

But he'd give her the promised sennight.

Seven days and nights to see the wisdom of his offer.

If not, he'd suffer the consequences to his own good name and haul her back to her drunkard sire in clanking chains, sackcloth, and ashes.

Then he'd blacken his reputation further by making his beauty his true lady the very next day.

And just as thoroughly and irrevocably as he meant to claim her body this night.

Chapter Thirteen

✦

PANIC CLAWED AT JULIANA'S HEART.

Hot, deadly talons digging ever deeper and spilling blood. She winced, tried her best not to see her candlelit chamber as a dark, empty place. The cold night, a vacuum of silence and regrets.

But the quivers of heated excitement that had been whipping through her for hours now slid as shivers of dread down her back, chilling her, as minute by passing minute, the evening that had held so much promise slipped into a timeless void of reeling uncertainties and doubt.

For long after she'd given up on her knight's arrival, she sat on the padded stone bench of her bedchamber's window embrasure, cuddling Mungo on her lap, stroking his soft, furry warmth, and trying not to keep peering across the room to the door.

Juliana frowned.

Nay, the unbarred and unmoving door, she amended.

She shifted on the bench, bit down on her lower lip, a

rush of heat washing over her as she yielded to temptation and slid yet another quick glance across the room.

Nothing had changed.

Despite the concentrated penetration of her stare, the
door did not swing open to admit her knight.

He did not loom up on the threshold, his braw self filling the doorway, dazzling her with his dimpled smile,
stealing her breath . . . his very presence vanquishing her
cares.

She swallowed, struggled to ignore the hot thickness
welling in her throat.

Faith, but the stillness played on her taut nerves like a
tight-drawn bowstring. Her heart pounding, she tore her
gaze from the door, drew her legs up onto the cushioned
bench, and tucked her borrowed bed-robe more securely
round her knees.

Naked knees . . . as was the rest of her beneath the voluminous folds of the furred bed-robe.

A fool concession she'd allowed her sauciest side to
indulge. A brazen act of nonsense that now made her
cheeks flame . . . as did the simplest glance about the
chamber.

Saints of glory, everywhere she looked, her gaze lit on
evidence of the hot-burning hope she'd vested in this
night.

The carefully tended peats glimmering red in the
hearth seemed to stare back at her, their usual warmth and
cozy comfort now a study in recrimination. Even the
well-loved smell, so dark and earthy-sweet, failed to con-
sole her.

And the branches of fine beeswax candles glowing on
the linen-covered trestle table appeared to laugh at her

folly—her belief that a dashing knight of gentlest birth could desire a maid of the glen.

That one such as he might see past her work-worn hands and good-for-birthing hips, to the shining-eyed lass within who only hoped to please him.

Pulsing heat swept up her neck at the thought and she drew another long breath, wished the cold air pouring through the shutter slats would cool her—if not her raging shame and other worries, then at least her flushed skin.

Instead, she tortured herself further by letting her gaze continue to wander. Even the simple act of poking her bared toes into the floor rushes cried her foolhardiness.

Had she truly sweetened the rushes with fragrant handfuls of dried heather and rose petals taken with permission from the herbarium stores?

In the hope of delighting her knight's senses?

To help set the mood if her own charms proved . . . inadequate?

Aye, she had.

Mortified at how easily she'd capitulated, she dug her fingers into wee Mungo's fur, tousled the softness of his floppy ears, and reminded herself of the supposed steel in her spine, the fortitude she'd e'er prided herself on.

And there could be no doubt . . . she *was* strong.

Resilient.

Some had even called her the most indomitable lass in all Glenelg.

Her mettle was legion.

Even if her considerable daring chose this ill-fated night to abandon her.

She shifted on the bench, smoothed the folds of her

bed-robe. Flown mettle or no, she would *not* look at the freshly made bed, its linens pristine and snowy white.

Nor would she glance at the untouched mound of cushions she'd piled before the hearth in such a flurry of passion . . . a hastily tossed-together collection of wantonness she'd arranged within the fire's circle of warmth, an indulgence she'd allowed herself in a moment of tingling madness and yearnings.

Yearnings.

Her heart split wide on the word.

Sitting up straighter, she swiped a hand across her cheek, refusing to let the scalding heat pricking the backs of her eyes well into tears.

Willing the sensation to recede, she pulled in yet another great, lung-filling breath and immediately wished she hadn't for, this time, along with the chill, peat-laced air, came still more reminders of her folly . . . the lingering scent of lavender.

Saints preserve her, even the decidedly pleasing scent of her own freshly bathed and oiled skin shot ribbons of heat streaking all through her. Just thinking about her painstaking ablutions intensified the blaze of her already-flushing cheeks and tightened the viselike clamp of disquiet crushing her ribs and squeezing her heart.

A laming disquiet not borne of shame for finally succumbing to the wondering awe that had been simmering so hotly and that she'd hoped would unfold in all its sweet beauty this e'en, but an ill ease brewing up from certain fragments of memory.

Quickening threads of persistence, stirring inside her and unwinding the past. Each one etching her night not with answers but questions that stared at her from the shadows, expressionless and intense.

Bits and pieces of all her yesterdays . . . unpleasant and puzzling truths sluicing iciest water over the dearest of her hopes and dreams.

Troublesome tidings she'd have to share with her knight at once . . . if even he yet appeared, at this late hour.

She hugged Mungo closer, rubbed absently at the back of his small neck, and took solace in his plump, warm weight in her lap. Closing her eyes, she tried to hear only the wind at the shutters and the splatter of rain on the window ledge.

Above all, she struggled to stop straining her ears for the sound of a man's eager footsteps on stone. Or the welcome creak of the heavy oaken door swinging wide, the telltale scrape of wood moving over the floor rushes to herald his return.

But no such sounds came.

Only the hollow whistling of the wind over the loch and the wet, restless breathing of the night curling ever so close around the tower walls.

Nothing else broke through her whirring confusion. The half-dreamed, half-remembered imaginings swirling through her like water tumbling over rapids.

Just little Mungo's stirrings as he squirmed on her lap, growing restless until she lifted him for a quick kiss between his ears, then set him on the rushes . . . there, just at the base of the window embrasure's opposite-facing stone bench.

Right where she'd also placed Devorgilla's healing cream.

Not surprisingly, the little jar seemed to wink up at her, all innocence and challenge, its fat-sided roundness daring her to retrieve it and smooth its creamy contents across her brow yet again.

Truth be told, she was certain that doing so would set the images to life again, each application of the ointment nudging another memory out of her.

Mayhap next time the one she most dreaded.

The one she did not want to know.

Her brow knitting, she pushed at the jar with her foot, using her toe to bury it beneath the rushes. And as quickly as she could for with just that simple contact, another disturbing round of memories came flooding back to assault her.

Her full name . . . Juliana Mackay.

Her late mother's name . . . Marjory Mackay.

And the name of the man whose lifelong largesse her mother had so desperately wished to repay.

"Lass?"

Juliana's heart stopped.

He stood leaning against the edge of the window embrasure, arms folded as he watched her, his most disarming smile soundly in place . . . and melting her.

She blinked, her mouth suddenly dry, her tongue too thick for words.

He looked wholly at ease, even amused, his gaze going unerringly to her outstretched leg, now frozen in place, her naked foot buried deep beneath the thick layer of rushes.

"If your feet are cold, sweetness, there are other ways to warm them," he said, dropping to one knee before her, his boyishly-dimpled smile turning deliciously lazy.

Dangerous.

"Shall I show you, Juliana?" He looked at her so deeply she feared he could see clear through to her soul . . . mayhap even to the dark and alarming things she now remembered.

Dread things she wished had ne'er come back to her.

"H'mmm, lass?" He lifted a brow, his hand already hovering over her naked calf. "Shall I . . .warm you?"

Juliana stared at him, so caught by the want and need beginning to spiral inside her that she could not move. Not even when the edge of her bed-robe slid away to reveal a goodly expanse of her bare thigh to go along with the already exposed nakedness of her calf and half-buried foot.

More alarming still, the cailleach's little pot of healing ointment had gone hot as fire and, she would swear, vibrated crazily against her toes.

Indeed, the wee round pot of fired clay sent streaks of prickling, white-hot flames shooting up her leg to burst onto her cheeks. A wave of molten delight to spill through her entire body and ignite a firestorm of heated tingles in certain unmentionable places.

A saturating, *dampening* intimacy Juliana recognized for what it was, and the shock of her arousal nigh undid her.

She cleared her throat, moistened her lips. "I—I . . . did not hear you enter," she got out, conquering her tongue at last. "I no longer expected you to come."

"Ahhh, but you did earlier, did you not, my beauty?" His gaze flickered to the pile of pillows before the hearth fire, the softly burning candles, the pristine expanse of the carefully turned down bed. "You even unbound your hair."

He touched the bright-gleaming strands, lifted a handful to his lips. "Aye, you prepared for me, Juliana, that I can see, and . . . you grew cold in the waiting. For that I am sorry, my heart." He looked at her, such an expression of mutual knowing in his eyes, she could scarce draw breath. "Never fear, sweetness, together we shall banish the chill."

"I am not cold," she spoke true, for she burned with the fiercest of blazes.

His heated gaze and the sensual promise behind his words set her to trembling, sent a rage of all-consuming fire sweeping through her, and made her heart beat wildly.

A small sound escaped her. She looked at him in the dimness of the window embrasure. "I am. . . ."

Burning.

I am aflame, she'd almost cried, only to have the admission lodge in her throat, held there by the same worries and cares that almost flooded her eyes with bittersweet tears again.

The unmentionable, unanswered concern still digging into her sides like greedy, hot-ripping talons.

No matter how much her knight's hot glances and sweet words might rouse her flesh. Or how fiercely brilliant need spurred her passion, making her ache to touch and taste him.

But even if her heart was already given, her mind cringed from what might be an even greater sin than desiring and lying with another woman's betrothed.

He leaned forward then, slipping his hand around her

neck to cradle her head. He stretched his fingers into her hair, and his gentling caresses proved an almost unbearable sweetness.

"You are troubled, lass, and you needn't be—all will be well, I promise you," he told her, resting his cheek against her hair.

She swallowed a sigh, wanting to believe him. *Needing* to trust him. Faith, just the underlying longing in his voice melted her, softening her like wax beneath a flame.

Still, his assurances let a surge of hope rise in her heart . . . but her confidence spiraled away again almost at once, its fragileness submerged by the uneasiness still beating inside her.

"See you, I have spoken with the lady Euphemia," he said, stroking his fingers through her hair, kindling the heat building inside her. "I am certain an amenable resolution can be found—and soon."

He lifted a section of her hair, let the strands spill through his fingers as he looked at her, studying her face. Possibly sensing the degree of her distress, he released her hair and framed her face with his hands, leaned forward to kiss her brow.

"Aye, to be sure," he promised, his expression one of absolute certainty. "You have no cause to be burdened, my sweet. I have given her a sennight—and two wise and good choices, the neither of which will bring her shame."

"And sorrow, my lord?"

She had to ask, and immediately knew a pang because she'd posed the question more for her own heart's peace than out of concern for the other woman.

Shivering anew, but with the night's true cold this

time, Juliana drew her furred bed-robe closer around her. "What will you do if she accepts neither of the suggestions you've pressed on her?"

"Ach, she will want the one or the other, I grant you," he supplied, sounding most certain. Still holding her face, he stroked her cheeks, traced the curve of her lips. "You must trust me," he added, his hand curling round her nape again, his fingers tangling in the heavy silk of her hair. "I say you, she has sharp wits, the lass does. She will see the sense in . . . acquiescing."

Juliana glanced aside, not sure of that at all—nor of how her knight might react to her own tidings, the question she must pose him.

And what *her* reaction would be to the wrong answer.

For a moment his fingers tensed against the back of her neck and his eyes darkened, his expression growing earnest. "That one will not be appearing on the threshold, never you worry," he said with a nod toward the door.

The closed and *barred* door, she noted, for he'd slid the drawbar soundly in place.

"You needn't keep casting glances that way," he added, clearly mistaking why she'd looked away.

"I was looking for Mungo," she improvised, blurting the first thing that came to her mind.

"Mungo?"

"Aye . . . he was just here," she said, looking round for him.

Not quite a ploy, but neither a full untruth, for she did wish to know where the puppy had gone since he'd already once sniffed a wee bit too close to the peat fire, his curiosity earning him burned paws and a bit of a singed nose.

"Have I seen your wee protector?" Her knight took the bait and cocked a jaunty brow at her. "Och, to be sure and the mite dashed over to greet me when I came in," he said, leaning forward to kiss her again, this time on the tip of her nose. "But just now, the wee beastie sleeps, curled in the warmth of the brazier near your bed."

Juliana nodded, and squelched the rising urge to follow the puppy's lead and flit across the room to her own great four-poster, dive in and yank shut the bed curtains, burrow beneath the coverings, and ne'er come out again.

Mayhap not even for air—until all her problems were resolved.

But she dismissed the notion at once.

She'd ne'er been one to run from difficulties.

In especial, not a strapping, dark-haired difficulty still whiling on bended knee before her, his sunniest smile beaming its dimpled way straight into her heart.

And lighting the dearest kisses on her face!

"Wee Mungo fares well enough, minx," he was saying, his gaze moving over her as he spoke, the slow deliberation of his perusal, and the softness of his kisses making her . . . needy. "*You* will soon burn with a heat much finer than the warmth of a brazier."

Juliana swallowed, shifted on the cushions of the stone bench, quite certain her heart would stop beating any moment. Mayhap even on her very next exhale.

He still held his hand poised over her bared calf. As if sensing how close she was to losing herself, he let his fingers hover but a scant hairbreadth above her skin.

So close she could feel the heat streaming out of him, feel its drenching possession flowing over her, pouring into her, and making her throb and ache . . . everywhere.

"I am going to warm you now, Juliana," he said, the smooth richness of his deep voice sending waves of dizzying heat whirling through her. "But only if you desire my touch. You must tell me the words."

He looked at her, the thrumming sensuality rolling off him thickening the air. "So tell me, Juliana . . . would you like me to touch you?"

She could only nod, every inch of her, inside and out, prickling with need. The hot pulsing building in the secret place between her legs made *that part of her* contract and tingle even as she ran hot with dampening liquid fire.

She opened her mouth to say something—anything— but the whirling sensations seemed to have tied her tongue in knots.

And he hadn't even placed a finger on her leg yet!

He was merely watching her.

But the heat in his gaze ignited a hunger within her such as she'd never known and its potency made her smolder and burn so deliciously she could scarce bear the anticipation welling inside her.

"I see your need, Juliana," he said, lowering his hand again so that this time only the merest sliver of air separated his fingers from the bared skin of her calf, "but that is not good enough. I would hear the words. Say 'Yes, Robbie, I want you to touch me . . . caress and feel all of me.'"

"*All of me?*" Juliana's brows shot upward, some of her bravura leaving her.

Especially when she shifted on the stone bench and the edges of her bed-robe slid back another few inches to expose still more of her thigh. "Your hand is hovering above my calf, sir, not . . . the entirety of me."

He gave her a look of feinted surprise.

"Och! Only your calf, is it?" He teased her, looked down to where his hand almost rested on her flesh.

"But you will enjoy my touch on the whole of your leg, will you not, Juliana? Every deliciously exposed inch of you."

"Of me?" She blinked. "Every inch?"

He nodded, his smile deepening into a wolfish grin.

Juliana gulped.

Wary now, she gave him a narrow-eyed look, something about the gleam in his eyes, the roguish uptilt of his smile setting the whole of her body in wild-spinning sensual turmoil.

"What do you mean . . . *deliciously exposed*?"

Dreading what she'd see but unable not to look, she glanced down, her breath immediately catching in both embarrassment and excitement.

As she'd suspected, the edges of the bed-robe had indeed fallen away from her thighs and the resulting gap clearly revealed the red-gold triangle of her lower curls.

In truth, almost the whole of her vulnerability!

"Oh!" She clapped one hand over her exposed heat and grabbed for the edge of the bed-robe with the other.

"Nay, Juliana. Do not cover yourself." He seized her wrists and returned her hands to the bench, pressing them in place before letting go, as if warning her to keep them there.

"I have seen your nakedness before—and in all its ripe golden sweetness—as you know," he said, the huskiness of his voice sliding beneath her skin, exciting her.

Chasing all else from her mind.

"See you, it pleases me to have you fully open for my

delectation," he said, his words making the lowest part of her belly tighten and grow heavy with hollow, hot-throbbing awareness. "And, my sweet, you will enjoy my touch all the more if I gaze on you, if you watch me looking at the most intimate part of you as I rub your leg . . . as I *warm* you, Juliana."

"But—"

He pressed two fingers against her lips. "You must say the words, minx," he urged, the focused heat of his gaze on her woman's flesh making her tremble. "Repeat the words for me . . . 'Yes, touch me . . . *caress and feel my nakedness.*' "

"Ooooooh, I cannot say anything suchlike," Juliana moaned, keenly aware of the wetness beginning to damp her inner thighs.

A female triumph she'd heard of from a scatter of married lasses in Glenelg . . . a wondrous glory she would have joyed in experiencing did she not have other troublesome thoughts plaguing her, casting dark shadows upon her happiness.

"You want me to touch you, Juliana," her knight was saying, his gaze still fastened on *that part* of her.

"Come, lass. Say the words and I shall . . . satisfy your wishes."

"My wishes?"

He nodded. "Any and all of them."

Juliana's eyes flew wide.

Her wishes!

Merciful saints, she did not ken what greater sweetness she could wish for . . . already, the very tops of her ears were on fire, the tips of her toes, equally a-blaze.

His words swirled around her, too. Seductive eddies,

each honey-sweet whirl bringing another bone-melting wave of deliciousness that undid her resistance and made her forget everything but his dark, heart-stopping beauty.

And how luxuriously exciting it was to feel his stare devouring her most intimate place.

"The words, Juliana."

"Yes, touch me. And keep . . . looking at me. Down there, as you are now doing, for I find your gaze on me— *excites* me, aye," she blurted, surrendering at last, the recently wakened wildness inside her making her angle her outstretched leg a bit more to the side—just enough to better his view.

And increase the deliciously hot pulsings weighting the deepest part of her belly. A sensation she recognized as mutual unbridled need. Faith, it pulled so taut between them, the sheer intensity of their passion crackled the chill air.

"Aye, do all those things—and more. Please," she breathed, aching for his touch. No longer needing to gather her courage, for the arousal spooling through her made her bold. "Caress and feel . . . all of me. *Everywhere.*"

"Everywhere?" That was a groan—soft and husky. "Och, but I shall, sweetness—and all the night through if it pleases you."

The barest of smiles quirking his mouth, he touched her at last, sliding his hand up and down her calf, letting his fingertips tease the backs of her knees, the light caress sending bolts of pure molten heat arcing straight to her loins.

All the night through.

The words rang in her ears.

Only four words, harmlessly spoken, but they stole some of the hot-thrumming pleasure from her blood, something about them affecting her as deeply as his soothing touch roused her.

She wanted more than one night . . . she burned for an entirety of such nights. An endless succession of intimate entanglings of their bodies and souls. Their hearts. But some lingering darkness taunted her, minding her with cold certainty that the melting sweetness he promised could not be hers.

Could ne'er be hers.

But he was still sliding his hand up and down her leg, stroking gently, the callused pads of his circling fingertips a thrilling contrast to the smooth sleekness of her thigh. Each slow, deliberate glide reverberating through her, driving her to madness.

Then he inched his hand higher, let his fingers slide inward so they reached the dampness misting the tender skin of her inner thighs. The musky-scented wetness oh-so-close to her throbbing woman's flesh. And the moment he touched that glistening dampness, the whole of her body came alive, tingling and spinning with his luscious discovery.

"Oooh!" Her hips lifted off the bench at that first near-intimate contact, the bed-robe now falling wholly open, its wide-gaping edges freeing the ripe swells of her full-rounded breasts. Her tight and proud nipples thrust toward him, a bold testament of her arousal.

"Oh, indeed, there is my precious minx," he agreed, arching a brow as he glided his fingers ever so close to her quivering heat. "Look down, sweetness, watch me touching you."

And this time she complied at once, swiftly lowering her gaze to where his fingers traced the most breath-stealingly delicious patterns in the wetness dewing her soft skin.

"The center of your womanhood is wetter still, Juliana. And softer," he murmured, his deep voice an intoxication.

Wetter and softer, indeed.

As if she could not tell—saints a mercy, he was melting her!

She moistened her lips, slid deeper down the bench . . . and let her legs fall apart just a wee bit more.

Nay, a lot more.

"Would you like me to touch *that* wetness, my sweet? Test and probe its softness for you?"

"M'mmm. . . ."

"I will taste you, too, Juliana," he told her, the look on his face revealing exactly *where* he meant.

Juliana's breath caught, her heart near stopping. She could not speak . . . too heady was such a notion.

"I will taste you there again and again if it pleases you."

That did it.

At once, her lower body developed a will of its own and her legs promptly opened even wider. Dear saints, she was dying. Of pleasure and lasciviousness. There could be no doubt. Ne'er could one experience such pure, unabated sensual bliss and wake up the next day to tell the tale.

"Say the words, lass." His fingertips were brushing over the tips of her nether hair now, that slight contact almost too intensely pleasurable to bear. "You must tell me this, too, my heart—that you wish me to . . . taste you."

His deep voice broke through the haze of exquisitely throbbing sweetness, and for one fleeting beat of time, the chill night breeze kissed her flushed and naked skin, cooling her flaming ardor, challenging what might be so very wrong . . .

"Come you, say me the words," he urged again . . . just in the moment her toes burrowed deeper into the rushes and nudged against Devorgilla's small jar of *all-cure* ointment.

Only rather than sizzling hot as it'd been earlier, the little earthenware jar was now possessed of a grinding cold.

An astonishing iciness that turned her toes to icicles!

Jerking back her foot as if she'd been burned, nay, *scalded* by the jar's frigidness, Juliana shot to her feet so quickly, her head spun.

She stared at her knight, purest desire still roaring through her veins, but another, deeper compulsion chilling her, turning her fast-pounding heart to ice.

Caught in a fearing dream, she dragged in a shaky breath and pressed her hands to her cheeks, uncaring when the bed-robe slipped from her shoulders to pool on the floor.

Scarce aware of the cold night air on her heated skin, she stood fully unclothed, naked save for the spill of her gleaming hair, rippling wildly to her hips, shimmering with the reflection of the candle shine.

That, and the suspiciously bright glimmer of moisture in her magnificent moss-green eyes.

"Guidsakes, lass!"

Robbie leapt to his feet with equal speed and grabbed her arms, steadying her. Saints, she was swaying, even looked as if she might swoon dead away on him.

"For truth, lass, I meant to set you alight—not bolting to your feet like a cornered doe." He touched her face, stroked her cheek. "I thought . . ."

He broke off, releasing her, heat scoring his own face now, shaming him for pressing her, for boldly assuming he'd won her heart and that she needed him with the same hunger he desired her.

"You thought I wished . . . that I wanted—"

She broke off, her gaze lighting briefly on the still-prominent lift in his plaid, but rather than color so prettily as she usually did, the last vestiges of her fetching blush drained from her face, the wonder of just moments before now replaced by a shadow that made his heart lurch.

"You *did* desire . . . this," he said, waving a helpless, frustrated hand. "I saw it writ all o'er you—God's bones, I can even *smell* your need."

He looked down, stared at his hand. Sakes, his fingers were still damp with the wetness of her arousal!

She followed his gaze, her eyes widening as she, too, clearly spotted and recognized the telltale glistening on his fingertips.

But to his dismay, she clapped a hand over her lips, swung about, and fair flew across the room to a little table near the hearth.

A table very close to where she'd so carefully arranged a veritable sea of cushions on the floor and strewn the rushes with so many dried rose petals and crushed heather sprigs.

Preparations even the dimmest of wits would comprehend.

So what madness had flown into her?

"Aye, I wanted you—*desired* you—and still do!" she cried, whirling around, the tatty old plaid from the herbarium clutched tight against her breasts. "But now, oh, how I fear—"

"Fear?" Robbie stared at her, eyes wide. *"Me?"*

She gave a choked cry and shook her head, her eyes brimming.

Thoroughly confused, Robbie crossed the room with swift strides and pulled her into his arms. He gentled her head into the crook of his neck, cursing whate'er demons plagued her as he held her close, rocked her.

"God's mercy, sweet, what is this?"

He pulled back to look at her, struggled to keep the dark from his own brow. By the Rood, he'd just told her he was certain he'd resolved the obstacle of his betrothal, and he knew she was not a maid to cower before the passion blazing so hotly between them.

Nay, his beauty was a magnificent full woman.

Well made and perfectly crafted for a man's vigorous loving . . . *his loving.*

And his every instinct told him she'd accept his love with pride and fully unashamed. That she'd e'er be herself, without every artifice, and that she'd give back her own ardor with a passion to match his own and all the generosity and fervor he'd come to cherish in her.

So what ailed her?

"My dear sweet lass," he murmured, using his thumbs to wipe the dampness from her face, "did you not hear me? I promised you that all will be well. I swear it on my life. Now tell me what troubles you so?"

She drew a great, quivering breath. "It has naught to do with you. Not directly. Nor with . . . *her.* Your betrothed. Or scarce little, anyway," she admitted, jerking away to clutch her middle as if she might retch. "'Tis my name, see you? I—"

"Your name?"

Robbie dragged a hand through his hair, disbelief making his head pound. "God and his saints aiding me, you needn't fear telling me your name, lass. You are my heart's blood, my sole desire—there can be no name under the heavens that would make me turn from you if that is your worry."

But she only shook her head and pressed the ancient MacKenzie plaid tighter against her.

"My name is Mackay," she said, her voice choked. "Juliana Mackay. And my mother's name was Marjory Mackay."

She paused to gulp, then said no more. She simply stared at him as if she expected the name to mean something.

But it didn't.

He knew naught of the Mackays save that they were a race of the far, distant north. Of Strathnaver. The wildest, most remote region in all the Scottish realm.

"The name Mackay means nothing to me, sweetness," he said, his own heart beginning to lift again—if indeed she'd fashed over the possibility his clan might hold some long-standing blood feud with the Mackays.

Truth be told, he doubted anyone in Kintail or even all

the Isles had e'er *seen* a Mackay much less drawn a sword against one.

"Sweet," he soothed, assuming a calm tone he hoped would settle her. "You have no reason to—"

"'Tis not my name that upsets me," she cried, snatching up the coiled braid. She waved it at him, then shook the frayed and ancient plaid at him as well.

"Nay, the good name Mackay has naught to do with my sorry plight. 'Tis the name of the man who sent aid to my mother that chills my blood."

She threw the braid and the plaid to the floor, turned her back on them as if she could not bear the sight.

"Oh, Robbie, do you not see? That man was your father," she revealed, her voice anguished. "Duncan MacKenzie, the Black Stag of Kintail!"

Chapter Fourteen

✤

"*My father?*"

Robbie's jaw dropped, a startling sense of bewilderment spilling through him. Her eyes widened in shocked surprise as he stared at her, noted her turmoil. So this was the heart of what troubled her. Still, it needn't be a path to disaster. Truth be told, such a turn of events needn't be fraught with significance at all.

He shook his head, refused to acknowledge the doubts and fear clouding her lovely face, the ill ease thickening his own throat. Like as not, his father had sufficient good reason for whate'er he'd done.

Had the Black Stag indeed been Marjory Mackay's benefactor.

By all the saints, no hint of any such relationship had e'er been evident, so he tilted his head to the side, strove for a calm tone. "You are certain you have the rights of this, lass?"

His beauty nodded, her magnificent eyes bright with the shimmer of unshed tears.

"For good or ill, I remember . . . most everything," she

said, wrapping her arms around her middle again. " 'Twas here, to this keep that I was bound when you found me. My mother's last wish was to pay recompense to the Black Stag . . . to clear her debt to him."

Robbie blinked, his head still too full to think clearly.

"I have ne'er heard of him sending monies or goods to a Mackay woman," he said, grasping to piece together what she was telling him.

Also why suchlike would even upset her.

She was Highland, ought know that all great chiefs looked after their own . . . kept a beneficent eye on even the humblest folk in the emptiest glens and corners of their territories.

"If my father aided your mother, he would ne'er have expected or wanted repayment, sweetness." He tried to reassure her, determined not to let contrary winds unsettle her.

In especial, contrary winds that needn't be the great coil she seemed to fear. Saints, he could almost hear the hard beating of her heart, nigh taste the cold chills winding through her.

"Nor would such a connection be cause for your distress," he emphasized, touching her face, smoothing his knuckles down her cheek. Willing her to believe him. "All lairds, even the smallest landed knight—"

"You do not understand." She jerked her head toward the plaid and the braid. " 'Tis not the coin or my mother's wish to repay your father that is ripping my soul. 'Tis knowing how much she revered yon relics of her past."

Robbie eyed the two objects he now wished he'd ne'er pulled from her travel bag, folded his arms. "So?"

"So?" She swiped a quick hand beneath her eyes, a

trace of her bold good looks and flashing-eyed vigor showing through her discomfiture.

"They were her heart's treasures. The black-haired part of the braid came from her lover's hair. That I now know to be true," she minded him, something about her tone making his breath seize. "And because she cherished the braid and the plaid so deeply, and now knowing it was your father who aided her all these years, I must ask myself if my father truly died, see you?"

He didn't.

Not at all.

But she raised a silencing hand before he could put his bewilderment into words.

Looking as if she were about to spiral out of control, she gave a deep, shuddering sigh. "Saints save us, Sir Robert," she cried, the title strange sounding, distant, on her tongue. "See you, I suspect my father could have been your own," she declared then, panicked anguish flickering in her eyes, her voice breaking on a sob. "The Black Stag hisself . . . which would make us brother and sister!"

Robbie's eyes flew wide, his stomach clenching on her words, his very guts twisting, but then, almost as quickly, his heart soared. Relief broke over him, washing through him like a tidal flood.

The lass was sore mistaken.

A more groundless fear had ne'er passed a woman's lips.

He almost whooped with joy.

Instead, he caught her to him and rained a welter of kisses across her face.

"A greater folly has ne'er entered your mind, lass, that

I promise you," he vowed, scooping her into his arms and lowering her to the mound of cushions before the hearth fire, his heart aching to soothe her, his body burning to take possession of her.

"On my soul, I swear to you. My father may be many things, but your father he is not," he vowed, willing nothing to e'er destroy the closeness fair pulsing between them.

But she only shook her head, clearly not ready to believe him. "How can you know?"

"The same way you would—and shall—once you get to know him," Robbie declared, shrugging off his plaid before stretching out beside her on the cushions, inordinately pleased when, despite her distress, she let him lay close, even draw her tight against him.

Her ill ease was beginning to slide off of her and seeing it slip away emboldened him, filled him with elation. Enough to let him smooth her hair away from her breasts, freeing them to his view again.

"My father is a hard man, 'tis true, but he is also a fair one," he said, taking a great chance by allowing his fingers to caress and linger over the exposed swells of her breasts. He tested their plump weight, teased her nipples until they swelled and tightened for him—until his tender ministrations began making her entire body grow taut, tremble.

A sweet distraction he hoped would soon consume her, just as he prayed his low-voiced words would banish her cares and settle her troubled heart.

"I grant you, minx, just as my father is e'er ready to help those in Kintail who may need a bit of lairdly looking after, so, too, has he e'er insisted that any man of this clan to sire a bairn outside his marriage bed not only support the wee one and its mother, but also acknowledge the bond."

Encouraged by the relief slowly spreading across her face, and the languorous heat beginning to reappear in her eyes, he smoothed his hand back and forth along the pleasantly lush curve of her hip, letting his fingers glide ever closer to the hot, wet core of her.

Already, the scent of her arousal wafted up between them, pungent and enticing. "Juliana." Her breathed her name, his senses drenched with the headiness of her female musk, the smoldering regard of her gaze. "Ne'er fret," he murmured, sitting up to yank off his tunic and toss it aside before he stretched out beside her again.

"There is naught but good between us . . . in *this*," he vowed, gently slipping his hand between her thighs to let his circling fingers stroke and toy with the softness of her damp, fragrant flesh.

"Trust me," he whispered, dipping a careful finger into her sleek, velvety folds, rubbing slowly and appreciatively, "I have seen my father sort the heads of more than one clansmen who proved reluctant to own up to a child he'd sired at the wrong hearthside."

At her tremulous sigh, he lifted his fingers to his mouth, savoring her essence, making sure she saw how much he relished the taste and scent of her. He used his tongue to wet his fingertips even more, then touched them to her nipples, smoothing the dampness onto their puckering flesh, circling round and round, caressing and playing with the beautifully hardening peaks.

"I say you, lass, ne'er under the bluest of Highland heavens would my father have allowed himself to sire not one but two children and then deny them," he said, his voice husky with his own burning need as he lowered his head to her breast, replaced his fingers with his mouth.

"That, I promise you with surety," he murmured against her skin. "There stands no reason we cannot be as one." The words spoken, he flicked his tongue over her nipple, then lifted up to brush a light kiss across her lips. "Nothing can keep us apart, my minx. We can have each other now, even this night, if you so wish it?"

And she did.

Of that he was certain, for she bloomed under his gaze, his caresses. She even began rocking her hips in unmistakable invitation when he stood to unbuckle his sword belt. Entranced, he let the belt drop to the rushes, then bent to remove his brogues from his feet.

His heart pounded, every inch of him drawn so tight he wondered he did not burst. Sakes, he was so close to spilling himself now, just from the overwhelmingly lascivious rush of filling his nostrils with the heady-sharp tang of her arousal and looking down on her lying so open amongst the pillows, her bright-golden ripeness full naked and spread so sweetly before him.

Well aware that he trembled with his own need, he latched his gaze on hers and rolled down his hose and braies, kicking them aside until he'd made himself as gloriously naked as she was.

Juliana looked at him, her heart welling at the tenderness, the want, in his eyes, love and desire streaming through her. His male scent excited her, drew her gaze to the granite-hard swell at his loins, his shaft run fullstretch, throbbing for her—drenching her with anticipation and need.

Yet still, he waited, watching her with a silent question until, in sweetest response, she opened her arms to him— her arms, and her legs.

And it was there, on the bright-gleaming curls at her very center that he turned his fullest attention, his heated regard making her tingle as he settled himself between her spread thighs and began once again rubbing and exploring her most private heat with the same deliberate touches he'd used before.

"Do you truly desire this, my Juliana?" He looked up to catch and hold her gaze as he lowered his head, nuzzled her intimate curls, drinking in the scent of her. "Again, my heart, you must tell me," he added, planting soft, wet kisses across her belly. "Putting your need into words will heighten your pleasure . . . trust me."

"You want me to speak of these things? This madness of pleasure you are spending me?" She stared at him, her eyes welling with tears again, but joyous tears, a great shuddering tremor rippling through her until the whole precious length of her trembled. "Put voice to the flames licking at me? Driving me from all reason?"

Robbie inclined his head, seeing her answer in the heat of her gaze, hearing it in the hitch in her voice, the undeniable quickening of her pulse, but he wanted the words.

And he needed her reassurances.

He would not take her unless she truly trusted and desired him with the same burning urgency that consumed him.

Had consumed him since the first moment he'd laid eyes upon her.

Saints, he could scarce breathe for wanting her, and his need to bury himself deep inside her made him throb so urgently he wondered if a thousand joinings would even be enough to slake his desire for her.

"Tell me true, lass, and if you wish, we shall wait," he said, some frightfully annoying sliver of honor forcing the ludicrous offer from his tongue.

He kissed her again, on the lips this time, quick, hard, and furious . . . slaking and deep enough to taste her fully and, hopefully, to rouse her beyond all ability to resist the feverishly hot desire snapping between then.

"But . . ." he finished, releasing her lips to settle back between her thighs, "whether we wait or nay, I shall still kiss you where you burn the hottest and where your fragrance gathers the sweetest. Thereafter, I shall leave you be—if you so wish it—not touching you at all until you are well and truly mine . . . and not as my leman, but as my lady wife."

"Your lady wife?" She blinked, the wondering pleasure in her eyes more answer than the three softly whispered words. "You are certain?"

"Nothing is surer," he said, reaching to caress her breasts again, rubbing and plucking lightly at her hard-swollen nipples before slipping his fingers beneath the soft fullness of her breasts' round lower swells, savoring the satiny warmth there.

"I will wait the sennight I mentioned to you, and then, if need be, I shall take other measures to make the lady Euphemia see reason. And I shall speak with my father at the soonest," he said, still playing at her breasts, lowering his head to capture one nipple to suckle.

Juliana looked down, a sweet sigh of pleasure slipping past her lips. "You are seducing me, Sir, . . . *Robbie*," she breathed, silently willing him not to stop. "Aye, you are bespelling me. I would hear why?"

"Because I love you, lass—only you, and have for long," he vowed, knowing he did indeed love her, and beyond all distraction.

She gasped, her eyes widening with disbelief, so he silenced any possible denials with a swift, soul-searing kiss to her lips.

"Ne'er you worry, minx, I will damn the world if I must to make you mine," he told her, returning his head to the welcoming fullness of her breasts, snuggling his face against her smooth, warm skin. "I would face down the devil himself, and at the very gates to eternity, if only I could forge a blade that would not melt beneath the flames of hell."

His heart now firmly laid bare, he swirled his tongue over the puckered flesh of her aureole, pulled the nipple deep into his mouth, suckling deeply and strongly until he felt her go pliant against him, her body shuddering.

Satisfied he'd banished yet more of her tenseness, and determined to win her love and trust, he released her nipple but continued to lick its hardened tip until sweet, soft little sighs began escaping her lips.

"But . . ." She attempted one last protest—a blessedly unfinished one.

"You will see, my precious," he murmured, the words a warm-breathed *hush* across the satiny skin of her lush breasts, "there will be a sound explanation for the aid my father gave to your mother. And whate'er his reasons—it will have naught to do with us."

She bit her lip and nodded, her thighs opening to accommodate his stroking fingers, for he'd slid his hand downward again, took much delight in toying with the wealth of damp, red-gold curls springing betwixt her thighs.

"Open your legs wider, lass," he urged her, his fingers seeking, then gently circling the tight, little bud swelling at the top of her sweetness.

"How wide?" she asked, the two words slipping past her lips on the breathiest of sighs, her arousal now reaching the point of abandon, the deliciously hot, urgent tingling at the very core of her plunging her beyond all reason.

"As wide as you are comfortable with . . . for it undoes me to look upon you there, between your thighs," he reminded her, near bursting when she opened her legs so far apart he could plainly see every damp-glistening curl and pink-fleshed fold of her.

He fastened his gaze on her, a groan rising from his throat, the unhindered view delighting and seducing him, just having her most intimate loveliness so freely exposed to his delectation, driving him to ever greater burning need.

"I cannot wait much longer, lass—tell me . . . you are certain you want this?" he asked one last time, not sure what he'd do if she naysayed him. "Now, this very night?"

"Aye, now more than ever! Make me yours, I beg you—let us have this night and claim it for our own, for I vow I am more than ready!" she cried, spreading her legs even wider, boldly giving him total, uninhibited access to her pulsing, quivering heat.

"Please." She lifted her hips, ground her softness

against his hard-muscled thigh, instinctively seeking a more urgent, steelier hardness.

"Och, aye, but I want you . . ." she breathed, her body arcing into his, begging without further need of words. "Please," she urged him again, all allure and sweet temptation.

"Then so be it," he fair growled, the hard, thick length of him stretching to an even greater, more demanding fullness on her acquiescence.

Wholly lost, he touched his lips to her honey-moist heat at last, swirling his tongue over her damp, tangy slickness to get the taste of her, then sending her sweeter, slower kisses back and forth across her tenderest flesh. Soft, barely there flutterings, just light flickings up and down the very seam of her with only the tip of his tongue. Tasting, dipping, and probing, but then giving in to his own ravening need and licking her with long, broad-tongued strokes.

Laving her repeatedly from the bottom of her sweetness to the top and back again. And with each lascivious sweep, he savored the taste of her, intoxicating himself on her rich, womanly scent until his tongue reached the center of all her delight and he took the hard little bud carefully between his teeth, licking and suckling its pebbled roundness until she writhed and moaned beneath him.

"Aye . . ." she cried, thrashing as he released the bud and began probing her hot, moist folds again, teasing her with careful licks, even sucking on her most tender flesh until, her delirium fast approaching, she dug her fingers deep into his hair and pressed his face hard against her, her firm grip keeping him there where she needed him as she ground and circled her aching, pulsing flesh against his oh-so skilled mouth in an unspoken plea for more.

Deeper kisses he burned to give her as he lifted his mouth from her dampness and began simply caressing her body again. But the *whole* of her body, his lips and tongue savoring her as he explored her every dip, curve, and hollow.

Looking up at her, he held her gaze with his and murmured words of love and adoration as he smoothed his hands all over her, skimming first the outer swells of her breasts, then hushing his fingers down her sides, over her sweetly rounded hips, worshiping with gentle, loving touches every sweet, ripe inch of her, admiring the smooth sleek feel of her fine, well-shaped thighs.

He let his hand glide upward, relished the slight roll of pleasantly rounded flesh at the top of her belly, creamy and oh-so soft. Then he caressed downward again, his fingers toying with the lush tangle of her red-gold curls, fragrant and damp.

Only when the rocking of her hips grew frenzied and her breathing began to come in faster, short gasps did he stretch out flush beside her again, this time covering her body with his own and taking her mouth in a deep, slaking kiss, all breath, tongues, and sighs.

She shifted beneath him and he drew back, looked at her. "Do not be afraid, my heart, I shall not hurt you," he said, reaching down between them to slide his hardness beneath her thighs, letting the length of his shaft simply rest against the hot slick moistness of her.

He kept his hand on her, caressing her damp softness with gentle, circular strokes, then rubbing just the tip of his phallus back and forth against her. She moaned her pleasure, clutching his shoulders, her increased wetness and the sharpening of her scent revealing her readiness.

Lifting up, Robbie caught her gaze, holding it as if he could look straight into her soul, see the deepest corners of her heart. Unable to wait another moment, he kissed her again, slanting his mouth over hers in a deep, claiming kiss as he eased into her, inch by sweet slow inch, pausing only at the resistance of her virtue, then drawing back slightly before plunging through to fill her.

He began building a rhythm of sweet long glides, in and out of her, deepening his kiss to match the strokes of their joining until she clenched and melted around him, their spiraling need finally bursting, shattering into a thousand bright-shining pieces as, at last, he fully claimed her.

Branding her his own for this moment and always.

Determined to keep her no matter what obstacles might rise up before them.

As he'd slayed one dragon for her this night, so would they face down and conquer all the rest.

Together, there could be no fiend dark enough to cross them.

Or so he hoped.

❦

Many leagues away, across the silent waters of Loch Duich and in a high and lonely glen, another MacKenzie faced his own demons as he camped for the night in the ancient ruins of Dun Telve, one of several hollow-walled brochs hidden deep in the woods of his beloved Glenelg.

A thin smirr of chill rain blew across the bracken and

heather pressing so thickly against the broch's thick, circular walls, but neither the damp nor the cold disturbed him. He lay rolled in his plaid on the hard, unforgiving earth, and even mourning as he did, he would not deny the heart-wrenching sweetness of being home again.

Even if he'd thought to be spending his nights in his *true* home . . . his onetime haven in all weathers and seasons, the little cot-house of stone and turf now standing in bereft solitude at the other end of the narrow, empty glen.

In the half dark of the rainy night, Kenneth shifted on the stony ground, drew his MacKenzie plaid closer about his grief-numbed body, and stared through a break in the walling at the moon-glinting burn rushing past so close to the ruined broch.

Precious fresh water for the broch-dwellers of old, but a sad reminder to Kenneth that he'd used water from the burn to slake his supper oats and quench his thirst—and not the icy-sweet water e'er gurgling up from the natural spring a mere few paces from the great outcropping of rock near his sainted mother's door.

A door whose threshold he could not bear to cross again for a goodly while.

Not until the lead weight of guilt left the pit of his stomach and the deep-biting sorrow lancing his heart began to lessen and heal. Too many memories lingered in the deserted little cot-house that still smelled of smoored peat and cook smoke.

A mother's love and . . . home.

Laughter-filled days, forever silenced.

And now, since he'd braved heavy seas and ridden night and day through the wildest, most desolate headlands to return, the place he held so dear also smelled of death.

Finality and emptiness, for he'd arrived only hours before his mother's passing, yet weeks since his sister's surprising and unfortunate departure to Eilean Creag.

Or so he'd learned from the glen good-wife who'd lovingly cared for Marjory Mackay through her last days and hours.

The pain in his heart nigh unmanning him, Kenneth curled his hands into the damp folds of his plaid and listened to the sound of the hurrying waters of the nearby burn.

Your fault, the fast-moving rapids seemed to call to him, the taunt reaching his ears despite the ceaseless keening of the night wind and the soft patter of rain.

His blame indeed, for his mother was dead, his sister gone, and he'd come home too late to do aught about it.

Kenneth's fists clenched and he tried to swallow past the dry ache in his throat—and couldn't.

The saints knew, he'd seen the egg-sized chinks in the walling of the cot-house. And he'd noted as well the soiled and matted condition of the roof thatch. The shockingly small height of the oh-so-crucial peat stack.

Minor faults, to be sure, and easily addressed, but sad and unnecessary neglect that had surely hastened his mother's demise.

A deep frown spreading across his brow, Kenneth ignored his weariness, the hot grittiness burning his eyes, and stared hard at the rough-hewn stones he'd carefully removed, then replaced from Dun Telve's curved inner wall.

A meet hiding place for his hard-earned money

pouches since hardly a Highlander lived and breathed who'd disturb the hoary stones of such an old and revered ruin.

That *he'd* committed such a transgression was a lapse he excused with the need to secure his coin—and the flood of prayers he'd sent the long-dead broch-dwellers, begging their benevolence and understanding.

Even so, his actions pinched his conscience and only added to his foul humor.

For one unsettling moment, he imagined he heard them. That ancient folk who'd walked and breathed and toiled here, but were now all but passed from human memory. The earth and stone might remember—might still see the litter and squalor of their days, or yet ring silently with the bustle of their work, the cries of children and the barking of dogs.

Kenneth shivered, burrowed deeper into the sparse comfort of his rain-dampened plaid.

In truth, all lay quiet around him.

And nothing but the hard thudding of his heart and the dark, undulating hills and moors had borne witness to his shame.

But on the morrow, so soon as the first gray light topped the mist-hung peaks, he'd begin remedying some of the crushing pain bearing so heavily on his soul.

It stood beyond his power and will to reverse the loss of his mother's life.

But his sister still lived and, as he knew her, she'd be livid and bristling o'er the inexplicable task their mother had lain upon her shoulders.

Repaying Duncan MacKenzie!

And with good coin Kenneth had spent years struggling to amass.

He scowled, gulped down the hot bile gathering in his throat. Truth was, he could do little more for his mother than beg God to have mercy on her soul and be kind to her, to grant her more grace and comfort in death than she'd known in life.

But he could ride to Eilean Creag and fetch his sister.

Rescue her.

Aye, that much he could do.

And tomorrow, without a glance thitherward, he would.

Chapter Fifteen

✦

A FEW DAYS LATER on a morning of chill wind and gusty rain, Robbie hastened across the outer bailey, all thought of dark and bedeviling fiends far from his mind. But his own sentiments came whirling back to haunt him when, pausing to dash the rain from his brow, a great hulk of a black-cloaked man stepped out of the darker loom of the high curtain wall to confront him.

"Ho, good sir! A word with you . . ." the giant called, coming forward, his towering bulk outlined against the drifting mists.

A fiend indeed . . . or at least a poor soul unfortunate enough to resemble one, even if he did speak with the softly pleasing voice of the Highland West.

But as the man neared, he threw back the hood of his cloak and Robbie recognized him as one of Lady Euphemia's guardsmen.

The one known as Big Red.

Big Red MacAlister. A quiet man if huge, he was square-faced and bull-necked, with a shock of fiery red hair and a thick-bristling beard to match.

"A word with you, Sir Robert," the man repeated, drawing up before Robbie and inclining his shaggy-maned head. "But a discreet word, if you will?" he added, his gaze darting about as if he expected some wraith might rise up from the thick-curling sheets of mist swirling round them.

Robbie stared at him. "Discreet you say?"

The man nodded—vigorously.

Forgetting the rain, Robbie crossed his arms, his curiosity piqued.

"I am not a woman to wag my tongue," he said, measuring the other even though he took care to keep his tone friendly. "But I was heading out to train my father's squires, so I'd just as soon hear what is on your mind and be on my way."

To Robbie's surprise, rather than stating his business, the giant looked down and began shuffling his feet on the bailey's rain-slicked cobbles.

"Come, my friend," Robbie said, clapping the guardsman on the shoulder. "Would you have us standing here in the rain and wind when the day's work is still before us?"

"You will not be wrath—"

"Wrath?" Robbie blinked. "We have ne'er exchanged a word. Why should I—"

"'Tis wrath with the lady Euphemia, I be a-meaning," Big Red said, his face beginning to glow a brighter red than his hair. "I care not if I incite your fury onto myself—there are few names I haven't been called in my time. And the saints know, I've deserved the most of 'em. But my Phemie—"

"Your Phemie?"

Robbie blinked again, comprehension flooding him . . . the heavy odor of strong masculine musk, sharp, and reeking of a man in rut, the unmistakable smell blended with the equally penetrating reek of the lady Euphemia's own arousal.

This man had to be her lover.

Mayhap even the father of the child Robbie was certain she carried. An innocent bairn Robbie suspected she meant to use to shame him, perhaps declaring the babe his, then glorying in knowing he knew otherwise.

An icy shiver ripped down Robbie's spine as realization tore the fog from his mind and all the pieces fell into place.

"You!" He stared at the guardsman. He was half torn between pulling him into a comradely embrace for providing him a reason to rid himself of an unwanted bride, and half seized by the urge to laugh at the incongruous image of his thin-bodied betrothed writhing in lust beneath such a bull-necked stirk of a man.

"You were with the lady just before I spoke with her not too long ago, were you not?" Robbie asked, hoping none of his true feelings colored his tone.

"I was with her, aye. A-hiding beneath the bed the whole time you were in her chamber," Big Red admitted. "God aiding me—'tis sorry I am, and begging your pardon, but I heard all you said to her and I would make you a third proposal—for I love the lass and would have her."

Robbie cleared his throat, tried to summon his most earnest mien, and feared he'd fail badly.

Too great was his mounting excitement.

His pleasure in this unexpected development.

"Then you heard the two offers I made her?" he asked,

swiping a raindrop from his brow. "To return her to her father's Castle Uisdean with her dowry intact and a boon to sweeten the broken betrothal? Or marriage to a Douglas in the south?"

Big Red nodded, began twisting his large hands.

"And what is your proposal?" Robbie asked merely from curiosity, for he was sore tempted to fetch the maid now and deliver her single-handedly into her lover's arms.

Regardless of what the man offered for her.

"I would ask you to grant her both of the proposals you made her. In part, at least," Big Red said, speaking so quickly the words almost ran together.

"Both? Havers, man, how can she have both?" Robbie's eyes widened. "I thought you wanted her for yourself?"

"Och, but I do," Big Red answered promptly, nodding his red-bearded head. "'Tis only that I am not deep-pursed, see you?"

"So you want her dowry and the boon to take her off my hands?" Robbie began to comprehend. And did not mind at all.

Indeed, he rocked back on his heels, almost enjoying the exchange. "If you swear to wed her so her child, and yours, I presume, has a name, the two of you can have her dowry and the boon I meant to give old Hugh Out-with-the-Sword for his trouble," he said, feeling more than generous.

But the giant was still staring at him, his broad face bitter-earnest and looking even more discomfited than before if such were possible.

"I thank you, sir, you are more than kind." Big Red inclined his head.

"Then we are in happy accord," Robbie agreed, his tone congenial. "I wish you both well."

But Big Red made no move to take his leave.

Robbie arched a brow. "You have something else to discuss?" he asked, remembering the man said he desired the lady Euphemia to have *both* proposals. "Since you claim to love her and have planted a child in her belly, I canna believe you would see her wed to a Douglas?"

As he'd suspected, the giant shook his head. "Nay, for truth, I would not—I'd rip the head off any sprig of that house or any other who dared try to take her from me—were she well and truly mine."

"But . . . ?"

"But I would go *with* her to the south—to the Douglases. If you, in your goodness, might be inclined to impress one of your southern friends of that ilk to employ me."

"Employ you?"

The big man shrugged, clearly having no need to flex his muscles or prove his worthiness as an able guardsman. "I would give my loyalty and best sword arm to whate'er Douglas might accept me as his own true man. And I give you my vow ne'er to make you regret having helped me."

Robbie eyed the man, his good sense telling him not to risk ruining his friendship with so mighty a house as Douglas. Yet his heart sensed the other's sincerity, making him want to help him indeed.

"Why do you not just return with her to Castle Uisdean?" He had to ask. "Or take her monies and settle hereabouts . . . in peace?"

"Because," Big Red began, flushing again, "I will tell you true . . . I have a dark past in these parts. See you, I was once leader of the broken men who dwell on the Isle of Pabay. And now, I wou—"

"You would put that past behind you," Robbie finished for him, not surprised when the man nodded.

Robbie, too, would be hungry to put such a dubious career behind him—all knew of the men of Pabay. The raids and other dark deeds e'er launched from that wee isle's heavily wooded shores were legend, the men greatly feared.

"I have shocked you." Big Red sighed. "You have changed your mind."

"Nay, far from it," Robbie reassured him, not quite certain himself why he sympathized with the man. "But I would ask a boon of my own—"

"There is one more favor I would beg of you," the giant cut him off, reaching to clutch Robbie's arm, clearly not intending to let go until his piece had been heard. "If you will allow?"

Robbie glanced at the huge fingers circling his arm. "Speak your concern," he said, looking back at the lout. "But pray stop cutting off my blood."

"The old man . . . Phemie's father," Big Red began, lowering his voice, "he is not the blackguard the prattle-mongers claim. I've kenned him nigh all my days and swear to you, 'tis not he who lowered his chain in the Kyle in recent years, wrecking galleys and charging tolls . . ."

Robbie cocked a brow. "But the MacLeod's *Girt of*

Strength, has been lowered—I have spoken to enough seafaring friends who've suffered damage, lost their ships, good men."

"Aye—but the old chief ne'er knew . . . leastways not in recent times."

"And this favor you would ask of me has to do with Hugh Out-with-the-Sword?"

Big Red nodded. "He was good to me when no one else would even look me in the eye," he said, shuffling his feet again.

He glanced up at the scudding rain clouds, blew out a quick breath. "Ach, I have ne'er felt more like a gowk!" he said, looking back at Robbie. "See you, he was once a most notable man and I would know him in better cheer, once Phemie and I are gone. I will honor you all my days if you swear you will send someone to look after old Hugh until the effects of the sleeping draughts he's been given wear off. He will ne'er lower his chain again, that I grant you—he requires naught but his ale and a lusty wench once a fortnight and he is happy as a lamb."

"And why did the lady Euphemia stoop to such treacheries? Why would she lace her own sire's drink with sleeping herbs?" Robbie asked, seeing the correctness of his guess in the giant's eyes. "How do I know she will not return and have her minions raise havoc in these parts again?"

Big Red flexed his muscles . . . and winked. "I will keep her too busy birthing my bairns to think long on old grievances and her fool plans for avenging them."

"Old grievances?"

Somehow Robbie knew *he* was meant.

"Ach . . ." Big Red ran a large hand through the tangle

of his red mane, "it will be no little surprise to you that the lass reviles you?"

Robbie dashed the rain from his brow again. "I have noticed, aye."

Big Red nodded. "My own self, mind, I see shame in bearing grudges so long, but Phemie . . . you cost her the great love of her life, see you? A young man she loved above all else and who, if she told me true, loved her with the same fervor."

"A man she could not wed because her father and mine pledged her to me?" Robbie asked, understanding at last.

The big man shrugged again, his gaze flickering to the dark and quiet tower across the bailey where they both knew the lady would still be sleeping at this early hour.

"That would be the way of it," Big Red admitted. "Mayhap her spleen toward you would not have grown to such poison o'er the years if the young man had loved her less. But he was as shattered by the betrothal as Phemie. Soon thereafter, he ran off to join the wars against the English. If the stories be true, he was felled by the cloth-yard of a Welsh longbowman in some skirmish too insignificant to bear a name."

"And the lady Euphemia ne'er forgot or forgave?"

Big Red MacAlister shook his head, but as quickly, he thrust out his hand. "You will not speak poorly of her? Not besmirch her good name?"

"Nary a word."

"Even though she sought to ruin you?"

Robbie clasped the other's hand. "I learned long ago to look forward, not backward, my friend."

" 'Tis agreed then? All of it?"

"I keep my word, MacAlister," Robbie assured him. "See that you keep yours."

Big Red pumped Robbie's hand, nigh crushing the bones in his enthusiastic grip. "To be sure, and I will, good sir," he said, a broad smile stealing across his face. "And I thank you, I truly do. But what is your boon? What would you have of me?"

"Naught that you will find too difficult, I am thinking," Robbie said, looking across the bailey to the lady Euphemia's window again.

"Only that you take your lady and be gone from here by the morrow's setting sun. Do that, and I promise a ready ear and helping hand if hard times e'er befall you."

Three days later, Duncan MacKenzie snapped. His famed black temper finally besieged the better of him as he paced about his solar, cursing beneath his breath. Gone were his cold looks and withering silences. The piercing glares he'd fastened on anyone bold enough to breach his self-imposed solitude.

Fury blazed inside him, hot anger burning in his eyes as he whirled on his son. "You have made your greatest mistake," he said, frowning. "Bursting into my privy quarters without so much as a knock—and with such fool contrive on your tongue!"

Robbie stood still, restrained himself with effort.

"Your blessing and goodwill is not required, Father," he said, speaking straight. "Such benevolence is only . . . desired."

"*Desired.*" The Black Stag gave a stern shake of his

dark head. "'Twas suchlike that started this—" he broke off, rammed a hand through his hair. "God save us, this is no piddling matter. 'Tis beyond all, is what it is!"

His scowl darkening, he went to stand before the fire, stared into the crackling flames. "Nay, nay, laddie, just because you've rid yourself of an unwanted bride-to-be does not mean you can take another so soon," he rapped out, his displeasure seeming to throb all through the solar.

The blessed sanctum where he'd sequestered himself for the past sennight, seeing no one and not even allowing his lady wife or the good Sir Marmaduke entry.

Only his favorite hound, old Roag, was granted such privilege and even he kept his distance, having claimed a comfortable spot of warmth near the brazier to stretch his shaggy self and sleep.

Stealth-by-dinner-tray had worked for Robbie, the ploy functioning beautifully this time . . . even if he was getting absolutely nowhere in gaining his father's favor.

"And you especially cannot take the maid Juliana to wife," the Black Stag declared, pacing again. "I forbid it and shall order her gone from here by the morrow. Highland hospitality or no!"

"Say you?" Robbie crossed the solar with great strides, coming up beside his father just as he paused at the table to pour himself a cup of morning ale. "And I say there is more to your spleen than meets the eye. You e'er relished having bonnie, strong-hearted women around you—why do you turn such a cold eye to this one? Especially knowing how much she pleases me?"

Duncan gulped the contents of his ale cup in one great swallow.

"It will do you nary a jot of good to keep dogging my

heels and peppering me with nonsense," he snapped, slapping down the cup with an overloud *clack*. "I will not change my mind. You cannot wed the lass. You are heir to a great and chiefly house—"

"Even so, I fail to see why you dislike her." Robbie's chest tightened with indignation, but he tamped down his own rising temper, fixing his gaze out the window on the rainy, torch-lit bailey far below. "You would do the better to be of greater heart," he said, biting his tongue before he'd added how much he knew of his father's generosity to Juliana's mother.

Instead, he gestured to the discarded and half-eaten victuals piled on the table, the scatter of emptied wine jugs and ale cups. The mound of rumpled plaids and furred skins near the hearth, where Robbie knew his father had been making his bed for some days.

Much to his lady wife's disapproval and concern.

Determined to get to the bottom of it, Robbie strode over to the table, picked up a dried crust of brown bread with two fingers, and waved it at his father before letting it fall again to the litter-strewn table.

"Simple perturbation at my wish to wed a lass who may not be a gentlest birth cannot qualify the need to hide away in here and subsist on moldy bread and black scowls," he said, pinning his father with a stare of his own.

The Black Stag bristled, shook back his still-magnificent mane of raven-black hair. "You ought not go poking your nose into places it does not belong," he groused, not looking at Robbie—or the mess on the table.

Instead he went to a shadow-hung corner of the room,

one little used and not illuminated by the flickering wall torches.

To Robbie's amazement, his father seemed to shrink as he stood before the dimly-lit corner. His great shoulders dipping, much of the Black Stag's bluster and fury appeared to slide off him, letting him fade and dwindle in their wake.

But as quickly, he seemed to recover. With a great flourish, he reached into the corner and retrieved a . . . stick.

Wheeling round, he waved the thing at Robbie, his aggravation palpable. Worse, his eyes now glimmered with a brightness that set Robbie's heart to lurching and made his stomach clench into a tight, cold knot.

As did the *stick* clutched ever so firmly in his father's hand.

Not a stick at all, but the toy wooden sword Robbie had so cherished as a lad.

A relic of a pain-filled past and one Robbie had not seen in more years than he could count.

A once-treasured prize, crafted for him by a father who loved him well, carved in the early days before Robbie's mother and her disastrous dalliance with his Uncle Kenneth had ruined all their lives.

Especially Robbie's.

Dark memories rushing him, he stared at the small wooden sword, his heart beginning to thunder. "Where did you get that?" he blurted, his voice hoarse with an emotion he did not care to examine.

Not with other more pressing matters plaguing him.

"I have always kept it," Duncan said, clutching the toy

sword as if his very life hung from its blunt wooden blade.

Robbie nodded, his throat too tight for words.

"I saved it as a reminder of the worst treachery to e'er stain these walls," his father revealed, smoothing a hand over the sword's child-sized hilt. "And so that I would ne'er forget how close I came to losing everything I held so dear."

His fingers still clenched around the sword, he looked at Robbie, his eyes shadowed with some dark and long-simmering emotion.

Robbie blinked, his own eyes beginning to burn the longer he stared at the sword. He swallowed against the swelling ache in his throat.

"Everything you held dear?" he got out, the words scarce audible above the roar of blood in his ears.

"You, son," the Black Stag admitted, propping the toy wooden sword against the wall and resuming his pacing, his hands clasped behind his back. "I lost my heart in those days, see you?" he said, shooting a glance at Robbie, his expression dark but no longer forbidding.

"And I almost lost *you*—ne'er my own love for you, which was always there, if buried deep inside, but I almost lost *your* love. Years later, you felt the need to leave us . . . to journey far from here, choosing to make your name elsewhere, rather than staying in Kintail . . ."

"You ne'er spoke of such concerns."

"Ach, well," the Black Stag said in an overgruff voice, "did you not spend enough time in the south and amongst the nobility and landed men thereabouts to ken great men hardly go about spilling their heart's blood for all and sundry to gawk at?"

Robbie shook his head, cut the air with a dismissive hand. "I believe the greater man *does* lay his heart bare—leastwise about the important things in life," he said, his gaze lighting on the wooden sword again. "I wish I had known your feelings."

"And now you do." Duncan poured himself another measure of ale. "Ten long years I waited for your return . . . ten years, I kept this clan—our family and home—free and safe from the taint of others, keeping away all hurt . . . even the barest tinge of a threat lest such grief and sorrow found its way to our door again."

"Yet now I am returned and you would snatch my own happiness out from under my feet." Robbie joined him by the table but refused the ale his father offered him. "You would deny me the bride I choose for myself . . . a lass I have wanted since I first glimpsed her. She is my heart's treasure, see you? Ne'er have I—"

"You cannot wed her. I—"

"You spent years sending monies and goods to her mother." Robbie threw down his gauntlet at last, slapped his hand on the table to emphasize the truth of the words. "Juliana has regained almost all of her memory now. She has told me what she knows. Including that she was on her way here—to you! To bring you a sackful of siller. Recompense from her mother for the aid you supposedly gave her."

Duncan blanched. "She told you this?"

The words fell as ice between them, his father's expression revealing he had known Juliana's identity all along.

"She told me that and more—but I would know what *you* have to say about it?"

His father turned aside, his clenched fists and the furiously ticking muscle beneath his left eye showing his distress.

"You knew who she was all along . . . yet you never said aught. I would know why?"

"For the love of Saint Columba!" Duncan raked a hand through his hair, stared at the ceiling. "I only *thought* I knew who she was. See you, she is the image of her mother."

He looked back at Robbie, the bluster gone from him. "I was not sure at first—only when she remembered her name . . . I knew her name, though I had not seen her since she was but a wee little lassie."

"Then you admit you sent her mother . . . aid?" Robbie pressed, tilting his head to the side. "You must've cared strongly about the woman's well-being to help her for so many years? And if you felt she was worthy of such attention, why deny my wish to marry her daughter? The woman is dead now, so you may as well speak true."

"Dead?" Duncan blinked when Robbie nodded. "Saints, I had no idea," he said, pulling a hand down over his chin. "She was e'er branded on my memory as a woman so full of life. Vibrant, and . . . good."

"Yet you would punish her daughter."

"I would punish no one," the Black Stag said, tight-voiced. "'Tis you who do not understand. I only meant to protect my own from further heartache. To be sure, Marjory Mackay is . . . or was . . . a fine woman. She was more than deserving of the help I spent her, and 'tis glad I was to do it. But she was also a woman tainted, branded with a stain so damning, I made her vow ne'er to come anywhere near Eilean Creag. Nor any living man, woman, or child of my blood."

Robbie could scarce believe his ears. "So you dislike her daughter because of this . . . stain?" he demanded, heat spreading up the back of his neck. "You esteem Juliana a threat to this house?"

The Black Stag heaved a great sigh, suddenly looking far older than his years. Tired, and worn. "Not a threat, son. Ne'er that," he said, his voice, too, sounding weary. "But she is a hurtful reminder of the darkest days to e'er pass beneath this roof. I worried her being here might unroll—"

"Guidsakes!" The protest burst from Robbie. "I thought you a man of sensibility and judgment! Do you not see she is like a freshening breath of bright summer air—full of warmth and smiles?"

When his father only stared at him, neither denying nor agreeing with him, Robbie seized the advantage. "Perhaps the old grief and shadows you speak of can be wiped clean by the good of my marriage to her?"

"You still do not understand." Duncan tossed back another measure of ale, then hastily dragged his sleeve over his mouth. "Even if I willed it so, you could still not wed the lass. Truth be told, you ought not even make her your leman!"

Robbie's heart began a slow rise to his throat and the walls of the solar started to inch close, creeping ever tighter around him until he feared he might lose the ability to breathe any moment.

"What do you mean . . . *even if you willed it*?" Robbie's voice thrummed with dread. Bile, hot and bitter, near choked him. "Because of the aid you sent her mother, Juliana feared you might be her father. Is that it? Are you her sire?"

Duncan's jaw dropped, his astonishment undeniable.

And seeing it, relief swept over Robbie in great waves . . . until he saw the sad shake of his father's head.

"Nay, I did not sire the lass," Duncan said, his gaze locking with Robbie's. "Would that I had . . . much sorrow could have been spared."

Robbie swallowed hard. "But you know who her father was, do you not?"

"Aye." The one word fell with laming precision.

A sickening queasiness began spreading through Robbie's innards. "Pray tell me she is not the daughter of my Uncle Kenneth?" Robbie's tongue somehow formed the words. "The man who was my mother's lover?"

And just as he'd known he would, his father nodded, that simple gesture extinguishing all the light and hope that had burned so brightly in Robbie's heart.

"Aye, I regret that is the way of it," Duncan said, in a slow, measured voice. "The lass is my half brother's daughter—she is your own first cousin."

Chapter Sixteen

❧

"AYE, THAT IS THE WAY OF IT."

The stranger's deep voice came from the solar door, his cold words tossed like a handful of ice into the heated discourse crackling between Robbie and the Black Stag.

Shocked silence filled the room, quickly shattered as father and son drew sharp breaths and spun round, their hands flying to the hilts of their swords—until the stranger stepped forward and a shaft of gray morning light fell across his face, the MacKenzie plaid draped across his broad shoulders.

"Saints, Maria, and Joseph!" Duncan stared, his eyes full wide. "On my soul, it is you! *Kenneth's son.*"

"To be sure, and I am," the young man said, his voice as frosty as winter. "Your forgotten nephew, also christened Kenneth—if you were not aware."

White-faced, Duncan strode toward him, reached out a hand, but let it fall as quickly. "You have come—"

"I am come from Glenelg and, aye, parts still more distant to fetch my sister," Kenneth coldly declared, even in seething anger looking so much like the other two men

Juliana might have found some amusement in their wide-eyed gawping if the reason for their astonishment wasn't so inextricably bound to her own greatest sorrow.

The dashing of her dreams.

The damning, undeniable heartbreak of her identity—a laming discovery that had shot through her like scorching hellfire the instant her brother had pushed open her bedchamber door and marched inside, his startling and unexpected arrival bringing full remembrance and, with the memories, an end to all her brightest, most golden hopes.

"Aye, good sirs," her brother said again, looking at the other two men as he wrapped a firm arm around Juliana's waist, drew her close. "My sister and I have the same tainted blood as your own flowing in our veins."

His agitation palpable, he narrowed his gaze on Robbie. "Wedding you, Sir Robert, is not only imprudent, it is the last favor I would allow her," he vowed, his face tight with disapproval. "Even if the two of you were not blood kin."

Robbie could only stare at him, wordless. His chest so tight he could scarce draw breath, he glanced round the circle of other faces, each one grim-set. There was a long pause before he spoke.

Striving for calm, he shook his head, pinched the bridge of his nose. "This is no time for heated words and lost tempers, my friend," he said at last, accepting a brimming cup of *uisge-beatha* from Sir Marmaduke who, despite the Black Stag's dark glare at him, had somehow found his way to Robbie's elbow.

"Aye, I vow 'tis all ill talk—perpetrated by malicious

tongues and naught else!" Robbie declared, looking round again, daring any in the little chamber to deny it.

None did, but enough of his long-nosed kinsmen who'd elbowed their way into the solar shook their heads with such forlorn sadness that Robbie's bravura collapsed.

In a rage of disbelief, he glared at them, then at Kenneth, and tossed down the fiery Highland spirits with relish, glad for the numbing warmth its welcome heat left in his throat.

"Curse it!" he railed, throwing aside the cup. "I am no fool—I ken you speak the truth. But, see you, the whole of it rips my soul. I ne'er—" he broke off, spun around to face Juliana, his expression bleak. "On my life, I love— . . . I need—"

"The only *need* I care aught about is my sister's health and peace of mind, *cousin*," Kenneth shot back, tightening his hold on Juliana. "If I can speak plain with you, I'll mind you that this house has a devil in it—and e'er has! If you wish the best for Juliana, say her Godspeed and accept that I must remove her from here."

"That may be one way, son," Sir Marmaduke spoke up, his deep voice e'er a river of calm, "but I hold there can be no good in hieing the maid to other bounds now, this very hour. Perhaps—"

"I do not know who you are, sir, but I trust myself to ken what is best for my sister," Kenneth rapped out, eyeing Sir Marmaduke with suspicion. "And while I appreciate your solicitude, there are others present who would be glad to be cleansed of us!" he added, with a scathing glance at Duncan.

"By God's good mercy, I understand your bitterness."

Robbie pushed past his stony-faced father to stand before Kenneth. "But I say you, I love your sister and I wanted to meet you. Just not under such circumstances. Nay, ne'er this . . ."

Kenneth arched a brow, looked skeptical. "I dinna see how you could have wished to make my acquaintance. You ne'er knew I existed. Your father made my mother vow that nary a word of my existence—or Juliana's—would e'er come to your ears."

A great buzz of talk erupted in the solar as yet more kinsmen and lesser castle folk pressed inside, each one eyeing Duncan, Robbie, and the newcomer, the whole of them craning necks and straining ears, clearly determined not to miss a heartbeat of the ruckus.

"What I hear and what I choose to believe is my own business, my friend," Robbie said, lifting his voice above the din. "As my blood cousin, I would have hoped you would have wits and heart enough to feel the same—to make your own opinions and not base them on ages-old tragedy nary a one of us can undo!"

"Hear me, I have been attempting to assuage the stain and hurt of that tragedy all my life," Kenneth shot back, squaring his shoulders. "The more fool you, if you do not believe me."

Letting go of Juliana, he went to stand toe to toe with the Black Stag. "Ne'er you worry, *uncle*," he said, a muscle beginning to twitch beneath his left eye, "I am man enough to thank you for the shelter and board you spent my sister until I could retrieve her, but I will take her to Strathnaver now. To our late mother's people, where I believe she will be able to put her time here—and her misadventures—far from her mind."

Robbie snorted, looked round at his gog-eyed kinsmen.

"You jest . . . surely?" he cried, catching Kenneth's arm and swinging him about. "You cannot take her so far north—she is of these hills! 'Tis here in Kintail, she belongs . . . in your own Glenelg, if not at my side as I would—"

"I know well the ache of leaving these hills." Kenneth jerked free his arm, brushed at his plaid. "Do not doubt it! And we shall return to Glenelg someday—but not before she has wiped you from her mind."

A man's deep voice, brimming with reason, rose from behind. "She—you are both—welcome at my own Balkenzie," Sir Marmaduke suggested, fixing Kenneth with a compassionate but piercing stare. "'Tis far and away across the other side of Loch Duich and would give you both the privacy and distance you need to . . . adjust."

To Juliana's amazement, some of the heat went out of her brother's face as he seemed to consider the Sassunach's words, but his hesitation lasted only a moment. As quickly, his jaw tightened and his features turned again to stone.

"You are a good man, I can well perceive," Kenneth said, the respect in his voice unmistakable, "but I deem it more wise if I deliver my sister into the care of our family in Strathnaver." He paused to flick a hot glance at Robbie. "Anyone who claims to care for her will not stand in the way of her healing."

"You must not take her," the lady Linnet urged, pushing through the tight-packed throng of clansmen. "I pray you, heed my words, young Kenneth," she besought him, holding out imploring hands. "The better healing will be found here . . . for the both of you."

But Kenneth only shook his head. "She shall rest happier far from here," he said, inclining his head in polite deference. "As will I—no offense meant to you, fair lady."

Juliana threw a panicked look at her knight, but he said nothing, his expression having gone as granite-hard as Kenneth's. Barely contained anger simmered in the rigid set of his shoulders and he'd clenched his hands so tightly his knuckles gleamed white.

Juliana's heart split. He was going to let her go—had sided with her brother that the only betterment for her could be secured in the wilds of Scotland's far north, where she kent nary a soul, blood kin or nay. And where she had even less desire to go!

Seeing his decision writ all o'er his face made the floor open beneath Juliana's feet, stole the breath from her lungs.

"You cannot let me go!" she cried, rushing forward to cling to him. "Not after . . . not after . . ."

"Think you I am glad-hearted?" He clutched her to him, stroking her back and kissing her hair and her brow, wiping the tears from her cheeks with his thumbs.

But then he disentangled himself, setting her from him. "Och, sweetness, my very own precious minx . . ." he said, shaking his head, a world of sorrow in his eyes. "Ne'er would I have desired such an end. I saw only our tomorrows, each one filled with hope and wonder—as you ought ken. But I would spare you the further distress that would surely befall you if you remain—would spare us both the grief of a long parting. A lingering . . ."

"Nay!" Juliana shook her head, his words crushing her soul and blinding her, tearing her heart.

But even as she staggered, backing away from him through the parting crowd, deep inside she saw the wisdom of his decision.

Knew that remaining at Eilean Creag, or even going with Sir Marmaduke and his Caterine to Balkenzie, would only prolong her agony.

The agony for the both of them.

That truth, she recognized with a woman's all-seeing soul, her broken heart seeing clearly the black-spinning void opening around her, draining her, and chasing all warmth and light from her life.

'Twas the fulfillment of her greatest dread, and, now, so swiftly on the heels of what should have been joyful days bursting with her most wondrous triumph.

Her bright shining love for her Robbie.

Faith, she could not even recall if she'd e'er even told him!

I love you . . . her heart cried, hurling the words at him when she could not push them past the thickness in her throat. *I will always love you . . . will ne'er forget . . .*

As if he'd heard, he ran after her, knocking aside his kinsmen as he sprinted forward to wrap his arms around her and drag her to him one last time.

"I am sorry, lass, my sweet Juliana," he cried her name against her hair, then slanted his mouth over hers, kissing her hungrily—regardless of who looked on and what they thought of him.

But when at last, he pulled away, his gaze found Kenneth. "I sorrow for you as well," he said, both cold steel and regret in his voice, "for I truly was looking forward to meeting you . . . to having you for my friend."

Before Kenneth could speak, Robbie wheeled around to confront his father, ignoring the stricken look on that one's blanched and grave-set face.

"And I am sorry for you—for whether you admit it or nay, you have lost yet again," he said. "A meet and fine good-daughter, and also a braw nephew whose friendship and love might well have lifted the *stain* you e'er dreaded."

The Black Stag said nothing. Turning away, he went to stand at the windows, his back to the room, his stance rigid as stone.

"You may keep the coin my mother wished you to have, good sir," Kenneth called after him. "I do not need it—I've earned and set aside more than enough to support my humble tastes and help my sister. On our way to Strathnaver and—"

"I have no wish to go to Strathnaver," Juliana cried, clutching the doorjamb to keep her knees from buckling. "I—"

"You cannot stay here." Kenneth was at her side in a heartbeat, grabbing her elbow and steering her through the circle of clansmen and servitors crowding the doorway before either Robbie, or his father, could grasp she was gone.

But even as Kenneth pushed on, dragging her down the long, torch-lit passage, something in the stubborn set of his jaw bothered Juliana.

As did a strange flickering in his eyes—his incredible haste to have her gone.

Unusual even in his vexation, for, as she now remembered so clearly, her brother was e'er a cautious man and great thinker, not one to do even the simplest task without much careful deliberation.

Yet he'd spirited her from the solar with such speed and force, she wondered her feet hadn't drawn sparks on the stone flags of the corridor's floor.

And the incessant ticking in the muscle beneath his left eye, a weakness he shared with his uncle and cousin whether he wished to acknowledge the similarity or nay, also revealed that not all was quite as it seemed.

Something deeper plagued him.

Something that gave her a wee shimmer of hope . . . in especial when, in a sudden burst of unexpected clarity, she recalled the rolled parchment her mother had pressed on her before she'd left their cot-house on that fateful day.

A missive of great importance her mother insisted.

Yet a message Juliana had regrettably lost while flailing about in the lochan, trying to rescue the ewe.

The near-drowned ewe whose frantic bleating and eventual rescue had landed her in Robbie MacKenzie's arms.

Arms that would ne'er reach for her, ne'er again hold her unless the saints took profound mercy on her and wrought some miracle. Granted her some magic that would undo the nightmare her life had become in the space of one ill-fated morn.

One ill-fated *hour* in truth, for Kenneth's arrival had been so swift and hasty, he'd stormed into her bedchamber and plucked her from its tapestry-hung walls with such speed she'd had scarce time but to snatch up her two travel bags, with the tatty old plaid and coil of braid stuffed inside. Faith, she'd barely had a moment to drop Devorgilla's jar of all-cure ointment into the leather bag tied to her belt.

The only memento she meant to take with her, for it proved the dearest.

A sweet reminder of the blissful hours spent in her knight's arms . . . a joy she'd ne'er truly believed could last—save perhaps only for a night.

✄

Days later, riding pillion behind her brother as he spurred his garron ever faster over the high moors toward the distant blue of the largest massed peaks Juliana had ever seen, the little jar and its sweet memories comforted the hollow ache inside her.

Struggling against another rush of hot-stabbing pain, she slipped a hand into the pouch at her skirts and circled her chilled fingers around the small earthenware pot, somehow not at all surprised when the round-sided jar began to vibrate and grow warm in her hand.

And this time, a not yet experienced accompaniment came along with the heated vibrations . . . a strange *humming* in her ears.

A sound that proved not frightening, but soothing.

Faint but distant, even when the humming altered slightly, blending with the cold, knifing wind whistling past her ears to become the high-pitched, reedy voice of a very old woman.

A crone's voice, ancient-sounding, to be sure, but persistent and strong. Determined, and threaded with *goodness*. Mayhap even love.

The parchment, the voice seemed to whisper at her ear.

*You must ask him what stood on the parchment . . .
then he will hide no more.*

Hide no more?

At the last three words, the little jar shattered beneath Juliana's fingers, the shards not cutting her, but the cream within oozing out to gush into her hand, seep into her skin and through her fingers, flooding her with incredible warmth and, she would have sworn, the most amazing golden light.

Hope.

And . . . confidence.

A definite surge of elation. Almost assurance that . . . all would be well.

And so it shall be, lassie, the crone's voice came again, but even more distant this time.

So far away, in fact, that it could only have been the wind.

But a *buoying,* joyous wind and one that made Juliana's heart soar as she pounded on Kenneth's back, yelled for him to draw to a halt.

The instant he did, she leapt to the ground, planted her hands on her hips, heedless of the hot-tingling *goop* dripping from her fingers, and fixed her most level stare on her decidedly guilty-looking brother's face.

And that was it.

Her brother looked . . . guilty.

That was what had bothered her back at Eilean Creag when he'd yanked her from the solar and dragged her from the castle faster than she could splutter a fare-thee-well to her knight or even a single stone of his great, forbidding keep.

. . . then he will hide no more.

"You are concealing something from me, Kenneth," Juliana said, and would have sworn the wind carried a delighted *cackle* past her ear the instant the accusation left her lips.

"There is something vital you are keeping from me, and I would know it." She began tapping her foot as she stared at him, noted well how the three vertical scars on his cheek darkened suspiciously the longer she glared at him. "Aye, you are sore troubled, and I am thinking it has to do with the parchment Mother gave me to deliver to the Black Stag."

The cackle on the wind became a gleeful hoot of triumph.

Kenneth sat up straighter in the saddle, gave her a look of studied innocence and denial that did not fool her at all.

"What parchment?"

As if he did not ken! Juliana folded her arms, an odd but incredibly uplifting sense of purpose beginning to pulse through her, warming her.

"The handwritten missive our mother entrusted to me and that I lost when Robbie rescued me from the loch," she answered him. "'Twas of great importance she told me—a privy word for the eyes of Kintail and no other."

"So?"

Kenneth reached a hand to her, tried to urge her back onto the garron. "Come you, we have many miles yet before us—let us be gone from here . . . we have not yet passed out of Kintail—"

"All the more reason for you to tell me what you know

of the message our mother wanted me to deliver to Duncan MacKenzie."

Kenneth swiped a hand through his hair, the gesture making him look so much like her knight that her heart split.

"How should I ken what she wished you to tell the dastard?" The three scars on his left cheek turned a livid red. "She gave the scroll to *you* not me."

"But you saw her before she died—you told me she lingered in the good-wife's care until you got there," Juliana minded him, the goop on her hand sending encouragement speeding all through her, the wind seeming to swirl protectively round her shoulders, steeling her backbone and giving her strength.

She lifted a brow. "Aye, Mother gave the parchment to me, but mayhap she told you what was on it?"

Kenneth compressed his lips into a hard tight line.

The sudden burst of increased ticking beneath his left eye spoke the truth.

His guilt.

Indeed, ne'er good at lying, he fair glowed with discomfiture.

"What did she want him to know, Kenneth?" Juliana demanded, certain now. Her pulse pounding, she narrowed her eyes at him, did her best not to blink. "Tell me true or I shall forget I have a brother."

"By all that's holy!" Kenneth swore, swinging down from his garron. He strode over to her and pulled her into his arms so tightly he near crushed the breath from her.

"I did not want to tell you—thought it best you ne'er know," he said, his voice filled with such agony she almost regretted pushing him. "I especially vowed not to tell you when I arrived at Eilean Creag and discovered you'd become the . . . er . . . that Sir Robert had taken a fancy to you."

"Hah—you say so!" Juliana lifted her chin, held her ground. "And I say I meant what I said—speak true or you are no longer my brother."

"Aye, but *that*, my heart, is the sorry truth of it!" he cried, letting go of her to ram both hands through his hair. "See you, I am not your brother . . . not your full brother, anyway. You have nary a drop of MacKenzie blood in your veins . . . only I do. You—"

Shock slammed into Juliana, the length of her running icy cold. She stared at her brother, her *half* brother, too stunned to speak. Then, as the full impact of his revelation hit her, she swayed, her legs giving out on her.

"How could you?" she cried out, dropping to her knees. "Ne'er would I have kept such a secret from you."

The blue world all around them began to swirl and dip beneath her and from somewhere distant, she heard her own sobs, loud and ringing in her ears. Heart-wrenching sobs of mindless joy, they ripped her dread to tiniest pieces and cast her cares to the wind.

Wind that hooted and cried in triumphant, gleeful delight.

"What are you saying? Who, then, was my father?" she heard herself ask, comprehension still washing through her, her voice coming from someplace so far off she scarce heard the words.

Just as she could scarce see her brother, for so many hot-streaming tears blinded her she could barely see her own trembling hands pressing hard against her cheeks.

"I am sorry, lass. I but meant to protect you—but I did

not harbor secrets from you." Kenneth's voice came to her, equally distant, but so warm, comforting. "I ne'er knew myself until our mother told me on her deathbed," he admitted, pacing back and forth in front of her as he spoke.

That, too, reminding her of her knight.

A reminder that filled her heart to bursting and let her spirit soar, despite her agitation at Kenneth. Looking away, she stared off at the great, moody hills, the heavy clouds resting on their peaks, so many questions still swirling through her mind. Then, glancing back at Kenneth, she dashed a hand across her cheek, drew a deep, quivering breath.

"I would know the whole of it," she said, peering at him as the cold wind scurried round her, pulling at her *arisaid*, and somehow, at times, feeling almost like caring hands trying to tug her to her feet. "Tell me true—if Kenneth MacKenzie did not sire me, who did?" she asked again. "Do you even know?"

"Ah, well," Kenneth began, his voice resigned, "if I understood rightly, it would seem that when my father's amorous attentions turned elsewhere, our mother, may the saints rest her soul, thought she might win back his affection if she told him she'd grown heavy with another child."

Juliana swallowed, staring at him. "But he was no longer ... paying her court?" she supplied, seeing the truth of her guess in her brother's nod.

"Aye, that will have been the length of it," he admitted. "So she sought the ... *assistance* of a pleasing man who was apparently fond of her, and when you were

born, she told my father that he had sired you as well—
which, of course, he had not."

"But the deception availed her nothing." Juliana made
the words a statement, comprehension striking her full in
the heart. "Her great love—your father, Kenneth
MacKenzie—abandoned her regardless."

Again Kenneth inclined his head. "By all accounts, my
father had wholly besotted himself in your Robbie's
mother. Beyond all measure and deeply enough to allow
his passion for her to ignite the heather with the greatest
scandal and shame e'er to stalk these hills."

"Our poor mother . . . to keep such sorrow locked in
her heart all these years." Juliana's own heart clenched
with memories of how good her mother's life had appeared on the surface.

Despite the harshness and toil, Marjory Mackay had
e'er brimmed with bright smiles and warmth, and her
home always rang with laughter and cheer, happy voices
e'er calling, each new day cozy and comforting as the
smell of peat smoke and fresh-made oatcakes.

Juliana blinked back the hot tears stinging her eyes. "I
had no idea. She must have faced unbearable pain, the
blackest days . . ."

"She was a strong woman. She had courage—as do
you. But this, she ne'er wanted us to know for fear we
would think ill of her." He paused, gave her a penetrating
look, his eyes warming with compassion. "With her end
approaching, she fretted for us, our future. She wished to
straighten her past . . . even implored me to go to Eilean
Creag, believing Kintail would accept me into his fold."

He glanced aside, shoved the hair back from his forehead. "That is what stood on the parchment, see you? She

hoped to win peace for us . . . see past wrongs righted. She felt the Black Stag might be moved to find a good match for you, whether you were his true-born niece or nay."

Juliana stared at her brother, not quite yet daring to hope. "But I am not his niece, am I?"

Her brother shook his head, the hard firm line of his mouth confirming it. Juliana's temples began to throb, her own mouth going dry. For one fleeting instant a bolt of white-edged fury shot through her, making her itch to wring his neck, pommel him with tightly-clenched fists until her face stopped burning and she could breath again.

Instead, she dug trembling fingers into her skirts and met his guilt-laden gaze with the most penetrating stare she could aim at him.

"It is true," she got out on a choking cry. "I see it writ all o'er you, yet you held your tongue at Eilean Creag— let us journey all this way! And that without the least thought to my own wishes, knowing how much I lov—"

"'Tis damnable, I will not deny," Kenneth jerked, shoving a hand through his hair. "But, see you, lass," he protested, looking miserable, "I but meant to shield you, to spare you grief at the hands of—" he broke off, scowled blackly as if he could find no more words.

"So—why did you tell me now," Juliana prodded, the sincere look of remorse clouding her brother's face dousing her own flashing burst of anger. "Come you, I would hear why," she added, the prickly golden warmth of excitement beginning to rekindle inside her. She lifted a brow, thrust her chin at him, waiting. "Out with it, Kenneth."

"God's holy bones!" Kenneth thundered. "I told you

now because I could no longer bear to see you in such despair. For truth, I vow you would pry a confession from a tree stump!" he added, glowering at her. "Saints save me—and have mercy on the MacKenzies, with the likes of you in their midst!"

"In their midst?" Leaping up, Juliana launched herself at him, hugging him as tightly as she could before reaching to wipe the surprising dampness from his cheeks. "Does that mean you are ready to take me back to them?"

Kenneth hurrumped, glanced aside. But after a tense moment, he nodded. "Think you I do not ken that you'd walk the whole distance if I did not?" he ventured, his handsome face lightening a bit.

And upon seeing his capitulation, the sweetest joy swept through Juliana, tightening her throat and blurring her vision. A great peace came over her, a precious golden warmth filling even the deepest corners of her heart with such bliss she wondered her happiness did not spill over to flood the vast moorland stretching so endlessly around them.

"So!" she cried then, blinking hard. "Our mother hoped the Black Stag would see me well settled?" She looked up at the sky, dashed the tears from her own eyes. "I vow he already has! Not that he knows it yet . . . or even my Robbie," she added, her voice thick with emotion. "But they will anon—so soon as we can return to Eilean Creag."

❧

A journey that took all of two days . . . one day less than the number of days they'd ridden north.

Juliana's breath caught in her throat when, at last, the great MacKenzie stronghold rose up out of the mists before them. Though she would have ne'er believed it possible, Eilean Creag Castle loomed even more dismal than it had on the day when her knight had galloped up to its forbidding gatehouse. When he thundered across its stone causeway with her, taking her into his home and his heart, only to lose her again so soon as love was found.

Indeed the castle appeared deserted, with nary a guard to be seen on the ramparts, the portcullis gate firmly in place, and only a scant few of the narrow window slits showing glimmers of light.

But as they raced nearer, a lone figure appeared on the battlements.

He watched them with apparent interest, staring at them as raptly as the Black Stag had glared down at her on her first arrival here. Although this figure was of the same great height and also cloaked in black, *this observer* stared in disbelief.

Disbelief, awe, and joy.

Bright-shimmering joy streamed out from him, lighting his handsome face even from this distance and warming Juliana to the roots of her soul.

Even wee Mungo, secured in his saddle basket, yipped in happy, excited recognition.

Aye, there could be no mistake. 'Twas her knight . . . and he'd seen them.

As they thundered closer, a great sob of joy gathered in Juliana's breast and she stared through her tears, watching as he whirled around and vanished from the battlements. The speed with which the portcullis began rattling upward bespoke of how swiftly he must have raced down the tower stairs, ordered the gates thrown wide.

Then he was there, bursting from the shadows to run toward her as quickly as his long legs would carry him, tearing her from her brother's horse before Kenneth could even draw to a full halt before the gatehouse.

"God be praised!" he cried, crushing her to him, not even sparing a glance for Kenneth or the many kinsmen now appearing from everywhere, the lot of them, circling round to stare. And cheer. "Saints! Can it be true?" He rained kisses across her face, murmuring endearments against her damp cheeks, holding her so fiercely he nigh squeezed the breath from her. "I thought I'd ne'er see you again, but . . . but . . ."

He set her from him, a shadow crossing his face, blotting his joy. "It may have been best if you'd stayed away," he said, the whole of his body trembling as he held her, the regret in his eyes lancing her. "We—"

"Nay, you err, my Robbie. I *had* to return . . . to tell you the best of tidings!" She threw her arms around his neck, beamed up at him, her heart swelling, her mouth curving in a shining, tremulous smile. "I am not a MacKenzie, not your cousin in any degree. I—"

Her words were lost in the crashing down of his mouth on hers and a furious, breath-stealing hug as he tightened his arms around her, pulling her ever harder against him.

"What are you saying, lass?" He broke the kiss, crooked his fingers beneath her chin so she could not look away. "You are not my Uncle Kenneth's daughter?"

"Nay, I am not," she said, lifting up on her toes to brush the tenderest kiss across his lips. "'Tis a long tale, best left for the fireside, but, nay, nary a drop of MacKenzie blood flows in my veins. There exists no reason I cannot be yours . . . if you still want me?"

"If I want you?" Robbie let loose a great shout of exaltation. "Does the sun rise each new day? Does—" but his words were lost in the joyous cries and hoot-hooting of his kinsmen. Loud, boisterous cheering, well peppered with a wet snuffle or two and the barking of the frolicking castle dogs.

But at last, when the ruckus began to lessen, Robbie turned to Kenneth, gesturing him near, for Kenneth stood alone, a good ways apart from the jostling, happy throng of his MacKenzie kinsmen.

"You, my friend . . . my good *cousin,*" Robbie called to him, laying especial warmth on the word, "come away in and help my lady tell me what this is about . . . o'er a fine cup of heather ale in our hall, if you will, eh?"

Kenneth looked at him for a long moment, hesitation and a touch of resentment still clouding his features. "You name me cousin—what makes you think I am? Now that you have heard my sister is not of your blood?"

"Hah!" Robbie hooted a laugh, a broad grin spreading across his face. He planted his hands on his hips, looked round at his grinning kinsmen. "Did any of you e'er hear a more fool question?"

No one answered him in words.

Every man present shook his head.

Looking supremely satisfied, Robbie strode forward, clamped a firm hand on Kenneth's shoulder. "See you, *cousin,* even if we forget your looks"—he slanted a glance at the Black Stag—"the stubborn set of your jaw and the twitch beneath your left eye give away your blood. Dinna tell me you will deny it? Turn your back on your own family?"

"Nay, I will not deny it, and I accept your offer . . . gladly," Kenneth said, the words choked, his deep voice suspiciously thick.

Then, to Juliana's amazement, his face suffused with pleasure. Seeing it, she blinked, her heart swelling as, equally startling as Kenneth's unexpected acquiescence, a smile began quirking at the corners of his lips.

A smile that widened, growing e'er brighter and more surprisingly *warm* by the moment. A smile that was joined by a shimmer of telltale brightness in his eyes when Duncan MacKenzie himself strode up to him and slung a strong arm around Kenneth's shoulders and began leading him beneath the gatehouse pend and into his hall.

"You, my son," the Black Stag could be heard to say by those walking close enough by him, "have been too long from home. Come, and let us welcome you properly and see if we can persuade you to stay?"

"Stay?" Kenneth blinked.

The Black Stag nodded, a smile of his own splitting his handsome face. "If you will have us . . . long as we have been apart?"

"And you, my sweetness," Juliana's knight whispered in her ear as they stood, still in tight embrace, watching as Kenneth and Duncan were swallowed up by cheering, *streaming*-eyed kinfolk. "Will you stay? Will you be my—"

"Not your leman," Juliana answered, a teasing light in her eyes. "But if you were about to ask me to be your lady wife, then, aye," she agreed, sealing her promise with a kiss. "A thousand times aye."

"For all your days, lass?" He put his hands on her shoulders, waiting. "Will you *love* me all your life? I warn you, I shall accept no less."

"And neither will you have less," Juliana vowed, throwing her arms around his neck. "My all and everything is and shall e'er be yours . . . for the rest of our days and beyond."

Epilogue

❦

EILEAN CREAG CASTLE, THE GREAT HALL
A FORTNIGHT LATER . . .

"*You KNEW ALL ALONG, did you not, my lady?*"

The deep voice came close to Linnet's ear, its well-loved benevolence bringing a pleased flush to her cheeks. Setting down her wine goblet, she tore her gaze from the revelry of her stepson's wedding feast and looked across the high table at her one-time champion and lifelong friend.

"And if I did . . . *have my suspicions*, Sir Marmaduke, I vow this e'en's celebratory feasting is not a surprise to you either?" She lifted a teasing brow, then returned her attention to Robbie and Juliana.

Glowing with happiness, the newly wed pair stood in the middle of the smoky, torch-lit hall, their hands firmly clasped through the near-perfect hole in the center of the MacKenzies' famed Marriage Stone.

"Aye, good sir, you ne'er cease to astound me," Linnet added for Sir Marmaduke's benefit as the young couple withdrew their hands from the large blue-tinted stone and embraced for the traditional kiss. "Indeed, if our paths should cross through a thousand lifetimes, I shall ne'er believe that you, too, are not blessed with at least a glimmer of *taibhsearachd*."

Sir Marmaduke shrugged, his own gaze resting on the beaming pair, now kissing most seriously, much to the delight of the circle of laughing, jesting well-wishers surrounding them.

"Bah! Me, with second sight?" Sir Marmaduke glanced down the length of the high table to where a diminutive, black-garbed old woman held court amongst a cluster of awe-struck MacKenzies.

"Were I so wise, I would not have required that one's assurances that all will be well with my lady wife and the son Devorgilla claims Caterine is carrying."

At the mention of her name, Devorgilla turned their way, a mischievous smile wreathing her wizened face. "The bride is of great beauty, is she not?" she declared, lifting her reedy voice above the din, a knowing twinkle in her eyes.

"And ne'er you fear, a great peace will soon bless this house as well . . ." she added, her sage voice tailing away as, at the head of the high table, the Black Stag suddenly shoved back his laird's chair and pushed to his feet.

A hush fell over the crowd, all looking on as he turned to the wall behind him and took down a great, ancient-looking sword that e'er hung in a place of honor beneath an equally old-looking swath of MacKenzie plaiding.

"Hear me, kinsmen and friends," he called out, raising the brand high above his head as he moved to stand behind young Kenneth's chair. "Behold the sword of my great-grandsire, Malcolm MacKenzie, great-great-*grandsire* to Kenneth MacKenzie, who, as *Sir Kenneth,* shall soon laird it at Castle Cuidrach, the long-empty holding on Loch Hourn, not far from young Kenneth's own Glenelg, that would have been his father's had not—"

A great, earsplitting cheer rose at his words, cutting him off as everywhere in the hall men leapt to their feet, every MacKenzie present unsheathing his sword to wave it high in the air in hearty agreement and jubilation.

Only Kenneth sat frozen, his features working, his hands gripping the table edge, until, smiling more broadly than anyone present, Robbie elbowed his way through the roaring throng and pulled his cousin to his feet.

"Come, my friend, kneel down," he said, his own voice thick with emotion, "my father is about to knight you!"

"By the Rood . . ." Kenneth got out, running a shaky hand through his hair. "I ne'er . . . I have done naught to deserv—"

"You are *you*," the Black Stag spoke up, easing Kenneth into position with a caring, almost-fatherly hand. "You are my own good nephew, a fine and braw young man, and ne'er has a knighting pleased me more," he added, raising the ancient blade above Kenneth's bowed head, then bringing down the flat of the sword to tap first one of the young man's shoulders, then the other.

"I, Duncan MacKenzie, Black Stag of Kintail, do solemnly salute you—and dub thee knight," he said, his voice, ringing, proud. "Be a good and true knight for all your days. Rise, Sir Kenneth MacKenzie!"

"And so I will," Kenneth gave the expected response, pushing to his feet, then extending his arms for the traditional embrace. "God willing, I shall ne'er disappoint you."

At once, the elation in the hall reached a fever pitch, the kinsmen's shouts of glee and the thunder of countless stamping feet nigh deafening. And no one amongst the grinning, damp-eyed clansmen would have doubted that with the dubbing of Sir Kenneth MacKenzie, a great peace had indeed settled upon Eilean Creag and all those who dwelt within its stout, sheltering walls.

And, mayhap, too, for one who once, long ago, had walked the castle's shadow-hung corridors and stood upon its tall, windswept battlements. Someone who now whiled unseen in the thickest gloom of a forgotten corner of the hall, a spectral goblet raised in grateful, heartfelt toast.

He, too, knew a great peace at last.

A healing peace that had been so long in coming.

For a very brief moment, the specter took his gaze off his son and looked toward the lady Linnet, willed her to see him, feel his gratitude. His appreciation for her forgiveness.

As if she saw him indeed, Linnet raised her own goblet in his direction, nodded, and took a thoughtful sip.

Go in peace and be sorrowful no more. The past is done and by with. From this night forward only goodness will grace these walls, he caught her unspoken words, hearing them with his heart.

And then, nodding at him one last time, she smiled.

Kenneth smiled, too, and vanished.

It was enough.

The *taint* that had so long plagued Clan MacKenzie existed no more.

About the Author

❖

SUE-ELLEN WELFONDER is a dedicated medievalist of Scottish descent who spent fifteen years living abroad, and still makes annual research trips to Great Britain. She is an active member of the Romance Writers of America and her own clan, the MacFie Society of North America. Her first novel, *Devil in a Kilt*, was one of *Romantic Times*'s top picks. It won *RT*'s Reviewers' Choice Award for Best First Historical Romance of 2001. Sue-Ellen Welfonder is married and lives with her husband, Manfred, and their Jack Russell Terrier, Em, in Florida.

More

Sue-Ellen Welfonder!

Please turn this page

for an excerpt

from her new novel

UNTIL THE KNIGHT COMES

available soon

from Warner Books.

The Legacy of the Bastard Stone

❧

*L*ONG AGO, IN ONE of the darkest periods of Scotland's history, but not so distant that time has blurred the memory, a great MacKenzie chieftain prided himself on his strong character and strict uprightness. An indomitable warrior, he was known to fame as Ranald the Redoubtable, his name commanding respect far beyond the Highland fastnesses of his own rugged Kintail.

A masterful man well able to maintain peace in this vast country of darkling hills and shadowed glens, he had but two disturbing weaknesses: a thread of greed that at times vied with the goodness of his heart and a distinct tendency to loftiness.

Susceptibilities that were to prove calamitous when a low-born by-blow of the clan lost his heart to the daughter of a neighboring chieftain. A mere cowherd, Cormac by name, the young man's physical prowess and skill rivaled even the fittest of Ranald the Redoubtable's sons, much to the puissant laird's annoyance.

Cormac's claim that the lass, a maid much-prized for her beauty and high spirits, wanted him with equal fervor only ensured that fate was to go against him. Indeed, when he approached his chieftain for help in amassing a suitable bride price, false hopes were given, empty promises cast to the fickle winds.

On a day of rain and strong winds, he was to journey to the farthest reaches of Kintail, the dark shores of Loch Hourn, there to climb to the highest point of the sea cliffs where a certain outcropping of rock resembles a giant door.

If upon positioning himself atop this natural-made arch, he is able to balance on one foot, he will be deemed worthy to claim any chieftain's daughter as his bride.

And to celebrate his daring and agility, he will be rewarded with double the bride price he'd desired.

Regrettably, as the seannchies so poignantly extol, just as Cormac completed his incredible feat and began the climb down, his foot caught on the edge of the door-like outcropping and he plunged to his death, never to know whether his liege-laird would have kept his word or no.

Only Ranald the Redoubtable knew, and over time his guilt overrode his greed and his pride, the true goodness of his heart triumphing to banish his darker side for the rest of his days.

In young Cormac's honor, the rock formation was dubbed *The Bastard Stone* and in its shadow, a mighty stronghold was raised: Cuidrach Castle, place of the forceful and determined.

And since these earliest times, Cuidrach stands as the proud inheritance reserved by Clan MacKenzie for the most valiant warriors amongst the clan's by-blows. One such stalwart in each generation is raised from his low-born status and granted the style of Keeper of Cuidrach.

A tradition upheld all down the centuries until in none so distant times one such favored bastard turned so blackhearted that the villainy of his deeds left the clan little choice but to withdraw the privilege, the sad forfeiture leaving Cuidrach to stand untended for decades.

But now a new Keeper of Cuidrach has been named.

A braw young clansman of the same strong character and

strict uprightness as his long-passed forbear, Ranald the Redoubtable.

And if along Kintail's wild coastal headlands, the windswept hills could stir, they'd surely be restless, the wind eddying about the rocks perhaps whispering of an ancient wrong.

And pleading it be righted at last.

❧

Drumodyn Castle
Scotland, The Far North
Autumn 1344

Hugh the Bastard.

The three words dealt Mariota Macnicol a smiting blow, each one lodging in her throat like searing lumps of hot-burning coal as she stood on the threshold of the tower bedchamber and stared at the man she loved more than life itself.

Certainly more than her own, for she'd willingly suffered the pains of scandal and ruin to be his lady, turning her back on her well-comforted existence to pave him the way to his dreams.

His lofty ambitions.

And now Hugh Alesone, Bastard of Drumodyn, was dead.

Or soon would be, for the twinkling blue eyes that had e'er besotted her were now full-glazed and bulging, the horror on his handsome face as he caught sight of her, an unmistakable recognition of his imminent end.

Aye, Mariota's golden giant of a Highland lover was about to die naked in his bed.

Naked in the arms of an equally unclothed whore.

And more damning still, with a rolled parchment clenched in his fist—without doubt one of the many love sonnets the well-lettered Hugh was e'er composing for her in supposed praise and adoration.

Shivering, Mariota stared, not trusting her eyes.

White-hot shock and disbelief crashed over her, stealing her breath until, in desperation, her anguish rose in a tide of fury, and the welling pain burst free.

"No-o-o," she cried, agony ripping her soul. "By the living God! *Hugh*. . . ."

" 'Tis m-my heart," he gasped, his precious scroll dropping from his fingers as his eyes widened even more.

Her own heart pounding furiously, Mariota bit down on her lip as he broke away from the sweat-dampened bawd straddling him and pressed both hands against his chest, its well-muscled planes, resplendent with a smattering of golden hairs, proving as drenched and heaving as his whore's fleshy, over-generous breasts.

His penis glistened as well, highlighted almost obscenely by the glow of the night candle. Flaccid now, and surprisingly small for such a great stirk of a Highlandman, the dangling appendage was clearly wet from vigorous love play.

A truth underscored by the disarray of the bed coverings, the flagon of wine and two half-emptied goblets on a fireside table, and the trail of discarded clothing littering the rush-strewn floor.

That, and the reek of passion sated still hanging so heavily in the chill air.

"Saints have mercy!" Mariota pressed her hands to her face, the only movement she could manage for her legs felt leaden, her feet as roots of stone.

The other woman suffered no such loss of agility, scrambling off the bed so swiftly her ungainly efforts to extract herself would have been comical if her very presence didn't feel like a vise around Mariota's heart.

All but spitting and snarling, the bawd flung the last of the bed coverlets from her naked body, knocking over the flagon of wine in her clumsiness, the blood-red libations splashing onto the floor rushes.

Watching her exodus, Mariota curled her hands into fists. The back of her neck throbbed, its tender skin blazing as her gaze lit on the spilled wine, some still-coherent part of her seeing a reflection of Hugh's ignoble demise in the quickly-spreading stain.

An irony the Bastard of Drumodyn would miss for he'd collapsed onto the bed sheets, lay staring at her from blank, unseeing eyes.

And just looking at them sent a bitter, piercing cold sluicing through her. "Dear sweet saints," she gasped, more to herself than the other woman still looming so naked beside the bed. "He is dying. . . ."

But Hugh Alesone was already gone, having left to join his forebears, breathing his inglorious last without a further word spoken.

And with his departure, a great gusting wind rushed into the room, guttering candles and sweeping across a work-table strewn with parchments, the icy blast scattering Hugh's treasured writings to every corner of the room.

Love sonnets, the most of them, but also painstakingly gathered accountings of the ancient line from which he proudly claimed descent—even if his bastardy had constrained him to subsist on little more than his own silvered words and broth of limpets and milk.

Good enough fare until Mariota's munificence enabled the would-be bard to indulge his higher tastes and live as befitted one who was believed to carry the blood of kings.

Scarce able to believe him dead, she swayed, reeling as if

she'd been running full-tilt only to hurtle headlong into a stone wall. A damning obstacle whose long unbound hair tumbled around her naked, generously-curved body.

And something about her prickled Mariota's nape.

"*You!*" she cried, awareness slamming into her. "You are—"

"Elizabeth Paterson," the whore supplied, her gray eyes cold and glittery as a winter dawn.

In numbed shock, Mariota recognized her with surety now. If not by name, then by reputation for the woman was none other than the notorious alewife of Assynt.

Widowed and slightly older than Hugh, Elizabeth Paterson ran *The Burning Bush*, an establishment of less than noble repute where the high-spirited widow was rumored to offer wayfarers much more than victuals and simple lodgings.

The air around Mariota grew colder. "You are the alewife," she said, the acknowledgment sounding faraway, her voice a stranger's.

"And that surprises you?" Nowise inhibited, the bawd made no attempt to cover her spurious charms. "Did you not know Hugh had dark, *lusty* tastes? Needs he could only quench with someone like me?"

Mariota gritted her teeth, her world splitting open to become a yawning void filled with naught but Hugh's naked, inert form and the triumphant little sneer playing about the alewife's generous, love-swollen lips.

"Be gone from here." Mariota flicked a hand at the crumpled clothes on the floor. "Dress, and take yourself from my sight."

The bawd ignored that, lifted her chin. "A pity you returned sooner than expected, Lady Mariota," she said, her throaty voice taunting. "You might have been left to your illusions had it been otherwise."

Mariota stiffened at the woman's haughtiness, something inside her cracking, turning her to stone.

"I turned back before even nearing Dunach," she admitted, the name of her home bitter on her tongue. "Praise God I did not plead my father's beneficence yet again—"

The alewife sniffed. "I told Hugh he'd seen the last of Archibald Macnicol's coin. Word of your puissant father's spleen with you is widespread."

Sliding a hand down her belly, the bawd let her fingers hover ever so briefly above the dark tangle of her nether hair. "See you, Mariota of Dunach, 'tis well Hugh knew you might return early, but he did not want to forego our *amusements*."

Mariota's eyes began to sting, hot gall swelling in her throat as searing heat burned her cheeks. Equally damning, she seemed unable to lift her gaze from the other woman's abdomen.

Elizabeth Paterson's decidedly swollen abdomen.

Her emotions churning, Mariota dug her hands into her skirts. "It would seem the two of you indulged often enough," she said, speaking without inflection.

The other shrugged. "That is as may be, but 'tis not Hugh's child I carry. Not that he cared. Truth be told, he took great relish in hearing of my *encounters* at the alehouse."

Mariota stared at her, wordless.

The alewife's lips quirked. "If you would know the whole of it," she said, reaching to trail her fingers across Mariota's stomach, "he gloried in my swelling form, even likened my sweetness to a ripening plum, his get, or no."

Recoiling from the woman's touch as well as her words, it took Mariota a moment to notice the multi-colored bursts of light suddenly flashing about the alewife's fingers, and yet another to recognize the bawd's true purpose in putting her hand to Mariota's waist.

"My dirk!" Mariota's heart slammed against her ribs at the sight of her bejeweled lady's dagger in the other's hand.

She fumbled at her skirts, her cold fingers finding the blade's empty sheath, the discovery sending chills down her spine.

"You've stolen my dirk!"

"Say you?" The alewife feigned astonishment. "Och, nay, my lady, 'tis not stealing it I am—only borrowing."

"*Borrowing?*"

The alewife nodded, her mouth curving in a satisfied smile as she returned to the bed and, with the dirk's blade, swept several of Hugh's wind-blown parchments onto the floor.

Spearing one that yet clung to the edge of the mattress, she waved the thing at Mariota. "See you, lady, to your face he called you his minx but behind your back he named you a fool," she said, her tone steeped in derision. "I was neither. Ours was an understanding of mutual fulfillment and I meant to use him as boldly as he used me."

Her eyes flashing, she yanked the scroll off the dagger and tossed it at Hugh's body, her mouth twisting in another mirthless smile when the parchment landed on his shriveled manhood.

But, as quickly, her attention flickered to the half-opened window shutters across the room, and something about the glint in her eyes iced Mariota's blood.

"Did you know that your precious Hugh carved footholds in the outer wall of this tower?" She spoke softly, her fingers playing over the gemstones in the dagger's hilt. "He cut them there to allow such as me to win in and out of this chamber discreetly."

"Indeed?" Mariota raised a brow. "I see nary a shred of discretion on you."

The odd look in Elizabeth Paterson's eyes intensified, her

expression hardening. "The need for suchlike is past, would you not agree?"

Mariota held her rival's stare and hoped her own features appeared as cold. Drawing a deep breath, she strove to ignore the tight edges of fear beginning to beat through her, the rapid hammering of her heart.

"Tcha, my lady, all that remains is my need for revenge." The woman's contemptuous glance slid over Mariota. "Aye, vengeance will be mine and served on you!" she hissed, hauling out to slap Mariota full across the face.

Mariota gasped, the smashing blow sending her reeling. She flung up an arm to stave off further blows, but her knees gave out and she sank to the floor.

"Not so proud now, are you?" The whore's face darkened with malice.

Mariota blinked, tried not to gag on the blood filling her mouth as Elizabeth Paterson's menace and her own pain slipped over her like a sheet of cloaking ice.

"Fie, but you have lost your wits, eh?" The alewife leaned close, spite pouring off her. "You'd best gather them, for when I climb out yon window, your life will be worth less than these floor rushes," she vowed, scooping up a handful and letting them drift onto Mariota's head. "A meet revenge, Mariota of Dunach, for with your untimely return, you have ruined my life!"

Mariota stared at her, the woman's gall restoring her tongue if not her strength. " 'Tis you who—"

" 'Tis I who could have made Hugh a master at barderie," the other boasted, waving the dagger for emphasis.

"You come of a long line of fighting men, warrior lairds who live by the sword," she went on, her eyes blazing. "I have the blood of poets, and a sufficiency of influence in bardic circles to have seen him on his way. So soon as he'd amassed enough coin for us to journey forth from this bog-ridden land of dark hills and desolation."

"Sweet Jesu, you are mad," Mariota breathed, her cheek still burning like a brand. "Hugh would ne'er—"

"Hugh would as he pleased, and he ne'er intended to make you his wife," the other flashed, bringing the blade dangerously close to Mariota's face. "But if it soothes your mind, I had no use for him beyond his promise to settle me with a new alehouse—a fine establishment to serve a better lot than frequent *The Burning Bush*."

Mariota struggled to her knees, silently cursing the light-headedness that kept her from standing. She did turn a blistering stare on the woman. "And now you, like I, have nothing."

"Not so," Elizabeth Paterson disagreed, whirling back to the bed, a *whooshing* streak of steel revealing her intent.

"No-o-o!" Mariota's eyes flew wide as the dagger plunged into Hugh the Bastard's chest. "In sweet mercy's name!"

"Not mercy, revenge." Her tone chilling, the ghastly deed done, the alewife calmly retrieved her gown from the parchment-littered floor and crossed to the windows.

Heedless of her nakedness and with her flaunting wealth of hair swirling around her, she tossed her gown into the dark night beyond, hoisted herself onto the broad stone ledge.

"Be warned. Hugh's men will have heard the ruckus," she said, looking pleased. "When they come, your dirk will be raging from the Bastard's heart. You will be thought to have murdered him. Vengeance will be mine."

And then she was gone, her parting words echoing in the empty chamber, the threat behind them giving Mariota the strength to clamber to her feet.

She staggered forward, intent on reclaiming her dagger

however mean the task, but the moment her fingers curled around the blade's jeweled hilt, the sudden clamor of pounding feet stayed her hand. Harsh male voices, raised in outrage and disbelief.

Hugh's men.

A half score of them pushed into the room, ready anger flaring on their bearded countenances, hot fury thrumming along every inch of their brawny, plaid-hung bodies.

Her own body chilled to ice, Mariota faced them. "God as my witness, I did not kill him. 'Twas—"

"Whore! See whose blade pierced his heart!" The nearest man pointed at the dagger hilt thrusting from Hugh's chest. The dirk's jewels sparkled, each colored stone screaming her guilt. "Think you we do not have eyes?"

"And lo! See the hand-print on her cheek," another yelled, seizing her arm. "They fought and she slew him in his sleep!"

A third man spat on the floor.

"Hear me, you mistake. . . ." Mariota protested, but her tongue proved too thick, the agony in her head, and now her arm, too laming.

With the last of her strength, she jerked free and threw a glance at the window. But nothing stirred beyond the gaping shutters save a thin smirr of rain.

Elizabeth Paterson may well have been a moonbeam—a figment of Mariota's imagination.

But the blade lodged in Hugh the Bastard's heart was real.

And it was hers—as all at Drumodyn knew.

She knew she was innocent. And that Hugh the Bastard was a bastard in more ways than one.

A murrain on the man and all his perfidy!

Her peace so won, she offered her arm to the guard

who'd seized her only moments before, let the fire in her eyes dare him into escorting her from the chamber.

Mariota of Dunach, proud if misguided daughter of the far-famed Archibald Macnicol, would be double damned if she'd tremble and cower before any man.

And she'd be thrice cursed, and gladly, if ever she fell prey to love again.

THE EDITOR'S DIARY

Dear Reader,

Like two magnets, lovers either attract or repel. And when they attract, heaven help whatever is caught between them. Don't believe me? Test out the science of love yourself in our two Warner Forever titles this July.

Romantic Times BOOKclub Magazine praised "you couldn't ask for a more joyous, loving, smile-inducing read" than **Sue-Ellen Welfonder**'s previous book. Well, hold onto your kilts—she's outdone herself with her latest, **ONLY FOR A KNIGHT**. The last thing Robbie MacKenzie desires is to abandon his bachelorhood and wed a complete stranger...but he will. For only the promise of this union has kept the peace between two rival clans and it is time for Robbie to face his destiny and claim heir to his father's lairdship. But on his way home, he sees a beautiful woman on the verge of drowning. He saves her and an attraction ignites within him hot enough to sear his soul. Though he is sworn to another, Robbie cannot bear to leave this bonnie lass who knows nothing of her past. But when the truth of this tantalizing stranger's identity and mission comes to light, can these two star-crossed lovers resist the love that burns in their hearts?

If your sister was missing, is there a limit to what you'd do to save her? Stephanie Grant from **Toni Blake**'s **IN YOUR WILDEST DREAMS** knows there are no bounds to what she'd do. So, as she steps onto the secret third floor of Chez Sophia, her resolve is only strengthened. Amid heady champagne, wealthy men, and stunningly beautiful women, Stephanie begins a dangerous charade to find her beloved sister. But she never expected to find an ally in Jake Broussard, the strong but sexy bartender and ex-cop. Since he reluctantly agreed to help her, she thought she'd feel only gratitude for him. But his gentle touch and soft Cajun accent send her senses reeling. Can she trust him? More importantly, can she trust herself with him? *New York Times* bestselling author Lori Foster raves "with sizzling sensuality and amazing depth, a book by Toni Blake is truly special" and she couldn't be more right. Pick up a copy today and find out why.

To find out more about Warner Forever, these titles, and the author, visit us at www.warnerforever.com.

With warmest wishes,

Karen Kosztolnyik

Karen Kosztolnyik, Senior Editor

P.S. Love doesn't always come before marriage in these two irresistible novels: **Kimberly Raye** delivers the wickedly funny story of a woman marrying to get rid of her mother and finds unexpected romance in **SWEET AS SUGAR, HOT AS SPICE**; and **Paula Quinn** makes her Warner Forever debut with the exciting and unforgettable story of a woman forced by the king to marry who soon vows to win her new husband's heart in **LORD OF DESIRE**.